Allan Massie

THE
HANGING
TREE

A Romance of the Fifteenth Century

Mandarin

A Mandarin Paperback
THE HANGING TREE

First published in Great Britain 1990
by William Heinemann Ltd
This edition published 1992
by Mandarin Paperbacks
Michelin House, 81 Fulham Road, London SW3 6RB

Mandarin is an imprint of the Octopus Publishing Group,
a division of Reed International Books Limited

Copyright © Allan Massie 1990

A CIP catalogue record for this title
is available from the British Library
ISBN 0 7493 0780 3

Printed and bound in Great Britain
by Cox & Wyman Ltd, Reading, Berks

For George and Elspeth

'Mr McCunn sought in literature for one thing only. Sir Walter Scott had been his first guide, but he read the novels not for their insight into human character or for their historical pageantry, but because they gave him material wherewith to construct fantastic journeys.'

Buchan

'Certain dank gardens cry aloud for a murder; certain old houses demand to be haunted; certain coasts are set aside for shipwreck.'

Stevenson

BOOK ONE

I

The wind, blowing in squalls from the south-west, had thrown up heavy clouds laden with rain, and the pony, a hairy-heeled sorrel, limping down the old Roman road with its tail to England, had cast a shoe an hour back. They had come through broken hill-country, dun-grey in the cold October. Once a skein of geese flew over, heading for the stubble fields or water meadows by Kelso where Tweed and Teviot meet. There were few other signs of life in that empty land. A blue hare sprang up a braeside and twice the pony's clip-clop startled a brace of grouse. A couple of times too the rider had seen a flock of sheep drawing up to the high tops, but gave their herds no wave. It was country a man was wise to pass through without drawing heed to himself. He saw a burnt peel-tower and farm buildings still reeking smoke across his way; and shivered.

The pony was tired and near done, and it was darkening to dusk before the Abbey tower of Jedburgh came into view. He had hoped for better time, but now he must lie at the inn there and find a smith in the morning to shoe his beast. He was worn out himself and had no wish to lame the pony. The realization of his fatigue was sudden. His shoulders ached and his head swam so that for a moment he had to take a grip of the rough mane to steady himself. It was no wonder he was in such a state, for it was only last evening he had been fit to rise from his fever-bed. The old herd's wife had urged him to bide another night, but he had been firm. He was eager to be gone, even more eager to be home, for it puzzled him to know why Clym had left him there with only one man to care for him, and why that man had deserted him almost as soon as his brother's back was safely turned. Or so the old wife had told him, but he could not know who the man was from her description; 'he was a middling chiel,' she had said, in an abrupt clackety voice, 'and he made off with never a goodbye or God bless you'.

3

It was the fever making him weak and nervous. He told himself that more than once. The wife had been right. He shouldn't have ridden that day. And yet he couldn't have borne to bide there, though he had no way of accounting for what perturbed him. So he had mounted the pony, and the wife had stuffed the end of a loaf of bread in his saddle-bag, saying that he maun eat sometime before he travelled far, though he had been too weak to do so when he rose, and she had seen him on his way with many a shake of her head. He had ridden warily, for a solitary rider had to keep an eye open for danger. You never knew when you might not fall in with a party of forayers spurring back to their Northumbrian bolt-holes. But the road had been as quiet as the grave or the long nights of Lent.

It wasn't, though, the same prudent wariness that his brothers would display which now formed bushes into threatening shapes and made him see movement on the hillsides that was only a trick of the failing light and gathering mirk. These were child's fancies or fever nerves. Telling himself that didn't disperse them however, and other fantasies invaded his mind, memories of winter tales by the fireside, of how the Queen of Elfland rade through the same hills in the same mirk night with Thomas of Ercildoune, the pair of them wading in blood to their horses' knee. It was the hour and place of enchantment; the great wizard Michael Scott might still lurk in the Eildon Hills that he had cut in three, those hills where Arthur rested with his knights waiting the hour of recall. And there were other spirits abroad, goblins and brownies and the ghosts of those killed in unjust quarrels.

He shivered and shook himself. He was too old for such fancies, no bairn but a man now and riding out with his father and brothers this past year, riding this last foray with Clym and five men under them in search of their reived cattle, and not knowing why they had left him in the herd's hut, wondering which it was who had deserted him, not maybe caring if he did indeed die of the fever. That was a matter to chew on rather than tales of that other world which marched beside theirs.

He shook himself again and sat straight on the pony, a slim boy with a soft mouth which the thin line of blond moustache he had been trying to grow couldn't disguise. His hair, mostly

4

hidden under the blue bonnet, was fair too with that glint of red-gold you often find in the Borderland. It was recognized in the family that he took after his mother as she had been when Walter had first brought her down from an upland farm thirty years back. He took after her and her folk in more than looks, for like her brothers he was given to making verses, and only the week before had made a ballad on his grandfather's great raid into Redesdale and his deeds at Otterburn that were a legend in the family to make them glow with pride. He was eighteen and his name was Robin Laidlaw.

Jedburgh was in a clamour. It had been market day and crowds still tumbled round the stalls which merchants were now dismantling. Groups of men, in serge tunics with blue bonnets on their heads, spilled out of the alehouses, some clutching leather jacks of beer. They jostled and shouted abuse at a party of monks making their way back to Vespers. The monks kept their eyes lowered. The abbey might own lands up Teviot and down Tweed, but market day when men came in from the Merse or the Forest was no occasion to parade their piety. Too many of those made bold by liquor were the abbey's resentful tenants. So the monks hurried with what speed they could to the Abbey gates.

Rob dismounted and led the hirpling pony down the hill to the house where he hoped to find lodging for the pair of them. It was prudence made him dismount, though he couldn't account for it, except by thinking he was less like to be noticed if he wasn't perched up on the beast.

Despite the bustle round the alehouses there was no hilarity in the town. The mood was raw. It gave off the sense of men bound together by an experience that was out of the ordinary and which had excited them and made them feart at the same time; it would have shamed them had they not been in a crowd. It had something of the tremorous mood you find before a battle, though there was no anticipation in it. Rob kept his eyes alert but his head still, as if he wasn't looking about him. Then, as he pushed through the crowd, past the piles of dung outside the houses, it began to rain, heavy drenching drops, and the wind rose. A man swore at him as his pony bumped against his stall and Rob, saying nothing, hurried on. He had caught and recognized the mood.

Once, some three summers ago, his father and brothers had ridden home towards the evening milking with just that edge on them. They wouldn't speak of what they had done, and it wasn't for a year that he learned of what had happened, one summer night on the hill with his eldest brother Clym. All of a sudden, without warning or introduction, that dark silent man had burst out with the story of how they had been reiving sheep from the Abbey lands round Minto and how a monk had galloped up on a fat grey pony and cried on them to stop. Walter had sworn at him for a fool, but Maurie (the second brother and ever quick in tongue and deed), 'Maurie outs with his sword and rams it down the holy gullet before the monk can cry the name of Jesus. "That'll stop your prayers," he laughs. I can hear that laugh yet, Rob,' Clym said and looked away from the boy into the mist rising by the waterside. 'Aye, and the fat grey pony's hooves clipping off into the mirk, till we heard it slough its rider off in a ditch. And Maurie, you ken, was gleg to be after the pony, but Feyther would hae nane of it. He pulls round his horse's head and sets spurs tae its sides, and we a' made for the Forest as fast as our beasts would carry us. Leaving the sheep tae, so that Maurie had killed the man for naething. Aye, Rob, it behoves us to gang warily when we're free of the Forest now.' And that was why a few weeks after that night Maurie had risen before dawn and with a word only to their mother had made for England without a backward glance. Rob shook his head at the memory. They had not heard a word from Maurie since; though he couldn't tell. He jaloused their father knew fine how and where he was.

Rob found a stall in a shed behind the inn for his beast and a stable-lad to fetch him hay, and he flung his own cloak over the pony's back so that it wouldn't catch cold in the night after their long ride. He tossed a penny to the boy. 'You'll keep an eye on the beast,' he said, 'and there will be another for you,' and he went into the inn to ask for food and drink and a bed for the night.

'There's mutton and a bannock and ale', the old serving-man admitted, 'but for a bed,' he smiled, 'you'll hae to stretch yourself on the bench theer, or the floor itself if the bench is ower narrow. Not but what you're a narrow lad yoursel.' He squinted at Rob. 'Aye, narrow enough, I'm thinking, to be riding the hills on your lane. And where do you come frae? Och, I ken fine what you're thinking, that it's nae business o' mine where you hail frae, but that's where you're wrang. Whae comes and gangs in this inn, and where they hail frae and whatlike's the purpose of their journey, is what I make my business. Precisely that, my mannie. We'll no hae just any folk here, you ken. And there's aye the Abbey guest-chamber for them my curiosity ill suits.' He leaned his beery breath into Rob's face. 'But maybe a spunky lad like you would no care for the Abbey and the monks. Aye, but you missed yourself here the day, lad. We've had a real auld-farrant Jeddart day the day. You'll no ken what that is, I'm thinking.'

He bustled away in answer to a summons and Rob was left to feel the full weight of his fatigue till the old man hobbled back – his right knee sticking out at an odd angle – with the food and drink he had promised. The hunk of mutton was braxy, but Rob was seized with hunger and gnawed at it and tore at the bere bannock and slaked his dusty throat with the sweet dark ale. The old man hovered over him, as if admiring his appetite, till he judged the boy's first hunger was appeased.

'Aye,' he said, 'a real Jeddart day. Ye'll have heard of what we ca' Jeddart justice, maybe? Aye, I thocht you might have. Hang 'em first and speir the crime after. That's our way. It saves the expense of a trial, you see. No that there could have been any need for yin the day. Na, na. Aye,' he plucked at Robin's sleeve, 'that's what we've had here the day. A hanging. It aye sets us up, a gude hanging. Folk are aye drouthy when they've seen another neckit. It's a rare thing, for trade in a Public. And this was a rare yin indeed. Gin you tak a turn doon by the Tolbooth you'll no miss a' the play, for you'll see four of the malefactors hanging in chains as they'll be till our next hanging, and the heid yin, that auld beast of prey and rapine, auld in blood and sin, Walter Laidlaw of Clartyshaws himself, still dangling from the gibbet on a hempen tow. It's a grand . . . hey, what ails ye, laddie? Mercy on us . . . Maggie, here . . .'

Robin had never fainted before, and, when he opened his eyes, feeling a damp cloth on his forehead, and looked up into a brown face with soft brown eyes and a frame of brown ringlets that brushed his cheek, he couldn't immediately think what had happened to him.

7

'Lie still,' she said, 'you're white as the driven snow.'

He obeyed, taking some comfort from the soft voice.

'But what's happened?' he said, and all the time heard the old man's voice muttering and sounding in his recovering ears like the Ettrick Water tumbling in spate.

'The lad's ower fine,' the old man grumbled. 'Can he no hear talk of a hanging. I was just for telling him of the day's ploys.'

'The mair shame to you, Calum Nixon,' the girl said, 'to deeve a young lad with your gallows-talk. You're a ghoul, that's what you are, a richt crotchety auld ghoul . . .'

'Hech, hech, what a business,' the old man said. 'What was I doing but giving the young lad the crack of the day? Folks are fine indeed when they canna bide talk of a hanging. And it's no every day an auld tod like Laidlaw of Clartyshaws is neckit. You wouldna expect me to keep rare news like yon to masel. I'm just wondering what way it affected the young lad so . . .'

A trembling like the return of his fever ran through Robin. He clutched the girl's hand. 'I've been sick,' he said, 'I'm just up the day from a fever, and I've ridden far and all at once I felt me as weak as a kitten. Is there no bed I could maybe have?'

'I tellt you, there's no a bed to be had in the house. This is a tavern, nobbut a tavern. Gin it's a bed you seek, awa to the monks with you.'

'And why should the lad no have a corner of mine the now? With the house in the stoor it's in, nor Jean nor Elspit nor me'll be bedded till the heich o' night. Come awa wi you, lad . . .'

'Folks is fine indeed, ower fine, what are loons coming tae, when they canna thole talk of a gude hanging . . .'

Rob was indeed in no state to go on. That was all he could tell himself to his credit, for consolation. He had been sick twice in the wooden bucket the girl Maggie had supplied. ('I tellt them thon mutton was past being fit tae eat,' she said the first time.) When she left him he lay for hours rigid but for the intermittent trembling that attacked him. In spite of the rough woollen blankets with which she had covered him, he was nipped and pierced by cold. The damp chill crept up from the river, seeped in from the moorland, through the thick walls, through layers of blanket and stocking, so that his feet were like lumps of stinging ice. He hugged himself for warmth. The sense of loss had hardly hit him yet, but the wretchedness with which his mind formed pictures of his father, with his hands bound behind his back, being roughly urged towards the rope, brought on new nausea. His father would not have spoken a word, neither of protest nor penitence, he knew that. Would he have prayed? Would they have let him pray or would the monks, neglecting their Christian duty, have urged him to his death unshriven? He had no doubt that this was the revenge of the Abbey and its agents. They had waited three years to avenge their Brother, but they had done so. Rob had loved his father, loved him still, feared him and honoured him, and he felt shame to be lying in a girl's bed while, only a few hundred yards away or less, Walter's body swung from a rope's end in the night air. He tried to pray for his father's soul, but the words stuck. He felt something more shaming still, and this was fear for himself. He was never to forget the fear with which he had listened to every movement in the house.

At last he fell asleep. He was so weary he did not hear the three girls come in and was not aware of them joining him with many giggles and some horseplay. He didn't feel them draw the blankets back or see them hold their candle over him to admire his body. But towards morning, with the wind now shrieking round the close and through the rooftops, he dreamed and dreamed horribly. He saw his father on the gallows with his legs stiff, his tongue huge and blue, and one eyeball half detached from its socket. He woke in damp horror, and lay in this mad empty crowded world of death and grief and girls. Hands caressed him and explored him, he responded as a dog might, and slept again. He didn't even know which girl it was and when he woke it was near light and he was again alone.

The brown girl Maggie brought him ale and bannock. He thanked her and made to rise, but she told him he was not fit to travel. 'You've still the fever on you, and had better bide.'

He had no will to resist. While he lay there, tended by the girls, he was acquit of responsibility. Until he moved he did not have to confront his second fear, that the hanged men in chains might be his brothers.

They kept him there for two days. He did not know how they concealed his presence, but presumed they did, and when he asked them about Calum Nixon, they laughed and said they knew a way of stopping that black gob. They saw to the shoeing

9

of his pony, and no doubt told a tale to account for it. They took their rewards in the dark night, giggling and tumbling over each other so that he never knew with which he was engaged. It was as much relief as delight for him, for during the empty hours of day, memory, imagination and fear all tormented him.

On the second afternoon the girl Jean, pale and blonde as a lily by the water's edge, slipped into the room and let a wet cloak fall to the floor.

'Maggie says you'll be off the morn,' she said.

'Aye, I maun.'

'I'm wet through,' she said, and slipped out of her shift. 'It's daft,' she said, 'I've had you in me, but I dinna ken your name, though there's muckle I ken and mair I guess.'

'It's Rob,' he said, 'Robin.'

'I'm that sorry for you,' she said. She sat down beside him and put her fingers to his cheek, and with her other hand took his and laid it between her legs. 'You talk in your sleep,' she said. 'That's how we ken. We're a that sorry for you, but me maist, for I was there and saw it. The others thought I should say naething to you, but I thought maybe I should. Was I right?'

He felt life throb below his hand and throughout his body and nodded again.

'He died right bonny,' she said, 'lifting his face up to the sky as if he was gazing on our Lady. Yin of the others, a wee lad wi' yellow hair, died whining, but no your Daddy. He might have been gaeing to his wedding. I thought you'd like to ken that.'

'Aye.'

'I said a prayer for him.'

He let the prayer lie a minute between them, and then moved his fingers.

'Jean,' he said, 'was there a tall black man with a scar on his cheek?'

'No, they were a' wee fellows.'

'And no yin with ae shoulder raised abune the other.'

'I ken what you're feared of, but na. They werena your brothers.'

She leaned over him and kissed him on the lips and let her hair fall over his face.

'You're nae all alone,' she said.

Later, she moaned and they clung together and she sighed, and then said, in a low voice, 'He's aye hanging there. Will you be able to pass him in the morn?' She ran her fingers over his lips and kissed his eyelids.

It was still black night, thick as a coffin-pall, when the three girls escorted Rob down to the shed where the pony was stabled. He bridled the mare in silence while they pulled their cloaks tighter round their bodies against the cold. Then Maggie lifted a lantern and held it up so that she could look him in the face.

'Aye,' she said, 'you'll do. Gie's a kiss.'

He leaned over and kissed each in turn.

'May our Lady watch over you,' Jean whispered. 'You've got the knife.'

'That I have.' He swung himself on to the pony's bare back. 'I'll no forget what you've a' done for me. Never.'

The pony's hooves slithered in the mud going down the hill. Rob was alert for sound or movement but the town was silent. It was hard to see the way and he was glad to move slowly to let his eyes get their night sense. Then he could just make out the looming shape of the Tolbooth and the gallows beside it. He put his hand up and took hold of his father's boot like a child crawling on the floor beside his Daddy's chair. The ladder was just where Jean had said it would be. He rested it against the transverse of the gibbet, and either gibbet or ladder, or perhaps both, creaked as he mounted. He swayed on the uncertain support. Steadying himself, he drew the knife from his jerkin, and, leaning precariously to his left, attacked the rope with a violent sawing motion. For a moment it resisted and he leaned more dangerously still to be able to apply more weight. Then, like a breaking dam, the strands tore apart. The body's dead weight fell like a sack of meal out of the corn loft.

Robin descended the ladder and dragged his father's body towards the pony which shied and pranced a bit, not understanding what was happening, and not liking the clumsy movement in the dark. Rob steadied the beast, and heaved the corpse upright so that it was propped against the pony. Then he bent down and swung the legs up so violently that it was all he could do to stop the body sliding off the other side. He stood, listened, one hand resting on his father's back, heard no sound at all.

Then, instead of going on down the hill which led to the town gate, he turned up an alley to the left. It was narrow and his feet slipped in the mire. He had to hold on to the wall to stop himself from falling. The next moment Jean caught his hand.

'I was that feart. I near came down . . .'

He held her hand tightly and allowed her to lead him up the alley. The buildings gave way to rough unfenced gardens and they stumbled through stony patches of kail.

They came to the wall surrounding the town and Jean led him along it, her fingers feeling the line of the masonry till they came to a wicket gate. She felt under her cloak and produced a key.

'It gives on to Calum Nixon's brither's field,' she whispered. 'He's lying fou as a puggy in the tavern. Beyond it you're on the town muir. They'll no look this way. Maist like, they'll scour the town first, for they'll ken naebody has passed through the town gate, and they'll no think that Dod Nixon would hae gied his key to a freend of your feyther. I'll hae the key back wi' Dod afore he wakes. But you'll no be safe till you win the Forest.'

She held up her face to be kissed. Rob pressed against her and their mouths sought each other. 'I'll no forget what you've done,' he said, and set his face to the east. As he marched by the pony's head, one thought hammered in his mind: 'How did my brothers let it happen?'

II

Clartyshaws at the back end of the year, in the rain and mirk, was a dour place. The mud that gave it the first half of its name came right up to the barred door under the peel-tower behind which the few thin shaggy cattle stood hock-deep in glaur and dung; and the shaws, woods of oak and hawthorn, birch alder and pine, tumbled down the precipitous slope behind the peel-tower that was indeed little more than a fortified farm. It stood in a little glen off the Ettrick Water, halfway up the hillside on a flat spur, the only level ground for miles but for the reedy marsh in the howe where building was impossible.

There had been Laidlaws in Clartyshaws for more than two hundred years now – a Laidlaw had ridden in to acclaim William Wallace as Lord Guardian of Scotland in Selkirk's Kirk o' the Forest, and another had been killed beside King David at Nevile's Cross, killed, some said, as he engaged himself in looting the English camp while the battle was still doubtful, before his king surrendered to be led into a long captivity in the South. The Laidlaws were most of them hard black surly men. Few would ride willingly with them, unless they had good cause, but even fewer chose to ride against them. They were thieves and killers, but not wanton killers for the most part, for some native decency kept them from the blacker and more cowardly crimes like rape and the killing of unarmed men. But they were ill to cross and no scruples would deter them from burning a poor man's house over his head, if they thought he had cause to spite them; and pity was an emotion few of them felt. Baptised Christians were rare among them, and their weddings were more like to be celebrated by the smith over his anvil than by the priest at his altar. For the parish priests though, mean peasants as most of them were, they seldom had more than an easy contempt. The abbey monks of Melrose and Jedburgh or even as far east as Kelso were another matter, fat chickens for the plucking, and the family's favourite exploit, to be recounted on winter evenings and sung at their Yule feast, was the time a Laidlaw – Dand, it was, old Walter's uncle – had robbed an English abbot or bishop of his treasure-kist and cope as he returned through the valleys from an embassy to King Robert. Then they would toast Dand's memory from a silver filigreed loving-cup that had been part of the bishop's treasure.

There was no toasting now though two of the four brothers sat in the hall with leather jacks of ale in their hands. It had been a long silence for Will had exhausted his recriminations over the past days and Clym was made speechless by shame and anger. He sat with his gaze fixed on the dancing fire, resentful as if the dance of the flames mocked his mood, a dull, heavy man with a black bushy beard coarse as a hill pony's mane, and a habit of fingering it as he listened to what men said and held back his reply. There was something solid about Clym that inspired trust, but yet that dead look in his eye repelled a man's confidence. He was the only one of the brothers to be married, and he had chosen a women of the same type as himself, Mollie, bred at a small place in the upper reaches of the Forest, no more given to talk than Clym himself, but devoted to her milking cows and her two bairns, Young Clym and the baby Ellen.

Even Mollie kept clear of Clym this evening, leaving him to his dull resentment while his brother Will, the third in age, sat whittling at a bit stick, to no purpose that Clym could see. It was an added source of irritation to Clym that Will should be of so little use to any purpose. He glanced once or twice at his brother's frank, open and yet empty face. The blackness of the Laidlaws had worn itself out in the two elder boys, Clym and Maurie who was now south of the Border, as if the gentle Ailie had proved of stronger stock, for both Will and Rob took after her. Now Will whittled at his stick, flirted with the hound at his feet, and now and then whistled the fragment of an air, as the wind howled round the peel and night closed over it. In the wee chamber off the hall their sister Isobel tried to soothe their mother into sleep.

For the tenth time Clym said, 'we'll hae to ride in and plead for his body. We canna in all conscience leave him to dangle there through the winter.'

For corbies to peck at, was Will's thought, but he said nothing and worked his knife at the stick-head.

Isobel joined them, a girl of twenty, pale and soft as the cheese Ailie made from the first summer ewe-milking. Her eyes were red with tears and her voice was slurred with grief and exhaustion.

'She's asleep,' she said, 'and fair worn out. And Clym, she's awful anxious for Rob. She says you're to go search for him in the morn.'

'It's to put our head intil the same noose,' he said.

'It's what the mither wants. She'll die if you dinna find him, if anything befalls him.'

She began ladling a stew of venison and hare and blackcock onto iron plates and set a kebbuck of cheese and a handful of oatmeal bannocks on the table. 'Ye maun eat,' she said, 'there's riding to be done by you lads onygate.'

'We'll no move,' Clym said, 'till we hear from Maurie. I've sent til him, and I'll no move till I hear.'

'Weel,' said Isobel, 'it's true it's Maurie as has the head.'

'Aye,' said Will, 'and whae but Maurie . . .' and then he broke off, and looked at Clym himself in reproach.

Clym gave him his gaze back and frowned, and the long heavy silence fell on them again as they thought of the absent Maurie, and remembered what their father had always said to excuse him, 'cripples hae a right to be cankered'. How he had repeated it even that night when they had all ridden back, Maurie with the priest's blood on his sword, and on his hands and on his right sleeve up to the elbow; and all of them had sat there, in the same hall only with no fire for it was summer, but all, even Walter, with fear in their hearts. Then at Walter's command Maurie had ridden for the border, and they had seen nothing of him since. The brothers had thought themselves well rid of him, but Isobel had pined. She had always felt for her misshapen brother a mixture of pity, admiration and fear. Maurie had dominated her childhood inventing games that were ingenious and frightening. She had confided in him though she knew he could not be trusted. Now it consoled her to think that Clym had sent for him. If anyone could mend matters in their trouble, it was Maurie, her crooked darling; she hugged the comfort to herself.

Clym stiffened, a chop-bone half way to his mouth, and the

dog at Will's feet, a lithe cross between deerhound and collie, leapt up, his birse erect, and rushed barking to the door. They could hear nothing against the sound of his barking and Clym shouted to him to be quiet, and, when he paid no heed, struck into his side hard with the toe of his boot.

His hand went to his dirk. The sound of horses' hooves came up the track to the door.

'Is it Maurie?' Isobel cried.

'It couldna be yet,' Will said.

'Hist,' Clym motioned them to silence, and listened hard.

'There's only the yin,' he said, and let his hand fall from the dirk . . .

Footsteps stumbled up the stair to the door. A fist banged.

'Let me in . . . it's me, Rob.'

'Rob . . .'

Clym's voice held a note of uncertainty, even dismay, but he unbarred the door. Rob fell through it and would have collapsed if Clym had not held him up, and then the boy gestured behind him to where the sorrel pony stood below. The moon was up and out from behind scudding clouds, a big straw-coloured hunter's moon. It lit up the side of the tower and glanced down on the burden the pony carried.

'Feyther . . . I won him back.'

Isobel embraced him and led him to the table while the others piled down the steps to the pony. They brought up the body with such care as they could, and laid Walter on the floor in front of the fire. Will disappeared to put the pony by, and Rob sank on to the bench by the table. His head fell into his hands. Timidly, with a sense of wonder mingled in her care, Isobel placed food and ale on the table before him.

'I'm that weak and hungry I canna eat. Let me tell . . .'

'Wait till Will's back,' Clym said. 'Ye maun eat. Man, it's a day's work you've done the day, no matter how . . .'

'Aye,' Rob said, 'and it was a rare day's work you did when you left me outbye in the herd's house . . .'

When he had told his tale he looked Clym in the eye, and for the first time Clym found he could not hold his younger brother's gaze.

'I shouldna hae left you,' he said, 'I ken that fine, but at the time . . .' There had been the cattle, he explained; he had been

16

feared to keep them there, lying by that exposed hut, on the bare hill. They had wrought hard to win them and he had feared pursuit. So he had first sent Nick of the Hangingshaws back to tell their father, and waited, anxious for his return. Nick had returned after two days, his whey face working with excitement, and said his father too was feared for the cattle. Clym was to take them by the back roads to the head of Ettrick where Walter would meet them. Meanwhile he, Nick, would look after Rob. It was but a day's ride, and when Walter had taken charge of the beasts he would send Clym back to fetch Rob. Clym looked at the weasel face and felt foreboding. There was something in it aroused his alarm, and even then he wondered why Walter had sent back merely his own messenger instead of coming himself with a body of men. But he was not accustomed to disobey his father, and hardly dared to question his orders. He looked at the table as he told Rob this. They rode hard to the meeting place and he was relieved to see his father waiting there as promised. At that moment his suspicions vanished, and he gave a great cry and spurred his pony up the pass. As soon as he did so the Forest was alive with men, men in livery, the Abbot's livery, maybe fifty of them. Walter had had no chance. He was thrown from his horse and pinioned to the ground, and when Clym drove at them, someone gave him a dunt on the head with a sword that would have cut it open if it hadn't happened to catch the raised ridge of his leather bonnet. His horse had panicked, and carried him, swaying in the saddle and dazed with the blow, right out of the skirmish. He had last seen the troop disappearing down the valley, and his own men, dead, captured or in fright. He hid up in the wood till all was quiet but when he rode back to the scene of the skirmish there was no sign of Walter.

'So it was Nick,' Rob said.

'Aye it was Nick. It was a' Nick. Weel is he called Nick o' the Hangingshaws. We'll hang him high as Haman ere the moon is dark on his deed.'

Rob scratched his head.

'But how,' he said, 'could Wee Nick deceive the feyther?'

'Aye,' Will said, 'but you see, he came back blubbering wi terror and gleg as a futret, to say you had a' been ta'en by Hob Cranmer o' Jesterslee, who, as you baith ken, has had an ill will at us langsyne. Weel, Hob's message was brief. He wad hang the baith of you wi a glad heart forbye the feyther paid a ransom. So Feyther rade oot wi that purpose in mind and a heavy heart . . .'

'And Hob had naething to dae wi it?' Rob said. 'It was a' Nick's villainy?'

'Nick's villainy and my ain folly,' Clym said. 'For I blame myself, and shall till my dying day . . .'

Isobel looked up. 'The feyther had a sair foreboding,' she said. 'He'd seen a hawk run down by a flock of rooks out on the hill and he wouldna take Will. He was that black there was no arguing wi him. And so he rode even though he kennt that Nick was as trustworthy as a fox in a hen-run.

'And then after Clym was back, word came to us. It was brought first to the priest at St Mary's chapel, and he sent the auld dame Grizzie Tomes to tell us, being feart to come himself.'

Clym drew his dirk and stabbed it into the deal table. The hilt quivered with the force of the blow.

'It'll be well for Nick o' the Hangingshaws,' he said, 'if he's seen a priest and been shriven, for he'll no live to let his eyes light on another kirk.'

The three brothers laid hands across the table, first Clym, then Will pressing on his and then Rob.

'Aye,' said Clym, 'that's a pledge, but first we'll wait for Maurie. We'll no strike wi'oot him for he has a right to share in our feyther's revenge.'

'Revenge,' Maurie rolled the word round his lips, savouring it like a glass of wine. 'Revenge is a dish to be supped cauld.'

They looked on him with the wonder accorded to the familiar grown strange. They took in the fur-lined collar and the two-forked beard he had grown, and the new polish in his manner, and then they looked from him to the English lord Edward des Moulins with whom he had ridden up in the misty sun of the October afternoon, recognizing where the polish came from. Des Moulins was a thin finical womanish fellow, that any of them, even young Rob, could have broken across his knee. He had light soft hair and a light soft voice, and a smile that came too quickly to his lips and danced in his eyes. They looked at the pair of them with their ringed fingers, at the jewels sewn in des

Moulins' doublet, at the little medal of St Pandulf that hung from Maurie's neck and occupied his fingers as he talked. They had wondered at him and doubted him, and feared him even while he had lived among them; now he was at the same time familiar and a stranger. They recognized that he had gone beyond them. They envied and were alarmed by the easy manner in which he spoke to des Moulins.

Yet they came together in the gripping cold of the hours before dawn, each feeling the madness that filled the others as they trotted their ponies down the hill-track. Before leaving they had gone in, one by one, to their mother, and knelt by her and let her lay her hand on their heads. They had said nothing of where they were riding or why; there was no need. Only Rob had leaned forward and brushed her lips with his, and she had then held him in a long silent moment of communion and blessing. But when Maurie left her, Isobel watched her mother make the sign of the cross.

They rode, in silence, to the west. Then, as the first grey light flickered into being, they turned up a rough rutted valley that led south into the Cheviots. They crossed a ridge and found a herd's cottage halfway down to the waterside, but the herd was from home, and his woman answered them only with a dumb look of ignorance and fear. Maurie was for putting a brand to her roof 'to gar her speak', but Clym pulled at his brother's bridle and they trotted off down the hill. At the bottom Rob looked back over his shoulder, and the woman was still standing there watching them.

Towards noon they stopped by a burn and mixed water with a little oatmeal from the leather pouch each carried strapped to his belt. They stopped at a manse to question the priest. He had seen them come down from the hills, riding in file, and barred his door, but when he saw Clym unhitch an axe from his saddle-bow he opened quick enough, and stood gibbering, a sad hedge-sparrow of a man, as they put the question. He knew well who they were and what their mission was, for word had gone round the country, but he denied any knowledge of Nick's where-abouts: it had been many weeks since he saw him, he averred, and no horseman had come that way in days.

They none of them believed him, but with that silent unanimity that marked all their actions that day, they rode off again, certain that his denial concealed his knowledge that Nick had indeed come by, and had been making for his brother's place at the end of the dale.

They rode faster now. Flurries of early snow swept across the hillsides. The cold bit into their cheeks and nipped their fingers. It made Rob's eyes water; he would never forget the smart of tears as they rode their vengeance. The ponies' breath rose in clouds when they paused on a ridge. Away to the left they could see flames climb to the low sky, but whether from a burning rick or building they could not tell. The sight urged them to quicken their pace again.

At last, up a side valley, they saw their goal, a moorland farm, a poor miserable place, with a few lean sheep dotting the hillside before them. Clym gestured to the others to draw rein. Their bridles jingled in the dead stillness.

'It's open,' he said, 'ower open. Nick will be half up the braeside cowering in a fox-hole afore we move.'

'Aye,' Will said, 'I dinna like the quiet. It's uncanny quiet.'

Maurie had no answer, but kicked his pony hard in the ribs so that it jumped forward, forcing its way past Clym, and Maurie set it at a hard gallop up the stoney hillside. The others had no choice but to follow, scattering the few sheep. Rob kept his eyes fixed on the hut, trusting his pony to choose her footing well, and still saw nothing move, but a thin smoke that soon lost itself in the winter light.

Without dismounting Will banged the hilt of his whip on the door and shouted. For a long time nothing happened. The world seemed reduced to the four brothers in the dead grey glen.

At last, with much fumbling, the bar was slipped. The half-door opened revealing a woman, ash-faced, with a shawl round her head, and dark eyes with half-moons under them. She raised her head to look Clym in the eye.

'Where is he then, your man's brother?'

'He's no been here.'

'Na, na, wife,' said Clym, 'we've the priest's word for it, the wee shilpit priest by the lochside.'

'The priest would hae been feart,' the woman said. 'He'll have lied to be rid of ye.'

Maurie leapt down from his pony and thrust himself past the

woman and the two bairns that were clinging to her skirts, and into the cottage. It was bare as a robbed tomb.

'Search as you like,' she said, 'he's no here.'

'Aye, but you'll tell us,' Maurie said.

'Leave her be, Maurie,' Clym said. 'We've nought to do wi' women and bairns. Where's your ain man then, wife?'

'Awa, weel awa, in a far place where the likes of you willna find him.'

'Is that so?' Maurie smiled. 'Maybe we ken better. Will, keep an eye on the wife here, while we hunt round the back.'

There was not much to search, no more than a couple of mean sheds and a pigsty. It was there they found him lying in the muck between the wall and a sow that had just farrowed. A bucket which had tumbled over scattering scraps of kale showed he had been feeding the pig when he heard the horses. Together they dragged him to his feet and round the front of the hut to where his wife still stood against the door-post gnawing a corner of her shawl to keep from screaming. Rob even then remarked her black and broken teeth, the dull pain in her eyes and the lasting defiance of her look.

Without a word Maurie fetched rope from the saddle bag and tied the man's hands behind his back. He took another, thicker, strand of rope and tested the big branch of the thorn tree in front of the house, fastening the rope to it, hauling a tight knot. Then, with Clym's help, he got the man on to Clym's pony and led it under the tree. He tied the end of the rope in a noose round the man's neck. And still, to Rob's horror, the man said nothing.

'Where's Nick then?' Clym said. 'It's Nick we want. You ken fine what he's done and why we want him.'

Still the man did not answer, though Rob willed him to speak, and even formed a prayer that he would.

'Ye damned stot,' Clym said. 'Will ye no speak?'

'For pity's sake tell him,' the woman cried, 'in the name of the Master.'

Her husband shook his head, with a slow movement that took his chin across the knot of the noose.

'Then I will,' she cried. 'We owe naething to him. He scuttled down the hill to the black tarn there, and left us to face you, the wee rat. That's where you'll find him cowering in the rashes. Now cut my man down.'

Maurie laughed. 'The wee rat indeed.' He brought the flat of his sword hard down on the pony's rump, so that it shot forward alarmed, freeing itself of the Goodman of Hangingshaws who swung there, suspended from his hawthorn tree, his feet well clear of the ground.

'Ye'd best catch your pony, Clym,' said Maurie.

But Rob was already off, galloping careless and hell-for-leather down the broken ground to the black tarn. Hearing him come, the little man hidden in the reeds panicked. Rob caught a glimpse of a white frightened face raised against him, and then Nick of the Hangingshaws ran blindly and stumbling into the peaty water. Rob kicked his pony after him and for a moment it near ran him down and Rob was like to trample him to his death. But instead the pony slipped, Rob flung himself from its back and seized hold of Nick, and the pair of them disappeared into the watery black.

It was like grappling with an eel. Nick twisted round and seized Rob by the throat. Both came like bubbles to the surface, their faces held inches from each other.

'It's you, is it,' Nick breathed, 'I'm glad o' that. I aye hated you worst of all. Devil on it, I should hae dirked you afore now. Well, I'm done for, but by St Bride I'll tak you wi me.'

The fingers tightened on the boy's throat. Rob twisted his legs round the little man and threw him over. But the grip held. Rob kicked wildly but felt himself being forced down and down into the black water of death. Then all at once the grip slackened, another hand grabbed him by the collar and pulled him up. He surfaced choking, to find Clym standing between the pair of them, thigh-deep in water, his other hand buried deep in Nick of the Hangingshaws' hair.

'You should hae waited, Rob,' he said. 'Drowning's nae death for this yin. Will, bring the horses. Christ's blood, Nick, were ye mad, man? Did you really think we wadna be revenged on ye? Did you no ken we would hae your blood for Feyther's gin we had to hunt you to the Gates of Hell itself? What sort of gold did they offer you?

'Where's Maurie?' Rob asked.

'He bided upby,' Will said, 'tae see the Gudewife didna cut down her man . . .'

They found Maurie and the woman fixed there, as if the world had frozen. Now she lifted her head, sensing Nick was with them, and directed a long, lingering and terrible look at the little man. 'I prayed him to send you on your way,' she said. 'I tellt him you brought naething but doom, that you carried death in your whey face. But he was your brother. "He's my ain blood," he said. Weel, look now on your brother and your blood. Look weel on the sour fruit of your work, Nick, and taste the blood that's on your ain hands and head. Look well and savour the sight afore you're bound over tae everlasting torment.'

'We'll hae your pony again, Clym,' Maurie said. 'Fetch him, Will. He kens the job noo.'

'Aye,' cried the woman, 'hang him, he was born to be hangit. But bear this in mind, ye black Laidlaws o' Clartyshaws, ye will rue the weird ye hae chosen for yourselves this day. The punishment ye mete oot tae this miserable wretch gangs against the king's laws and the laws of mortal men, but what you have done tae my gudeman whae never harmed a hair of your family's head, whae committed nae offence but to give shelter to the bairn brother his dying mother commended to his care, flies in the face of a' justice like chaff blown by the west wind. There's nae penance can quit you o' this deed, and sae I command you to heed my words, the words o' a woman widowed by your cruel spite and left wi bairns made feytherless by your same spiteful nature, but a woman too whae has trafficked in the dark mysteries and won herself the power to invoke the dark and revengeful and masterful spirits that control the destinies of men. Listen well, Laidlaws of Clartyshaws, while I cry this murder to the skies. Murder will no sleep easy. I call my Master's vengeance on you, and I say to you, you four black-hearted brothers, that when you lie dying in fear and grief and laneliness and loathing, in a cauld o' love that has never been or o' a love that you have stifled and slain with your ain cruelty, mind you weel o' my man and o' the widow-woman you hae made the day and the orphans you hae deprived of their feyther. I lay my curse on you and my Master's curse and I deliver you to him I serve, and I tell you, with the fruits of all the dark knowledge I hae won me, that all of you will die mad, or feart,

23

or graveyard cauld, cheated o' whatever you desire even in the moment you hae thocht tae triumph, all of you in sad confusion and misery, and maist especially you, you cankered cripple there that has had a gallows-look since the day you crept forth deformed and vile frae your mother's womb . . . I curse you in your joy and your ambition, in your work and in your love, in the field and in your bed . . . I call on the skies, the moon and stars and all familiar spirits to bear witness to my curse, that in the moment of death you will mind what you hae done this day and tremble for it even in the corruption of your spirit . . .'

Rob could not meet her gaze, but Maurie looked long at her, and then fastened the noose under Nick's chin.

'Aye aye, woman,' he said, 'those are brave words, but we have business to do now,' and he brought the flat of his sword again against the pony's rump.

Isobel could not settle the whole day. She envied Clym's wife Mollie for her ability to go on as if the brothers were merely out tending the cattle or sheep. As for her she was in and out from her mother's bedside time and again, till she realized that she was bringing her to the same state of fretful anxiety she was in herself. 'Let her be,' Mollie said, 'let the woman rest, and you fetch in the twae milking cows. There's nought women can do but their wark. And if you care to take that peely-wally English lord of Maurie's wi you, you would hae my thanks. I canna dae wi having him in the kitchen, aye sipping at his ale and haeing my sark off wi his een. As for Clym and his brothers they will dae what has to be done, ye can rest assured of that, lass.'

So Isobel went to fetch the cows, but though she asked des Moulins to accompany her, he took one look at the bleak damp of the day, pulled his furs around him, and declined. Yet in a little while as she sat on her three-legged stool, working the red cow's teats and getting what comfort and assurance she could from the warm pressure of its flank against her brow, she heard his soft cough behind her and was aware of him settling himself in the straw by her side.

Edward des Moulins looked at the girl's rounded cheek, at her soft full lips, at her warm breasts, at the red hands massaging the cow's teats. He whistled a little tune. When she had finished he placed his hands on her shoulder and languidly began to

24

stroke her, leaning over her as she sat still on the stool by the cow. Sensing no resistance, he drew her against himself. He pressed her head against his groin and then drew her off the stool down on the straw. She wondered at his soft cared-for hands, at his light voice and gentleness; his effeminate authority was something she had never met before, never imagined, yet found herself welcoming. She lay safe in his arms in the deep straw and the dark of the stable. He dillied, dallied, toyed and ployed, teased and pleased, and sighed with the expectation of pleasure. His soft white fingers played on her breasts, then his lips found a home there, gently as a sucking child. He drew her on top of him and his hands found their way under her skirt and stroked her thighs. She played with the yellow hair that fell over his forehead, and he moaned with joy at her strength and firmness. 'Now,' he said, 'now.' Warmth and tenderness overwhelmed her as his hands found their way between her legs. 'Now,' he said again, and they rolled over, and he thrust against her. She yielded to his thin nervous urgency and her lips opened to say 'yes'. Their tongues met and they twined together, with the dark around them and the hot sweetness of the new milk in the close air.

The four brothers looked back from the end of the valley. They saw the hovel and the thin smoke, and the tree standing out clear. One body still swung from the hanging tree and they could just see a black shape crouching on the earth while the breeze brought them the wailing of the woman and her children.

'Weel,' Clym said, 'Feyther can rest now.'

Will nodded his head. Rob shivered. 'Rest,' a voice said in his head, 'will we rest again after what we have done the day?' But he kept silence; it was not a thought to share.

Maurie said, 'Happen we should have strung the auld beldam up wi her man.'

'Aye,' Clym said, 'and like as not you'd hae slit the bairns' throats tae.'

Maurie nodded. 'Deeds likan ours are better covered wi a shroud.'

With one accord they turned their horses' heads and rode off at a shabby trot down the valley. Night closed round them as they headed for home.

III

Maurie rubbed his cheek against the fur collar which disguised his crooked shoulder. As he sat waiting for Des Moulins to move his piece, he toyed with the jewelled relic (St Pandulf's finger in a gem-encrusted étui) which he wore on a silver chain round his neck. The tops of his slippers, made of the finest kid, were also fringed with fur. He stretched out his right hand to the goblet of Gascon wine. Beyond them in the hall many of the company were still at table, but their shouts and occasional snatches of song and laughter no longer disturbed him as they had in his early months in the castle. Now he waited for Edward to move. As for himself, he was content, well satisfied with his position.

Edward moved his rook as Maurie had intended he should. That let him bring his bishop into play to support and cover his queen. He had identified the key square on the board, concentrated his forces against it, and prepared a trap from which Edward could not escape.

These games of chess were necessary as well as pleasant. From the first Maurie had seen that he must establish a moral supremacy over the lord he had adopted. Chess, counsel and a deference that hardly concealed his superiority were his weapons. Now he leant over the table, moved the bishop to take his master's pawn, then picked up the jug of wine and refilled Edward's cup. It pleased him that the young baron drank three to his one. Courtesy was another weapon, and humour; Maurie could relieve Edward's depression with mockery of those his master feared and resented.

Maurie had come far in the twelve months he had passed at Castle Greer. He had arrived a skinny fugitive, speaking in a Scots accent they mostly detested. He remembered that ride up the north Yorkshire dale, and in memory could again experience the apprehension he had felt. It had been a bold measure, justified by his desperation. Of course there was nothing remarkable in his decision to seek fortune south of the border. There was a frequent coming and going. Many families had connections on both sides; wanted men found it convenient to slip across out of the jurisdiction of those they had offended. Moreover, except in rare periods, few Borderers were so infected with national spirit as to make service on the other side seem disloyal; it was common for great nobles to maintain such connections across the frontier as might come in useful should they chance to offend their own king. In fact the Border was a great convenience for all those who had little respect for the law or for royal authority.

All the same, as a young man who had killed a priest, Maurie had cause for apprehension. The Church was loth to abandon the pursuit of those who had offended it, simply because they had put themselves across a frontier. His father had been blunt with him. Maurie had imperilled them all and must run for it. Was it to be France or England, he had asked, expecting the boy to say France. But Maurie, looking him in the eye, had plumped for England.

Now, looking at Edward's thin, light-featured face, at his too-ready smile, at his long, constantly moving fingers and the soft hair he was forever flicking back from his brow, Maurie thrilled again at the choice he had made, trembling with pleasure at the knowledge that he could dominate his lord.

'Mate in two moves,' he said.

The thin fingers moved in the air before him, then swept the pieces from the board. Too little stamina, too many nerves, Maurie thought; well, he could provide what was lacking.

'If only winter would end,' Edward said.

Walter had questioned his son's decision. It was easier and safer to go to France where there was a constant demand for Scots soldiers in the long war against the English that the heretic-burning Harry of Monmouth had resumed with his invasion of France. Maurie nodded and touched his shoulder. 'I'm no warrior, Feyther,' he said. 'Whae would recruit a cripple?' Walter shrank from the subject, which he had never been able to talk about to the boy. Then he nodded. There was, he said, a family in England might welcome Maurie. Had he heard of the des Moulins? Maurie shook his head. His father was not surprised. It had been three generations back, even four, but once, the des Moulins had been lords of much of the Scottish Border. 'We ourselves were their lieges,' Walter said. A great part of the estates now held by the puissant House of Douglas, to whom the Laidlaws now owed fealty, had once belonged to the des Moulins. But the des Moulins, with extensive estates and many manors south of the Border too had supported the English in the long wars that the Scots would come to call Wars of Independence. After the death of Robert the Bruce, the des Moulins had been among those who supported Edward Balliol, whom Edward of England tried to establish on the Scottish throne. They had suffered with Balliol, losing their Scottish lands when he was driven out. But, Walter said, like all the Disinherited (as these lords were called) they had never relinquished the hope that one day they would be restored to their old estates. Walter ran his finger down the blade of his dagger. Who could tell how things might fall out? The family might well benefit from having a foot in both camps. Maurie should go to Castle Greer, now the stronghold of the des Moulins, and present himself as a member of a family once loyal to the des Moulins, now himself anxious to resume his old allegiance. That had been his father's scheme, and now, sitting in furs and sippng Gascon wine, Maurie marvelled again at the old man's wit, at his knowledge of the ways of men.

'If only winter would end,' Edward sighed again.

The snow had lain for weeks now, since soon after their return from their Scottish venture, on which Edward had embarked in a spirit of levity, and from which he had returned at once nervous and conceited. It had not taken long for Maurie to discover what had happened. Within hours of their return he had suspected it. He knew the truth when Isobel blushed as Edward spoke and could not meet his own eyes. He took her aside and questioned her. 'Pray God you're no with child,' he said. 'The Lord Edward is a great lord, affianced to a great heiress.'

'Take me with you,' she pleaded. 'I know I canna marry him, but take me with you. There's no place for me here.'

For a moment he was tempted, but shook his head. 'It's madness what you speak of,' he told his sister. But he made it his business to get Edward away quickly. There was no telling

28

how Clym would behave in his unsettled state if he found out what had happened. He promised Isobel he would send for her, if there was trouble, and rode off, never meaning to keep the promise, but pleased with the new knowledge he had acquired of his lord.

Edward drew his cloak around him and shivered. He hated the cold. There had been a fresh fall of snow on Sunday last, and though Castle Greer was big enough, Maurie thought, to be a town in itself, though the outer bailey had been cleared of snow that the men might exercise, the denial of bodily freedom and the constraints of winter told on Edward. He was a boy who needed hard exercise to compose his mind. Now he fretted. His hand moved under his short tunic. Maurie looked at him feeling a contempt he kept out of his eyes.

'You were telling me about your great grandfather,' he said.

'He was the last great man of our family,' Edward said, smiling at the thought but not moving his hand. 'My father, God rest or rot him, was nothing. I never knew him for my sister and I were born in his old age, but he was by all accounts, a tired, timid man.' Edward giggled. 'So was his father, both with no more guts than a rizzered herring, my uncle said. And yet they held on to what they had, while my great grandfather, the Lord William, lost all his lands in Scotland, pawned his English estates to raise a company to fight in France alongside the Black Prince, and lost them too, along with lands briefly granted him in Gascony. Yet William was considered a hero, a paladin of war. Can you explain that, Maurie?'

'The world loves a flourish,' Maurie said. 'How came you then by Castle Greer?'

'My poor thing of a father married the heiress. She was his first wife. The marriage was arranged by the Prince to compensate us for what we had lost.'

Maurie took a coin and spun it. 'Heads or tails?'

'Oh . . . tails.'

'Heads it is. You see,' he said, 'it is chance. Chance rules all, rules the world and controls our destinies. Your great grandfather followed Balliol?'

'I have told you so.'

'And thus became one of the Disinherited. If the coin of fate had fallen otherwise . . .'

'I would be Lord of the Douglas lands . . .'

Maurie smiled: 'And may yet be, my lord. Chance will tell. As it is, you have already suborned the loyalty of one whose fathers have followed the Douglas for a hundred years, and whose brothers still follow him.

He held his smile, happy in his smoothness, taking pleasure in the English accent he had laid across his rough Scots tongue, happy in the future he saw unfolding. Edward nodded, not yet convinced. His hand crept under his tunic again.

'Oh this winter,' he sighed. 'We should have had your sister ride south with us.'

'My sister? What has a great lord like you to do with the likes of her, a milky maid, a poor ignorant country lass . . .'

Des Moulins had a sister too, a slim girl with yellow hair and a petulant wilful mouth. Her name was Clare and she was consumed with boredom as she waited to escape from the prison of her girlhood. Her boredom took a strange form. She had an odd fancy to learn to read. Edward of course mocked her for it. Reading was clerk's business. But their guardian, their mother's brother, Sir Guy de Grange, a solemn solitary man, who had travelled far, making pilgrimages to Rome and Compostella in Spain, nodded a sleepy approval. He assigned one of his secretaries, a young clerk named Nicholas, as tutor. Nicholas, a red-faced garrulous fellow, whose breath was greasy with pork and beer, babbled to Maurie of the beauty of his pupil. Not only of her beauty, but of her . . . he dug Maurie in the ribs . . . her willingness. He would swear to that. These girls with dark blue eyes set far apart and thin legs were eager as stoats. They would go at it like whores in hell, he said, and grinned at Maurie and licked his lips. 'And my lad,' he said, 'they think a clerk's safe. They licence us to all kinds of toying liberties, as long as we stop short of the final act.' He sucked juicily on a pigs's rib-bone. 'Rumbling and tumbling and fingerplay,' he said licking the illustrative finger, 'she's hot for it, boy. Don't you envy me?' He slopped his beer in his excitement. 'And I'll tell you another thing, boy, my own secret what I've learned myself and one that will be useful to you, cripple as you are. I'm telling you because I've taken a fancy to you, Maurie my boy. Listen I'm fat and ugly and sweating and my breath stinks worse even than my feet. You think that rules me out as a lover? Not a bit. It used to dismay me till I put it to the test. But girls like it, boy, you know, it's Beauty and the Beast. Shall I tell you something more, boy. When the Beast turned back into a beautiful and noble prince, she was soon bored and disgusted. There was no relish in it for her, and she herself turned to the stable for an ostler stinking of horse-piss and horse dung, or to a fat beery pot-bellied clerk like me. These well-born girls with their virgins' faces and clean linen are panting and sobbing for a spot of corruption. Specially when they have those dark blue eyes set far apart . . .'

'Have some more ale,' Maurie said.

'I don't mind if I do.' Nicholas winked. 'I never mind when I do. You're a hunchie, Maurie, a misshapen, misbegotten creature with a sharp wit and no morals. I can read you like a book, better really. Take my advice, and take heart. You've a great career as a lover. I speak,' he hiccuped 'with all the sublime authority of Holy Church.'

Maurie encouraged him to drink and talk, and gabble and drink himself into deeper confidences, boasts and indiscretions. Then next morning, in bright new spring sunshine, Maurie splashed his face with water from the well in the courtyard, had himself shaved and decked himself in a clean tunic and surcoat of Lincoln green, a livery supplied by Edward. He crimped himself and scented himself to remove any lingering beer fumes, though he had himself been moderate as usual, and requested an audience with Sir Guy.

The old man – he was near fifty and had lost all his teeth and most of his hair – was in his chamber, engaged in the passion of his old age, accounting. Maurie addressed him humbly, in his most honeyed voice, his Scots accent subdued to inaudibility but for the occasional long vowel. He begged pardon for the interruption, would not have dared to approach him but for his deep respect and care for the family, his sense of duty and the urgency of what he had to relate, yet hesitated to broach the matter, alas; nevertheless he must, in whatever trepidation, for it concerned the Lady Clare, concerned indeed her very honour.

Sir Guy, who had been shifting with the impatience of a man drawn from his passion, bridled. 'My niece's honour. What can you have to do with that?'

'Nothing at all, my lord, being myself so humble in your

household, and when I say honour, I must protest that nothing I may say should in any way be thought to impute anything that might in any way sully what I am as certain as I hope for immortal life can be nothing but immaculate. Nevertheless, my lord, that clerk Nicholas . . .'

'How? My clerk Nicholas? What of him?'

'. . . who has been teaching her to read . . . has also been talking filth. He lies in his teeth my lord, doubtless, I am certain of that. Nevertheless what he says, what he asserts, what, my lord, he boasts of, though empty words, are words such as should not be employed of any lady. My lord, he has been traducing your niece, uttering the most foul and malicious slanders . . .'

Sir Guy pressed him. Maurie was firm. The clerk Nicholas had, he said, grossly deceived his lord, grossly abused his trust. Maurie's quiet determination coupled with his respectful demeanour, finally convinced Sir Guy. He swore he would confront Nicholas with his accuser. Maurie held up his hand, palm towards Sir Guy, and begged to be excused. 'My lord,' he said, 'I am your most loyal and obedient servant, and the Lord Edward's also, and would fain be the Lady Clare's, but, for that very reason, I must implore you to proceed otherwise with this matter, and excuse me this meeting. The fact is that the Lord Edward has asked me to test his men for disaffection, to sound out their views. If it becomes known – as it would be known – that I have reported my conversation with the clerk Nicholas to your lordship, why then, my value to both you and my lord Edward will be reduced. I have no doubt in any case that the clerk Nicholas will have babbled in the same lewd and insolent manner to many others. There is no reason, my lord, why he should learn from whom you have heard of his grossness.'

As he spoke Maurie lowered his eyes, trusting in his words and humble tone of voice to convince Sir Guy. He kept very still and silent as the old man deliberated.

'Very well then,' Sir Guy said, 'your argument is good. If the villain was not a clerk in Holy Orders I should have him flogged from the Castle gate to the parish church.'

'He's no' a priest, you ken,' Maurie said, lapsing momentarily into his native idiom. 'He's nae even what they ca' a deacon, is he?'

He watched Sir Guy struggle with temptation. 'No,' he said

at last, 'I dare not . . . he still has protection of Holy Church. But I'll have him stripped and ducked in the moat.'

An hour later, Maurie, resting on the little balustrade that surrounded the well in the courtyard, watched the fat clerk have his cassock torn off, saw him dragged through the gate, and listened to his yelps of protest turn to screams as the boot of a Flemish sergeant sent him flying into the icy water of the moat. He splashed with difficulty to the land in his clinging shift amid laughter and cheerful insults.

'Do not coom this vay again,' called the sergeant. 'My orders are, Nicholas, to give you a goot dooking any time you coom near the castle. So Gott speed you, you fat whoremonger . . .'

Two days later Maurie approached the Lady Clare and humbly offered himself as tutor.

'You,' she said, fixing her gaze on his raised shoulder, 'you are no clerk, my little Scot.'

Maurie smiled.

'Can you even read?' she said.

'That I can. And Latin and French too, and play the virginals as well as I can beat my Lord Edward at chess . . .'

'Oh come,' she said, 'Latin and French . . .'

'I was taught,' he said, 'by a renegade and criminal priest who took refuge with my family a few years back. He taught me well. He assured me reading would open the door to undreamed-of delights.'

Her tongue touched her lips. She pressed her hands over her breasts.

'Delights?' she said. 'I fear the priest was deceiving you. Besides,' she said, 'I have lost the fancy. It was a girl's whim, nothing more.'

'A girl's whim, my lady? Surely fat Nicholas has not satisfied that?'

She blushed and lifted her chin.

'Fat Nicholas,' he said, smiling, 'was a dull and clumsy teacher, I'll be bound. He would smother any interest, douse the flame with his stinking breath. Perhaps a new tutor would reanimate your . . . enthusiasm.'

'Little Scot,' she said 'be careful. I heard Nicholas shriek at the coldness of the water . . . and he was protected by his clerk's status.'

'Oh my lady, he said, 'I speak of Latin and French, nothing more.'

'My ladies tell me French is an immoral tongue.'

'I have found it,' he said, 'interesting.'

'Tell me,' she said, 'is it true what my brother boasts of, that he seduced your sister?'

Maurie shrugged his shoulders and spread his hands.

'He took his pleasure, my lady.'

'While you were avenging your father's death, he says.'

'That is so.'

'And you are not angry?'

'My lady, she was my sister, and I am a humble man. My lord Edward is my lord, and a great one.'

'How,' her tongue touched her lips again, and he felt the intensity of her thin frame, 'how did you avenge your father?'

He smiled, 'we hanged the wretch and a woman cursed us.'

'Perhaps,' she said, 'Nicholas was a poor teacher.'

IV

Of all the brothers Will amounted to least, and so Will became a wanderer. He had nothing but a few half-bit talents, and would sit for hours whittling at his sticks or playing little tunes on his fiddle, tunes that would break off like as not in the middle of a stave. In the weeks after the brothers' ride Will's isolation seemed ever more marked. It was Rob who was consulted by Clym, Rob who worked with Clym, Rob who rode out with his elder brother, while Will, who should have done so, skulked indoors, vacant-eyed as if he had been a natural. Years later Rob wondered if Will hadn't felt the enormity of their deed more than any of them, even though he knew that Will slept sound of nights while he himself was kept awake by the wild sounds of the dark and the pictures that tumbled over in his mind and oppressed him. Yet once or twice Rob caught a look of fear in Will's eye; he was like a man who cannot stop his gaze from turning to the far horizon that marks a frontier. It was clear to Rob too how Will missed their father, not with the deep loss he knew himself, but rather as a man who had aye had a quick command for him that filled his day. Clym wouldn't, it seemed, be troubled to see that Will was occupied. He left him whittling at his stick and playing his half-tunes and never asked him to do more than maybe keep an eye on the beasts when they were let out on the thin sour moss-grass of a false spring.

Even their mother had never had much time for Will – he had been a bairn that never called attention to himself and one that responded neither to petting or scolding; so she had formed the habit of letting the boy drift in no especial airt. 'A fushionless loon,' she used to say shaking her head. But now she had no mood for even that comment, but sat long winter hours gazing at the blank walls. She had coughed her way through the coldest weather and was spitting disordered blood in February dawns. Her flesh fell away, her voice, always soft and gentle, grew faint, her will to live dwindled. If she noticed Isobel's condition she said nothing, and Isobel herself told Rob and Clym of wakeful nights disturbed by Ailie's racking cough. They told each other that she would pick up with the mild weather, but hardly believed their own assurances, and when he heard them, Will shook his head and said nothing. The false spring seemed to disconcert her indeed, and one night early in a March that had crept in soft and lamb-like and sunny, her soul slipped away in the dark to join the Maker in whom, alone of the family, she had warmly trusted. They buried her by her husband and Clym and Rob rode out to Yarrow to pay the priest to say a mass for her grieving soul. When they got back and saw smoke rising from a fire where Isobel was burning the cloths from their mother's bed, Rob felt the sword stab of realization that he had no guides but his equals and his own judgement left, no sure comfort beneath the wandering sun and moon.

Two days later he came in from doing a round of the cattle to take his breakfast. He found Will laying a saddle-bag across one of the galloway ponies.

'What's this?' he said.

'I'm for off too.'

'Oh aye,' Rob said, 'and where to?'

'I'm for France.' Will looked at the ground.

'For a soldier? You?'

'Just that,' Will said. 'There's nowt for me here, and the warld's room.'

'But you'll no be off like this,' Rob said. 'Without a word, had I no happened by.'

Will shrugged his shoulders.

'There's nowt for me here,' he repeated. 'You and Clym are thick as they twae reivers either side of the Holy Rood. So,' he paused again and scuffled his toes on the ground, 'I'm for the wars.'

He held out his hand, Rob felt a surge of shame. Will was surely right, they had treated him as of no account, and here he was for France to fight the English. Rob seized his brother's hand and pulled him hard against him.

'Bide a minute, will you?'

He found Isobel in the kitchen scrubbing a pan.

'Have you spoke to Will?'

'Aye.'

36

'Is that a' you can say?'

'Aye,' she said again, keeping her eyes down.

'Can we no stop him?'

'What for should we?'

'Are you saying he's right to go?'

'Happen he's daft. But there's nowt for him here.' She laid her damp hand on her belly. 'Happen there's no muckle for ony of us. But there's nowt for Will.'

Rob hesitated.

'Well,' he said, 'will you gang outbye and keep haud of him a minute. We canna just let him ride aff on his lane.'

Isobel looked up at last. Rob saw she had been weeping and felt a tear prick his own eye.

'It's a lang road he'll hae to travel on his lane,' she said, 'but I'll do your bidding.'

Rob climbed the stair and fished in the kist by his bedside and found an amulet with an image of the Virgin.

'Here,' he said to Will, 'it was the mither's, wear it for safety and for memory. And here, I'll ride you on your way as far's the heid ower the Swire.'

So they mounted their ponies and rode down the hill, clip-clop at a trot too eager for Robin's mood, and climbed till they halted on a ridge where they could look back to the folded hills of the upper valleys. Will gazed south a long minute and said, 'I canna get thon auld wife's words oot of my mind. Happen they'll no hound me tae France.'

Then, giving Rob no chance to reply, he tugged at his pony's head – he was ever a sudden clumsy rider – and said, 'I'm tellt I'll maybe find a ship in Leith. So, brother, happen I'll be back wi my fortune made.'

Rob watched him descend to the valley in the direction of Yarrow, from where he would turn up the water before heading for Tweed. He watched him till the distance swallowed him up and knew for sure that Will's last words were no more than whistling in the dark to keep his courage up; and knowing this, Rob wondered what fears lay behind the half-music Will had been accustomed to make.

All the time he rode back Rob found his eyes turning to the southern hills, and he tried to remember how Will had looked at Hangingshaws and searched his mind too for any signs of guilt or perturbation Will had shown since. But it was no good.

Will was a brother he had hardly known. He had accepted his presence as you might a dog's, and it was only now he was gone he felt his place in his life. Clym however said nothing when he heard the news, just gave an abrupt nod of the head, and it wasn't till the evening that he referred to it.

'So there's just the twae of us,' he said then.

They had been seeing to the horses and the air was warm with the reek of the midden, but below them in the valley a chill mist was rising. A bit moon was half-masked by shifting clouds, making its light pale, and a barn owl cried further up the wood. Without saying anything the brothers walked side by side to the grave where their father and mother lay. It had been dug on a little knoll that let them look right into the valley.

'The daft fool,' Clym said, 'tae run tae France. I had no words with him you ken, and yet I ken fine what was troubling his mind. How could we baith no ken?'

He leant against a branch of hawthorn tree that glistened black in the half-light.

'As if you can flee from . . .' he said, and stopped as if to listen. But the owl was silent and there was no sound but a dog barking behind them. 'A man maun dree his weird,' Clym said. 'You and me winna run.' He paused again. 'And what of our sister? The bairn'll be the English lord's?'

'Ah well,' Rob said, thinking to comfort or divert him, 'nae matter whae the feyther, it'll be no but a bairn, and the sister'll care for it fine.'

'I've my ain bairns,' Clym said. 'Have you no a lass, Rob?'

Rob laughed. 'Time enough,' he said.

'We'll no hear from Maurie, you ken. He's gane frae our life tae. Maybe there's nocht that binds us but the auld wife's curse. But this bairn of our sister's will be born in an ill-chanced hour . . . do you think, Rob, you that has a poet's head on him, that the English lord lay with her in the same hour as we . . . and what would the Feyther say?' He lay face-down a moment on the rough wet turf that covered the grave. 'Would he talk of our sister's honour tae be avenged?' He ran his hands over the grave. 'One minute of cruel madness frae Maurie, one ill choice o' mine that I'll carry like an open wound till I die.' He held his hands up and licked his wet palm. 'There's a dew,' he said, 'a heavy yin. It'll maybe be fair the morn.'

V

Rob's hand moved in the water and rested, chilling. The cold
ran up his forearm to the elbow. He let his hand creep forward
as if floated by the stream, and began to work his fingers under
the speckled belly of the trout. The fish responded to the tickling
till Rob was able to close his hand round it, and then, with a
flick of the wrist that caught the fish by surprise, howk it on to
the bank where it lay squirming. He caught at it again and
banged its head on a stone to break its neck. The tail continued
squirming a few minutes. Rob lay back on the short grass and
looked into the pale blue of the spring sky. A verse started to
make itself and run in his head:

> Where by the bonnie waterside,
> As the broom came into yellow,
> I sought my love near eventide
> An' we twae twin'd by Yarrow . . .

They were only words, for he had no love. Down the valley
the farmhouse lay still in the dark deeds of the back-end of the
year. Isobel had withdrawn herself, brooding. He could not tell
whether she sighed for her English love or not; there had, as
Clym had foretold, been no word of him or of Maurie. Isobel
had taken to going at twilight to sit by their parents' grave, and
though Rob knew well that a lass in her condition was better to
guard herself against thoughts of mortality she merely shook her
head and stayed silent when he sought to divert her. He had
consulted old Goody Tomes, who had eased more bairns into
the world than any other wife in the valley, and laid out more
corpses too, but, though she had promised to hold herself ready
for the moment of the birth, she had had no words of comfort or
even good counsel now. Rob could see the old woman purse her

lips, and her eyes glittered, he was sure, at the way Isobel's thoughts were turning.

Mollie was no help either, for she had enough trouble on her hands with Clym, who had grown harder and more sullen in the weeks since their mother's death. Rob knew well that he blamed himself for the troubles that had come on the family, and though he had heard Mollie urge that all their misfortunes should in truth be laid at Maurie's door, Rob knew that Clym's self-hatred would not be appeased by reason. Clym had cause too for his self-reproach; it had been his lack of judgement had killed their father.

Rob knew too, without needing words, that the Gudewife's curse lay ever more heavy on Clym. He was earth-bound and all the more fearful therefore of the world beyond nature which he did not understand, which he could enter in no way. So Clym lived in a state of pent-up emotion, fear, guilt and resentment all disturbing him. He had taken to long days on the hill, either alone or with Young Clym, and Rob could only guess what thoughts he fed his son.

Rob himself felt a hollow in his bones. The curse laid on them did not disturb him, for he believed that a man's path was fixed in the world from the hour of his birth, and could not be altered by what he did or by the ill-wishing of others. Life, Rob thought, was a form of walking in your sleep; you went where you were directed by a power outside yourself. If you were wise you could read your fortune in the stars and conjunction of planets, but you could not divert your destiny. All the same, he was lonely now; he had known no girl since he lay at the inn in Jedburgh, and he dared not return there.

He fell asleep, and woke shivering; there was only a fringe of pale gold at the edge of the sky. He rose and shook himself like a dog, and whistled up his lurcher bitch that was nosing for rabbits in a patch of broom and whins. He tied his trout to a line running along a stick from which four other fish hung, picked up his staff and turned down the valley, the bitch Brownie nosing at his heels. Rob moved quietly for it was the hour of evening when you might likely see the fairies if you did not cause them to take fright. Rob had no fear of them, unlike Clym, the big stolid man who never feared mortal man but who had come into the house with his face the colour of skimmed milk after he had seen them dance in Carterhaugh. But Rob as a poet was on good terms with the other world, and now he kept his eyes alert for a sign of them.

Brownie set up a barking at a briar bush, her birse up, and her hind feet scraping the ground as she backed off from it. It was no fairy who stepped out from a clump of hazel behind the bush to accost them, but a sturdy grizzlehaired man with a red beard and a cast in one eye. He carried a stout stick and wore a surcoat of hodden grey, and he was no shepherd Rob had ever seen in the valley. He stepped right in the middle of the track that ran beside the water and greeted Rob with a sharp nod of the head. Rob gave him good evening and waited, standing a couple of paces clear, and the dog backed behind him her haunches low and her tail between her legs.

'Yon's a fine catch you have,' the man said.

'Fair enough, though they're but wee things.'

The main smiled and spoke in a clipped voice Rob couldn't place.

'You'll be Rob Laidlaw of Clartyshaws I'm thinking.'

'And if I am, ye hae the advantage of me, for there's no name I can put to you.'

'There's no name you need,' the man said, and looked at Rob as if daring him to ask again. But Rob was canny; he let the stranger guide the talk. For a moment, though, the man showed no sign of proceeding. Instead he sat down on a fallen tree, pulled a loaf of bread and a hunk of cheese out of his pouch, and began to eat.

'Will you join me?' he said.

Rob shook his head: 'I'll no do that.'

'Just as you like, then.'

The fallen tree lay across the path. Rob made to climb it and pass by the man.

The man took the cheese from his mouth. 'Bide a moment, friend.'

Rob hesitated. 'You're no from these parts,' he said.

'That I am.'

'What way have I no seen you then?'

'What way indeed?'

'And you hae the advantage owre me.'

'That I do. You're the lad whae lay at the inn at Jeddart the night his feyther was hangit.'

The sun dipped behind the hills and Rob's shadow no longer lay between him and the man. Had he seen the man cast a shadow at all?

'What's that to you?' he asked. 'My feyther was falsely killed.'

'I've heard different,' the man said. 'It's naething to me though. I'm nobbut a messenger, my friend.'

'A messenger? Whae from?'

'That I'm forbid to say.'

'Forbid?'

'And my message is brief, friend. You're to be under the alder tree in the Goodman's croft on the far side of the wood the morn's night at moonrise.'

And with that he put the cheese to his lips again and munched like one who had dismissed the conversation.

Rob was restless through the next day, so that even Clym, self-absorbed as he was, noticed it. He chided him first, and then, good nature breaking through like a rainbow, mocked him for being 'surely lovelorn and I didna ken.' That morning they worked side by side more happily than at any time since their father's death, till Clym's mood was changed black again towards noon by the sight of a man riding up the valley on a black-and-white shelt.

'It's the laird's jock,' Clym said. 'Mind what you say now, Rob.' He told Mollie to take the bairns back in the house (though young Clym objected) and stood there rubbing the back of his hand against his nose and watching the pony climb the hill. When Rob asked him what he was thinking, he only shook his head.

The horseman greeted them without dismounting.

'Are your ponies shod?'

'Aye, that they are.'

'I'm blithe to hear it. The Douglas would hae you ride.'

'Aye.'

'When the moon's past full. Be ready then to present your-selves at Hermitage,' and the man trotted off to carry the news to other followers of the Douglas.

'Weel,' Clym said, 'it might hae been waur,' and Rob knew that all winter and spring his brother had been fearing a summons to answer a complaint that the Wife of Hangingshaws might have laid against them. He smiled at the innocence of the thought.

'Aye, we'll ride,' Clym said, but there was no relish in his voice. He was never the man Walter had been; he would just as lief be a quiet husband and father. The moon was pricking over the hill as Rob left the peel with Brownie beside him and turned in the half-light through the Black Wood. He climbed for some half an hour through the trees, beech, hawthorn and chestnut giving way to Scots pine, silver birch and rowan. It was a soft evening with a bit of the day's warmth clinging to it, and it was still warm walking. Brownie put up a hare on a stretch of open turf and twice startled roe deer in the trees. At last Rob emerged on the moorland where springy turf alternated with clumps of heather. It was still light there, out of the wood; the moon was climbing high, and whaups were sounding their melancholy cry of vacant places. He paused a moment on a ridge. Down to his right he could see a small expanse of lighter ground, that the moon fell on, ground that was green and close-cropped all the year round, by deer doubtless. It was ground that as a child he had never dared approach, for there was an old ruin stood at the corner of the field, a place of which a tale was told of a deserted wife cursing the land with her dying blood as she still looked for her lord that would never return; the field itself had long been one to beware of, for it was known as the Dark Master's land. There was something uncanny about the pale patch with the moon throwing the shadows of the tall pines athwart it. Rob clutched his staff tighter and set off down the slope.

At first the silence oppressed him. He thought he had been brought on a fool's errand. Then Brownie set up a barking, her birse rose, and she darted towards the ruin. She stopped again, barking wildly.

A cloud crossed the moon and the light dimmed. Rob called out, and Brownie fell silent. A figure detached itself from the gap in the cottage where the door had been, and a girl's voice spoke.

'I kennt fine you would come, Rob. The wee man would hae it you were owre feart, but no my brave Robin, I said. Whisht dog, I'm nae spirit, but flesh.'

43

Brownie was whining now and Rob laid his hand reassuringly on the dog's head.

'Do you no ken me, Rob,' the girl teased.

'Aye,' he said, 'that I do,' and the picture came into his mind of her face in the light of the lantern in that grim dawn when he had his father's body slung across his saddle-bow. She held up her mouth for a kiss. They embraced and sank wordlessly on the turf and made love, still in silence, first urgently and greedily as men slake their thirst after long travelling, then again with a slow tenderness, exploring each other's bodies in a manner that brought back memories of the inn-chamber to Rob, so that he knew at last for certain which of the girls had pleasured him most. For a long time they did nothing but murmur, while Brownie sought out rabbits in the ruined stones and the fringes of the wood, and then came and lay beside them and slept.

In time they slept too under Jean's plaid, but Rob wakened long before dawn dew-drenched and chill, to look in the gathering light at Jean resting in his arms and wonder at the means she had chosen for the meeting. He touched a little froth at the corner of her mouth and she stirred in her sleep. He felt himself as if he had awakened from a dream, only the manifest reality of it lay in his arms. She had said nothing of herself, as she had not done in the inn. He knew neither whence she had come nor whether she intended to stay.

Then she woke too, slowly, reluctantly, like one for whom sleep was the natural state. He was seized with urgent desire, but when he would make love to her she pushed his hands aside.

'I'm feared for you, Rob,' she said, 'I'm feared for what I see ahead of you. There's a dark fate hangs over you, and, for all the love I have for you, I canna see how you will escape it. Listen, my love,' she said, 'you maun sleep again. When you awake I shall be gone, but I shall return when I can, and when I do so, I hope it will be to tell you how to cheat what has been decreed for you. Believe me, my lover, except I intercede on your behalf you are a lost man.'

Then she leaned over, and closed his eyes with soft fingers, and laid her lips on his eyelids, with as light a touch as a moth, and he felt himself drift back to sleep, though it was against any conscious will of his.

There was no sign of the girl when he woke again, but he

44

found a sprig of May twined in his bonnet. But for the May he might have persuaded himself it was all but a dream and the girl a Princess of Elfland. He was stiff and sore and, when he had won his way back to Clartyshaws, all Isobel's teasing could elicit no answer but a shake of a head and the information that he had gone hunting with Brownie and passed the night in the woods.

VI

The Great Court of Hermitage was crowded with retainers of the mighty House of Douglas, who had ridden in from the Forest, from Liddesdale, from the softer lands of Annan and the high lands of Lanark. Rob and Clym arrived there with half a dozen followers towards evening, guided to the Castle from miles off by smoke rising from the oxen that were being roasted on spits in the yard, that all men might have a dish of meat from their Lord. They would, Rob thought, be poor creatures to roast after their wintering unless maybe they had been brought from the Western grasslands where it was possible to keep the beasts out in all but the foulest of the winter weather.

Clym had spoken little on the way, only saying, 'Mind your tongue here. The toun's no going to be short of those that are ill-disposed tae us.'

Rob was surprised by the number assembled. It was like a muster of all the Douglas men.

'Are we no in a time of truce?' he asked.

'That we are.'

They found themselves a corner of the courtyard where they might hope not to be noticed, and there fed their horses, attended to their wants and sent two of their men to fetch meat and ale. Clym had given a few acquaintances his grim nod as they rode over the drawbridge, before they were stopped at the gate and asked to identify themselves. This was normal procedure, not so much to guard against spies and infiltrators (for it would be a bold man who dared to spy on such a force) as to enable the Douglas to learn which of his adherents had neglected to obey his summons.

Rob respected the cause of Clym's uneasiness. His brother was used to being lord of his own kailyard. He was nervous too lest their reprisal against their father's betrayer might be resented, even though their action was fully justified by the

46

custom of the Borderland. That custom though was hardly sacrosanct. King James had inveighed against the lawlessness of the Border and men knew that Archibald, Earl of Douglas, was far from eager to offend the King. Moreover, there was the Church to be reckoned with. Not all the Laidlaws' long record of loyalty to the Douglas would protect them if their action seemed in any way to threaten his position. Earl Archibald was known to be a canny politic man, no bold spirit like some of his fathers, but one who preferred to have the law on his side.

Nevertheless Rob could hardly share Clym's alarm. It was the first time he had seen a great army assembled, and his senses and imagination thrilled at the sight. Ignoring Clym's advice, he fell into talk with a group of old soldiers who had fought in the French wars alongside the Earl Archibald's father, and he listened open-mouthed to their stories, all the time wondering if his brother Will might be having the same adventures.

One of the soldiers, a lean man with a face indented by the scars of sword-slashes, especially caught his attention. He was a man of about forty maybe, hardened and soured by the wars, bitter against the French and the Great Ones of the World.

'I served this Earl's father ten years in France,' he said, 'ten years of hard fighting and no thanks for any deeds you might perform. You may think lad, it would sicken me of war, but believe me, when you have tasted it, it's like wine. It maddens you and you wish for nothing else. They called him The Tineman, you ken, for there was hardly a battle he didna lose and ill fortune dogged him wherever he went. He was a wanchancy leader tae follow. And, boy,' he said, breathing wine into Rob's face, 'I learned only ae thing in my ten years and mair in France. Trust naebody but your ain wit and your ain strength and your ain courage.'

He passed a leather-jack of wine to Rob, who lifted it to his lips and tasted for the first time the thin sour liquor that sustained men of war throughout the long horror of the French campaigns. He spluttered to drink it, and the veteran clapped him on the back.

'They say the Earl here's feart of King James,' he said. 'I canna blame him. I was aince near hangit by the King himself, Scot though he kennt me to be.'

'How did that happen?' Rob asked.

47

'Aye tell us, old soldier,' cried another.

'Tell us how you were no hanged,' said a third, 'for, Christ man, you have the true gallows-look.'

'Gallows-look, is it?' the old soldier said. 'If you had the hauf of my experience, my friend, you would ken fine that there's nae look condemns a man tae be hangit, and there's nae look can protect him if the dice fall his way. Why man,' he said, gripping Rob by the shoulder, 'look at this bonnie boy here. By the look of him you might think him safe frae the gallows. Nae siccan thing. This lad even might swing frae the tree if his fate sae decrees. You'll no read a man's fortune in his face.'

'Aye,' said another voice, 'but tell us how King James came near to hanging you.'

The old soldier sucked at his wine-flask.

'Is it a story you want then?' he said. 'Very well. Listen. You maun ken how our present King, the noble and puissant James, as some ca' him . . .' he paused, waiting for the laugh that would greet his irony, 'was taken prisoner as a bairn by the English. You may recall that his brother, the Duke of Rothesay, whae all loved as a blithe lad wi whom to crack a bottle, had been spirited from this world while in the loving care of his uncle the Duke of Albany. Prince James's father, poor King Robert, was afeared that the Duke's embrace might likewise prove owre warm for his surviving nephew. So nothing would do but the lad be sent to France to finish his education, as it was put about. But as I say the lad was taken by the English and shut up in the Tower of London where he remained many years, never troubling us his countrymen and subjects. Well, to cut my preamble, you will ken that some years syne, the young King of England, Harry of Monmouth, a cold man who took pleasure in nowt but the singeing of heretics' flesh and the screams of his enemies dying in battle, took a notion to eat some frogs, and repaired to France for that purpose. Now you might think that we in Scotland could find nought but comfort in the King of England being occupied in France, but not so. There was nothing for it but we Scots had to be off to fight in defence of our auld allies of France, though little good we have ever had from the connection, and little respect they have ever felt for us. Why, I aince heard a fat French priest talk of Scotland as a cauld barbarous land where the sun never shines in winter and there is nae flesh to eat . . . but yon's another story for another time. Sae, to resume, I was amang these whae followed the Tineman across the water, being young and silly and eident to fight the Sassenach, as if I couldna hae done the same mair profitably by tiding owre the Cheviots. And it happened, the Tineman being as ill-skilled as ever, that I was taken prisoner, and whae should I be brocht before but oor ain King James sitting side by side wi yon dour brute Harry of Monmouth. How came he there, you ask? Weel, Harry had bethought him of the King of Scots as soon as he heard there were Scots in the French lists, so he hied him frae the Tower and carried him to France telling the royal loon that it would be a rare privilege to study the art of war by side of its greatest living master, meaning himself, the modest mannie that he was. Moreover, says he, mark my politic stroke, gin you fight by my side, why then, Jamie, says he, those wretched Scots o' yours now fighting in France will be rendered traitors to their rightful King and lord. Well, King James was blithe to agree, though you might hae thought that he wad hae said summat to the effect that it was but a puir king allowed himself to be carried bag and baggage in anither's train. But no' oor royal liege, he was gleg as a foumart to be aff to the wars.

'Sae the wee man travelled tae France wi a high heart and the Lion Rampant of Scotland flew owre his pavilion in the camp, nodding in harmony to the three leopards of England, while we Scots swacked blood on behalf of the lilies of France. Eh, but I'm dry, fetch me mair wine, my bonnie boy . . .'

Rob hung fascinated on the story, seeing as the old soldier spoke, the whole panoply of war, in its splendour and misery, unfold before his wondering eyes. He felt in touch with the great and terrible movements of the world, and again he thought of Will wandering, struggling, perhaps even dying, in France.

The old soldier drank his wine and rubbed the back of his dirty hand across his lips. 'But I tell you,' he said, 'I tell you, friends, the twae kings were well-matched, Our King Jamie, saving his grace, being every bit as harsh and as siccar that he himself could never err frae the paths of justice and righteousness as even Harry of Monmouth was. So he stood like a wee supporter on a coat of arms by King Harry's side at Troyes where the English king was recognized as heir and regent of France – the reigning king ca'ed Chairlie haeing fewer wits, poor soul, than a mad march hare. And it was oor King Jamie was first, after Harry's brothers, and an unco crew they were and are, for some still survive, to kiss the bonnie cheek of the new Queen of England, Catherine de Valois, that was sold in marriage as the price of France. Before long King Jamie found himself at the siege of Melun and it was there he issued a command to all us Scots whae were fighting in the army of the Dolphin of France, that we were to lay doon our arms or incur the dread penalties of treason for having presumed to bear weapons against our lawful king. The Earl of Buchan, the king's ain cousin, that was our general there, cocked a sneck at the order, and his was maybe the only laugh in the poor disheart-ened camp of France. But a number of Buchan's men, friends of my ain, had cause to resent it, for they were taken in the siege and set to decorate gibbets by their royal master, whae was eident to prove himself a worthy companion of cauld Harry of Monmouth.

'They were firm friends now, the twae kings. At the banquet after the Queen's coronation, King Jamie was put on her left side, and Harry invested him with the Order of the Garter on St George's Day. "Honi soit qui mal y pense" is the Garter motto, and I tell you friends, there was many a Scot thought shame of the king for accepting it.'

'What does it mean?' a listener asked.

'Shame be to him what thinks evil of it. That's the meaning. Black shame, say I, to the Scots king that welcomed it.' He paused again; the camp was falling silent as men drifted into sleep. 'Well, friends, to cut my story short, for I could tell of the French Wars till the cock crows three dawning times, I myself had the ill-fortune to be captured by a troop of English soldiers – or rather Welsh, for the leek-eating lickspittles were thick in Harry's army, and, when they found I was a Scot, I was hied before my royal liege for judgement. Eh, but that was a black hour, all the blacker when I saw Harry of Monmouth glowering by his side, ready, as I thought, to hold King Jamie to his royal purpose, lest he should slide into pity or tenderness for his fellow Scot. Not that there was muckle likelihood of that, for pity, that tenderest flower of man, has never taken root in our monarch's heart. So, picture me, friends, in my sark-tail, chained and deprived of all that might mark me as a soldier but for my unconquerable will.

'Well, I kent fine I was in sair trouble, and I saw the gallows' rope swing afore my eyes. So, says I to myself, boldness, be my friend. And I spoke up.

'"Your Grace," I cried, "there is nae mair loyal subject of the King of Scots than your humble servant. I am no, I said, properly speaking a captive at all. I am in fact a deserter. Certainly I came here to fight in France, as a loyal retainer of the Earl of Douglas, a potent allegiance as your Grace will grant me. Nevertheless, my lord, when news was brought to me of your Grace's presence in this camp, and I heard tell, as took some time in the hearing, of your Grace's command to all loyal Scots, why then I was grieved to find myself in siccan false a position. I had thocht I was fighting the English, which, saving your other Grace's august presence," says I, wondering if I dare give a wee wink and prudently deciding against it, "saving your other Grace's august presence, is a fit activity for a man of war, prohibited in nae article of war that I ken of. But then I was appalled, fair affrontit, to discover your Grace's presence, and that I was indeed fighting against my rightful king. What's mair, I was made speechless to discover that my lords of Buchan and Douglas didna immediately lay down their arms. And sae, I determined to desert at the first opportunity and join myself to your Grace. And I was doing just that when I was taken by English soldiers, or rather the . . . Welsh."

'"In the act of robbing an old wife's poultry yard and raping her daughter, look you," pipes up the wee Welsh sergeant.

'"Na, na," says I, 'living off the land and furthermair the lass was willing. She was mair than willing, gleg as a stoatie."

This earns me a steely look frae Harry of Monmouth. "I have hangit men for less," says he.

'"Sae I have heard," says I, 'but that was when the wars were young I'm thinking."

That was a rash thing to say, to remind the Frogeater of a' the debauchery and distress his lust for power and glory had inflicted on the fair land of France.

But now friends, obsairve the workings of Providence. Just as I spoke these words, a hideous grimace came owre the Frogeater's countenance. He groaned, clutched his belly and hurried frae the tent, leaving his words "I hae hangit men for less" dangling in the air ahint him. What, you ask, had happened? Harry of Monmouth, the frogeater, had been smitten with the dysentery that killed him but thirty-six hours syne. His death reprieved me, for withouten him to please, canny King James saw little to be gained by hanging a repentant subject, and instead took me into his service. But, friends, since I had masel' but scant confidence in his enduring patronage and protection, for apairt from other considerations, he was aye a prisoner of the English, I thought it mair prudent tae abandon him in Calais as he made his way through thon dismal burgh accompanying the Frogeater's body to glorious burial in England. So it happened that I missed the boat while dallying with a tavern lass, a muckle Flemish blonde called Katje, and then I continued to sodger in France for many years. So, friend, never say that I hae the gallows-look. A man saved from the hanging by a king's timely death has won the right tae say that the saints watch owre him. Yet I am laith to make siccan claim. In the affairs of this warld, chance governs all. Here endeth the first lesson: there is nae sic thing as Destiny. Man is born tae die, but the manner and hour of his death can never be foretold. Whae, I ask you, wad hae thocht that the Frogeater wad be cut doon in the hour of his sinful pride? A' the same, our Earl is wise tae fear King James, and I myself, for all my courage and fortune in the wars, am no exactly eident tae look him in the een again.'

'And what brought you hame?' Rob asked.

'What brought me hame, lad? Nought but a desire tae see again the soft hills of my ain countrie. The wines and women of la Belle France, as they ca' it, are braw indeed, but the heart pines for its calf-country and there's never a wandering Scot but desires to feel the sough of his native air again.'

He gave a great sigh, as if to prove his words, wrapped his cloak around him, rolled over on his side, and turned his face to the wall. One by one, slowly, his listeners followed suit or picked themselves up and slunk off to places they had earlier marked for sleep. The camp hushed. At last Rob was left alone, the sole man waking, it seemed to him, gazing into the embers, pondering on the old soldier's story. The Gudewife's words echoed in his mind, fighting for mastery there over his innate sense of fate and the soldier's assertion that chance ruled the world. He thought too of Jean on the hillside, lying in his arms in the Dark Master's land. She would return; yet how could he be so sure of that, if Chance was Lord? At last he slept, but woke early to hear the cock's crow.

Clym came to him before the sun was up with a dark look on his face. He had had talk with the Earl's steward and had heard that the Abbey, not content with the revenge they had taken on Walter, was now demanding that the son who had actually been guilty of the monk's murder should be surrendered to justice. 'I'm feared we may have to answer for his absence,' Clym said.

Rob stretched himself in the sun.

'And how could we do that?' he said. 'Maurie's safe whaur he bides.'

'I dinna like it,' Clym said, and Rob felt pity for his brother but no fear himself.

The Earl looked up at them with a watery and wandering eye. He shifted his corpulent body on his seat and his red face ran with morning sweat. His hand strayed to the jack of ale that sat on the table in front of him. Two or three times he refrained from lifting it, but at last, with a sigh, did so, and drank deep. He replaced the jack and began to cough, holding his left hand flat on the table to steady himself. A little thread of mucus ran down his chin.

He hardly seemed to listen as Clym made his case. His father, who was innocent, had already suffered for his brother's deed; and that brother was no longer to hand. Did the monks demand more innocent blood? The blood of his brother here, or of himself, both loyal vassals to the great house of Douglas.

'Oh aye,' said the Earl, 'loyal vassals that rob and hang as they think fit. Forbye, the company your brither keeps in England tells a different tale of loyalty. I'm thinking. Has he no attached himself tae ancient enemies of my noble house?'

'My lord,' Clym said, 'I canna be my brither's keeper.'

'Weel,' said the Douglas, 'you're no awfu' gude at it, that's for sure.'

He belched with laughter, drank more ale and gave a sour smile. But his rejoinder (or the ale, or the combination) had, Rob saw, lightened his mood. He preached a little homily on the respect due to Holy Church, all the time though supping ale, which seemed to Rob to betoken no great respect on his own part; and then talked of the obedience due to himself. But it was evident that he could not take the monk's death too seriously. It had happened, a couple of years back, and that was that. Moreover, he shared the respect for the brothers' swift revenge, which respect, Rob had become aware, was general in the camp. In the end it became a question narrowly argued of how many cows they should pay the abbey in recompense. It hurt Clym to part with these, but Rob was indifferent. Cattle were easy to come by; they would soon make good their loss. Nevertheless, seeing the Earl was bored by the pettifogging insistence of the Abbey's man of business, Rob hazarded a suggestion.

'We're talking of but yin monk, my lord,' he said. 'Would a stot no be a fair recompense?'

'A stot?'

'Aye, you canna make a milking-coo or bull equal to a monk. Would a stot no be mair suitable?'

The Earl burst out laughing.

'A stot it is,' he cried. 'You hae a fair impident wit, young Robin. I like it weel. Come, let's hae a sup of ale. But I warn ye fair, it'll gang hard wi' your brother gin he should find himself afore me.'

VII

Rob was surprised when Clym pulled his horse's head round and turned off the track that would lead them home. He followed his brother without a word, not liking the set look on his face, but reluctant to question him. It was raining hard, thrown in their faces by a wind from the south-west scudding up the valley, and Rob hunched his shoulders and let his pony pick its path. It slipped now and then in the mud, but he trusted in its inborn surefootedness.

Clym had hardly said a word since they were dismissed from the Douglas' presence, except to tell the six men they had brought from Clartyshaws to make their best way home. Rob suspicioned he was brooding on Maurie, blaming him for the mishaps that had befallen the family, as the only way to avoid blaming himself. But he was to blame too; he couldn't escape from that and knew it fine. Rob felt for his brother in his turmoil, and so was content to follow him as he listed if his company would ease Clym's mind.

The light was failing before he was sure where Clym was heading, and when he realized it, he felt a cold grue on the back of his neck. Was it some sort of penance Clym had in mind? The wind had dropped and mist was closing round them as they turned up the valley of Hangingshaws and there was a dead silence in the air when they drew up their horses. For the first time Clym turned his head to look at Rob as if inviting him to accept his judgement or maybe – Rob couldn't tell – asking his pardon for it. Then Clym kicked his horse and made off at a shambling trot.

The woman wasn't there. The house stood with its door open and hanging from one hinge. Clym stopped gap-mouthed as if he hadn't thought such a discovery possible, then blundered past Rob and out into the night air again. There were a few bits and pieces on a chest in the corner of the room. Rob let his fingers play over them. He could hardly see what they were, and he didn't know why he troubled himself with them.

Then he heard a cry from outside, a great roar in which seemed both pain and fear, and hurried out to join Clym. At first he didn't see him, and then noticed a shape dangling in the air, and for a blind moment mistook it for his brother. But it wasn't, of course. It was Little Nick abandoned there by his brother's wife, and Clym had perhaps stumbled against it and was lying on the ground. Rob knelt down to help him up and, as he did so, became aware that he was still clutching the object he had been fingering in the house. It was a lump of wax – he could tell by the feel – with four bumps, like heads, and four slivers of sharp metal protruding from it. He threw it out of sight lest Clym ask what it was.

The next morning Clym said, 'I was daft. I thought she might lift the curse if I set out to deliver Maurie tae justice. My ain brother.' He leaned over the bridge and stirred the water with a stick. 'But I would do it,' he said, 'for the bairns and Mollie, aye and for you too, Rob and puir Will that kens so little of anything. I wad do it. It's Maurie has delivered us to our weird. It's Maurie killed the wee monk and Maurie whae brocht about our feyther's death, and Maurie, naebody else, whae hangit the Gudeman. The rest of us had liefer let him live, for we had business only with wee Nick. But she's gone and her words aye hang heavy on my heart.'

Rob thought of the wax figure he had lifted with its crude representation of the four brothers cursed and impaled, and shook his head.

'Aye,' said Clym again, 'it's Maurie has brought doom on all of us, and puir Isabel tae, carrying the English lord's bastard bairn.'

Summer came on at Clartyshaws, with the broom and whins yellow, and birds chuckling in every bush, the young lambs out on the hill and the burns full of trout that were hardly as shy as an old ewe. It was that brief season for rejoicing when all the earth seems fruitful, and Rob could hardly fail to respond. But he knew there was no joy in Clym's heart. Isobel's growing belly seemed a mockery to him, and he was often away from home scouring the countryside. Rob knew fine that he still pursued his search for the Gudewife, and knew it was vain. She had vanished. She might even be dead, but it was more likely she had taken refuge in the depths of the forest among the broken men and women who eked out a living there. That was the best that might be hoped for. In his night fear Rob saw her differently, one of a troop who held to the Old Religion and communed with the dark spirits of the woods and the other world. Everyone knew there were such women, and the prudent man steered another course. He had even wondered if his own Jean might not be one of them, for it was uncanny how she had slipped into his life, touching it with a mood he had never known before, and then as suddenly and completely vanished. Only a fool mocked such possibilities. There were too many cases of dying cattle being cured by strange words and potions, of bairns being snatched from cradles, of dark strangers and simple girls . . . not all the spirit forces were kindly.

He sighed, stretched out his hand to a rose bush and plucked a flower. For a moment he pressed it against his nostrils, then crumbled it in his hand.

A voice from the shadow said: 'Laddie, dinna pull another . . .'

He had sensed no one there.

The voice spoke again, sweet as mountain honey: 'Why pu's the rose, Rob, and why does your hand break the wand it holds? And why have you come here, Rob, to Carterhaugh withouten I send you word?'

He couldn't have replied if the voice had promised him all the treasure Michael Scott had buried in the Eildon Hills.

The sun, a deeper red than the rose petal that still softened itself in his fingers, now showed only a rim above the western hills. It dipped behind them and the valley darkened. A chilling mist crept from Yarrow on one side and Ettrick on the other. No wind rustled the leaves, the birds were silent and the lines of the trees were dim. He swallowed and choked out the words, 'I'm free to come by Carterhaugh, and dinna need speir leave . . .'

As he spoke, the silence deepened as if an attendant spirit had withdrawn. He found he was wet with sweat, and Brownie crept out from under a briar bush, her tail between her legs and her whole body curving in abasement.

Rob told no one of what had happened, but he could not

leave off thinking that if he had answered differently he would have been spirited away, for he had no doubt it was the Queen of Elfland who had spoken to him; and her voice caressed his dreams.

He could not resist returning, night after night, to the lonely little plain above the meeting of the two waters. On the seventh night he lay near sunset by the same rose bush. Again he picked a rose and let its petals fall between his fingers. Again the voice came to him in the same words: 'Why pu's the rose, Rob and why does your hand break the wand? And why do you come here, Rob, to Carterhaugh, withouten I send you word?'

This time he steeled himself and replied, just as the sun dipped behind the hills and the valley darkened and the mist closed round.

'Whae is it that speaks? Are you wife or Spirit?'

But the only answer was a soft laugh as of a mocking music; a thin tune sounded and he heard horses' hooves in the long wet grass, and then the sudden silence. This time he advanced beyond the bush but the grass had not been trampled and the branches were neither broken nor bent. His own pony trembled when he mounted it and Brownie skulked right under its hooves till they were clear of Carterhaugh. But this time Rob felt no fear and the thin music still sang its mournful enticement in his ear.

At Clartyshaws he found a horse standing by the well. It glistened milk-white in the moon that was rising over the hill now that he had left the waterside, and he had never seen it before.

Isobel met him at the door.

'There's a lass to see you,' she said, and he could tell she was displeased. 'Whae is she?' she said. 'She was no for telling me.'

'How can I tell till I've seen her?' he said, and pushed past her into the hall.

Jean was crouched by the empty hearth with a shawl round her head. Mollie sat by her but in such a way as suggested she was putting as much distance as possible between them, without the inconvenience of shifting her stool. Clym was slumped on the bench by the table, and, not looking round as Rob entered, kept his gaze fixed on the girl.

Rob had never expected to see her there. She had been even

in his imaginings, apart from his family, belonging to his secret life. She came to him in his dreams, he fell asleep thinking of her, he knew her flesh and nature, but nothing of her past. He could find no words to explain her to his sister and his brother's wife beyond saying she was one of the lasses that had tended him at the inn in Jeddart.

When they still looked cold, he said, 'If it wasna for Jean here, we wouldna hae won back Feyther's body.'

That silenced any protests, though Clym pushed the bench back hard and stalked out, and Rob could see his words didn't dispel the stormy clouds gathered in Isobel's face.

He asked Jean if she had ridden far and she nodded as if hardly risking speech after long silence.

'I'll put your shelt by then,' he said, 'come wi me.'

The velvet of the pony's nose pressed into his open palm.

'Are you angry I came then, Rob?'

'Why would I be that?'

'I'm no aye welcome.'

'I'm blithe tae see you.'

He turned and kissed her. Her lips sought his and she pulled his hand hard against herself so that he felt the bones of her mouth driven into his, and then her tongue searched for his and they clung hard together.

'And you'll bide,' he said at last.

'Oh Rob, I'll bide. Robin, Robin,' she sighed and held up her mouth to be kissed again.

Isobel, as her time approached, remained sullen and angry – jealous – but Jean either did not notice her mood or affected not to. She did not grumble either when Mollie assigned her the dirtiest and dullest chores about the place, though she knew fine why they were given her, and shared her knowledge with Rob in sly, secret half-smiles. She rarely spoke to the other women, though when she did so, her voice was always courteous and low, as if she accepted their hostility as natural and was neither hurt nor offended by it. She didn't even protest when Mollie snatched her youngest child from her and told her sharply to leave the bairn alone.

Clym, sunk in worried thoughts as he was, seemed long indifferent to this new strain in his household, but, at last, high on the sheep pastures with Rob one day, he said. 'Isobel's no' happy, you ken. Nor is Mollie neither.'

Rob waited. He watched a lark soar, then hang a moment level and steady in the air, then soar again. He heard the curlew call and the oyster catchers. He waited till his brother should speak the words the women had given him.

'Isobel is of the mind there's that that's no canny about your Jean.'

Rob smiled. He lay back on the springy turf with his shoulders propped against the dyke of the sheep-fold. The smell of sheep dung mingled with the scent of broom, wild thyme and hill flowers.

'Are you for marrying the lass?' Clym said.

'In a kirk, dae you mean? Wi' a wee priest to say a blessing owre us?'

'Dinna lauch at me, Rob.'

'Oh I'm a lang way frae lauching, and we're a lang way frae the kirk. Jean's no ordinar lass, I ken that fine.'

'Happen she's less that than you think.'

Rob twisted his neck to look at his brother whose eyes slid away.

'When you were gone, Rob, they twae-three days up the valley, Isobel tells me Jean wasna in the hoose a' nicht. She met her twae mornings coming hame when the sun and the full moon were in the sky thegither. There was a live look in her een she didna like.'

'I've yet to see the day Isobel liked the look in Jean's ee.'

'She speired where she'd been, and your Jean answered her in a high spirit that she'd been wi' her Maister, where else? Then, when she saw the black look Isobel gave her, she tried to turn it off as a jest. "Is it no a grand morning for worship?" she said, "or just for a walk in the dawning?" And then, as if like to mak' peace, she offered Isobel to gie her a hand milking the kye, but when she touched the paps of the red coo, nae milk wad flow. "I jalouse Hob's been here afore me," she said, and then lauched again. My Mollie's sair alarmed tae. She says she's seen Jean look at the bairns as if she wad ill-wish them. And then when Young Clym was feverish, she made a broth frae some herbs. Mollie was loth to gie it to the bairn, but he grew waur,

60

and at last she did, and in twae shakes of a rat's tail he was sleeping quiet, and when he woke the fever had left him.'

'Well,' Rob said, 'that surely canna hae distressed your wife.'

'Aye, but it made her feart. It's hardly canny, she said. Will you hae a word wi' Jean, Rob. I'm no saying what's wrang but the women dinna like it. And women hae a sense for sic things that we men dinna.'

But Rob said nothing to Jean of this conversation. He was afraid to do anything which would disturb her. She herself never spoke of her past and he was ready to respect her silence. He sensed too that her strangeness, her sense of belonging elsewhere, was at the heart of her appeal; if he broke that otherness, his idyll would wither. He was content not to know; Rob was a poet and could never content himself with a dull-beast marriage like Clym's.

In the summer evenings Jean and Rob walked the hill with the dog, but they never lay again in the Dark Master's land, though they made love by the waterside, on the braes and under the pine trees. It was a rare June of great day-long heat when bees hummed late in the evening, beyond dark, and the day's warmth never quite died away. Rob and Jean were caught up in the blessedness of summer and of passion.

One night he told her of the voice he had heard in Carterhaugh. She lay beside him on a bank fringed with violets; a daisy-chain she had made rested across her naked thighs. When he spoke of the voice, she twisted the upper half of her body round, so that she lay athwart him and kissed him full on the lips. Her kiss was like summer roses.

'Is that no better than the Queen of Elfland's kiss? Oh Rob, am I no glad you didna hearken. I would hardly hae wished to pine seven years till you rode back to your ain country.'

'Aye you can lauch that didna hear the voice. But it was true, strange and uncanny.'

'Rob, Rob, the hale world's uncanny. We're surrounded by mysteries we canna fathom, or canna fathom on our ain. Are you intent to learn mair?'

She moved her lips lightly over his like fluttering wings

'Will you teach me?' he sighed.

Hay-making came on in the same day-long heat. It was a summer of peace and richness such as none could remember.

There were no raids, no rumours even of English invasions; even private feuds seemed stilled, war and the strife of faction as distant as the depths of the azure sky in which the eye could lose itself. The hills shimmered to the west and gleamed blue and gold in the evening sun. In the benign atmosphere even Clym relaxed, as if sucking on the hope that the fates would relent and this endless summer would let him live as the quiet farmer he longed to be. Isobel too seemed calmer now that her time was approaching, and Mollie, taking her mood from Clym, softened even towards Jean. Rob himself, enthralled by his love, worked hard, loved long in the evenings and through the warm gentle nights, and made verses to delight his Jean. The voice of the Gudewife of Hangingshaws no longer sounded through his dreams.

By harvest, which that miraculous summer came on as early as the middle of August, a bare two weeks after the Lammas tide, they knew Jean too was with child. Clym again raised the question of marriage, but Rob gave no more than his slow secret smile in answer. He and Jean had never talked of it. He was content to live in the present and abide what the future would bring. All his life he was to wonder if he had been wrong.

The weather broke when they were a bare week into harvest. The air grew sultry so that the work with the scythe seemed twice as hard. By evening the western sky was laden with heavy clouds, and towards midnight the first thunder cracked.

The storm grew in intensity, lightning sending its shafts through the peel-tower so that the dogs cowered under the table whimpering. At the moment when the thunder seemed right overhead and there was no gap at all betweeen the lightning and successive roar, Isobel screamed with the first of her labour pains. Mollie hurried to her side, but when Jean would join her drove her back with angry words. The girl received the rebuke and insult silently. She nestled against Rob and put her fingers to his lips so that he could not reply to Mollie.

His mind seemed to him to be split in three. He was conscious of the raging storm as the wind continued to beat the rain against their house and the thunder moved down the valley. He was conscious of Jean's warm, soft and inviting body. He was conscious of his sister's pain, of the skin stretched tight on her brow as the sweat stood out on her temples and her body heaved and shook. All three impressions were quite distinct to him and it seemed as if he also stood outside himself observing everything that happened but part of none of it.

And yet at the same time he knew they were all caught in a singular and single drama, that the life trying to force itself out of Isobel's body and that other he could imagine when he laid his hand on Jean's belly were both part of him, part of old Walter too, already actors in the chain of circumstance and happening that had been formed even at that moment when Maurie, riding in high fury in the Abbey fields, had thrust his sword into the monk's belly; he saw them all bound together and helpless, and he lifted his head, his eye meeting Isobel's frightful and frightened gaze, gave a great cry, and charged out into the storm.

He came to himself standing by the barn. Jean had put her arms round him again. 'Come,' she said, and drew him down into the sweet meadow hay, and let him kiss her breasts.

'Rob,' she said, 'my man, I couldna but think it was me. Rob,' she sighed again, and he responded to her urgency, her wordless plea that they should accept the dark, but still deny death and assert life; and his world expanded again as he sank into her, and heard her sigh his name, again and again and again . . .

The storm dwindled down the valleys, leaving dawn mists behind, and then the sun crept over the hill to a new and shining world. They lay in the sweet hay, Rob asleep in his love's arms, and Jean wept as she looked on his face that was still a boy's and looked also beyond the valleys of the present and the high hills he strode so finely, looked beyond the new day's light to the dark ahead.

It was Clym who roused them, a bottle in his hand and a wild and wandering look in his eye. He shouted and swore, and Rob could not at first understand what he was saying. His mouth was full of vile words and he threw them at Jean, cursing her for a catastrophe he was unable to reveal. Then he stopped, looked about him, and, as if he had come to the end of words, seized a pitchfork and launched himself behind it straight at Jean. The action broke Rob's entrancement. He hurled himself sideways, deflecting the weapon and then knocking hard into his brother so that he crashed down on top of them. They struggled for the fork in a welter of confusion. Rob felt Clym's grip slacken. He threw his spoils aside. But Clym was not done. He had transferred his grip to Jean's neck, and lay pressing down on the girl, choking her life out. Rob grabbed his brother's hair, but the grip held. Rob looked round for a weapon, saw only the pitchfork and hesitated to use it. But he could see his brother's pressure growing, and Jean's legs kicking and threshing about as she struggled to free herself. And then Rob picked up a hammer and hit Clym hard on the head.

For a moment he still maintained his grip. Then, very slowly, it loosed. Jean's hands were at last able to prise the fingers from her neck. Her face was a little blue and her lips were bruised and swollen and a streak of blood ran down her right cheek which the pitchfork had struck just missing her eye. She lay a moment panting. Rob dragged his brother off her and looked down. Her legs had fallen back apart, her shift was torn in the struggle and a line of milky thigh was exposed. He knelt beside her, laying his hand inside her thigh.

The baby would live, but Isobel was dead. Mollie met them with the news and a face that was like a dykeside in rain. 'Clym says there's a curse on the house,' she said.

She looked hard at Jean who met her eye candidly so that all at once Mollie dropped her gaze and brought up the corner of her apron to rub the corner of her eye, and at that moment it came to Rob that perhaps Clym had never told his wife everything that had happened at Hangingshaw. Perhaps even now in his madness he was trying to shift the blame on to Jean. That was an explanation which at least made sense.

Jean now passed by Mollie without a word, and crossing the room to Isobel's bed picked up the baby, which was screaming but broke off as soon as she had it in her arms. Mollie however could not bear the sight. She darted over to snatch the child back. For a moment it looked as if there would be a tug-of-war, but Jean stopped, smiled, and let Mollie have the prize. Rob knelt by his sister's death-bed. No one was to blame. Women died in childbirth as often as not; the kirkyard was full of such corpses. At the thought he felt cold with fear for Jean. Then he laid his fingers on Isobel's face; he had never seen her like her mother till now. Well, she was gone. Could the four of them bide together at Clartyshaws after what had happened? He didn't know, didn't see how it could be done, but couldn't think beyond that.

Mollie was crooning over the babe in arms.

'Andrew,' she said, 'we'll ca' him Dandy . . .'

VIII

'I tell you,' said the fat priest, 'it is a cold barbarous land. The sun never shines in winter and there is little flesh to eat. They have no wine. Imagine that, my friends, no wine. How could they have when there is never sun to ripen a grape? Instead they live on oatmeal mixed wilth cold water from the streams. Sometimes, my friends, when they feel rich, they heat the water first and then they call the mixture porridge. My faith, but I was cold there. And yet, they fight, these little men. We have seen how they fight the English Goddams, like men possessed. There is a saying in their Borderland, 'it is harder to chew a goose then kill an Englishman'. I can well believe that, for their geese are tough indeed. How now, my friend Scot, you find me praising your countrymen's fighting qualities.'

The speaker turned to Will who had joined the little group round the fireside. There were perhaps a hundred men in the valley, stragglers who had regrouped after a pell-mell retreat before the English forces led by the young king's uncle, the Duke of Bedford. The rain, which had been turning the whole valley of the Somme into a morass, had at last abated, and a thin watery moon was reflected on the flood waters spreading around them.

'Aye,' Will said, and nodded, thinking that they could have done with some fighting qualities from their smart French knights. He remembered what a colleague had said: 'They'd run like rabbits if their armour let them move that fast.'

The talk continued. It was the talk of tired and frightened men, trying with jokes and gibes to recover their spirits and regain their nerve. Will sank to the ground creeping as near the fire as he could get like a yard-dog that has made his way into the kitchen. His shoulder throbbed where an arrow had nicked him. Maybe he had an ague coming on. But the real pain was in his heart and in the discovery he had just made, that he could

66

run heart-in-mouth from an engagement, and that war in this flat marshland had none of the joy and adventure his father had found in a Border raid.

The march had been bad enough, by roads calf-deep in mud, past the burned huts that told of near twenty years of warfare, with the Army of France, – or what was left of this division of it – being denied entry to two towns and provisions from them, even though they were held and garrisoned in King Charles's name.

They were marching with their eyes down and bellies empty through a bird-silent land, where the trees were stripped of leaves, past big low fields there were no peasants to plough. They had come on one village or manor and the men had raised a cheer, hoping for food and drink, which had died away as they entered the first hut and found three corpses, an old woman, a stout man and a child; the dread cry of 'plague' had been raised. Then no one dared enter another hut, but, with all the speed they could still muster, they had put the place behind them and stumbled on, Will ignorant of the direction and purpose of the march. He had been reduced to a pair of moving legs with each step painful, his pinched and frozen-wet feet slipping in the mud.

That was how they were when the arrows again spattered among them, like a new shower of rain. A Brabanter routier, trudging before Will with a curse at every step, sank to the ground right in his path, his oaths worth nothing now. Will himself stumbled against him and fell over and lay there grateful not to be moving. For a moment he felt nothing but that relief, and then some comfort from the mud and the new warmth of the body he was couched against. Then more legs shuffled past him and he heard yells of pain and fear as the line broke. The sergeants howled curses and abuse, but only briefly. Before Will fully knew what was happening, their voices were drowned in the general panic. They abandoned any attempt to steady the men. 'Sauve qui peut' came a cry, and that was taken up by others. Most of the men acted on this advice but when Will lifted his head from the belly of the Brabanter where it had cradled itself, he saw a small group still held together and moving in ragged but somehow still cohesive fashion off to his left. He looked ahead and to the right and there was no

67

movement. He had no idea even where the arrows had come from.

For a moment he hesitated, on his knees in the mud. He felt a bee-sting in his upper arm and heard the whish of an arrow. He screamed, but the fear and pain brought him stumbling to his feet. He didn't think that, by rising, he made himself a target again. He didn't think at all. But even as he stood a moment, lost as a rabbit in a bright light, another arrow plunged into the fat Brabanter body at his feet, with no more impression than if it had been a sack of meal. Whimpering, Will turned away and began to shamble off in the direction of the group of men who were now taking a stumbling, cursing way towards a patch of scrub and hazel over to the left. He found he was sobbing as he ran, and he held his right hand pressed against his wounded arm; the arrow had only nicked him, though. Then there was a dip in the land and they were out of sight of the road.

The shouts of the English fell away behind them; then the last screams of the camp women were heard no more. Looking back, they saw smoke rise to the low sky. Then, still without a word, the little group – there were perhaps thirty of them now – turned away and began to push forward. Will had no notion where they were going, but then he had marched blindly for days now, caught up in the mindless motion of the army, that might, at some impossibly remote distance, be thought to be fulfilling a commander's plan, though to the weary and broken men that was altogether beyond any understanding. They had all surrendered their freedom long ago, and been compelled to march, now here, now there, but always where they did not choose; now, through the enemy's intervention, they had regained their freedom, and were even more lost and mindless than before.

Gradually, a group here, a group there, they fell in with other stragglers and broken men, till their band swelled to perhaps a hundred. Then, as the afternoon died, it dwindled again as small parties detached themselves to hunt for food in the occasional isolated or ruined village; but the main body held together, and night fell.

Someone organized a fire. Will sat with his back to a wet beech tree, and closed his eyes. His wound ached and stabbed, and his sleep was fitful. He had come to France, unthinking, simply, if motive could be discerned, to escape the weight of things, to cut free. He had but escaped the servitude of fate and landed himself in the servitude of circumstance. His dreams were sour; a noose dangled from the branch that overhung him. He was roused, easily as soldiers at their limit of endurance are, by a light touch; the apprehension that conquers fatigue. A hand was tugging at the leather pouch he wore at his waist, slung from his shoulder band. He snatched at the hand and found himself clutching a wrist that seemed impossibly thin. He twisted the arm round and found that his prisoner was a child. How could she have come to be there? Dismayed, he let his grip relax and the girl twisted free and darted into the darkness. A man who had been watching from a few yards off, approached.

'You were quick enough, man.'

'She was nobbut a bairn,' Will said.

'This mad aggrieved land is full of such children. Where the Four Horsemen of the Apocalypse ride are many such victims. You're one of the Douglas men, by your livery.'

'Aye.'

'We are countrymen, though I follow no lord but belong to the Free Company of St Christopher, now broken, scattered, consigned to heaven or hell – which I neither know nor care. I have passed a dozen years in this accursed war and would count myself lucky to be alive if I still saw any purpose or advantage in existence. Yet something drives one on when even hope is gone. Where's your Douglas lord?'

'Lord kens,' Will sighed. 'I found myself cut off in the last stour but ane. Weel, we're a lang way frae Yarrow kirk and St Mary's Loch, and that's a' I ken. Would they hae ony food owre by the fire?'

'We can but see.'

And so they found themselves listening to the fat priest, though as the Free Companion remarked, his words seemed to bear testimony to their native ability to survive on next to nothing rather than to promise to supply their wants.

'Have you remarked,' he whispered, 'how these sleek ravens keep their plumage while we poor soldiers are plucked clean?'

'Aye,' said Will, 'we've nae love for thae capons in our family.'

And, even as he said the words, he saw again the gaping surprised face of the monk with Maurie's dirk buried in him up to the hilt, and his father red and angry and fearful at what Maurie had done.

No food was offered but a wineskin was passed to them. Will drank deeply and shuddered as if to banish the image. The talk jabbered round him in a mixture of French patois and Flemish. Furtively he slipped his hand into his pouch and withdrew a handful of meal. He fell asleep munching it.

He was woken by a gentle pressure on his temple and felt a hand placed over his mouth. The moon was up now and he could make out the features of the Free Companion who, seeing that Will was awake, brought his mouth to his fellow Scot's ear.

'The wee priest's asleep in the dell wi a belt of gold and a fat pouch. Are ye game, my man?'

Will blinked. He felt his shoulder shaken again and struggled to his feet. It was hard to keep upright in the mud. The moonlight lay on the priest's face giving him the look of a happy child. Will saw the Companion kneel down beside the little man who had praised the courage of their nation. A gloved hand was placed on the priest's mouth. The Companion beckoned to Will.

'Ripe his sark. The belt's beneath'.

Will drew his knife from his belt and lifted the cassock. He stuck the point in and ripped the cloth round, revealing the belt. His fingers trembled as he tried to unfasten it and then he felt the man stir beneath him. The man's belly rumbled and he moaned and the body thrust itself convulsively upwards knocking Will's hand away a moment. He waited till it was still and then let his fingers creep back to the belt. His hand was all warm and wet but the belt was loose. He had it off the body and saw the Companion wipe the blade of his knife on the grass. Then he leaned forward and removed the pouch the priest had used as a pillow. The two Scots stole away into the dark.

IX

The Laidlaws of Clartyshaws were small men such as would not
feature in the public history of their times, though a few might
be remembered in ballads. But they touched the fringes of that
history and had done so for some two hundred years. A Laidlaw
had ridden with the good Sir James Douglas, the friend and
lieutenant of King Robert the Bruce, and a Laidlaw had died
beside the good Lord James in that battle against the Moors in
Spain into which the Douglas had thrown the Bruce's heart,
that so King Robert's vow to lead his men against the Infidel
might be fulfilled. And Laidlaws had fought in all the Border
Wars, and distinguished themselves in many battles. It was left
though to this generation of Clym, Maurie, Will, Rob, and the
next one, to insinuate themselves in history, and they did so
through their ambitions, talents and the working of their good
and evil fortune.

There were a few years of peace on the Borderland which
would have suited Clym fine had his mind been still steady. But
he was perturbed by fear and guilt and was often found moping
on the wildest braes of Ettrick. He could never say just what he
feared, even to Mollie, for in the months after Isobel's death, he
was imprisoned in a dour silence. Rob could only look at him
with pity. He had no hatred for his brother despite that attempt
to murder Jean, for he knew that Clym was in a manner
possessed; it was not, he reasoned, Clym that acted, but a
malign spirit that now inhabited him. All the same he was loath
to have him near Jean, and took care they should not be left
together.

Jean's pregnancy was easy, and a boy was born at the first
lambing time. They called him Walter after his grandfather, but
he was soon known as Wattie. He was a small baby, douce and
unnaturally well-behaved, and it seemed to Rob that something
of Jean's remote mystery had left her. When he saw her giving

suck to her babe, she was just a woman with a child; though his woman. She and Mollie had established a way of living together, perhaps more easily indeed because of Isobel's death. Mollie worried over Clym's state of mind, but no household with two babes like Wattie and Dandy, and a strong wee boy like Young Clym, six years old when his cousins were born, could be a dreary place. For Rob the two years after his son's birth were happy ones. The past seemed to him to have slackened its grip. Even the fairies no longer spoke to him.

Yet all paradises on this earth can only be for fools. They could not live detached and isolated from the world. Rob, lying on his back under the sun, would often find himself thinking of Maurie and Will and wondering how they fared. Clym, he knew, blamed Maurie for Isobel's death – and had reason to do so, for it was he who had brought the English lord to seduce her. Yet Rob could not do so. He knew that Maurie merely acted out what he was and he never forgot his father's words 'cripples hae a richt to be cankered'. As for Will, Rob's heart ached when he thought of him soldiering in France; Will was no more cut out to be a soldier than the salmon in the bridge-pool he had been watching the past half-hour was made to live on land.

It was on account of their allegiance to the House of Douglas that the Laidlaws could not escape history. The Douglases had long been the greatest lords of the Scottish Border and their relations with the Crown were unstable. On the one hand the King depended on the Earls of Douglas to secure the middle and western border against England; on the other the Douglases were well on the way to being greater than the king.

King James I distrusted his greatest vassals, all the more so because they were eager to maintain the French alliance, having been rewarded for their loyalty to that cause by the grants of lands in Touraine; while the King, who had long been held as a hostage in England and had grown to like and respect his jailers, and had indeed acquired a cockney accent and an English wife, Lady Joan Beaufort, saw no advantage for him or his kingdom in supporting the French cause, but instead hankered after good relations with his southern neighbour. In his mind one of the obstacles to such relations was the unruly nature of the Borderland.

So, in the early summer of 1436, he called on the Border

chiefs and barons to meet him at Melrose Abbey that he might repeat the message he had given them when he returned from his English exile twelve years before. Rob attended with the other Douglas vassals, but Clym, shaking a gloomy head, had pleaded a sickness ('a sickness of the brain, I'm thinking,' said the Earl's man who had brought the summons) and took to his bed rather than obey his lord.

Rob then waited the king's pleasure ('or displeasure, mair like' was the general view). He saw a thick set man with a sharp-pointed beard streaked with white and a cold grey eye, who looked on his Border subjects 'like a wild-cat in a dykeside'. His voice was clipped and English. 'We know well,' he said, 'your Border inclination to strife and turmoil. When I returned to our kingdom we observed how our Peace had been broken and our subjects abused in our royal absence. Then we swore that, with time and God's help, though we must lead a dog's life to attain our end, we should yet make the key keep the castle and the bracken-bush the cow.'

'Howtie-towtie,' muttered a voice behind Rob, 'but you've made sair wark o' it, and it's been sair wark for the likes of us tae.'

The king frowned and rough men who had learned to fear that frown grew silent. 'We made that pledge in this same Holy Abbey of St Mary of Melrose. With the Holy Virgin's help we are on the way to making it good. We would remind you too that we have drawn up a Treaty with our English neighbours, ratified here in Melrose in the sight of you all. Our principal purpose here today is to remind you, our lieges, both great and small, those who hold land directly from us, and those who are no less our subject-lieges though their lands are held from our greater barons, of those clauses which relate to life on the Borderland and to the regulation of disputes between Scots and English. We are sorry to learn that many have been flouted.

'We would remind you that we have concluded a reciprocal agreement with our brother of England for the punishment of criminals and evil-doers of either nationality, according to the usage of the laws of that country which they have transgressed. In plain language, this means that a Scot, who in defiance of our royal command, reives cattle or burns homesteads or commits any form of rapine, theft or malefaction in our sister

73

country of England will be hanged by an English rope at order of an English judge, and there is no form of appeal from such a sentence.

'Furthermore, we would remind you that there now exists provision against the harbouring of evil-doers fleeing the rightful jurisdiction of a realm against whose laws they have offended. On demand they shall be taken and conducted to the Marches, to be there delivered to the offended authorities. The property of these fugitives will be forfeit and any ill-advised man or woman who shall in any way aid or abet such flight, whether by counsel, concealment or any other means, shall render themselves liable to share in this same condign punishment. We have provided that the Warden of the Marches shall provide a safe conduct for persons crossing the Border in pursuit of such malefactors. And we have provided that no person shall escape the consequences of his crimes by becoming denizened as subject of the other.

Be it well understood: the king's writ shall prevail: the key shall keep the castle and the bracken-bush the cow . . .'

There was a general silence. Then the Abbot of Melrose, John of Fogo, called for a service of thanksgiving for the securing by the King's Grace of a blessed peace for the troubled Borderland. But, as a Douglas retainer remarked sourly to Rob, 'what else could ye expect from a priest.'

Yet the king's words, though they had met with little general approval, had set Rob thinking. He couldn't forget Isobel's face the day Edward des Moulins had ridden south with hardly more than a backward wave; it had been wistful as a lily in the rain. And then there was Dandy, an orphan and landless bairn, with no birthright. A wrong had been committed on him and on the whole family. If the king's words meant anything, might there not be a way of obtaining recompense? Rob as a poet and a farmer was a practical man: he knew you couldn't make verses out of nothing any more than you could starve a beast and bring it fat to the table. Private revenge on so great a lord was doomed to failure, and anyway private revenge would avail them nothing. To stick a knife in Edward des Moulins' back might give satisfaction; it would hardly provide for Dandy's future. But, if the king's words meant anything – At the very least they might rouse Clym.

Clym was like an ox and took some rousing. When Rob expounded his plan, he looked at him with dull stupidity and Rob had to repeat himself three times before his head nodded in assent. Still having made up his mind to action, Clym's eye brightened.

'Aye,' Mollie said, 'but the real villain is your brother, and you winna touch him.'

'And if we could,' Rob said, 'we wouldna think of it. This law is no a thing to be invoked against a man's ain blood.'

A silence came over them. They were sitting in the vaulted kitchen. A joint of meat turned slowly on the jack attended by Young Clym. His father looked into his ale as if the future might be written there. Two years of moping and inactivity had made Clym fat; there was a dull suet look to his complexion. The two bairns, Dandy and little Wattie, were asleep. Rob thought of that other evening when they had resolved to ride in search of wee Nick. But it was not that night which had unleashed the forces that still gripped them. Brownie came and laid her head on his knees. The dog's melancholy eye searched for meaning in his face, and Rob searched his own heart. There was a strand that attached all a man's acts to the core of his being, so that as soon as you had made a choice it seemed impossible that you could have chosen otherwise. He scratched the dog gently behind the ear; her delighted muzzle pressed harder on his leg. A man was the sum of what he did and thought and dreamed as certainly as a dog was bound to its master. Was it that knowledge which ailed Clym? If so, he could only pity him.

That night he held Jean close in his arms and made love as if for the first and last time.

In the morning when he saw young Dandy playing in the dust he was certain he was doing the right thing.

Archibald, Earl of Douglas looked at the brothers in a long silence. 'It's no' our way,' he said. 'Thae ideas of King Jamie's look braw and sound braw when he expounds them, but I'm damned if I ken how they may wark. I ken fine your cause is just and you hae sair grievance, but. . .' he scratched his head. 'What do you say, my lord Abbot of Melrose?'

John of Fogo was round and shiny as a Dutch cheese.

Statecraft sat smugly on him like a chain of office round a bailie's neck.

'Your family's tenderness to our holy house of St Mary is well known, my lord.'

'Aye aye,' said the Earl, 'my unfortunate feyther commended the monks and lands of Melrose to my care afore he left for France.'

'So,' the Abbot said, 'your benevolence encourages me to be open.'

'Open he might be,' Rob thought, 'but I wouldna trust him ony mair as a fox in a poultry-yard.'

The Abbot smiled. 'Long residence at the court of His Holiness in Avignon has deprived me of intimate knowledge of the wicked feuds of my native land. I have heard though of these suitors of yours, my lord. Predatory as rats in a barn, I am told. And yet I have also heard that these two are among the least evil of that nest of adders.'

'And our brother Will,' Rob interrupted, 'is even now fighting among the remnant of your feyther's men in France.'

'That'll no commend your cause to King Jamie, I'm thinking,' the Douglas muttered.

'All the more reason to proceed carefully in this matter, my lord,' the Abbot said. 'I have heard too that the brother now domiciled in England is the most venomous of the unruly clan and he is, according to my information, coadjutor to familial enemies of yours, my lord, indeed serves the very lord against whom these poor sinners complain. That is a weighty but perplexing consideration. Then, my lord, we must ponder the implications of this request. Certainly, our royal Grace has wished to substitute due proceeding of law for the exercise of private vengeance, and their decision to appeal for formal justice is a matter of some moment and one which we must commend. On the other hand, my lord, we must consider also whether even such a request that the Lord Edward des Moulins should surrender himself to the Marches Court for judgement is not politically inadvisable, and finally, my lord, we must consider whether the case advanced by these brothers is not in fact of the flimsiest. We have, my lord, only their word that the Lord Edward des Moulins has in fact committed such an outrage.'

Rob interrupted: 'My lord, our family have aye been loyal

vassals of yours. My grandfeyther or my feyther would have responded to the wrang done to us by calling on the Earls of Douglas to aid their vengeance by themselves crossing the Border in search of our enemy. Weel, times are changing, the king tells us. It's a' to be done now by due process of law, and sae we appeal to you for a wee bit writing, I dinna ken the legal terms, and while we thus stand on the law as the king bids us, we hae to hear the Abbot here traduce our family.'

'Aye, aye,' the Earl sighed, 'they're changed days. But listen, Rob, here's your brother Maurie the bosom friend and right-hand man, by what we hear tell, of this same English lordie, and here's the Abbot telling me that the Church has high cause for complaint against Maurie, and sae what's to be done?'

He spread his hands wide, and finding the right one encounter a goblet of wine, lifted it, drank, wiped his tongue over his lips, and sighed again.

'Sir,' Rob cried out, 'I have a sister seduced by this English lord, and dead leaving an orphan bairn. Is that no a cause for him to answer?'

'Aye, aye,' said the Douglas, 'it's a cause, there can be no denying that. I'll hae my clerks draw up the wee bit document you seek, but, Rob, mind this well: I wadna put owre muckle trust in its efficacy. I'm thinking this legality's nobbut a bit whim of King Jamie's.'

X

'If I believed in the effect of curses, I'm a dead man,' Maurie said. His voice had acquired a drawl when he talked to the Lady Clare; it was a male version of hers. The similarity emphasized the intimacy that had developed between them. She, without knowing it, had picked up habits of thought from him. He had taught her to read her world at an angle. She lay now on a couch well away from the slit window which admitted a shaft of summer sunshine, against which she was naturally careful to protect her face. When Maurie spoke she moved her legs lightly within her silk gown, rubbing her thighs against each other. It gave her pleasure to do this and to know that the movement was invisible to him, yet might be sensed. Her white soft hand held a fan of painted gooseskin; its gentle movement would command his attention when she chose. Meanwhile the fingers of her left hand played in her lap but she had cast a muslin wrap over the lower part of her body.

She found Maurie delightful and fascinating. She knew he was aware of this and knew also that he itched for her. And she felt then that what was between them would remain exactly as it was, that they would never so much as touch each other, except when she extended her hand to him and he brushed it with his lips (so red, so curving, she could bite them) or when, greatly daring in company, he held it against his mouth and pressed those lips on it a little longer and harder than was quite seemly; yet never so much so that anyone but she would be aware of it. She found all this knowledge, everything she sensed of the delicate and corrupt mood they created between themselves intensifying and exciting. So her fingers danced in her lap and she looked at Maurie, who was gazing in half-profile over the terrace and moat (how black his eyes were) and she knew he felt as she did. They were happy in their alliance, which was the most delightful secret of her life, and he would serve her all his days.

For it was of course her duty, and would also be her pleasure, to marry a great lord. But, with Maurie's help and counsel, she would so dominate her lord as to live with a freedom denied most ladies. She would taste – her pink tongue protruded to lick her lower lip and savour the slight saltiness left there by the almonds she had been eating – she would taste power.

'What curses have been laid on you, my little tutor?'

'Ah, you would like to know, wouldn't you, my lady?'

He turned away from the window so that his face was obscured in shadow, crossed the room and perched on the end of the couch.

'My father was hanged,' he said.

His eyes danced. She touched her lower lip with her tongue again.

'A great uncle of mine, or perhaps one generation more, was executed with the other favourites of King Edward II. They say he died a coward as so many of that sort did, whining for mercy . . . perhaps he shat his breeches . . .'

She smiled at him, beckoning approval of her obscenity.

'Ha,' he said, 'my father died like a man and I revenged him like a man,' and he told her of the brothers' wild ride, of the dark tarn where little Nick had sought refuge, of how he himself had driven the horse from under Nick and his brother too, and of how the Gudewife had cursed them, and him especially. He told his tale with relish, conscious of her growing excitement, delighting in his own vanity and her admiration.

'With that curse lying across my path, I fear nobody and nothing,' he said. 'No worse harm can come to me than its fulfilment. And the time is not ripe for that. A spaewife told me I would be long-lived and to fear nothing but a bairn that was born to a dead wife. And that canna be. So, my lady, to your Latin studies if you please, horum, harum, horum . . .'

'Harum-scarum, hocus-pocus. She made a little pout. 'It's too hot for Latin. Let us rather have a cup of that chilled Gascon wine and talk of the future.'

It was a subject that pleased and provoked them. Both were dreamers, for all Maurie's view of himself as a practical man; both also felt what they might do together, longed in fact to do,

79

and yet both enjoyed the delicacy that restrained them; that compelled them even to stop just on the threshold of saying frankly what they thought or giving overt expression to their desires. It was a game and they played it with delight mingled with trepidation such as a child might feel dancing across a frozen river; the possibility that the ice might crack added to the intensity of their pleasure.

They were interrupted by a knock on the door. A servant, bowing so low his head all but scraped the ground, informed Lady Clare that her brother, Lord Edward, presented his apologies, but required her tutor's services. She pouted again, delighting Maurie.

'I must yield to my brother in little things.'

He bent over her hand.

'And am I such a little thing?' he murmured.

Their eyes met a moment. As he left her she turned over on the couch, pressing herself hard down against it and kicking her heels into the air.

The servant knave led Maurie by the corkscrew stair, then turned off halfway down, opened a heavy iron-studded deal door, and indicated where Lord Edward could be found on a little battlemented terrace formed where the wall of the old keep abutted on the more magnificent and modern castle built from the profits of the first French Wars. This terrace commanded a view that stretched north and east to the hills. Immediately below them was the bailey, as usual full of activity that would have been confusing to an unpractised eye: horses were being groomed, a smith was shoeing one, maids were crossing with bundles of laundry, others were carrying buckets from the castle well to the kitchens, and a pair of soldiers were practising quarter-staff, for recreation rather than for any use that might now have in war. There were the usual loungers round a couple of pedlars who had been permitted to offer their goods for sale within the castle. The three great mastiffs snoozed in the afternoon sun. Swifts and martins dived and swooped overhead.

Edward was pacing the little terrace, cracking his finger-bones as was his habit when agitated.

'Well,' he said, seeing Maurie, 'I trust my sister was not displeased by the interruption to her studies.'

It occurred to Maurie yet again what an odd mixture these people were: absolutely demanding, yet strangely polite.

'Have you heard,' Edward said, 'of your sister?'

'My sister?' Maurie laughed. 'Come, my lord, I know you are bored, but you surely cannot be pining for that milky maid. Why, my lord, your own marriage is fixed at last, and if you cannot abide to wait that long, there are serving-wenches to do you pleasure.'

'You are pleased to jest. I wish you would not.'

'Very well, my lord, I have not heard of my sister since we crossed the Cheviots.'

As he spoke, he remembered Isobel's pleading face, saw the tear-stained cheeks, heard her beg him to let her ride with them. He pushed the memory aside. What had he to do now with his family? Let them make their own life.

'She is dead, it seems,' Edward said, turning his eyes away from Maurie and letting them wander to the hills.

'Dead? Well, it's common.'

'She died in childbirth.'

'My lord, how do you come by this knowledge, and why does it affect you so?'

'A son survived. They say it is mine.'

'My lord, how can they tell?' Maurie smiled. 'It's but natural a maid will father a child on the best-born man she's lain with.'

He could see Edward was nervous, twisting the fingers of his left hand in his right, as feart, Maurie thought, as a fowl that finds a polecat in the barnyard. He couldn't understand why. Then Edward burst out: 'I am summoned to the Marches Court to answer charges of rape and paternity laid by the Douglas on behalf of your brothers. They have summoned me, me, can you imagine that, a great lord, on the strength of the testimony of a pair of uncouth peasants. It is the greatest insult.'

Maurie bit back laughter. 'You'll not go, my lord,' he said.

In that moment however, seeing Edward twisting his fingers in indecision, hearing the whine of wounded pride in his voice, he knew that this was not the man who could guide his steps further upward. He had long known of course that Edward was worthless, but he had thought he could manipulate him to his profit. Now he no longer believed it. Nothing else had changed: the same swifts and martins darted round the battlements, the same figures stretched themselves out in the sun below them, the same dog barked in the distance. Only life had suddenly shifted.

'You'll not go,' he said again. 'There's none that can compel you to answer such a summons.'

'You think not?'

'I know I speak truth.'

'Well,' Edward said, still moody, 'I never found you false yet.'

'Trust me, my lord.'

'Come,' Maurie said, 'let me see the summons.' He examined it carefully. 'This is nothing,' he said. 'It is the empty fruit of what I have heard the King of Scots is attempting, to substitute the rule of what he calls law for the old law of the Border. My lord, if my brothers or their Douglas lord wish to make good these charges, which rest, as you observe, on no testimony but their own, on neither a jot nor tittle of evidence except their word – which is worth little – then, let them ride against you, and prove it. Come, we shall reply in these terms.'

XI

Rob woke to a morning of dancing loveliness. Larks soared to heaven's gate. Peesies and oyster-catchers skimmed over the sheep-cropped turf. Cushie-doos cooed in the pinewood below, and then, in a moment of the stillness of the summer dawn, he heard the cuckoo.

He looked over at Clym still sleeping, though two or three times Rob had woken in the night to hear his brother moan and mutter in a broken sleep. Well, they had cause to be apprehensive. It was a mad venture they rode, and one which had little sense in it that Rob could see. He had only agreed to come when he saw that Clym was fair-set, even to madness, on riding whether he came with him or not.

He thought back to their last meeting with the Douglas, when word of Edward des Moulins' impertinent answer had been brought. Rob had heard Maurie's voice in that reply, clear as a bell, but there was nothing to be gained from revealing that. The Douglas heard the letter read to him, and fumed and stamped, but Rob could see that he had no mind for action. Clym appealed to him, as was his right, to espouse their cause. They had tried King Jamie's law, he said, and had received naught but insolence. He called on his lord to follow the old way, and lead them to their revenge. The Douglas chewed at his moustache and went red in the face, even redder, and spluttered. He cast a quick glance over his shoulder, even as if he expected to find King Jamie standing there, and Rob knew he was mortal feared of the king. Clym glowered, the Douglas hummed and hawed and looked for a way out, and Rob waited.

'I can dae naething myself,' the Douglas said at last, speaking as if each word was drawn from him as painfully and reluctantly as a tooth. 'Naething. I have a duty to you, certes, but I hae a deeper and more urgent duty to my house and my whole vassalage, and I canna, indeed, I'll confess it, I daurna, invite the king's wrath. I have no mind to share the fate of those lords like Malcolm Boyd of Cumbernauld whae have defied him.'

So, shamefacedly, he had let them recruit a troop of men, secretly, to launch themselves on Clym's mad plan.

Rob looked on his tormented brother; he could not believe that even success in this venture could lift the shadow from Clym. How was it that he, the dullest of the brothers, should be the most oppressed?

When Rob agreed to accompany him, he said, 'There'll be nae killing, Clym. Nae gallows justice. We'll hale them back north wi' us and afore the Douglas. I'll no ride gin you dinna swear that.'

'Aye, aye,' Clym had said, sharpening his knife on a boulder.

'It's our ain brother after a' . . .'

'And was our ain sister . . .'

'Aye, but we've enough to answer for without adding the sin of Cain to our load.'

'Just so,' Clym had muttered, whetting away at his blade.

'Revenge,' Rob persisted, 'dae you no think we've supped our fill of revenge?'

'Do you mind what Maurie said? That it was a dish to be supped cauld?'

'We'll no do that . . .'

But had Clym agreed? The conversation was clear in Rob's mind. He couldn't answer for his brother.

He got to his feet and made his way down to the little stream, stretched himself on his belly and slapped water on his face. Then he cupped his hands and drank. What was it Clym had said last?

'You ken fine I'm no a man that ettles to see blood flow. But you'll mind there's justice to be done and a sair-abused sister to be avenged. You'll mind on that, Rob . . .'

How could he forget, and yet . . . he wished Jean was with him, he wished he was anywhere but here in this valley that opened on the spur where Castle Greer stood, and where they had now waited for two days, to see the Lord Edward ride hawking. He approached the watch. 'Is there any sign of movement?' The man shook his head. 'Maybe they'll no ride the day either.'

The sun rose higher. Two of the Douglas men threw off their

jackets and slept again, lying back, mouths open, on the turf. The birds fell silent. Smoke rose from the distant castle which now glistened in the sun. Clym sat on a rock a little apart from the rest of them and kept his gaze fixed on the keep. Rob caught some of the men glancing at him and read doubt and suspicion in their eyes. He knew word had gone round that there was something nae canny about Clym. He inspired awe now, even him, Clym the farmer; it was the dread men feel for a man whose mind no longer moves on a normal plane. They didn't trust him, for they feared he had abandoned reason. Could they be trusted themselves, Rob wondered.

Clym's plan was simple, to the point of being an idiot's. But maybe it was an inspired idiot. Sometime, he said, the Lord Edward would rise out hawking, and he would choose to fly his birds in this valley where they were protected from the prevailing wind. They would let him enter the valley, some two hundred feet below them, where they lay concealed, behind the little grove of scrubby rowans. Then they would ride down and block his way out. He wasn't expecting trouble, and would be taken easily by surprise. Then, Clym promised, they would carry him north of the Border. He spoke as if he saw no difficulty, and in such a way that no one, not even Rob, dared protest.

So they waited. Clym would wait for ever.

The world was held in a noon hush. Unbidden, the words of the Psalm came to Rob's mind: *non timebis ab incursu et demonio meridiano* – you will not fear attack or the midday demon. But there was no midday demon, he knew that. This was not the hour of enchantment, nor the place. Spirits haunted the lakes and rivers and their hour was twilight . . . he watched his brother gazing down the valley, listening for the sound of the horses' hooves that would not come. Rob drifted into sleep.

He must have slept for two hours, by the movement of the sun, and when he woke he was thirsty and hungry. He had a sour taste in his mouth and he had dreamed badly. He had ridden a lame pony into Jedburgh a second time and seen a body swing from the gallows, but it was not his father and he could not tell who dangled from the rope. 'Is there any movement?' he called to Clym.

First the mist, then the night, closed round them. They dared not light a fire even in the corrie, and so they mixed their meal with water from the burn and ate it cold. The Douglas men sat apart from the brothers, their faces turned away. 'They'll come tomorrow,' Clym said.

Before dawn, unknown to the brothers, a troop of horses left the castle by the south gate and rode three miles to the south before striking up a side valley. Word had come from a shepherd of a group of men camping in the hills, and, by taking this route, the way back to the north could be cut off. They rode at a brisk moorland trot, and by the time it was light, they had put themselves across the valley. Their leader, a sergeant called Bartholomew, smiled at a job well done; and they turned their horses' heads and moved into cover.

The chief of the Douglas men, Hob of the Wynd, approached Rob in the cold dawn. They had waited too long, he said. Word would have gone out of their presence for such things could never be long hid. Clym's plan had failed and it was time to look to their own safety. There was no profit in staying, but one of them had noticed a small herd of black cattle some ten miles to the north and, if they seized them, their journey would not have been in vain. Rob tried to argue: they had instructions from the Douglas to place themselves under their command. Would they break their word? Hob heard him out, then spat sideways, and shook his head. It was time to be gone, he said.

'Aye,' said Rob, 'happen you're right. I'll speak tae Clym.'

He approached his brother, who still sat, motionless and weighty as the rock under him, gazing down the valley. Rob put Hob's argument to him. Clym gave no sign that he was listening. Then, very slowly, he turned his great head, once to the right, then back to the left.

'We'll no budge,' he said. 'We've that tae do that we've sworn tae do.'

Rob felt a surge of exasperation. There was something in Clym's obstinacy which seemed to him like an abandonment of choice; as if, having ridden here and committed himself to this plan, bare and mismanaged as it was, he had surrendered himself to whatever . . . Rob broke off in his reflections.

There was a glint in the distance, as of the morning sun striking metal, then a cloud of dust and Rob saw a score of horsemen emerge from behind a grove of trees, coming at a sharp trot towards their valley. It was no hunting-party, for there was a different air of urgency and certainty about the way they moved.

He shook Clym by the shoulder and pointed at them. Clym stumbled to his feet and called out an order to their men. For a moment no one moved. All gazed down at the troop that was approaching so quickly. Now they could be recognized as men at arms. Hesitation gripped them, and Clym shouted out again. Rob saw the leading horseman draw rein, saw his head turn to the hillside where they lay, saw his arm wave in an enveloping sweep, saw the hindmost part of the troop halt while the leaders advanced.

Clym swung his arm, beckoning his men forward. Again, no one responded. At that moment young Will Douglas of Crummlinghaugh who had been posted as look-out further up the brae crashed down the hillside in great bounding leaps.

'There's another troop coming doon the valley,' he cried out. 'We're trapped.'

'To the braeside,' shouted Hob of the Wynd, running to his pony.

Again, a moment of hesitation, while no one knew what he would do. Then Hob was mounted and setting his pony to the brae down which Will Douglas had bounded. All at once the others followed suit. Rob tried to grab hold of two of them, but they shook him off. He was aware of a wide white eye and gaping mouth and then a fist bursting in his face. He picked himself up, rubbing a shoulder which had struck a boulder. He was alone with Will Douglas on the braeside, and Hob and the rest were halfway to the ridge.

Where was Clym? For a wild moment he thought he had been headed off by the others. Then young Will touched him on the sleeve and pointed a finger toward the valley. Clym on his pony was descending, unsteadily because of the rough ground. He had drawn his sword and held it point forward in front of him. The horsemen below had halted, as if amazed by the mad intensity of what they saw.

Then he was among them and they jostled round him and Rob saw the sword fly through the air. Shouts rose to them watching on the braeside, and then silence, and then Rob felt a score of faces turned towards him and Will. The sounds of the

87

fugitives had died away, but, looking to his left, Rob saw that the other troop which Will Douglas had seen descending the valley had now fanned out over the hillside in such a way as to cut many of them off. A whimper came from the small figure beside him; young Will, a boy of maybe sixteen, had realized the hopelessness of their position. Rob put his hand on the boy's shoulder.

'Whisht,' he said, 'no harm will come to you.'

If the boy hadn't been there, he wondered later, would he have tried to cut his way though and died fighting?

As it was, he mounted his pony, and gesturing to Will that he should accompany him, eased it down the hill to their surrender.

Neither Maurie nor the Lord Edward was among their captors. Rob almost smiled at Maurie's caution – though he could be bold enough when he had a mind to it, and Rob knew it was Maurie's boldness had loosed the family's troubles.

They tied their hands behind their backs, and turned their horses' heads to Castle Greer. Clym seemed to be stunned by what had happened, by the suddenness with which the world had been turned upside down. Misfortune had maybe made him an idiot, and Rob felt a stab of resentment. He should never have let Clym have his head.

The troop rattled and clattered over the drawbridge, into the shadow of the gatehouse, and Rob heard a heavy clang behind them. It was cold out of the sun and his shirt was wet on his back.

XII

The rat had been watching Clym for a long time, crouched not more than two of a man's paces from his head, and it disturbed Rob that Clym didn't seem to have noticed it. He picked up the can they had brought his drinking water in, and slung it at the beast. He thought it missed, but at least the rat scampered into the shadows at the end of the dungeon. Rob settled himself against the wall again, waiting.

He was already losing touch with time. He thought they had been there four nights. The uncertainty shook him; he had heard how easily prisoners lose that sense of time and of how that loss can disturb the mind. Finding a bit of flint he scraped a notch on the wall. He would do that each time they brought food which was, as he thought, only once a day.

But he was more worried about Clym, who had not spoken since their capture. Clym sat motionless for hours staring down at the ground, which, Rob was certain, he didn't even see. He hadn't eaten either. Rob had tried to spoon some of the thin cabbage soup they were given into his mouth, but he hadn't swallowed it and the liquid dribbled out to dry in his beard.

It was cold and damp in the dungeon. Rob hugged himself and heard young Will Douglas whimper in his sleep at the chill. His own feet stung with the cold, though the shaft of light that crept through the little grille at the top of the dungeon indicated there was sun outside. He slapped his arms around himself and against his sides, and cursed Clym for his daft determination. And he was worried about Jean: if he could only get word to her that he was still alive.

Three guards burst into the dungeon, and two more stood armed at the door – as if they could offer resistance in their plight! A lantern was hung in Rob's face and arms heaved him to his feet and pinioned his hands behind his back. The three of them were shuffled out, and though it was hardly light in the passage outside the cell, Rob found himself blinking as he tried to accustom himself to what light there was.

They were hustled along the passage and up a winding stair. The guards used them roughly, as if with pleasure. They paused on a landing where the air was fresh and Rob breathed it in deeply. It started him coughing and for a moment he thought he was going to be sick. Then a door was thrown open and they were pushed into a chamber.

Sunlight struck his face and dazzled him. He blinked and opened his eyes again slowly. He had an immediate impression of softness: there were cushions and tapestry hangings and a bowl of red roses stood on the table.

Edward des Moulins and Maurie sat behind it. The English lord's face was half hidden by the flowers. His fingers drummed a little tune on the wood. Maurie leaned back in a carved chair. The elbow of his right arm rested on it and he cradled his chin in his hand, two long jewelled and elegant fingers lying on his cheek. His eyelids were half-lowered and there was an elaborate and insolent detachment in his gaze. Rob shifted his shoulders under his dirty and stinking shirt.

He glanced at Clym. Clym was staring at his brother but as if he didn't see him.

Maurie spoke: 'Ye daft gommerils, to set yourselves up against me.' He turned his eyes on Clym, then back to Rob. 'What ails him? Is he gone in the head now?'

'You ask what ails him?' Rob lifted his chin. 'What you have brought on our family.'

Edward des Moulins said, 'Are these really your brothers? I wouldn't have recognized them.' His voice was peevish. 'And they really thought to try to summon me before the Marches' Court. Tell them I think them insolent.'

'I hear you,' Rob said, 'there's no need for Maurie to act as your spokesman. Our sister's dead. There is a boy. Your son.'

Des Moulins shifted in his seat, drank wine, tried to meet Rob's eye, failed and shrugged his shoulders.

'Perhaps,' he muttered.

'He's a healthy bairn. We've ca'ed him Andrew.'

'Andrew . . .'

'Aye, Drew or mair like Dandy.'

Maurie rapped on the table with a silver knife.

'Enough of this talk,' he said. 'Whatever charges you may have insolent thought to advance against my lord here, there is no question of your own guilt. You are found bearing arms in England, contrary to any statute, lying in wait or ambuscade, conspiracy against the life of my lord here, all heinous crimes.'

'And is this a court then?' Rob said. 'Whae made you a judge owre us, Maurie? Man, you were her favourite amang us a', may the Lord hae mercy upon you.'

Maurie smiled: 'Ah Rob, I fear you have entered a world you don't begin to fathom. You should have bided on your hillside, tending the cattle and making your little songs. But, enough of that. You are both of you clean guilty and the question is, what's to become of you?'

'Holy Mother of God,' Rob thought, 'he's eident tae hang us. Our ain brother. And would that fulfil the curse?'

Sweat trickled down the back of his thigh. Maurie leant forward, as if to speak confidentially, but then his left hand snaked out to a dish concealed behind the vase of roses. He withdrew a peach, held it up a moment between thumb and forefinger, so that Rob saw the small indentation made by his brother's thumb. Maurie bit into it; juice trickled down the side of his mouth.

Rob lifted his chin. 'We rade into England,' he said, 'for one reason only. Having found that your lordship here' – he moved his gaze from his brother's face and looked straight at Edward des Moulins, whose eyes slid away and would not meet his – ' was loth to answer the charges brought against you according to the terms of the Treaty signed between the twae kingdoms, we determined to escort your lordship to that same court. Yon was the sole purpose of our journey and you canna mak it oot otherwise . . .'

'And who gave you men of low degree the right to make demands of me . . .'

Rob felt Clym raise his head. 'The laws of God and the laws of man and the laws of honour.'

These were the first words he had spoken since their capture, and the room fell silent on them.

Then Maurie laughed. It had an ugly sound in the echoing room. Edward des Moulins beside him relaxed. A muscle in his cheek that had been leaping like a landed trout steadied itself.

91

Rob looked sideways at Clym; it was as if he hadn't heard his brother's laugh.

Rob took a step forward. He said: 'Maybe we've done wrong, brother, and wrong to you too, my lord, taking this matter the way we have. If so, we can only confess our fault and beg pardon. But, gin you see it frae our side, gin you had seen our sister dee, clutching the babe your lordship fathered on her, tae her dying breist, gin you had seen a' that, and heard the wails of lamentation that sounded round the chamber when we kent she was indeed deid, why then, you would understand our anger, and maybe how it disturbed our judgement.' He swallowed, lifted his eyes and continued. 'But, when a' is said and done, there's naething can bring back Isobel tae life. We ken fine we have offended the laws of England by this ride, and gin you choose tae punish us, we maun thole it; but afore ye so decide, I would ask you to consider weel why you would be punishing us. Is it your ain guilt, my lord des Moulins, that would drive you to it? And I would ask you tae consider weel the bairn whose rights we defend, consider your son.'

Maurie laughed again. 'Fine words,' he said, 'fine words, but fine feathers dinna mak' the bird. What has his lordship to do with the bastard bairn of a country lass? Here you are, taken in armed invasion of this realm of England, with the full and fell intent of effecting the capture of his lordship, as you confess yourselves, making yourselves guilty out of your ain mouth, and you prate of this bastard bairn. You would do better to fall on your knees and beg for mercy. And,' he paused, 'you might still look for it in vain.'

Clym gave no sign that he had heard his brother.

'Why do you hate us?' Rob looked Maurie in the eye. 'Are we not bairns frae the same womb? What have we done to mak you hate us as you do?'

Maurie met his gaze.

'What have you done, you ask. You are. Is that no' enough?' He swivelled in his chair to bring himself round to face des Moulins. 'My lord,' he said, 'it is clear this is only a private venture. They have had but little backing from the Earl of Douglas, or they would even now be threatening you with his vengeance.'

'Vengeance,' Rob interrupted. 'I shall be happy to leave that to the powers that rule this world.'

'Oh aye,' Maurie said, 'will you now.' He smiled again. 'I'll be blithe to let you. Sergeant, take them away, while we determine their fate.'

Will Douglas leapt up as they were pushed back into the cell, and held Rob a moment in his arms, burying his face in his shoulder.

'I was afraid,' he said, 'afraid they would . . . and I maun bide here alone in this dreadful place.'

Rob smoothed the boy's hair. 'Never fear that,' he said. 'There's no harm will come to ye, in our absence.'

Night came on them but only their weariness told them it was night. The boy Will snuggled against Rob for warmth and Rob heard him breathing in an even sleep. He was aware of Clym still sitting in the corner, with his knees drawn up and his arms folded round them and his head bowed. He had hardly moved since their return to the cell, and Rob had long abandoned the attempt to rouse him. At last he drifted into sleep himself, an unquiet and uneasy slumber, disturbed by wild dreams.

The Lady Clare pulled her furs around her and purred.

'Tell me again, little tutor,' she said, 'tell me again what my brother said.'

'Your brother is afraid,' Maurie said, 'afraid to act. All he has to do is give the word, and he will be rid of two enemies.'

'Your brothers . . .' she dwelled on the words, and brought her fingers to her mouth and touched their tips with her tongue.

'But he is afraid. He says he has blood enough on his hands.'

'Blood on his hands,' she repeated and licked her fingers again.

The castle was silent as the tomb around the pair. Both knew they were lovers in all but the act. This talk, in which they played with the same notions and played with them again, as in a round dance, was their form of love-making. Both relished the restraint they imposed on themselves even while it irked them. Restraint, self-discipline, could be enflaming. That was their discovery and their secret. They had only to glance at each other in the presence of others to feel their power, to delight in their separateness.

'Does he not like the taste?' she said.

'Not he.' Maurie could not take his eyes off her. He watched the fur move in the shadowy light, the flickering flame from the fire, as she shifted her legs, one over the other. 'I fear, my lady, that in attaching myself to your brother, I have been in error. He is no bold man to make my fortune.'

'Must it be a bold man as does that?'

'Must it, my lady?'

'Feel this fur,' she whispered, 'feel its softness, its rich warmth, feel its . . .'

'It's what, my lady? Its promise?'

'If you like, little tutor . . .'

'Someday . . .'

'Ah someday . . .' she sighed and nibbled her index finger.

'Would you dare hang your brothers?'

'Would I?'

'For me . . .'

'My lady, what would I not dare . . .'

'Yet, if you hang them, do you not bring nearer fulfilment the fate the old wife saw for you . . .'

'My lady, I don't give a pish for the mad words of an old wife.'

'Little tutor, little tutor, what lessons you will teach me.

Will Douglas tugged at Rob's sleeve. 'Are you awake?'

'Aye,' Rob said, 'hauf and hauf.'

'He hasna moved,' the boy pointed at Clym, 'he hasna moved and I've been watching him for . . . I dinna ken how lang but it seems an awfu' time.'

Clym indeed still crouched in the corner in the same position he had adopted the night before. He was quite silent, and though his eyes were open he seemed to see nothing.

'I'm afeared for him,' the boy said, and Rob saw that he was shivering.

How long had they been there? How long would they have to wait? The meeting in the chamber had chilled Rob. Hope was feeble as a dying candle. How long had Maurie been filled with this bitter hatred? Did it matter? He recalled their father's words: 'a cripple has a right to be cankered.' But such a right!

'Come here, Rob, come owre here.'

94

The boy Will had grown restless while Rob looked at Clym and brooded. He had been moving around the cell in what seemed a fever, but now he was still and tense. He grabbed Rob's elbow and squeezed hard in his excitement.

'This stone,' he whispered. 'It doesna fit. You can move it.'

Rob knelt down. The boy was right. There was a crack between the stones and by pressing hard one could be made to move, ever so slightly, but still it gave. Rob ran his finger down the join.

Will had left his side and crossed over to the far corner of the cell where there was a pile of rubbish and debris that had lain there unregarded for a long time, covered with dust and cobwebs. He ferreted about in the heap and emerged with two pieces of flint.

They lay down facing the stone and each began to work at one side of it. It was hard work scraping the cement or plaster that held them together, and Rob's knuckles were soon raw and bleeding as they rubbed against the wall or floor. They worked hard and silently for a long time. Then Will threw down his flint and groaned. 'It's nae gude.' He pointed at the tiny pile of dust that was all the reward of their labours. Rob nodded, smiled, reached over to clap him on the shoulder, and resumed work. Rub, scrape, rub, scrape. His shoulder ached and he found he had to shift his weight more and more frequently. Rub, scrape, rub, scrape, Will was at it again too, either shamed or encouraged by Rob's example.

Rob put his hand against the stone and shoved. It moved a little more, seemed looser, and he transferred his effort to the top right-hand corner. Dust fell in his hair, got into his throat, making him cough and splutter, but he worked on. He stopped to suck the blood from his knuckles and drove himself back to work. The flint dug deeper. He pushed it hard into a crack and heaved sideways. A chunk of cement pattered to the floor. He dug again and a larger chunk fell. He dropped the flint, and pushed his finger against the dusty wall. It broke through the dust and waggled free. He withdrew it, but there was no light on the other side.

They were interrupted by the sound of footsteps in the passage. Will scrambled to his feet and threw himself down on the pallet bed. Rob merely turned over on his belly and lay there as if asleep or too distressed to respond to sound or movement. The door opened. He sensed the change of air and heard the sound of bowls being pushed in. The guard withdrew without a word. Rob sat up and Will brought him the thin cabbage soup. It tasted good. Both realized their hunger and drew strength from the drink which was indeed hardly more than tepid water with a few cabbage stalks in it. Clym made no move. When Will took his bowl of soup over to him he paid no attention. They watched him in the dim light. Then Rob said, 'You need the soup, lad, more than him. Drink it.' The boy offered to share it with him, but Rob said no, and resumed work.

He would not let himself up, and worked without ceasing. It was at the least something to do, better than brooding. He sensed Will's spirits lifting and approved, while denying himself the same feeling. Even if they could move the stone, and the next one, and clear a hole big enough for them to squeeze through, they might be no better off, for they had no idea what lay beyond, whether they would find themselves only in a neighbouring cell. But there was no responsive noise beyond the wall.

They had no sense of time. Existence was reduced to that patch of floor and wall, the movement of the flint, the pain in the working wrist, hand and fingers, the ache in the elbow which supported them, the choking dust that filled their nostrils, mouth and throat, that got in their eyes and made them smart and water.

But the pile of dust was growing around them. The stone was looser. Rob struggled to his feet, seized by a sharp cramp in his right calf. He hopped and stumbled about the cell to ease its grip. He muttered an oath, cursing the pain, and was rewarded by a laugh from the boy. That was good, the laugh was natural, and held no hint of desperation or hysteria. He must look a fool, hopping about like a heron.

He fished around in the heap of rubbish. If only he could see properly! But his hand encountered metal. He tugged. It freed itself. An iron bar, almost as long as his forearm. How had it come to be there? How had they come to leave such a weapon in the dungeon? He didn't stop to consider the matter. It was a new and better tool.

But the sound it made was terrible. It seemed to resound like a ring of bells. After one blow he stopped, and listened. No sound came from the passage. He had no idea how distant the guard-room might be. The iron dislodged another chunk of cement. He inserted it at an angle and found it was now possible to work it behind the stone. He heaved. The stone moved, surely it moved. He dug in again. This time there could be no doubt. Groaning the stone was urged forward, to stick out perhaps the depth of a man's thumb at the top corner. Encouraged, they fell to again, working faster than before.

It still took a long time, but at last they were able to dislodge the stone and tear it out. It made a hole big enough for a man's head, but not wide enough to get his shoulders through. The boy said, 'Maybe I could do it', and lay down and poked his head into the blackness, but his shoulders stuck too.

'There's nothing but blackness,' he said, 'but listen.'

He withdrew and Rob took his place. The boy was right. He heard the sound of rushing water.

'What does it mean?' Will asked.

Rob shook his head, and considered the question. He struggled to picture the position of the castle. They had been led in by the East gate over the moat. That could not account for the sound they heard. Castle Greer stood on a rock, and although the approach from the East was gentle enough, it must be steep from the other side; and if it was steep, a river or stream might run round the rock to the west. That must be it. He told the boy what he thought.

'I canna swim,' Will Douglas said.

'We'll cross the river, laddie, when we come to it.'

Meantime there was the other stone to be removed, one more at least, before they could force their way out of the dungeon. And Clym useless! Could they even get him to move? He lay there like a sack of meal now. And they were both weary. The boy was near to dropping. He had no idea how long they had been working, but the boy must get some sleep. And he had no idea either how long they had to make their escape. When would Maurie persuade des Moulins to decide their fate?

He listened. A rat moved in the cell. He sensed it was approaching their soup bowls. Apart from the scurrying of its feet, all was still. He turned back to the wall.

It must have been hours later that he too fell asleep, his iron bar still in his hand, his face pressed against the hole they had made. He still hadn't managed to move the other stone more than an inch or two. His mouth was full of dust, and he coughed and choked in his exhausted sleep.

His senses though remained sharp despite his fatigue, for he woke at the sound of footsteps beyond the cell. The heavy key was fitted in the lock, there came a rattle of metal, and Rob heaved himself to a sitting position, his back to where they had been working.

The door opened. For a moment he was blinded by the lantern, though in fact its light was feeble and it hardly illumined more than a few feet of the cell, and could not see who was carrying it. He was aware that three or four men had entered on them.

Then Maurie spoke from behind the light. 'Well, brother, the dice are cast, your fate is determined, and it only remains to fix the hour of your death.'

He couldn't see Maurie's face. For a moment he wondered if he was dreaming, but this was real enough.

'You have played and lost,' Maurie said, 'I told you you were fools to set yourselves against me.'

There was nothing to say. The question he had asked Maurie in the Chamber would never be answered. 'Cripples have a right to be cankered,' but such a right! And yet he tried again.

'Why?' he said.

At first it seemed as if Maurie was not going to answer. The men-at-arms who accompanied him shuffled their feet. There was no movement from Clym and the boy Will Douglas still slumbered on the bed.

'Why?' Maurie picked up his brother's question, and threw it into the dank air where it seemed to hang between them. 'I could ask why is any action undertaken. I could ask why you pursued me in this mad fashion. But I have an answer. You are my past, you pursue me as the ghosts of dead actions and a dead life. Is that not answer enough? In your mind, you wonder what I seek. I seek freedom, to be myself, untrammelled, my will free as the wind on the hills, and you come, with your demands and memories and cries of responsibility, and I will not have it. Oh your offence against the laws, your insolence, these are excuses, serviceable and fortunate excuses. But I must destroy you to be myself, you and Clym, always you and Clym and your memories standing between me and myself.' ˙

He had started quietly and spoken more and more quickly and loudly till the final cry 'me and myself' rattled round the cell, howling his expression of a self-consciousness that was something new to both of them, and would be new to anyone who had heard it, like a wounded beast crying its lonely pain. Rob shivered. He tried to see his brother's face.

'You would have me fear you,' he said, 'but I fear for you, brother.'

Maurie laughed, 'you fear for me?'

'I fear for your soul.'

'Fear for your own.'

'Aye,' Rob said, 'that I do, for there is innocent blood on my soul too. There is the blood of the Gudeman of Hangingshaws, and that, I am afeared, is a death we shall a' have to answer for. A death we had nae richt to bring about. But, Maurie, my guilt, is like a bairn's sin compared to yours, and gin I can see a priest and confess, why then, I shall face the darkness with an even mind, but, as for you, man, you have condemned yourself to live in a darkness that will grow ever more profound, till you meet with the cauldest and laneliest death a man can contemplate. And how will you hae us die? You'll no' dare to hang us, I ken that fine, for fear of the auld wife's curse.'

'And why not? Am I a man to be afeared of curses?'

'Are you no'?'

'The curse of a demented auld wife? Learn this, brother, there are no words can daunt me, and no dreams that disturb my nights. As for the manner and moment of your death, that is a matter I have not yet decided.'

'You . . . decided?'

'And why not me? Is it not my right? Know this however, it will be sudden and in the dark. As for a priest, you will see no such man. Are you our father's son to prate of priests?'

Saying this, he picked up his lantern, swung it round the cave, limped over to the crouched figure of Clym and kicked him. Clym did not move. Maurie laughed again, barked out an order to the soldiers. The door clanged, the key turned, the footsteps receded.

The world closed in around them again. Maurie's words caused Rob to intensify his efforts. Will woke and came to help him. They dug, scraped, hacked and heaved, and at last the stone moved.

'I promised him it would be sudden, but it will not be sudden.'

'Not sudden?' Clare sat up, throwing back the blanket of furs that lay on her.

'A sudden death,' Maurie sniffed a rose, 'is suddenly over. There is a moment, and then, snap. We would all wish for a sudden death. The mind's pain, even the fear, have a sharp limit. And hope dies before the body but hope is the greatest and most painful delusion. Why should I grant them sudden death? Let it be lingering. Let them hope and fear, and grow weaker and more fearful and perhaps die raving. I have read of the great King of Numidia, Jugurtha, how he was imprisoned by the Romans and left to starve to death, and how in his agony he consumed the greater part of his left arm. On the other hand, there is another death I have read of, of how malefactors are confined in a sack with a fighting cock, a monkey and a viper and thrown into a river, that they may die in one of at least three noisome ways.'

'Which will it be, little tutor?'

'Which should it be, Lady Clare?'

It was a hard job forcing Clym through the hole they had made, for he seemed to have lost the use of his limbs, along with his will, and Rob had to drag him through while young Will pushed from the other side. Rob knew that the boy must wonder whether they would not be better to leave Clym behind: he was near death, it seemed, he would impede their flight, and there seemed to be no way in which he would be anything but a burden. Yet he couldn't bring himself to do so. To abandon Clym, would be to accept a heavy load of guilt for the rest of his life. What would escape be worth if he saddled himself with his brother's death?

When they had got him through, Rob crawled back and heaved at the two great stones. He pushed them sideways through the gap, and crawled back again. Then, sweating with the labour, he urged them very roughly back into place. They would not long disguise their flight, but they might do so for a little.

They struggled to their feet. They were in what must be a passage, for when each extended his outer arm, standing side by side, it encountered the slimy wall. The roof of rough and jagged rock was just higher than their head. They heaved Clym to his feet and each got an arm round his shoulders, and so, stumbling and slithering, they began to advance. Rob still held the iron bar in his right hand and used it to feel their way like a blind man's stick. Soon, however, the passage narrowed. It grew lower too, and once they banged Clym's head against an overhanging seam of rock, but he made no sound. It was hard going. Both would have liked to rest, but dared not.

At last they saw light ahead. It was faint and flickering but natural light. They tried to quicken their pace. It seemed that the passage must have been cut through the rock to emerge over the river, for the sound of water was louder now.

Unmistakably, Rob recognized a star. He had almost forgotten night and day, but he blessed the fortune that had seen to it that they were attempting their escape under cover of darkness.

A whiff of fresh air came upon them. The passage rounded a corner, and they saw the whole field of the starry sky before them, and a rising moon. But they saw also a barrier. It was a gate, let into the sides of the rock and reaching almost to the roof of the passage. The boy Will groaned at the sight. Rob told him to rest with Clym and himself advanced on the gate, the iron bar in his hand.

He paused for a moment. The river rippled far below and the moonlight danced on the fields and woods beyond. The night landscape extended like a promise. He listened. Apart from the water music there was silence: no tramp of sentries above, no human or animal voice. Even the night birds were not calling, though the light was owl-light.

He ran his hands over the wood of the gate. It felt damp. He inserted the bar diagonally where a horizontal joined with an upright and heaved. To his delight it gave: the wood was rotten. It would not take long to demolish the barrier. He tried to gather the wood as it broke, and lay it aside, but one large piece escaped him; it slithered and jumped down the rock, but he did not hear it strike the water.

When the gate was broken, he lay on his belly and looked out. The rock fell abruptly, but he could not doubt that, the gate being positioned as it was, there must be some way of escaping the sheer drop. The moon slid behind a cloud, and, though the light was dimmer, yet in the absence of shadows, he thought he could make out a path away to their left. It was where he could see it hardly more than a ledge, and there was a perilous drop of perhaps four feet to it. A man would have to let himself down backwards, clinging on the floor of the passage, and holding himself there till he had secured his footing. That done, he would be able to edge along till, as he saw, the path widened before beginning to descend. It could be done. But could it be done with Clym in his condition?

Maurie turned in his sleep and moaned, dreaming of virgins and young thighs.

Rob slapped Clym on the face. At least his eyes opened, but there was no other response. He looked at Will and read in his face the hope that he would choose to abandon Clym. He shook his head. It could not be done. If only he had a rope.

He said to Will: 'We maun bide here a little. It's a gey hard descent and we shall need a' our strength.'

The boy did not dare to say what he was thinking. He leant back against the rock. He was shivering and there was a tremor in his cheek.

Rob took off his shirt and, using his teeth and hands, tore it into strips. Then he wound the strips tight and tied them together. He tugged at the knots till they were small and hard as pickling onions. He circled it round Clym under his armpits. It was no good, far too short to give sufficient length to hold him up by. He repeated the operation with Clym's own shirt. This time, having fastened the knots and the two lengths of cloth together, he gave one end to Will Douglas and sent him back along the passage till the improvized rope was stretched out between them.

'Pull as hard as you can,' he said, and did the same himself. The rope held. It would have to do.

He fastened it round Clym again, and together they forced him upright and walked him to the opening from the passage.

'You first,' he said to Will, 'dinna be feared and remember that your life depends on your courage and skill.'

The boy lowered himself. His feet scrabbled for a footing and then he was steady. Rob got Clym to the edge, turning his face against his own. For a moment there was a flicker in the eyes and then the face went dead again. Binding the other end of the rope round his own body, Rob put his arms under his brother's and, as slowly as he could, eased him into the empty air. He felt Will grab hold of the legs and let them slide through his arms. He was now flat on his own belly, but for the moment Clym was safe. They had got over the first difficulty.

He was soon on the lower ledge himself. A flash of moonlight showed him the fear on Will's face. Then again the moon was gone, and as they stood panting and pressed against the rockface, it began to rain in heavy drops that blew against them. They turned back to face the rock, and with Clym held dizzily upright between them, began to edge their way along.

It couldn't be done. They had come to a halt and Will stood frozen by the narrowing ledge. How long they remained motionless Rob had no means of judging. He dared not speak, even to encourage the boy. He must find his own courage. But if Rob had gone first, the boy would have had to take the weight of Clym. And anyway there was no room to change places on the ledge.

At last Will took a step. Rob forced Clym along. At least he seemed still to be able to move his feet, if only just. He heard Will give a moan in which he read relief, and the next moment they were on easier ground, away from the sheer drop below the gateway.

Again they paused. They now had to nerve themselves for the descent, but at least there was now a path, a rough track, overgrown and stony, but for some yards falling shallowly enough. Bushes and briars brushed against their legs, the rain beat in their faces and made it difficult to see, but they crept downwards. It became steeper. Clym lurched forward and fell over Will's shoulders. Rob strained to hold him and the boy stumbled, cried out and vanished from sight. For a moment the rope held and Clym swayed below Rob, and then, with a wrench, he felt it tear and Clym too slid tumbling down the cliff. Rob himself was pulled forward on to his face and began to be swept downwards. He threw out his hands and caught hold of some bush. He held on to it as his legs came round, and he came to a stop panting and appalled in a heap in the middle of the bush, which was gorse. There was no sign of the others and no sound either.

Just then the rain stopped as abruptly as it had begun. The wind threw the clouds clear of the moon. Rob collected himself, struggled to regain the path, and listened. Only the rush of the water and the wind came to his ears. No sound from below, none from the castle above. A silence of failure and death.

Halfway down the rockface he came on Clym. He had been caught in a stump of thorn-tree growing out of the rock. Perhaps, somehow in the fall he had regained consciousness and struggled to free himself, or perhaps it was an accident, there was no means of telling, but the cloth Rob had tied round his body had worked itself over his shoulders and round his neck, and he hung by it now, the other end being round the thorn tree and his feet swinging free, kicking the empty air. Rob lay flat out on the path, but he could not reach him, and, the moonlight catching his brother's face, knew it for wasted effort.

There was no sign of Will Douglas; he had vanished into the black water below.

Maurie smiled as he watched the masons at work, and sipped a morning cup of canary wine.

The Lady Clare whispered, 'Did you not want to see them a last time, to tell them their hour had come?'

Maurie said, 'There are pleasures of the imagination, my lady. Think. They will hear the masons, but they cannot be certain just what is being done. Dwell on their wondering. When will it be that they know for sure they are immured. Will they cast back their minds in a few hours and say, 'Was that what that sound meant?' And then they will feel fear like an empty place, and the truth of Death like a ghost stealing on them in the night. While I . . .'

'Yes, you, little tutor, what of you?'

'I shall gloat.'

'And I with you, little tutor.'

They watched the mason smooth the cement with his trowel and the wall rise against the door of the dungeon.

*

A man alone can move fast and unseen. Weary, half-naked, distressed and soaking from rain and river, Rob had yet reached the hills by daylight and found a dell to rest in, in a wild and lonely place with a long view. He lay up there through the day, and moved again the following night.

It was not for two days that a soldier looking over the battlements saw a body swinging halfway down the cliff. He raised the alarm, and the news was brought to Maurie, who turned pale at the word and began to stammer. The messenger, fearing his anger, slipped away and left him to his thoughts. Maurie told himself, 'At least only one was hanged and the others must be drowned', and, as he said so, his hand strayed for comfort to St Pandulf's medal around his neck.

On the fourth day, Rob fell in with a tribe of beggars who took him for one as unfortunate as themselves. He travelled with them a week thinking their company good enough disguise from any pursuers, then, finding their pace slow, and their direction turning westward, slipped away from them in the night, stole a horse from a moorland farm and turned its head to the Border.

XIII

Rob's return to Clartyshaws was grimmer than any he had made, grimmer even than after his father's death. Then at least he had brought back Walter's body, and, with it, something of his honour. He had come home, to the house where his mother and sister lived, where his brothers waited to ride with him in pursuit of his father's betrayer. This time, as he turned from Ettrick into the bare lands his family held, he felt shame. He hesitated to confront Clym's widow and fatherless bairns. He brought neither body nor honour, and the family was destroyed and scattered: Will vanished in the mists of the French War; Maurie their enemy now, and Clym's swollen face still before his eyes. Even his own deliverance seemed to him to have something of shame in it. The thought came to him: but for Jean I would have turned my horse's head another airt.

The widow came to the door at the sight of the lone horseman, and Rob, getting down from the pony with the leaden movements of fatigue, knew this for the worst moment of his life. She said nothing to him, as if his mere lone presence, grey with dust and shaking with weariness, told her all she feared to know, but she gathered her bairns to her and with a slow nod of the head left him alone in the sunshine which was no sunshine for him.

He looked for Jean to come running, but there was no sign of the girl.

When he had seen to the pony and stumbled into the house, Mollie set a bowl of porridge and a jug of ale before him. The children came pulling at their uncle's legs, and he picked them up and kissed them, but found nothing to say, and waited for them to call for Clym.

At last, towards night, when the bairns were bedded, he told her what had happened. There was no way to soften it, and he felt the cruelty of his short account. But the cruelty was in things, not in words. Mollie cried then, but only for a little, and then her face hardened again, and Rob saw it as a mask she would wear the rest of her days. She had accepted what there was no way of denying, but she would neither forgive nor forget. Rob's guilt sharpened: did the survivor always feel less than a man? Then, at last, Mollie told him what he feared himself but had not dared to ask.

One day an old woman had come to Clartyshaws and called for Jean. She was a grim vagrant-like wife that Mollie could not recall seeing before. Jean had been up the hill with her bairn and the woman had insisted that Mollie send young Clym to fetch her, and had then settled herself on the lip of the well with no more words, and had declined Mollie's offer of food and drink. Jean came down the hill at last, with young Wattie in a sling across her back, and when she saw the woman 'her cheek paled and her ee grew wan', but she said never a word to Mollie. Instead, she and the old wife talked a while, their voices never rising above a whisper, so that Mollie had no notion what they said; and then, in the gloaming, Jean had picked up Wattie again and the pair of them had set off up the valley with the old wife.

'And did she say nothing? Had she no word for me?' The words burst from Rob, from his very heart.

Mollie shook her head. 'Never a word. But as she reached the bend in the road, your Jean looked back, aince, as if she was loth to go. And the bairn was crying. And not a sign hae we seen of either of them since; and that was the night of the new moon that's now auld.'

Rob struggled through the next weeks. Tending the farm was heart-breaking work, for every job was associated with Clym. They made the last hay because it had to be done, but they worked with none of that season's pleasure. When Rob rode by a neighbouring farm and heard girls singing at their work, he felt numb; it was as if his own life was held suspended in a bad dream. Even the children caught the mood and were quiet and subdued, shy of shadows.

He waited for a sign from Jean, for surely she would learn he was still alive. That thought gave him his one shaft of hope: that Jean would know, and would return or send for him. He took to wandering the hills at night, half looking for her, half killing his hope, until Mollie begged him to bide home at nights. She was afraid, she said, even of what she knew lay in her own heart. He did not question her, but did as she wished, and was glad enough indeed to give up his aimless seeking. One night, in her grief and loneliness, she came to his bed, and he was ready to respond, out of his own loneliness and grief and pity and the shame he could not shake off, but she drew back from his first caresses, and they lay, side by side, but not touching, appalled by what they had been about to do, though there was no sin in it that Rob could see.

From that night forward Mollie seemed to change. Resolution formed like a scab over a wound. She was brusque and hard with the bairns, but she was alive again, an eye on the day Young Clym would be a man.

Rob knew her mind, knew how she was schooling the boy in hatred and revenge, and once at least tried to warn him against letting such passions dominate his mind. But the boy's face was hard and Rob saw he was not heeding him. And why should he? It was right Mollie should have his ear.

All the same there were affairs to be settled. After harvest he presented himself again before the Douglas, and besought him to bring the family's case again before the Marches Court. He reminded him of the wrong they had suffered at the hands of des Moulins, and he asked that meanwhile he be made guardian for his nephew Young Clym who was now lord of Clartyshaws. The request was granted, but beyond it he got nothing but sympathy. The Douglas felt obliged – or was obliged by his clerks, for he was himself ill-versed in legal matters – to point out that Clym and Rob had offended by their attempt to take the business into their own hands with their raid into England; that the Marches Court would take a sour view of such behaviour; and that Clym himself, taken in the act of rapine, as would be averred and could doubtless be proved, had received due punishment, even if his death was self-inflicted. All this the Douglas muttered in a confused and rambling way between swigs of ale, and of his own part in the business and the help he had reluctantly given them, he said nothing.

Rob could not be satisfied. He lingered in the Douglas household. At least he was free of Mollie's accusing eye there, and at least he was free of a place where every corner and every lovely spot reminded him of Jean. The farm work could be done by the hinds; Mollie was fully capable of directing them and the prospect of a winter at Clartyshaws was intolerable to Rob. He was not, like poor Clym, a man born to be a farmer but cheated by circumstance. He craved something wilder and more colourful, and, sighing for Jean, resumed his old habit of verse-making. There were love poems and laments springing to his lips, and he earned his keep as it were by celebrating his lord's ancestors. Something of his new melancholy found its way even into this work, and it may be that Rob was the minstrel who supplied that most moving and mysterious verse of the Ballad of Otterburn where the Douglas, woken by his little page cried:

> 'O I hae dreamed a drearie dream
> Ayont the isle of Skye,
> I saw a dead man win a fight
> And I thocht that man was I.

It was Rob too who composed at least one version of the Tale of Thomas the Rhymer and his encounter with the Queen of Elfland, and in making these verses he sighed for Jean who had offered him a glimpse of that far country of magic. The crow-priests who infested the household (for the Douglas had a great fear of death and was forever telling his beads and seeking comfort from them) had an ill-will at him and listened to the stories that were told of his dealings with faeries and the secret world. But Rob cared nothing for their sour looks.

He lived there two years, and all the time there came no word from Jean, no news of Will in France, who might be dead in a ditch or tumbled in a tavern bed or indeed hanged by his neck, and, as for Maurie, he had, in Rob's view cut himself off from the family by his actions. Did he hope by so doing to cheat the curse laid upon them?

Rob knew something had snapped in him with Clym's death and Jean's flight; it was as if in the brief years of early manhood he had suffered such harsh experience that he had lost the capacity to act. Instead he dreamed and pondered the reason for his state. He could find no solace in orthodox religion, for he suspected that that would outlaw his Jean and instruct him to deny her. Some followers of the English friar Wyclif, whose disciples cold Harry of Monmouth had taken such delight in burning, attracted his attention for a while, as they roved through the Borderland preaching, when they were allowed to, a purer Gospel and a poorer Church. Yet Rob found something lacking in them too: an absence of the mystery at which Jean had hinted.

He had spells when he took to wandering the moors and valleys, and this was recognized as his right for he was freely granted the license due to a minstrel and tolerated as such. So he came to know the Borderlands better than most, for he travelled in peace, with no defence but the stout staff that helped him up hills. For choice he now travelled on foot, as humble folk did, and he came to know many of those who lived beyond the bounds of settled society and travelled the roads and bypaths: pedlars and discharged soldiers; near-crazy preachers who risked the wrath of the Church to deliver their message; the bands of gypsies, those strange tribes that had arrived in Scotland none knew whence, speaking a tongue none could understand, thieving from poultry-yards and horse-lines; outlaws and broken men, and the poor mad women who had taken to the roads for reasons that none could account for. Rob came to know them all and was made welcome by them.

Three or four times he visited Clartyshaws to cast an eye over Mollie and so discharge his nominal guardianship of Young Clym. But he never stayed long. There was a sense of purpose that he found alien, and frightening. Ideas of revenge on Maurie had died on him, and it distressed him that Mollie was bringing the boy up to the harsh duty of vengeance. He said to her: 'Maurie has made his ain pact wi' the Deil. Let the Deil look after his ain.' But she would have none of it.

One day in April, when the laverock soared high in the blue lift and the whaups cried on the moors, when the last snows of winter were still found nestling in the corries and could be seen on the rim of Cheviot, he found himself in a little glen at the head of Yarrow. A pair of buzzards hung above a pine wood and, in the wood's lee, there reared the broken arch of an abandoned chapel. The little valley was silent, but for the bird-song, and quiet as the grave.

But a thin smoke was rising from within the broken walls. Such a sight would have made many strike off for the further side of the valley and hope to pass unnoticed, but Rob had made a habit of seeking out new acquaintance, for there was always the chance that he might learn news of Jean.

As he approached, he heard singing. It was a man's voice, a full baritone, and the words, he thought, were French. Then a second voice, the reedy quaver of an old man, took up the refrain, and the song was in full, if discordant chorus, when Rob rounded the corner of the burnt wall, and came on the singers.

There were indeed just the two of them. The baritone was a thickset, red-faced fellow wearing a leather jerkin and high boots with a heel missing from one of them. He looked up at Rob with a bright insolent smile on his face:

'Are you alone, friend?'

'I am that.'

'Then join our company and share our table.' He gestured towards the broken altar of the church. There was a cooking-pot suspended from a chain across a tripod that straddled a wood fire underneath the altar, and a rich savoury smell was issuing from it. Rob was hungry. He sat down.

The other man was dressed in a robe of rough brown stuff. He had a long thin beard and long straggly white hair. When he waved his hands, which were also long and thin, Rob saw the bones stand away from the flesh. He had drawn back, as if frightened, on seeing the stranger, but now, apparently reassured, gave Rob an oddly gracious bow.

'A brace of blackcock and some moorfowl and the end of a roebuck's haunch,' the baritone said. 'Brother, you shall feed well among us wayfarers, outcasts from our fellow-men though we be. What do you do in these wild and dubious parts?'

Rob, taken by the flourish of the man's speech, smiled. 'I can scarce tell you that, for I scarce ken myself.'

'Are you condemned, like us, to wander the hills and waste places of the earth?'

'No' exactly,' Rob said, 'though I canna call myself a man of settled life.'

'You are young to be a victim of misfortune.'

'Well,' Rob said, 'I can hardly call it misfortune that lets me happen on so savoury a stew in a desert place.'

'Ah, a philosopher and humourist! Well, friend, to add to your philosophy, let me say that the man who minds not his own belly will mind nothing.'

And he began ladling the stew onto thin metal plates.

They set to with a will, and in silence, in the manner of hungry men, and there was no further talk till their plates were clean. Then, with the sun now hot on them, and a woodpecker drilling in the pine trees and small birds chirping about their nests in the undergrowth, the old man drifted into sleep. His companion filled a leather flask at a spring behind the church and offered it to Rob.

'There's a well inbye,' he said, 'but I misdoubt me of it.'

He watched Rob drink. 'You'll be thinking we're a motley pair. Faith, and I think that myself. Little did I ever dream the day would come when I wandered my native braes which I hinna seen these twenty years with an auld man reft of his wits.'

Rob lay back. 'You'll have been a soldier, I'm thinking,' he said.

'Aye, I am one that has done great deeds and suffered sore wounds in the service of Mars, an old soldier of the French Wars.'

He stood up, threw his arms in the air and blew out his chest. Then, as he spoke, he swaggered around the confines of the broken chapel before coming to rest on a fallen column, and, as he told his tale, Rob no longer saw a broken-down ruffian with the words braggart, liar and cheat written plain on his countenance, but instead caught something, an acrid whiff, of the glamour of courts and great battles, of the beauties and miseries of France, of a rich world of poetry and despair and cruelty and wild courage that made his own life seem but a dark shadow.

'As a young man,' the old soldier said, 'a fledgling calf from the braes of Lammermuir, I was in that small company of men who ran with torches by the stirrup of Louis of Orleans as he rode through thon black November Paris to be cut down and treacherously slain by the bravoes of his cousin John of Burgandy. Aye, and I was myself thrown in the ice-cold waters of the Seine with a knife-wound in my side, and left for dead if I hadna managed to struggle, God kens how, but with the aid of his angels, it may be, to the other side. That was a wanchancy business, that night, and yin that left the fair realm of France, bonny land as it is, riven through the heart. Thereafter, friend, I served the Duke's son Charles of Orleans, him what makes verses wi' mair joy nor war, and whae was briefly married to

Isabella, the widow of England's King Richard, a point to which I will animadvert at some later stage of my story. Then I was taken at the bloody battle of Agincourt, where the English arrows flew thicker than the mist ever lies on Lammermuir, and then I secured my freedom by declaring my willingness to adhere to the English side, and since it happened that our King Jamie was then or soon after the companion of the Frogeater, I enlisted under his banner. Yet I misliked me of that, and soon found opportunity to cross over again to the other side, and fought in the French armies for mair years than I care to think. For, besides my eye for my own fortune, which is the indispensible requirement for all true men of war, I could never thole to find myself on the same side as the black Dukes of Burgundy who had murdered the one master I ever loved, in so foul and treacherous a fashion.'

Then he told Rob of how he had returned to Scotland – 'a man has aye a hankering after his ain calf-country' – and found his father's house occupied by a stranger and his brothers dead. He had then struck south-west and fallen in with his present companion at a village in the Tweed valley where a group of boys were mocking the old man and threatening him with a ducking. 'They called him kingie, and something in me took a scunner at them, so I carried the old man off with me, and now I'm stuck with him, like a festering sore or like the sailor in the Arabian tale. Common humanity – it's a gey queer state of affairs that has reft me of my will. And the auld man daft as the March winds.'

Mostly, though, he said, he was a quiet decent-like body, with no vice or rage in him. But he suffered from a sad trick of fancy. And what was that? Rob wouldna credit it. He thought he was King Richard of England, him that had been deposed by Henry Bolingbroke, the Frogeater's father, some forty year syne, and then murdered, as most men believed, in Pontefract Castle. But the old man would not have it that way. He insisted he was indeed King Richard, and had been wandering the moors of Scotland these long years. Did you ever hear the like?

A hush fell on them both at the question. The claim was staring mad; but staring and not stark. Stories of the deposed and humiliated king had been legion; Rob had heard many. Some said he had fled to the Holy Land, others that he had taken refuge with the Emperor in Byzantium. A handful of

Pretenders – false Richards – had appeared. One had even passed a season with the Douglas and had been carried by him on an invasion of the northern counties. It was said Richard had come to Scotland to do penance for the burning of Melrose Abbey; that he had turned holy man; that he lived with a community of believers in the Old Religion; conversely that he had been a sacrificial victim of that cult.

The old soldier shook his head. 'I have an interest,' he said, 'seeing I have taken the old man into my protection, and seeing that I served the king's widow Isabella, but it's all havers. Yet I have gotten a fondness for him. It harms nobody gin he thinks he is a deprived king, and he's a decent gentle body.'

They sat with their backs to the old stone, and let the spring sun play on their faces. The old man stirred in his sleep. 'Ye shall have no captain but me,' he muttered, 'I am your king . . .'

'You hear how it runs in his mind – '

But Rob heard other tunes. He heard a voice clear as the evening bell in another valley; he heard the deep sigh of loss. He closed his eyes and saw a lone heron fish by a grey water, and again sniffed the rank odour of the rat-infested cells of Castle Greer. He drifted towards a light sleep, and everything he had sought for in his verses, glimpses granted him as he lay with Jean as summer dew touched the dog-roses, flitted moth-light through his mind.

He stirred to a cool breeze. Both his companions were still asleep. Rob got to his feet and looked down at the old man: his face was like parchment and his breath came in quick uneasy gasps. The lips wrinkled as if his dozing was disturbed by argument. Rob leaned against the wall, looking up the valley as evening came on. Verses formed themselves in his mind.

> The grey man lay by the bracken bush
> Upon the dying o' the day,
> I am the king of auld England,
> There's nae childe my rights can gainsay.
>
> They pulled me frae my gowden throne,
> The leopards and the lilies froze,
> They cast away my gowden crown,
> And tore the petals frae my rose.

> Sceptre and crown they reft frae me,
> And gave unto my fause cousin
> My heart alane they left tae me . . .

But the next line wouldn't come. He toyed and played with it, then sighing resumed for fear he should lose the last verse:

> yet no' my heart alane was left
> I hae a voice can prophesy:
> Nae heid shall wear a siccar crown
> won thus by guilt and falsity.

The moon rose and the three huddled round the fire they had revived with branches from dead trees. Again the old man slept while Rob and the soldier talked into the night. Rob, his tongue loosened by a flask of wine the old soldier had produced (and where had that come from?) told him of his search for Jean, even hinted at his fear that she might be a witch: 'That she's flesh and blood, nae spirit, I canna doubt, and one that has borne me a bairn, and yet there is that sae uncanny about her . . .' His words died away as the soldier poked a stick into the fire and stirred it so that the flames leapt high.

'Have you heard,' the soldier said, 'of her they call the Maid of Orléans?

'There were three of us', he said, 'me that was known through France as a proud Scotsman, Dirk, a Fleming, and a man from the south called Jehan . . .'

They were, he told Rob, the remnant of a company that had starved to death in a great winter when it froze hard for nine-and-sixty days and the crows dropped stiff-dead from the trees, and an army could have marched along the frozen rivers if any army could have found the will to move in that dead season. So at last there were just the three of them, and they moved like skeletons awakened from their grave.

One day they sat under a hawthorn tree on a great lifeless waste in Lorraine. That morning they had passed through a village deserted but for a few starving hounds that sniffed around the frozen middens. There was not so much as a cabbage stalk in the gardens – the man shivered at the memory – and when they entered a hovel, they were met by the sight of three corpses frozen round a table with an empty bowl before them. They were all used to death, but something in that grouping of the figures made them take to their heels and they fled the village of Death.

'And yet,' Jehan said, 'we might have waited to meet him there. At least we were out of this evil wind.'

Dirk shook his head, 'I am ready to meet him here. We are three naked men. O Mary, Mother of God, take pity on us'.

Jehan said: 'If the Pope at Avignon were to intercede himself, there would be no grace for the likes of us. It is a different master lies in wait for you here.'

Then he tore a branch from a dead tree and began to belabour Dirk, crying on him to rise and march. But the Scot pulled at his arm.

'It's no use,' he said, 'he has the will of death on him. Let him be and let us march.'

All this time Dirk just sat there, unmoved by the beating, like a man who was dead already.

'I tell you this,' the old soldier said to Rob, 'by way of preamble that you may judge my state of mind and so judge the story I unfold.'

So, with Jehan he left Dirk under the hawthorn tree and the pair of them resumed the rutted road that ran across the plain. It was with great slowness, pain and difficulty that they walked, and they were near the end of their strength. When they looked back, Dirk was still crouched where they left him.

That night, as if by a miracle, the frost lifted. The wind eased, and shifted to blow from the west, becoming a soft rain-laden breeze. It grew warmer. Though their feet stung with pain and their bellies clove to their backbone, yet hope entered their hearts with that shift in the wind. They lay that night in a ruined chapel – 'aye, like this one' – and sheltered there from the warm rain that darkness brought.

They woke to a limpid morning in a valley that was taking on a pale and weary yellow colour from the rain. The way being now downhill, they were able to continue their march, though they were weak as newborn kittens, and there was no sign of life and no sign of man in all the wide country.

Then they saw a grove of trees, poor lifeless things, and, beneath them, a flock of sheep. A lean dog set up a barking, and

Jehan shifted his hand to his sword-hilt for he had a great fear of dogs. But the Scot advanced on the beast and offered the back of his hand to it as a sign of peace. The dog, an ugly wall-eyed brute, sniffed at the hand, and smelling no fear on it, pushed his nose against it.

A girl's voice addressed them: 'So you're not afraid of my dog? Are you soldiers?'

He hesitated. The girl advanced from behind a tree where she had been watching them. She was a tall girl, with mousy hair cut short, and wore a brown smock or tunic girdled up at the waist, and thick yellow stockings made of wool. She smiled at them, and he couldn't remember seeing such a smile on a peasant's face.

'You look fair exhausted,' she said. 'If you give me a hand with the fire, I'll heat some soup for you.'

'There's no bread,' she said, as if the lack of it was occasion for surprise, 'and a meal without bread is but a poor communion, I'm told, but we had a visit from the Goddams soon after harvest and they took our grain. We've been living on cabbage soup and milk and cheese from the sheep ever since. You get tired of cabbage soup, don't you, and long for bread. Still, we must bless what our Lord provides and be grateful. And eat it of course. That's the true gratitude.'

Well, of course, she was mad, the lass, we both saw that, but her soup was good. There had been a mutton-bone in it, and it had body and true goodness. We felt life coming back. And then she said, 'You'll get an ague, the state you're in,' and went into the wicker lean-to constructed between a couple of oak trees and brought them sheepskins.

She asked them if they were soldiers. The Scot was loth to confess, but Jehan spoke up and told her they were maybe all that was left of the Dauphin's army.

'That poor lad,' she said, 'my heart grieves for him, done out of his rights. I'd like fine to be a soldier myself.'

Jehan smiled. It was his first smile since the frost began.

'A lovely girl like you has better things to aim for.'

She screwed up her face. 'I don't like being spoken to like that,' she said. 'Your friend's very silent. Has he lost his tongue? I've known them do that, the Goddams. They cut out men's tongues. Some say they eat them the way we do sheeps'. But I can't believe that. Not even the Goddams surely! Though I know for a fact they sometimes eat human flesh. Children mostly. How can they? Oh, I know what you're thinking. I do run on, don't I? It comes of being here on my own with the sheep, with no one to talk to but them and the blessed Saints. Though it's the saints as do most of the talking. My task's but to listen.'

Then she asked more about the two of them and when the Scot told her he had come from across the sea to fight for 'la belle France' she clapped her hands and cried out, 'Is that not grand? To come so far for the sake of our poor abused France. I am sure the Saints will be pleased when I tell them about you.'

'You seem to talk a lot to the Saints,' Jehan said.

'Well, of course, I do, doesn't everybody? Especially Saint Catherine, she's my special friend. They tell me what to do. Shall I tell you a secret?' She smiled at them. 'I think I will. After all, it's not going to be a secret much longer. But first, tell me how the war is going?'

Jehan shrugged his shoulders. 'It is all but lost. The English boy king will soon be master of all the fair land of France, thanks to the bloody Burgundian traitors.

Her face clouded. 'I never saw a face,' the old soldier said, 'that told you so truthfully what she felt.'

'That's what I was afraid of,' she said. 'It's what the blessed Saint Catherine told me. And Orléans is being besieged, isn't it? So I'm right. Well then, the Saints have told me I must go to the Dauphin and offer to lead his armies – and then – when he has given me command – I am to relieve Orléans and crown him king in Rheims. What do you think of that? Isn't it exciting?'

'The girl's mad,' Jehan said.

They watched her stride up the hill, directing her dog to collect the sheep that had strayed.

The Scot shook his head. 'I'm not so sure of that,' he said. ('And I'm still not,' he said to Rob.) 'After all she knew of the siege of Orléans. It's hundreds of miles away. How could she know?

'There are a hundred ways she could know,' Jehan said. 'Besides, whoever heard of the saints speaking to people like that? I know what the priests would say. They'd say she is possessed. When people hear voices, it's usually the Devil.

'Does she look as if the Devil inhabits her?'

'We all know Satan is cunning. He is the Devil, after all. He's clever enough to inhabit a nice girl. Don't tell me you believe her.'

The dog had succeeded in rounding up the sheep. It brought them back to the flock and trotted up to the girl, and sat down before her. She knelt and let it lick her face.

'I rather think I do,' said the Scot.

'And I still do.' He rose to his feet and looked out through the arch to where the pines stood out black against a pale sky. 'I still do, and yet who can tell? Does this lass of yours hear voices?'

'I think she may,' Rob said.

'Aye, and are they from God or Devil, or from . . .' he broke off. 'That's what none can tell,' he said.

The girl returned to them, and stood over them, smiling. 'Yes, I am right. You must come with me to the Dauphin. It will be very convincing if I have two old soldiers with me.'

Jehan looked at the pair of them. 'You are both mad,' he said, 'but I suppose I must accompany you. But as for the Church and what it will say. . .'

'The Church,' the girl said, 'but why should the Church question what the Saints tell me? Surely that is not right?'

The old man stirred: 'I too put myself at the head of my people,' he muttered.

'Peace, old man,' said the soldier. 'Go back to sleep. There is naught here that concerns you.'

'And then?' Rob said.

The soldier had paused and was looking into the fire. He scratched the back of his neck.

'I have heard,' Rob said, 'that she did indeed relieve Orléans.'

'Oh aye, she did that.'

'And crowned the king.'

'Aye, wee Charlie. She did that . . .'

The night before the Coronation of Charles the Unfortunate as he had been called, the soldier and Jehan were in a tavern in Rheims. They were all drinking deep, but Jehan's mood was different. The soldier mocked him for his lack of faith in the Maid, and told him he was like a crab apple, sour because he had judged wrongly.

Jehan lifted his eye from the wine-smeared table: 'Wrongly?' he said. 'If I had indeed judged wrongly, my mood would be lighter now.'

'How can you claim that? You aye mocked my faith in the maid.'

'And now I fear it. I fear it more than ever. Oh at first I hoped she was just a daft country lass, whose talk of the saints was merely the imaginings of a green girl; but now I know otherwise, and I am mortal feared. Do you not see, you dumb northern ox, that her Voices are real. There can be no doubt of it. And yet, can you believe that the Saints speak directly to her in contradiction of the teachings of Holy Church? That surely cannot be, and yet the Voices are real enough. So I ask myself, whence do they come? What is their source? And fear the answer.'

'Judge a tree by its fruit,' the soldier said.

'And then the Maid herself entered the tavern, with her closest friend, the great noble Gilles de Rais.'

The soldier hesitated on the name, as if he feared to pronounce it but it might be, Rob thought, that he just didn't call it to mind at once.

The Maid wore a leather jerkin, breeches and top boots and her hair was cut short like a boy's. De Rais' blond hair in contrast spread over his shoulders, and, though he was a veteran of twenty battles and scores of skirmishes, he still looked like a lovely girl when he smiled at the maid. He was dressed in purple velvet and there were rings on his fingers, and the two of them made a pair you couldn't look away from.

She called for milk for herself, and the best Gascon wine for her Gilles, and she cried to Jehan and the soldier to join them. 'Come, my old friends, tomorrow is a great day, when we shall crown Charlie-boy and the first part of our work is accomplished.'

'I mind her like that, rosy with joy,' the soldier said.

And Rob saw the picture and it mingled with Jean lying on the braeside showing him her milky thighs, or standing in the water of the Yarrow with the water lapping her calves and her gown tied up to keep it dry.

Within months she was on trial for her life. The Burgundians had taken her and sold her to the English who surrendered her to the care of the Church. There was a long list of charges, and the soldier repeated them word for word, as if saying his prayers.

They said: she frequented the enchanted fairy-tree of Bourlement. She went there alone and at night, sometimes also during the day at the hours when Divine Service was celebrated in the village Church.

They said: she would dance round the tree and hang garlands of herbs and flowers in its branches, and then chant incantations invoking the God of the witches; and the next morning the garlands were nowhere to be found.

They said: she received her mission at the tree of the fairy-ladies of Domremy.

They said: she was instructed by certain old women in the use of witchcraft, divination and magic arts, so deeply that she herself confessed before her trial that she did not know the fairies were evil spirits.

They said: she had attacked Paris on a feast day.

They said: she had stolen the Bishop of Senlis' horse.

('And why not?' thought Rob.)

They said: she had leapt from a high tower and not harmed herself.

They said: she wore male costume.

They said: that when a priest called Brother Richard had encountered her and made the sign of the cross and sprinkled holy water, she replied, 'Approach boldly. I shall not fly away.'

When they asked her why she wore male attire, she answered that she did so by the advice of no human man. 'Everything I have done I have done by my Lord's command, and if he ordered me to assume another dress, I would do so, according to what he commanded.'

When Jehan heard the articles of accusation against the Maid, he stole a horse and rode away from the army. He tried to persuade the soldier to accompany him. 'We have been through too much together, my northern ox,' he said, 'for me to be happy to watch you fall victim to such impieties.'

But he shook his head – as he did again now telling the story – and said: 'The maid is a good lass. I cannot desert her now.'

Rob pondered the words.

So Jehan rode to the south and safety, but the soldier presented himself before Gilles de Rais to urge an attempt to rescue the maid. He was ushered through long grey corridors, up a narrow twisted stair, and told to wait. He could see the river blood-red in the evening sun.

Gilles lay back on a bed of roses. One page-boy manicured him, another sprawled over his heart, a third read to him from a book of verses.

'Is this how you disport yourself,' the soldier asked, 'while the Maid's life is in danger?'

Gilles inspected his polished nails.

'That lass has saved France, she has set the king on the throne, she has made you a great man and Marshal of France, and now she lies in peril of her life, while you amuse yourself with page-boys and verses.'

Gilles smiled. The soldier stood there, as if to demonstrate by his presence that the Marshal's debt to the Maid should hang heavy as a millstone on him. But the Marshal smiled.

'What we have chosen,' he said at last, 'we have chosen. The Maid and I. The Maid knows that. If you were an initiate, you would understand. We follow the same master, she and I. Interpret that how you will. Why have you never joined us?'

The owl called from down the valley and a gentle wind moved the upper branches of the trees. The fire was dying as the old soldier finished his tale, with the Marshal's question hanging in the air. There was no need for Rob to ask what the Marshal had meant. He knew too well, and, as he sensed the soldier had known, he was aware that what was revealed was already known. The thought puzzled him.

'And yet the Maid was a good lass,' the soldier said. His voice was quiet, wondering, yet sure.

'I saw her die,' he said. 'I had to. I stood in the rain and watched them lead her in a white dress they had forced her to wear out from the castle towards the faggots piled round the stake. And there was innocence in her eye, and they murdered innocence. I would have liked fine for her to see me, that she might know there was one friendly face but her eyes neither dropped nor searched the crowd. She was staring up in the heavens as the smoke rose and hid her. Maybe she saw Saint Catherine smile at her. I pray she did. Then the flames broke through the smoke and lit up the grey morning. There was an awful silence and it rained harder.'

He paused again.

'She has marked my life,' he said. 'Aye, and marred it maybe. I have a last memory of that night. I was in a tavern, drinking cannily, as is my wont, for I have seen too many men die in tavern brawls. There were English soldiers there, and they were not merry, for it was as if shame lay on them because of what had been done that day. But then a whore, a slim lass with auburn hair and pale blue eyes, leaned over one of them, caressing him, and then whisked his jerkin and leather cap away. She draped the jerkin round her, crammed her hair under the cap and pranced up and down the room, sticking her arse out. "Come on, Goddams," she cried, "follow me and I'll see your little king Henry king again of our lovely France." The soldiers roared with laughter, as if their shame was wiped away, and the one whose cap she wore pulled her back on his knee. "A pretty whore has better things to do," says he, cramming his mouth on hers. "Come on," he cried, withdrawing a moment, "give me a real French kiss." "Go on, Lisette," they cried, "that's more than the Maid could do, I warrant." "Oh no," shouted another soldier, "she would have been a rare one for the kissing. Her sort always are".'

XIV

'If I am to marry him, you must come with me.'

The Lady Clare pouted at Maurie. She crossed the room, with a walk that was half a dance, and laid her head, as a dancer might, on his raised shoulder. 'Promise that you will, my little crookback. Promise you will cleave to me and not to my brother, and that you will not suffer me to go alone to that cold castle and that heavy lumpish lord.'

She languished over him, fluttering eyelashes, twisting her fingers in his hair, play-acting yet sincere. A quiver ran through his wrists.

'Oh my lady,' he said, 'what if my lord requires me?'

'He may require you, but you find him dull.'

'And certainly since he saw the equanimity with which I received word of my own brother's death, my lord has been shy of me.'

'He may require you, but I . . . I want you. Besides, little crookback, you will die of boredom here without me.'

'And you there without me.'

'Precisely. Now tell me what you know of him who is to be my lord, my husband, but never, while there is breath in my body, spirit in my heart and wit in my head, my master. Tell me of him.'

She threw herself down on the couch and nestled her head in the cushions and smiled at him.

'You have seen him.'

'I have seen him, and I have seen oxen in the fields, but I know nothing of them, nor of him.'

Maurie said: 'He is everything that is most suitable. A great lord, with the great castle of Mirabel, a dozen manors here in the north and lord knows how many in the sleepy south, a trusted confidant of my lord Bishop of Winchester, they say, a hero of the French Wars, and a great booby to judge from his conversation.'

'And old, little tutor. Thirty if a day.'

She caught his eye and shuddered.

'Aye, and married twice, but, mark this well, with no issue.'

She opened her eyes very wide, and her tongue played between her lips.

'No issue,' she said and giggled. 'Do you think he can't?'

The marriage was celebrated on May Day. Simon, third Earl of Boscobel, was almost sober during the ceremony. He was quite drunk by the time the lady Clare retired to bed, and had slid under the table before it was thought right that he should join her.

'Marriage,' she said to Maurie. 'So this is marriage. I tell you, sweet, a sow in a sty experiences more than I with that great boar last night.'

'My lord Bishop of Winchester is wearing a heavy frown,' Maurie said.

'Why, so he is. He came to me this morning and lectured me on the duties of Christian marriage. Why,' she plucked at Maurie's sleeve, 'look at them now.'

The cleric, red as a fox and as sharp-featured, was engaged in close conversation with the lump of English clay that was Boscobel.

'Do you think he is lecturing him too on Christian marriage?'

For all that they joked and for all the Lady Clare's apprehension, which she hardly tried to conceal from Maurie, both of them were pleased enough by the turn of events. Simon Boscobel might not promise much as a husband; he would be neither companion nor lover; but, as one of the greatest lords in the north of England, he would offer his wife a position of great dignity. Moreover, as both Clare and Maurie knew, it was possible for a wife to concentrate a deal of power in her own hands, if she learned to master her lord. The opportunities were there for a trusted and confidential agent too. And both Clare and Maurie had discovered a relish for the sweet taste of power.

She was soon disillusioned. Arriving at Mirabel she was taken to the ladies' apartments and there met her husband's mother. The Dowager Countess was a tall hook-nosed woman who walked with the aid of a stick, but was otherwise young for her fifty years. She greeted Clare by extending a gloved hand towards her; Clare felt the jewels below the kidskin.

'I'll have you know, daughter-in-law,' she said, speaking in that broad-vowelled Anglo-French which had survived as a custom in the household of old John of Gaunt where she had spent her youth, 'that Mirabel is mine by inheritance, though of course my son now holds the fief. I have been accustomed to direct the household these thirty years, and I shall not abandon my charge to a chit of an ill-begotten girl. Your two predecessors learned to accept how things are done here, and you will do the same. My son is a great soldier but he had no idea of management. He is wise to leave these matters in his mother's hands. I must tell you too, girl, that it was with great reluctance that I gave my consent to this match. Your family's antecedents hardly impress me. Now turn around that I may look you over closely.'

Clare bit her lip, but kept silence.

'You'll do,' the Countess said. 'You are over-narrow in the flanks for your purpose.'

('As if I was breeding-stock,' she snapped to Maurie later, 'the old bitch.')

She soon learned, however, that her mother-in law spoke nothing but the truth. Everything in Mirabel was done as she commanded, in the fashion of a generation back. The Dowager Countess had, on her marriage, surrendered all ambition to shine at the royal court, even after Gaunt's son Bolingbroke seized the crown. She preferred domination of a narrow sphere to whatever interest and rewards might be found in a wider. As for Boscobel, he was a mere cipher. His mother ruled all, as she had promised, and she had a sharp and bitter tongue which she liked to employ on Clare.

'I see now,' Clare said, 'why my lord has been twice a widower.'

There was neither pleasure nor compensation in her marriage bed. When Boscobel was drunk, he was brutal. They had been wed near a month before she lost her virginity, and then it was an act of rape. She felt from the first an intense aversion. The sight of her lord's beefy thighs striding towards the bed where she lay, of his red beery pock-marked face, with a great hairy wart to the right of his mouth, looming over her, brought on nausea. Yet she lay still, and after that first night learned to submit. He grumbled of course, called her a whey-faced bitch that was cold as chastity; she kept silent. When she was with her mother-in-law – and the old lady compelled her attendance at a daily sewing session – she kept her eyes lowered, and spoke little, answering only direct questions, and these as briefly as possible.

She complained to Maurie, of course. Meetings between them were however rare and stolen. She knew that her mother-in-law viewed everything she did with jealous suspicion; he was conscious that his position in the household was precarious. Encountering on the stairs, they would brush against each other, give a quick squeeze of the hand. Once in a passage quite dark except for a single rushlight, she held him in a quick embrace; it was the measure of her loneliness and fear. He put his tongue to her ear: 'We must find means to talk,' he breathed.

It was not easy. Their lessons had been discontinued, and, if he had a status in the household now, it was as a sort of steward. But this was hardly recognized; he had rather slipped into the position of being one of those ill-defined beings to be found in every great household, men who ate their bread there, were ready for any service, and yet had no real function. As such, he might be dismissed, sent back to Castle Greer, driven out, at any moment. He tried to attract as little attention as he could.

He chafed. He had felt his powers and was denied their use. He tried to ingratiate himself with Boscobel; in vain. That dull ox glowered at him through bloodshot eyes. Maurie shifted his tack and craved an audience with the old lady. It was granted; he found her erect, stiff-backed in a high narrow-winged chair.

He began with compliments, speaking of her kindness and his zeal to do her service. She fixed cold eyes on him, as if dismissing his words as flummery. But he persevered, and at last, when she had motioned him to make a stop, she said:

'My lady Boscobel trusts you, does she not?'

'I have that honour, I believe.' He bowed low as sin. 'If I can be of any service to your Grace,' he repeated.

'The times are difficult,' she said. 'You will know nothing of high politics.'

'Alas, my lady, how should I?'

'It is necessary,' – she seemed for an instant to be talking to herself – 'that my son has an heir.' Then sharply: 'Will she conceive?'

'My lady, how can I tell? I know nothing of such matters.'

'No, of course not.'

A log caught in the great fireplace. Flames leapt. The Countess's shadow danced on the wall. She smoothed her hands over the beaten-gold taffeta of her gown.

'If I could be sure,' she said, 'that she will not play him false.'

So that was where the old bitch's mind was tending!

'I am sure my lady is as anxious for an heir as Your Grace is.'

'Too anxious, I fear. I distrust eyes of that colour.'

Her own were dark in the shadows. Maurie, not waiting for an invitation, drew towards her, exaggerating his limp.

'Your Grace, I am ready to watch. As you say, my lady trusts me. I can report . . . anything . . . untoward or otherwise.'

So Maurie, little by little, became the countess's spy. The reports he brought were intended to reassure; Clare was circumspect, aware of the danger of her position; they concocted the reports together. And Maurie was soon able to extend his sphere. The Countess, finding him, as she thought, reliable, perhaps more important, discovering something sympathetic in his manner, began to employ him in other ways.

She sent him on a mission to Henry of Winchester. The bishop, a cousin of the dead Frogeater, being descended from John of Gaunt by his morganatic marriage to Catherine Swynford, was now the most powerful man in the Council. He liked, men said, to see himself as a great spider spinning a web to entrap his enemies, and Maurie's skin pricked and throbbed at the thought. Everything about the court excited him. He saw the boy king dribbling at the mouth as he struggled to understand what his elders were saying, and he heard a great noble mutter 'That lad has a look in his eye of his grandsire, the mad king of France, that I care not for.'

There was a caress in Henry of Winchester's voice. When he discovered Maurie was a Scot, he questioned him closely, even though, or perhaps because, he understood the young man's eagerness to be rid of his nationality.

'We have an interest,' he said, 'in the condition of your native land.' Maurie bowed. 'It is a personal interest, you must know, as well as a political one, for our niece is the queen-regent. To which lord does your family owe allegiance?'

'To the Douglas, Your Grace.'

'And yet you yourself have been attached here in England to the des Moulins, old enemies of the Douglas. How is that?'

'Your Grace,' Maurie lifted his head to watch the effect of his words. 'It is as fortune has willed. There is nought for me north of the Border. Moreover the Douglas failed in his duty to protect my father, who had been his loyal retainer. That failure severed my obligation, and freed me to follow fortune and my own judgement. So I have come to England, and loyally served my lord Edward des Moulins, and now my Lady Clare, who is my lady of Boscobel, and I serve also the Countess of Boscobel who has entrusted me with this message to Your Grace, and I pray that my Scots blood be not held against me.'

'Fine words,' the Bishop said. 'We fear the influence of the House of Douglas. Do not let me forget you. You are a man that may be useful to us. Would you dare undertake a mission for us in Scotland?'

'Dare? Dare, Your Grace? What way would I not dare?'

'There is no cause or impediment that would prevent you?'

'Armed with your Grace's warrant, there is none.'

'We shall not forget you,' and he extended the episcopal ring, a garnet set in rubies, for Maurie to kiss.

'I hate the thought of what is growing here.' The lady Clare stretched in the sun and stroked her belly. 'Will you tell that thought to my mother-in-law, little spy?'

'If I am her spy, it is in your interests.' Maurie smiled. 'For one thing, now that I am her spy, we are permitted to spend time together, than which I have no other or greater pleasure.'

'Lord, I have such a lust for apples.' She dug her even white teeth into the sour green fruit. A little juice spurted down her chin and her tongue searched for it, as Maurie watched. 'I do not think my husband will live long,' she said.

Maurie smiled again.

'Maurie,' she said, 'he disgusts me. Our coupling . . . it was all I could do to force him to insert his prick into the right hole. He had never done it before.' She pushed her bare toes against

129

Maurie's thigh as he lay on the grass beside her. 'It excites you when I talk like this, crookback, doesn't it?'

'My lady delights me always.' He chewed a long stem of grass. 'Go on,' he said.

'He prefers the other way.'

'It's an old soldier's habit, they tell me.'

'Crookback,' she said, 'little crookback . . . how will you do it?'

The Lord Boscobel fell sick in the early autumn; of a wasting sickness, his physician said. Naturally the physician bled him to draw off the evil and noxious humours. The Lord Boscobel weakened; he lay dumb as an ox in the shambles. His mother, who had concentrated the last passion of her selfish life in her soldier-son, dismissed the physician and summoned others, who bled him again, so that he weakened further.

Maurie approached the Countess.

'There is a friar I have heard of in York,' he said, 'who has travelled in the east and acquired great store of curious learning. They say he has a way of applying unguents drawn from rare herbs which heal even the sharpest diseases. I know nothing of him directly; only hearsay. But, Your Grace, my lord weakens. His physicians cannot treat him. There seems no hope. With your ladyship's permission I shall ride to York and fetch me that friar here.'

He found him in a low tavern crouched beneath the wall of the Minster. The friar was holding court to a group of young men whom Maurie took for novices or artisan apprentices. He settled himself in another corner of the room and called for Gascon wine. He watched the friar: a big, lean man with pendulous jowls and blubbery lips. He wore, in defiance of the rules of his order, a rich chain of gold around his neck. Given him by a grateful patient? Or client? Or stolen? There were rings on the hand that fondled a pert blond boy beside him. The little group laughed at the friar's words and the blond boy giggled and nestled against him. The friar picked up a mutton chop-bone and gnawed at it; fat slid down his chin, dribbling from the ruby lips. When he had taken enough to fill his mouth, he offered the bone to the blond boy who bit and sucked at it in

the friar's hand. 'There's a friar's kiss for you, Ned', cried one of
the novices, and the blond boy squirmed against the friar.

The next night they were there again, and again Maurie
sipped his Gascon wine and watched. His gaze did not disturb
them; this tavern was a free part of the world. But, when they
left, Maurie crept after them, his lantern shaded under his cloak.
It was misty dark in the narrow cobbled lanes, and he came
near to losing them. Curfew had sounded and in the distance he
could hear the town guard bidding wanderers retire to their
beds, and rousting others out of the taverns. Then he heard a
sound, something between a sob and a gasp, followed by heaving
panting. He tiptoed into a stinking alley, ankle-deep in glaur
and dung. The sounds were louder. He fished the lantern out
and held it up. The friar's back was to him and his habit was
hitched up to reveal his bare calves. Maurie coughed. The friar,
alarmed, stopped his stroke and turned round. The blond boy
was spread across a barrel with his breeches down about his
ankles.

'You'll be at the Lord's work, brother,' Maurie said.

At that moment they heard the town guard. Maurie dowsed
his lantern, and, taking the friar by the sleeve of his habit,
hustled him and the boy behind the barrel. They crouched
there, pressed against each other, and Maurie laid his hand over
the boy's mouth to silence his whimpering.

'You take risks, brother,' Maurie said, when the guard had
marched off.

The friar chuckled. The boy hitched up his breeks and would
have darted off into the darkness if Maurie had not grabbed him
by the elbow. 'Not so fast, child, we have matters to discuss.
The three of us. But we are hardly safe to do so in the streets. I
am a stranger to York. Where can we go?'

The friar laughed again. 'We were on our way to Goody
Tuke's lodging-house and stew when I was overtaken by impor-
tunate desire that would not delay. Friend, I must thank you.
My ardour was such – Pastor Corydon formosum Alexim
delectat – that, but for your intervention, the watch must have
seized me in flagrante delicto ... and what delicto – ' He
sniggered and dug Maurie in the ribs. 'What delicto! Have you
ever chanced on so delicious a wenchy-boy, such limbs of
delight, such a veritable Cupid, or rather Ganymede? Come,

friend, accompany us to Goody's where we shall find ale, if not the Gascon wine that is your preference, and there we can pledge our thanks, Ned and I, before discoursing pleasantly on whatever matters it is that you wish to bring to our attention.'

So speaking, he thrust himself between them, placed his right arm round Maurie's neck and his left round the boy's, and guided them by a succession of noisome wynds, following what seemed a circuitous route, but one evidently well known to him, till they were near the river. They descended a flight of greasy steps where they surprised a covey of rats squabbling over cabbage-stalks. The moon crept out from behind heavy clouds. It was reflected from the water, and Maurie was impressed to see his companion's face alight with amusement.

'Surely this is the very man for my purpose,' he thought. 'Why, he is as ignorant of shame, and therefore of scruples, as I am myself.'

The friar tapped gently on the door, and after a few moments, a panel slid back. The friar whispered a few words and the door opened. The woman, Goody Tuke herself presumably, a buxom red-haired wife in the prime of life, greeted the friar as an old friend.

'Brother Ambrose,' she cried giving him a smacking kiss on the cheek, 'this is rare delight. You have been absent too long. Is it one of my girls you are wanting or have you more private pleasures in mind?'

'How well you know me, Goody my love,' the friar said, 'but for the moment set the three of us down with a jug of your best nut-brown. We have great affairs to discuss. See that we are not disturbed, heart of my heart, and when we are off with our business, then who knows what larks and sport we may be inclined for. Though, my angel, there is not one of your girls, blithe though they be, that can compare with their mistress. Would I were a poet to sing your charms!'

He raised her hand to his lips and slobbered over it a moment. 'Be off with you,' she said, 'sauce.' 'Sauce for the sweet,' he sighed and motioned to the others to follow him into a small room with a fire that smoked and a black cat beside it. She brought them ale and tankards herself and then left the room, bestowing an arch look and a loud laugh on the friar as she did so.

'Now, friend,' the friar said, 'your proposition.'

'What makes you think I have a proposition for you?'

'Come off it, me old cock.' Brother Ambrose dispensed the ale. 'You don't sit watching a man for two evenings and then follow him down a lane to disturb him at his pleasures – for which interruption I am in the circumstances grateful though in others I wouldn't thank you – you don't behave thus unless you have business with a man. Besides, I knew you had from the first moment I felt your glance on me.'

'My business,' Maurie said, 'is of a private and confidential nature.'

He looked at the boy Ned who, no longer perturbed by what had happened, had picked up the cat and set it on his knee, and was stroking it with a smile on his face.

'Ned?' The friar said. 'I have no secrets from Ned. Ned is my heart's delight.'

'Nevertheless . . .'

'Nevertheless as you say, there are things that a sweet child might be better not to know. If it is such things you wish to lay before me, very well. Ned, my angel, would you leave us a while. You take my heart with you, give me a kiss first.'

'Certainly,' the boy said, 'under protest.'

He kissed the friar and made for the door. Before leaving, he turned and winked.

'Isn't he exquisite?' The friar spread his hands wide. 'You know, my dear, I am all of a flutter, not just because of Ned – by the way he does exquisite wood-carving too, he's apprenticed to a master who doesn't appreciate him in any way – but also because I sense that you have something of great interest to impart to me.'

'I could see you hanged for sodomy,' Maurie said, 'or do they burn clerks?'

'Tut, tut, my boy, is this friendly? Your word against mine too.'

'And would Ned be silent if put to the question?'

'The thought appals me.'

'Of course, I merely mention it to demonstrate that your position is – shall we say – insecure.'

The friar smiled.

'We who traffick in deep designs court insecurity. But come,

133

my boy, cease from this foolery and expatiate. Besides, let me assure you, I am not, like some, born to be hanged. Or burned if it comes to that. I may say with the Archpoet, 'meum est propositum in taberna mori.'

'Many,' Maurie said, 'may be hanged or burned who are not born to it.'

'A philosopher I see. One who believes in the freedom of the will.'

'Or in chance,' Maurie said. He took a pull at his ale. 'I have a lady . . .'

'Fortunate youth. Fortunate lady.'

'Not so fortunate as she might be. This lady, who is of high degree . . .' The friar kissed the tips of his fingers to him. '. . . has a husband. A noble lord. Since last summer her lord has been ailing, a wasting sickness they say. He has been bled, to no avail. Physicians, learned and orthodox physicians of the school of Galen, have tended him. Under their care he grows neither better . . . nor worse.'

'And the lady, your dame of high degree, looks for a change in her lord's condition?'

'Precisely. Now I have heard tell of you that you have a rare and canny skill as a herbalist.'

The friar smiled: 'There is none like me this side of the Alps. Nay, why should I be so modest? None north of Naples. I have studied under the great masters there, and, but for an unfortunate incident – which I shall not weary you by describing – I should be living in luxury and splendour such as my genius and learning warrant, not skulking like a thief in this miserable northern town. Oh, to have the sun on my back again . . . to see the deep azure of the Mediterranean, not our grey north sea. Your lady could not have sent for a better man, whether she seeks cure or . . . is it? . . . kill. Ah, I thought so. How happy I am to read which it is in your face. I was sure a wise youth like you had not sought me out for a mere cure, such as would hardly try my genius. I shall require silver, much silver.'

'And, on your part, silence.'

'Silence is said to be golden, but never silver. Let us have Ned back and tell him of our good fortune and devise a scheme to prise him from his unappreciative master. Tomorrow we can discuss the details of the case, but tonight shall be given over to revelry. I assure you that you have put yourself and your lady in the best of hands, and to prove my gratitude, you shall be free of Goody's stew – at my expense, unless of course you resemble me in having Greek tastes. You don't? Perhaps we should . . . but . . . who told you of my genius by the way?'

'A fat filthy clerk by name of Nicholas.'

'Nicholas? A fat rogue with stinking breath like a week-old herring? Well, he has served me ill in the past. Once indeed he tried . . . ah but here is the beauteous Ned. Enough . . .'

Brother Ambrose made a deep obeisance to the Dowager Countess of Boscobel. His face gleamed with humility.

'If your ladyship pleases,' he said, 'I must know the hour of your son's nativity. Mine is a deep and exact science. His lordship is in low state. These quack physicians you have employed have near put him beyond the point where even my lore may save him. I must therefore cast his horoscope with unusual speed that I may know which remedies to employ.'

'He talks like a wise man, your friar,' the Lady Clare said. 'He is clear what is required.'

'My lady,' Maurie said. 'He has arrived just in time. Your husband will rally, for, Brother Ambrose informs me, he is already regaining his strength though this is not yet visible. He will be near rising from his bed. All will praise the skill and sagacity of the friar, and then alas your lord will fall back again, grievously sick. All the herbs of Arabia will not sweeten his state, nor will he last the night. Then, my lady, you must see to it that the false physicians who have so weakened him that he could not respond to the friar's medicine are punished.'

The lord of Boscobel looked with wild eyes on the world contracted to his chamber. His mother spoke to him. His eye roved from her, and when he tried to reply, he babbled nonsense.

'Alas my lady, his wits stray,' Maurie said. 'Brother Ambrose, you must redouble your efforts, try new remedies,'

'I fear he escapes even my skill. The furies have him in their claws.'

The friar, behind the countess's back, winked at Maurie

Did the dying man catch the movement? Did he understand

what was happening? Maurie thought he did, for Boscobel's body arched upwards and a scream tore itself as if from his very soul. Then he fell back. The friar applied cooling unguents to his brow. The man made a feeble gesture to reject them. His mother's face was white as a winter mountainside. Maurie heaved a deep sigh of distress. Boscobel groaned. It seemed that the scream had borrowed his last ounce of strength.

Boscobel died whining the next night as his wife went into labour. The child was born two hours later, a misshapen rat with a head the size of an apple. His grandmother whose eye had been dry as she watched over her son's agony screamed when she saw the child. Her screams rang and echoed through the long corridors of the night. She called for men-at-arms to bring the treacherous friar before her.

'This is his work. He has slain my son with poison and worked some evil magic on my lady's womb.'

But the friar was nowhere to be found. He had approached Maurie within minutes of drawing a cloth over Boscobel's face, told him his work was done, requested his reward and announced that it was time for him to depart.

'Where will you go?' Maurie said, handing him a fat purse of silver.

'To Ravenspur, and there take ship for France. We have two palfreys ready at the village inn. I trust in you to secure our passage from the castle.'

'I have my lord's seal,' Maurie said.

The friar smiled. 'I trust you because we are bound together. If anything unfortunate or untoward would happen, if we should be hindered in any way, why then I can only hope to save my neck – and Ned's which is dearer to me than my own – by animadverting to your part in our little affair. And need I say how loth I should be to imperil one I esteem, whom indeed I regard as a kindred soul, in such a way?'

'You may rely on me,' Maurie said, and himself accompanied the pair beyond the main gate of the castle to a little wicket normally used only by the kitchens. He advanced before them and, flourishing his authority, despatched the gate-keeper on an errand, assuring him that all would be well in his absence, and that he himself would take full responsibility for the security of

136

his gate. Then he summoned the fugitives from the shadows, and wished them all speed.

'I trust,' Brother Ambrose said, 'your life will run so smoothly that you do not require to avail yourself of my services again, but if you do, contrive to let me know, and I shall speed to your side. We are twin hearts, you and I,' and he leaned over to embrace Maurie.

So, when the Countess called for the friar, there was none could find him nor knew where or when he had gone. She sent to the village, but the friar had taken the precaution of bribing the innkeeper to stay silent. Then she turned her anger on Maurie. Her examination of him was close and prolonged. He swore his innocence and urged that the friar had rescued her son from what seemed like certain death, 'drew him back from the gates of mortality', but how in the end even his skill had failed to master the disease. 'If anyone is to blame,' he said, 'it is those physicians who so weakened my lord that he could not respond even to the friar's most potent medicine. They should be whipped out of the castle.'

'And how,' she said, drawing her lips back so that he saw her black and yellow teeth, 'do you account for the child's deformity?'

He felt her eyes fixed on his own raised shoulder.

'My lady,' he said, 'it ill becomes me to question the ways of the Almighty.'

But his position was dangerous, and a new anxiety was now added to it. Childbirth had weakened Clare and brought on a fever. For three days she tossed and turned in a high sweat unable to find rest. If she should die . . . he wished now that he had not permitted the friar to leave. They piled blankets on her to expel the fever. They physicians were ready to bleed her. The Countess was eager that they should.

Maurie called the sergeant Bartholomew to him. He had been impressed by his conduct in the affair in which his brothers had been captured and had brought him from Castle Greer. Now he met him in the hawks' loft, where such a meeting might not arouse suspicion. For a little they discussed a sick tassel gentle with the falconer: then, on the pretext of showing Bartholomew a merlin he had newly acquired as a gift for his lady, he drew the sergeant to the far end of the loft.

'How many men can you trust?'

'There's the three we brought from Greer. Maybe another ten. No more.'

'Enough,' he said, 'more than I thought.' He drew a letter from within his jerkin. 'I have a dangerous enterprise for you, Bart. Are you game?'

'That depends.'

'Depends on what? The danger or the reward?'

'Maybe a bit of both.'

'Both are great. The stakes are high. Look, I have here a letter under the seal of our dead lord. Open it. Can you read? No, then I must read it to you, or give you the sense. It commands me to use what agency I require – that's you, Bart – to take, seize and imprison the Dowager Countess of Boscobel on a charge of attempted poisoning. Well, man? Look at me.'

The sergeant kept his eyes averted.

'Look at me,' Maurie insisted. 'Look at the seal. Is it not authentic?'

'There's nothing wrong wi' the seal,' the sergeant muttered.

'Bart,' Maurie laid his hand on the man's sleeve and pressed his arm, 'we are playing a great game, the Lady Clare and I. Help us bring it off, and you shall be well rewarded. If we fail, then we are all done for, for by St Pandulf, I shall see that you are pulled down and suffer with us. But, if we are resolute, it will not come to that. Come, she is only an old woman when all is said and done. She is no witch to curse you. And, if you have scruples – though why you should, I confess I can't imagine – she will not be clapped in irons or harmed in any way ... merely restrained. When that is done, I have another and more important missive for you to carry, a letter to the Bishop of Winchester, which will lay bare to him the gross wickedness that has been attempted, and will explain how we have thwarted it. Trust me, Bart, and make your fortune. Play the man and throw the dice.'

They chose the hour before dawn. Bartholomew crashed the hilt of his sword on the door of the Countess's chamber and, when it did not open, called up two soldiers with a battering ram to break the lock. The Countess sat up in bed, grey hair like rat's tails on her shoulders and her mouth wide open as if to scream; but no sound came. They rounded up her ladies and had them led away except for one maidservant. At last she found words and asked by whose authority they acted. Bartholomew shrugged his shoulders and told her that could wait; meanwhile she was to be permitted no communication with the world beyond her door.

'That cripple has done this,' she cried. 'That weasel Scot. I should have trusted my fears and hanged him from the castle gallows.'

'Too late for that, Countess,' Maurie said, appearing from behind a curtain where he had slipped in the confusion of their first entry to the room.

He bowed to her and smiled.

'Besides, Countess, I do not act on my own authority but on that of my dead lord.'

'My son, you dare to say . . .'

'Aye, Madam, your son. And I dare, having a letter under his own seal. Your son, fearing that you would not have due regard for the interest of his widow and child, left such instruction.'

'My son would never have done such a thing. He cared nothing for that whey-faced bitch. And as for the deformed rat, why who is to say it is even his?'

'Rant as you wish, madam, you will not contradict the authority of my instructions given under my lord's seal. Furthermore, there is now a new and graver charge to answer. You are accused by the Lady Clare of attempting her death by poison and of causing the deformity of her child by witchcraft. Answer those charges if you can. Escape them if you can.'

He hugged himself. Everything that might be laid against him had now been charged on his enemy. It was with relish that he penned his letter to the Cardinal, rolling the phrases round his delighted mind.

'Can we keep the old bitch quiet?' Clare asked.

She was pale after her fever but her eyes sparkled as she drew Maurie to her and urged his hands to fondle her breasts.

He leant over and kissed them and licked their milk.

'I have humbly and respectfully asked on your behalf, that she be commanded to pass her last years in a nunnery. She has played, lost and we have won. It is not for us vindictively to demand punishment for her crimes.'

'Oh crookback, my little crookback, when you assume that saintly face, I cannot doubt our success.'

XV

'Her sort always are . . .' The words rang in Rob's mind, playing
a little tune, as, the lark's hour succeeding the owl's, he took
leave of the old soldier and the old man who might once have
been a king, but whose wits had anygate gone the way of King
Richard's crown – and mightn't his soul have more hope of
Paradise without either wits or crown? – and strode up the
valley. He felt a new lightness, like the lark's song, and a new
expectancy. He had no notion where he might find Jean; yet the
soldier's story had somehow given him new hope, and for the
first time his search was purposeful. He could not understand
why this was, yet his mind seemed cleared of the mists that had
enveloped him since Clym's death.

He was still torn between his own sense of fate and the
philosophy that chance governs all. On the one hand was his
conviction that he and Jean were bound together; on the other
the fact that he still had no clue as to her whereabouts, and was
indeed relying on chance to show him the way. On the one hand
was Clym's death which so horribly confirmed the fate the
Gudewife of Hangingshaws had wished on them. On the other
was Rob's own refusal to consent to death, and his notion that
maybe the Gudewife's curse was an act of will. Fate, chance,
will – who could disentangle them?

Of a sudden, pondering these thoughts as he set himself at a
braeside, he thought of Maurie, and, to his amazed disgust,
found himself longing for him. Maurie had outlawed himself
from the family, chosen to become their enemy, and yet, Rob
wondered at himself, now Rob would have given a night's sleep
to talk with him about these matters. Maurie had the sharpest
intelligence he knew; but that wasn't the only reason. He
pictured his brother's keen features, the cynical droop of his
eyelid and his twisted smile, and he remembered how, when
they were children, Maurie had aye been able to make him

laugh. That was what couldn't be wiped out of mind; that Maurie could make him laugh.

That morning was the start of some three years' wandering for Rob in the course of which he traversed the whole of the Borderland. He was welcome as a minstrel wherever he found himself, and the songs he made were kept and remembered in the villages and farms. He went as far north as Forth and south over the Border beyond the Tyne and down into the rich vale of York. Sometimes he travelled alone, sometimes with a band of pilgrims or pedlars, from whom he learned many strange stories of distant lands. He learned of the great cities of Italy where men walked the streets without swords and where goods were bought and sold without coin. He learned much of the French Wars, though nothing ever of his brother Will, and also of that war fought against the pagans in the marshes of eastern Europe. He fell in with roving bands of gypsies, and learned something of their language that none could understand. He heard tales of devils and witches, kelpies and bogles, ghosts and unquiet spirits. But in all this time he learned nothing definite of Jean.

Once he thought he had got a trace of her in the headlands of Tweed, and hurried there; but the woman he found in a shieling which the shepherds had left with the gales of the autumn equinox was younger than Jean, and a mad lost soul who, when she saw Rob, tore at her bosom and begged him to board her. He shook his head, and threw down a coin, though whether the poor creature would be able to put it to any use he misdoubted.

Then the next spring he attended as was his custom the Beltane Fair at Peebles. There was ever the hope of getting word of Jean at a fair where there would be a gathering of folk from all districts, and he was also used to earn money there, gratefully given him by those whom he entertained with his songs and music.

The second night he was sitting in a tavern when he felt a hand fall on his shoulder. He looked up from his ale to find the old soldier of the ruined church.

'With your leave, friend, I shall take my ale and cheese beside you,' the soldier said. 'You have travelled far and wide without success, I hear.'

'Just so,' said Rob, 'but the warld is room and I'm a patient bodie.'

'Yet,' the old soldier said, 'I have often thought of you and of that night we spent thegither.'

'I mind fine the story you told me of the French lass,' Rob said, 'and I have pondered it deeply. There is a part of life beyond good and evil it seems to me, and your lass inhabited it.'

'Just so,' the soldier said, 'and is that the land you would fain win yourself?'

Rob sighed. The soldier clapped him on the shoulder again and called for more ale.

'Where's your old friend that would be the king of England?' Rob asked.

'Deid,' the soldier said.,

'Weel, he was maybe glad to go, for there can have been little for him here.'

'Little, friend, for many years, but pain and fear and hunger. He suffered none of these at the end, though he died in a snow-wreath at the back end of the year. But he passed over as lightly as the sun sinks behind the hill, though still babbling of royalty. Ah well, if he was a king, he was a rare one, for he lived many years and did no harm to any man, and there's few of his fellows could claim as much. Aye, and he knew the nakedness of man too, and there again, there's few that could say that either, save aiblins Charles the mad king of France that was my Charley-boy's feyther. But, friend, I am blithe to see you, for your sake as weel as my ain pleasure. And I think I may be able to set you on your path.'

And he told Rob he had heard a tale from the auld herd on the Whitmuir that lay on the west side of Eskdale of a faery-woman who had bided with him through a lang winter. They had happened on his hut on a night of driving snow, when the wreaths were such as might bury man or beast. The herd had never known who they were nor where they had come from, but had accepted them as he might have accepted a stray ewe and her lamb that had attached themselves to his flock. He was an old man who had resided these twenty years or more in solitude and he reckoned no more for the vagaries of human kind than for the shifting winds. They had stayed there through the winter, and in the spring the woman had fallen into a fever and been like to die; but the laddie fetched her strange herbs and she regained her strength. And when she did so there was a wild look in her eye as if she maun be off. And then the gypsies had come – a band of these wild Egyptians speaking an unco tongue which the old herd could not understand, but the woman seemed to. They had camped a sennight in the valley below the buchts. It was the lambing time and he had been fearful of their presence, and had spoken of his fear to the woman who had smiled as if it meant nothing. She had descended again to the gypsy encampment, taking the laddie with her, and when the mist rose from the valley bottom the next day he saw that they had departed. So he had that to be thankful for: that she had laid a spell on them and spirited them away, though he never saw her nor the laddie again.

The soldier paused.

'She may not be the she you seek,' he said, 'and it comes into my mind that it will profit you little to find her if she is. But who am I to deny you the chance of coming to your goal? So, my friend, you maun speir for the Egyptians, and may the saints guard you in your quest.'

XVI

Towards evening Rob came on the gypsy band in a little dell in an oak forest. He sniffed their cooking pots before he had sight of them, and the smell of the rich stew simmering there reminded him he was hungry. Then a half-dozen dogs of the lurcher sort set up a barking and rushed forward, dancing widdershins round him, keeping their distance as he continued to advance. Old women sat by the pots under makeshift tents. Three or four men sat apart making snares and whittling at sticks. They were all dark and wore moustaches and were dressed in red and yellow. They looked at Rob with a level sort of stare that had hardly curiosity in it, but a silent challenge. Only the dogs kept up their angry defensive barking.

Rob sat on his pony and waited. It was less than he had looked for: a straggly gang of game-thieves, no more than a dozen and a half in all.

Then a boy who had been sitting cross-legged by the fire rose and approached him.

'What do you want?'

He spoke the words haltingly.

'I am a traveller,' Rob said, 'let me speak to your chief man.'

The boy shook his head.

Rob dismounted and looped his reins over a thorn bush. He spread his hands wide to show that he came unarmed in peace. Without saying anything more, he crossed over to the fire and sat there. The dogs sniffed round him a moment and then, satisfied, slunk back to their places. Rob nodded and smiled. They seemed to find it natural that a stranger should ride into their camp and settle himself. The old women went on with their task; the little group of men bent their heads. Somewhere behind the tents a girl was singing in a tongue Rob did not know; there was sadness and longing in her music as if she remembered something loved and lost.

The boy brought Rob a platter of stew and a mug of spring water. Rob took them, and nodded his head. The stew was rich and savoury – some lord's warren had suffered to provide it.

When he had eaten, he lifted his head. The boy was still standing by his side.

'I am seeking a woman,' Rob said. 'She is the mother of my child. I was told she was with you.'

The boy put his finger to his lips. Then he asked if Rob had travelled far.

'Far enough and too long,' Rob said. 'From the north, from another country.'

The boy turned away, across the clearing, and crouched down beside one of the old women. She listened to what he had to say, shook her head two or three times and listened again as the boy jabbered at her. She pointed at one of the men and the boy crossed and repeated his tale to him. The man too shook his head, and looked at Rob, who felt himself again the object of scrutiny. He sat still and waited.

Presently the boy slipped from the clearing. He was gone a long time and the light began to fade, blue-purple and grey where the shadows lay. Rob sat still, trying to look unconcerned, knowing from past dealings that there was no hurrying these folk. His pony cropped the grass by the thorn bush. Where had the boy gone?

He was answered at last. The boy emerged at an opening on the other side of the clearing, followed by a number of men. He pointed towards Rob. The leading man, a big broad fellow with a black beard, laid his hand on the boy's shoulder, as if to thank him, and advanced on Rob.

'So,' he said, 'so you are the boy's father? So we meet at last?'

Rob looked again at the boy whom he had taken for a gypsy. He was thin and dark and he saw nothing of himself in him. He pushed himself to his feet. 'And you?' he said.

'I am Giorgio, king of this sept of the Romany people.'

He spoke English confidently, and swept his hand round to display his mastery of his little flock.

'And the boy's mother, Jean?'

'Is my woman.' The gypsy grinned. 'One of my women,' he corrected himself.

'I have searched long for her.'

'And I found her. She was mad when I found her. She is not mad today.'

'Can I see her?'

'Perhaps? Who can tell? Why have you come? Do you hope to take her away?'

'Aye.'

'Good,' said the gypsy. 'I like a man who is honest.'

He clapped Rob on the back.

'You are our guest,' he said, 'you have eaten our meat. Now we shall drink.'

He smacked his hands together and called out in the Romany tongue. One of the old women brought liquor, good ale and a distillation of herbs that was strange to Rob. Giorgio pledged him and they drank. The liquor was both sweet and sharp and warmed Rob's stomach.

'She is afraid of you,' the gypsy said. 'No, that is not right. She is afraid for you. And your son,' he said, 'is he not a fine boy?'

'We are wanderers,' the gypsy king said, settling himself against a tree, 'and all Christian men turn their hands against us. That is our fate, and we combat it as best we may. The woman we speak of has been condemned to wander also, for she too is an outlaw. But what of you? You are a seeker, and that is a different thing, for you long for a settled habitation. Am I not right?'

'Aye,' Rob said, 'and yet I have wandered far from that whilk I hae, and it may be I have learned that whilk misfits me to enjoy my ain hearthside again.'

The gypsy nodded.

'As to the matter of the woman,' he said, 'how shall that be decided?' He frowned. 'She was yours, she is mine.'

Rob laid his hand on his belt and remained silent. The boy's eyes were fixed on his face.

'She is not of our tribe, and yet she belongs to the tribe of outcasts.' He fixed his gaze on Rob's hands fingering the belt beneath his tunic. 'We could fight, but you are but a poor thing and I should certainly conquer. You think you could buy her, but then if you have money – is it silver you finger? – why should I not slit your throat and keep the money and the woman?'

146

He clapped Rob on the shoulder again. All round them the gypsies, satisfied that nothing of any great moment was about to happen, were wrapping themselves in their cloaks and preparing to sleep. The old women crawled into the tents. The fire sank low. The birds were still. Rob wondered where Jean was concealed.

'We shall talk of it again in the morning,' the gypsy said. 'Meanwhile you are welcome as our guest for we have long expected you, having heard of your search and being acquaint with your movements.'

'Well,' Rob said, 'let me say just this, and then we may sleep on it. I hae travelled many weary miles, owre hill and dale, in foul weather and fair, in thirst and hunger, often thinking I followed naething but a fool's errand, a will-o'the wisp, like a man led astray by the fairies; but now I hae come upon her, I shall be like a bulldog tyke that winna let go.'

'Very well,' the gypsy said, 'I understand you.'

'Does the boy ken he is my son?'

'I do not think so.'

'He looks searchingly at me.'

'He is a strange child with many fancies and of much penetration.'

The gypsy left him. Rob composed himself for sleep. His mind was still. He had reached a point on which life would turn and he was powerless to affect the issue. He had laid himself at the mercy of these foreigners, who would kill him, drive him forth or grant him his wish as they desired. Yet he felt a deep certainty. Jean and he were bound together. She had sought to evade that destiny by flight. He had pursued her and found her. They would live or die together. He closed his eyes.

He slept through the first awakening of the camp, and light sparkled green and gold through the leaves. Violets, anemones and cowslips glittered in the dew and the first dog-roses were in bloom around the little clearing. The boy brought him a flat bread and a platter of last evening's stew on which to break his fast.

'What do they call you?' Rob asked.

'Wattie.'

He was a funny little fellow, thin as a sapling and supple as one too. His eyes were dark and revealed nothing and his mouth was a bit twisted as if he had already learned to expect little of the world. When he spoke it was in a faraway voice that seemed to summon words from a deep memory. Rob questioned him about his upbringing, but either the boy remembered nothing or experience had schooled him to hide what he knew.

All the time there was a bustle in the camp, a coming and going of men. They moved in such a way as hardly to attract attention, but Rob was aware of it even though he scarcely saw them arrive or depart. It seemed to him though that the mood had changed; that there was a fear he couldn't account for.

When Giorgio approached him his face too seemed changed from the night before. It had lost its ease, and the surprising friendliness had vanished from it.

'I fear you have brought trouble on us,' he said. 'There are soldiers searching the forest.'

'Soldiers? How can that be?'

'You spent the night before last in the environs of the castle of Mirabel did you not?'

'They told me that was the castle's name. What of it?'

'Fool! Did you reveal your name?'

'And why should I hide it?'

'Do you know who is the lord of Mirabel?'

'No.'

'Your own brother, and a brother who hates you with a mortal fear.'

'How can that be? My brother is no lord.'

'Lord in deed, if not lord in name, and feared throughout the country for his cruelty and vice. That is your brother. And he is known for his hatred of our race. By coming upon us in this rash manner . . .' he paused and threw his hands wide. 'I fear nothing for myself,' he cried, 'but for those who depend on me. You must leave us.'

'I'll no leave without Jean and the bairn,' Rob said.

The gypsy scowled. He drew a thin leather thong from his belt.

'Perhaps I should kill you, hang you from that tree,' he said. 'Then when the soldiers came I could display your corpse. That might appease your brother, and cause them to stay their hand against my poor tribe.'

A woman's voice rang out: 'If you touch a hair of his head, I shall lay such a curse upon you that your tribe will hold your name bloody to the third generation.'

Rob spun round. There was Jean before him, thin and wild-looking, her hair loose about her shoulders and her feet bare.

'Jean,' he said, 'oh Lassie, I hae looked that long for ye.'

The gypsy had taken a step back; now his eyes moved from one to another.

'Aye,' Jean said, 'but your coming here brings sair trouble on these good folk whae have been kind to me and to our bairn. Oh Rob, I kenned fine you were seeking us, but I had prayed that for your ain sake you would never happen on us. But now I see that my prayers were vain. I should have kenned they would be, that we are indeed bound together by a bond that naething but death can break, and indeed no even that for I fear we shall ligg in the same grave.'

She turned and spoke to the gypsy in his own language. She laid her fingers on his cheek and her voice crooned to him, and it seemed to Rob that she was not pleading but was rather soothing him and telling him what must be, what they could not control. At last he heaved a sigh and bent his head.

'I'll have his silver though,' he said, and Jean turned to Rob and said, 'Give him your belt.'

He did so, and got Jean on to his pony with Wattie up behind her. He held out his hand to the gypsy, who, hesitating a moment, took it.

'I am sair vexed to hae brought the soldiers on ye,' Rob said, 'But gin we are gone, happen they winna trouble ye.'

'They are still beating the far side of the forest. Follow the stream till you come to a parting of the ways, and then strike northward,' the gypsy said. 'I canna wish that your God goes with you, for . . .' and he broke off and waved them on their way.

The path ran close beside the stream for perhaps half a mile. It was narrow and climbed up and down. The pony baulked at one of the rises, not liking the drop to the side. Rob had to leave its head and squeeze round behind it risking that it would start suddenly and push him off the path. He gave it a smack on the rump and it half-reared so that Jean had to cling to its mane. Then he put his shoulder against it and and it sprang forward and scrambled up the bank leaving Rob sprawling behind. It was easy going after that though, as the path wound down again through oaks and chestnuts. They paused. There was a silence in the near forest and the sounds of the soldiers were far away.

Then the trees thinned and they saw a meadow spread before them. The burn ran along one side and on the other the ground rose in a gentle slope dotted with broom and whins in its upper reaches till it met the trees again. There was no path running round the fringe of the wood and it would be hard to push round keeping in cover, for the way was blocked by a tangle of thorn and briars.

Rob misliked the look of the open space before them, where they would be visible to anyone who had taken the high ground to watch for fugitives. It was a long meadow, three or four hundred paces. Bees and butterflies buzzed and fluttered round the flowers, buttercups, tall daisies, clover, and wild orchids.

'What's that?' Wattie said. 'Listen.'

Rob heard nothing. Then, borne on a sough of wind, came a sound which caused his heart to miss a beat and the sweat to start on his temples.

'Dogs,' he said, 'they have put hounds on us. They must have found some piece of your clothing – or the boy's – at the gypsy camp.'

The meadow still lay innocent in sunshine. A pigeon beat its way out of the trees above their heads, smacking the air with its rush of wings. Rob looked at the thorn and briars to the right, and the tangled undergrowth to left. There would be no need of dogs to follow their track if they went that way.

He took the pony's head and led it to the verge of the meadow, then turned to the left following the line of trees and keeping in their shadow. There was just a chance that they might still be hidden from anyone watching from the hillside, but now that he heard the hounds behind he thought it unlikely there was anyone posted there. He forced the pony into a trot and then the stream was before them.

The pony didn't like the water, for the bed of the burn was covered with flat stones on which its hooves slipped. But Rob forced it into the stream. The water came halfway up his calves. The pony tossed its head, but Rob kept hold of the bridle. He hesitated a moment, then he pulled the beast's head round and turned it downstream, back the way they had come. The dogs would, he reckoned, follow them easily to the water's edge, and it was likely that their handlers would guess they had gone up the water.

They moved slowly, for the pony was shy of the slippery footing, and all the time the cry of the dogs grew louder. The trees hung low over the water and Rob had to push branches aside to let them pass. Jean flattened herself over the pony's withers with the boy in front of her, so that he lay against its neck and her face was pressed behind its ears. Rob could hear her breathing.

They had gone perhaps a quarter of a mile and the stream widened. That made the going easier for the bottom was sandy now, but it also left them exposed to any watcher. Then, in a couple of hundred yards, they met another stream, coming in on their right, and this time Rob turned the pony up the new valley. In a little it narrowed and it became hard to follow in the water. Twice Rob had to lead the pony onto the far bank and scramble up the footpath that ran down by the water. Each time he returned to the stream itself as soon as he could. The sound of the dogs was fainter, but the wind was now blowing it away from them.

Rob paused and cupped his ear. There was silence but for the rustle of the wind in the leaves and the water lapping against their legs. He looked up and smiled at Jean.

He gave them a few minutes to rest and then they went forward again. The glen narrowed and a cloud swung, like a great ship under sail, in front of the sun, and the world darkened. Then they heard a great roar ahead, and rounding the corner, saw the stream stretch out level before them, and straight ahead, a great curtain of falling water. The sides of the valley were steep and the cliff by the waterfall sheer. They could not advance beyond it. The water fell perhaps thirty feet, hitting the pool at the bottom in a ferment of white and yellow spume.

Rob drew the pony onto the narrow track that ran alongside the pool, and tied the reins to a stump of alder.

'Ye maun bide here,' he said.

Jean nodded, and he crossed the burn again and began to climb the bank opposite. He went as fast as he could pulling himself up by the saplings and clumps of young bracken that grew there. His hands were torn and bleeding by the time he made the top of the ridge. He looked back. Jean had dismounted from the pony and was standing by its shoulder. The beast had his head down and was snatching at the rough grass. The boy was on his knees by the waterside and drinking from cupped hands. They looked as calm as a summer afternoon.

He turned round, and did not like what he saw. A moor stretched out before them, a rolling level of heather, young bracken and coarse grass, with not a vestige of cover. No one could hide there. They would be as exposed there as a boat dotting on a loch. Beyond the moor were hills, but it was a long tramp across the moor to win them. It could not be done safely before dark.

He listened. There was no sound but what was natural. He breathed out. Then the sun emerged from behind the cloud and away over to the right, where the trees fringed the moor, a glint of metal caught his eye. He watched a moment. There it was again.

He dipped under the rim of the hill, and, skipping and scrambling, pressing one hand against the ground to steady himself, hurried to the head of the waterfall. It was possible to descend, though there was no way up there; as he had feared. If the glint of metal betokened soldiers, then they were in danger of being caught in a trap of their own making.

His foot slipped and he felt himself sliding into the rush of water. He threw out his hand and caught hold of a hawthorn bush that hung at the very edge of the fall. Trusting to it, he heaved, swung his legs round, and felt rock. He lay there panting, then found a hold for his left hand in a slimy cleft and eased himself upwards. The spray wet his back. He had arrived at a point when he was almost behind the fall, for the rock on which he lay was a spur, and he could see behind the water.

Looking down, he saw the rock stop, and give way to blackness. At first he thought it a trick of the light. He lowered himself, only able to move a few inches at a time till his feet came to rest on a ledge. From there he was able to reach his head behind the water, the spray battering his face. It was hard to see, but there could be no doubt; there was a cave behind the waterfall.

He was eager to be down now, and careless, missed his footing and tumbled the last twenty feet, ending half in the water, breathless and shaken. There was no time to consider his injuries however. He picked himself up, and, entering the water just below the falls, plunged across to where Jean and the boy had been watching him while the pony continued to feed.

He told Jean what he had seen and found in a few sentences. Once again he was struck by the calm with which she received the news. This time Jean heaved the boy on to her own back while Rob urged the pony back into the water. They kept to the edge of the pool but it was still deep. Once the pony lost its footing and would have been under the water if Rob had not pulled him up. He swore at the brute. It had crossed his mind that they should strike it on the rump and let it run loose; but he feared lest that suggest to anyone who found it that they were still in the vicinity; their best hope was that the soldiers sould think they had slipped through the noose before it was tightened.

'Up there,' he called to Jean and she swung Wattie off her back and on to the ledge by the waterfall. It was wet and slippery and the boy dropped to his knees and watched his mother, as she flipped out of the water with the ease of an otter. Rob pointed. She touched the boy on the shoulder and the pair of them crawled over the ledge till they were behind the water.

It was too steep for the pony and its panic was growing. It reared up trying to break free, but Rob held on. He heaved. The pony rolled its eyes and held its ground. He tried again with the same result. So he stepped back into the water, turned the pony's head and urged it to the other side. The bank was shallower here, though he hadn't noticed this, and the pony, if still reluctant, was able to scramble out. It stood shuddering, and then Rob coaxed it behind the water and into the cave.

It was cool, dark, and wet, and the noise of the falling water tremendous. Rob handed the reins to Jean and pushed forward to explore the cave. It ran straight for some ten paces into the rock, and it was impossible to see the back wall before he felt it. He paused a moment to let his eyes grow accustomed to the darkness, and then, running his fingers along the rock followed the wall. He came to a point where his left hand was still in contact while his right touched empty air. There must be a passage running out of the first cave and deep into the hillside. He followed this stumbling sometimes over fallen pieces of rock and always keeping his hand on the wall. He had to bow his head, but at least it was possible to travel on two feet and not bent double. There would be room for the pony. The passage gave way into what he sensed was a second cavern. He could see nothing there and the only sound was the now fainter one of the thundering water. It would do; they were as safe there as anywhere they might find till night fell and they could move.

XVII

Maurie had grown a great man. The Lady Clare left the management of her household to him. That was pleasing in itself. He stroked the thought as he stroked the fur round his cuffs. More important, she now slept with him, though secretly, and was submissive to him. He had proved himself to her as a man of action and his ruthlessness enchanted her. Best of all, he was able to use his position to find his way on to at least the fringe of great affairs. He had established relations with the Bishop, and the Great Man had hinted that he might find him of use. Maurie purred. Life was moving, and in the way he desired.

And yet . . . he frowned, and even shuddered when he thought of his past. He was filled too with a hatred, that he couldn't account for, for his brothers. Perhaps the real reason was his consciousness that he had done them wrong, that it was his actions which had brought trouble upon them; but Maurie was not given to trying to account for his feelings. He had known a savage joy when he saw Clym's body swinging, even though at the same moment he had felt fear like a fleshless hand on his arm. Wasn't Clym's death proof that the Gudewife's curse was working?

There was a way out. He saw it when his agents reported Rob's presence in the district. If he could take Rob, he could hold him safe, and while Rob was safe, then the curse must be suspended. Or if Rob was killed by a sword or arrow, why then, it was disproved.

'She said we would all hang,' he said to himself. 'If one of us escapes hanging, why then, she was lying, her curse is vain, and I . . .'

He passed his hand across his neck.

*

At last the boy Wattie fell asleep. Jean stroked his brow. 'He sleeps ill,' she said, 'his nights are disturbed by dreams.'

Rob listened. Evening was coming on, and there was no noise beyond but that of the falling water. They had seen no sign of the soldiers. He could almost think they were safe, and that it would be wise to move long before dawn. Meanwhile, however, they too should rest. But before that, he had to ask Jean why she had fled from Clartyshaws.

She would not meet his eyes in answering, and he knew that her words were false. And then at last she lifted her face to his and whispered, 'I was feared for you, Rob, for I saw I could not save you from your fate.' Yet he knew this was not the whole truth, that she had a secret she feared to yield to him. He held her close, happy to have found her again, but still mystified. Why had she hidden? Why, having been discovered, had she accompanied him without a word?

XVIII

It was impossible Rob should settle with Jean and the boy Wattie at Clartyshaws. His nominal guardianship would soon be over, for Young Clym was near of an age to manage his own affairs; but there were deeper reasons than that. The boy, it was true, had grown up hard and mistrustful. His mother had taught him too well, and he had a harsh taste for revenge that disturbed Rob. There was something of his father's dourness to him, but he added to it an ambition and a deep wildness that reminded men of his grandfather Walter. Even as a young man he was quick to quarrel, eager to strike the first blow, and not over-particular from which quarter he dealt it. Rob discovered that he had already got himself a name in the valleys as an ill lad to cross. A few months back, he was told, thinking himself cheated by a merchant in Selkirk, he rode into the burgh at the head of a dozen men, 'wild chiels from the forest'. The fat merchant quaked to see them, but Young Clym was too wary to shed a burgher's blood in his own town. He had his men lift the merchant's kist and set a fiery brand to his roof-tree, and all the time sat his grey horse steady as a statue in the market-place. Then, when the house was well ablaze, he called for the merchant, and his men bound him, and stripped him to his sark (acting all the time without new instructions so that all men could tell Young Clym had planned what would happen well in advance) and put a lighted torch to his feet. 'The rogue's led me a pretty dance,' Young Clym said, 'weel, we'll gar the chiel dance himsel.' So the douce merchant hopped and skipped as they poked at his feet with the flaming torch and hollered like the damned in hell, fit to wake the kirkyard, while Young Clym sat with never a smile on his face to see the man skip like a hen on a hot girdle. 'Aye,' he said, 'and noo you ken it's a wanchancy think to bate a Laidlaw of Clartyshaws.'

Clartyshaws and the land were like a passion for him, and he was like his father in that. But whereas old Clym would have been blithe to have lived as a simple farmer had his fortune permitted it, the boy saw land as power. All his life he would be adding a bit here and a bit there, gloating over his fields like a miser with a pot of gold. At the age of sixteen he had had Mollie fix him a bride – in his guardian's absence – and arrange that his Lord of Douglas approved the match. She was a poor shilpit thing but the only child of her father who was tenant of Deloraine in Ettrick. She was thin and small with a squint so crooked that they said she could see round corners easier than anything put before her nose (which was long, pendulous and given to dripping), but, when he looked at her, Clym saw none of this, but rather a douce farm and acres that were broad for the valleys, and her father's herd of shaggy black cattle and flock of hill sheep. Rob pitied the girl for he saw that Young Clym had no tenderness for her, and his judgement was right. She died within two years, whimpering in childbirth (the child was stillborn) and was shuffled into a grave her husband never troubled to visit. And why should he? Had he not got the lands for which he had married her?

Rob soon knew that Young Clym disliked him. They were of different types, but there was more to it than that. Somehow Rob was included in the resentment Mollie had bred in the young man. Rob knew fine that if he had had his way, Old Clym would never have made that fatal ride into England. He knew too that he had risked his own life for his brother, but the boy did not know this and there was no way of telling him.

He was disturbed too by the fascination with which Young Clym regarded his Uncle Maurie whom he had been brought up to hate. The boy was dazzled by what he heard of Maurie's rise in the world. Here was villainy indeed – but what rewards it brought! A young man with his appetite for power could hardly resist such an example. At the mention of Maurie's name, his eyes sparkled. Hatred was well mixed with envy, and something more than envy; there was approval there too. But Rob had learned to fear and abhor power, and Young Clym looked on him as something less than a man for doing so.

There was a final reason for their estrangement, and it was the most serious of all. Young Clym, careful by nature, was the first of the family to be on good terms with the Church. He might even be called devout. Though he wouldn't trouble himself with his wife's resting-place, he would soon give money which in most cases he parted with as willingly as a man might offer to have a good tooth drawn from his mouth to a chantry up Yarrow, so that masses might be said for his soul in the event of his death. Men laughed to see one who was hardly more than a boy do that, but others said that Young Clartyshaws was a douce too making siccar he had gear in heaven as well as on earth. Yet Rob thought it went deeper. Young Clym's dull imagination was insensible to stories of faeries and brownies but the terrors of Hell were real enough to him.

Being like this he was wary of Jean. His mother had fed him with her fears and suspicions, and when Rob caught him casting dark looks at Jean, his own blood chilled. He could not doubt that Young Clym saw her as an enemy of his religion and a danger to his salvation; and he himself feared for Jean.

So it was natural that Rob, Jean and Wattie shouldn't stay at Clartyshaws, and natural too, that having no land of their own, they should gravitate to the Douglas Court. Great nobles could always accommodate any number of dependents, and the Douglas was growing in power and esteem and influence with every year that passed. He was a greater man than the king in the Borderland, all the more so because the king was now a child, King Jamie having failed to make good his boast that the key should keep the castle; at least as far as he was himself concerned, for he had been murdered in Blackfriars Abbey in Perth some years back, despite the efforts of another Douglas, a lass called Catherine to hold off his enemies by inserting her arm through the bars of a door from which the bolt had been removed. She had won the name of Barlass for that exploit but it had hardly even delayed the murder, and though the chiefs of the conspiracy Sir Robert Graham of Strathearn and the old Earl of Atholl had been put to the torture and then hustled to the block, the royal authority was, as it were, in limbo, with the English Queen-Regent that had been the Lady Joan Beaufort (the Bishop's niece) unable to rule sternly – as who would expect a woman to do? – and dominated herself by the two Keepers, Sir Alexander Livingstone who held Stirling Castle, and Sir William Crichton who held Edinburgh.

So, anyway, Rob and Jean and the boy Wattie found a niche

in the Douglas household, where Rob was made welcome as a loyal retainer and a bard. Candlemas saw always a great feast at Hermitage. The first fish of the new season were taken from the rivers, and smoked or baked in the clay ovens, or boiled in great vats of water. The salt beef from the autumn was soaked to make it palatable and then roasted on spits in the courtyard over fires of birch wood. Even in the hardest winter there would be fresh game – roebucks and blackcock and wild duck. Big barrels of wine which the Douglas had shipped from the Loire and his own estates in Touraine were tapped. There was an abundance of ale matured throughout the winter, and now strong, dark and yeasty. Though winter was not yet by, and food would be short throughout February and March and into April too, it was still a time for rejoicing. The rigours of Lent would follow. Candlemas offered the last chance for some weeks for all to fill their bellies.

One year though it was different. A seven-night before the feast, three Dominican friars had presented themselves to the Douglas. They came, they said, bearing a commission from His Holiness in Avignon (for Scotland, as the ally of France, recognized the French Pope there, not the usurper in Rome.) They had been sent, they said, to extirpate heresy, in particular the foul practice of witchcraft, from the northern kingdom.

They were lean dark men with chilled unused faces, and they cast a gloom over all, for they had death on their lips and in their eyes. The Douglas himself was agitated by their arrival. He had no dealings himself with what many called the Old Religion, being fearful and pious as a great lord should be, and yet, in a fashion for which he could not have found words, he knew it as an element in the life that surrounded him; it was part of that tapestry of custom, incantation, awareness of the parallel world of magic and faery, of which none could doubt the reality. His disturbance at their arrival was instinctive. They came to break custom with abstraction, and their faith was founded, it seemed, on a sour enmity to whatever they could not sense, and had therefore perforce to explain.

They demanded his help and he dared not refuse. He tried to temporize; in vain. They produced letters patent under the royal seal instructing all to give the Pope's commissioners whatever assistance they required. Two miserable shoemakers, professed

Lollards, disciples of the English heretic, Wyclif, were taken and accused of heresy and tried and found guilty by their accusers; they were handed to the Douglas for burning. The poor brutes babbled prayers as the faggots were lit; the stench of the burned offerings to the authority of the Church made cruel men sick at heart. A pall of fear fell over the country, but the examining friars were not appeased. Lollards were but poor stuff; they had set their sights on a more formidable foe.

Rob was infected by fear as much as disgust. In his dreams he smelled the smoke, mingled with the stink of the inn at Jeddart where he had lain as his father's body swung from the gibbet. He looked at Jean's pale face and dared not ask her if she too was afraid. Then their boy Wattie came to him with questions written in his white weasel face, and, as if some nerve had been struck the way Moses struck water from the rock in the wilderness, he poured forth talk.

He told Rob of how he had once woken in the night to find his mother absent. They were staying in a village high in the valley of the Upper Tweed. He could give it neither name nor description for they had been ever on the move in those years and he had little sense of anything solid or lasting. He had another 'Father' then, he told Rob, a big black-bearded man with a streak of white 'like a magpie' in his raven hair. This Father too was missing and Wattie, rising fearful from the pile of straw where he lay, stepped to the doorway of the hut. Down the hillside, he saw the river mist broken by a shaft of flame, and then heard the music of pipes. He crept down the braeside, as gleg and wary as a young fox, and all the while the fire and the music grew wilder. The kirk-tower sprang up before him and he got himself behind a sheep-dyke that ran round the kirkyard, to a point where there was an opening between a pair of yew trees. And a sight met his eyes such as he had never seen before.

He gave Rob a quick smile, as if to excuse himself, and went on, saying that they were dancing round the gravestones, each of them holding a candle, but though the breeze blew hard, the candles stayed lit even as the dancers whooped and skirled and leapt. They burned all with a blue flame, the candles. Then they placed the candles on the tombstones and formed themselves into a ring, and danced in a circle, widdershins, faster and faster, the last one being The Father, him still playing his pipes and leaping higher and faster than any of the others. The white magpie streak shone in the darkness like a wreath of snow on the braeside in moonlight, and when he leapt high, Wattie could see that his feet were 'nae canny'.

The music stopped and the ring closed and they lifted the candles high above their heads. The Father stood on a grave-stone with his back arched towards Wattie, and he saw his mother approach the Black Man with the magpie streak, on her knees. She put her hands on his hips and pressed herself against him; but what else she was doing he could not see. Then the whole company let out an eldritch screech, the candles were doused, and, with a clatter, they ran faster than a shelt's gallop out the kirkyard, all bearing broomsticks, and they cried out in a tongue Wattie dinna ken, and flew into the air and filled the night sky.

The boy's weasel face was set fast as a trap, but he pushed his hand into Rob's for comfort. Rob smoothed the boy's hair and told him he must have been dreaming.

'Aye,' Wattie said, 'I dream often and I have a dream to tell you too, but this was nae dream, for when my mother brought me porridge in the morn her hand was all scratched and torn as if she had torn it through a bramble bush.'

'And what liken proof is that?' Rob asked. 'Could she no have been outbye afore you waked?'

But the boy shook his head, and said only, 'that was the last time I ever saw that Feyther.'

A noise came from the courtyard, and distracted Rob.

'But I maun tell you the dream I dreamed last night,' the boy said.

'Tell me later, if you maun, but laddie, say nothing of a' this tae anybody.'

He descended into the yard. A group of crones were being herded into pens by the soldiers. He asked who they were and was told they were old wives against whom charges of witchcraft had been laid by their neighbours. 'But they're a hauf-dizzen or so short, I'm thinking,' the soldier said. There was a solitary man among the women, a sturdy grey-headed fellow with a cast in his eye, and at the sight of him Rob felt his limbs drained and his belly turn over. It was years since he had seen him, but he was unmistakable, and in that instant everything he had feared and known and feared to know rose up before him like a great rock in a flat country. He asked one of the soldiers if he could have a word with the man.

'They're a' due for profound examining by the friars,' the soldier said, 'and my orders is tha nane may so much as exchange the time of day with them.'

'It would be information I would be seeking myself,' Rob said.

'Aye, and I'm thinking, Rob, it might be information you would be safer without. It's a sair time, lad, and he whae kens least, kens best.'

So the feasting was dull and wary, for men feared to show joy before these black examiners, and there was no singing at the Douglas board. There were no verses and no music and Rob sat unregarded in a corner of the hall.

The next morn the friars proclaimed a solemn season of penitence. No one dared gainsay them, but Rob took himself to a loft from where he could look down on a scene in which he could not bring himself to take part. There was music now, but a cold and doleful music, that broke into a penitential chant. The friars' acolytes swung censors and a sickly perfume filled the air. The company was on its knees and with much wailing and lamentation all offered their sins to the Almighty. Even the Douglas himself was there, and he had stripped the shirt from his back and was scourging himself with a little five-thonged whip as he howled his wickedness in sight of God and his estates. The friars set a good example applying the scourges to their own backs and crying on the Lord and the saints to witness that they humbled themselves that they and other sinners might achieve salvation. It was a grey morning with a gusty wind spitting from the west. Rob watched the scourges rise and fall, heard them lapse into a rhythm like drums urging on an army, and the blood ran from the torn flesh as if virtue could grow from its watering.

A hand stole into his and he found Jean by his side. She was shaking like one with fever, yet he had not heard her approach. She pressed herself against him.

'What hae I done?' she moaned. 'I never knew there could be sic a lust for blood.'

They stole away that night, for Rob knew that Jean could never rest easy again in that place, and he feared also that her life was in danger. They sought Wattie before they slipped out under cover of darkness, but the boy was nowhere to be found. He suspected that he had chosen to go into hiding, and it occurred to him that perhaps he would be safer without them. As for him he had no clear plan. It was necessary only to get away. He was still unwilling to question Jean. He knew that she was seized with a double fear: fear of what might lie in wait for her there, and fear too of those with whom she had been involved in the past and from whom she had fled: for his sake, as he believed.

Wattie had taken himself to the kennels and found a couch among the great deerhounds. The beasts accepted him easily, for he had a way with dogs as with all animals and birds. So he lay among them as if he had been one himself.

As he lay he dreamed. He saw a clearing in a forest and a little hut huddled against a rock face with a goat tethered before it. A thin old man came to the doorway of the hovel and made a sign of the cross as he saw Rob and Wattie approach. He spoke to them in a slow voice as if a rusty key was opening a long disused door. But Wattie could not understand what he said and knew only that he spoke in the Latin tongue. The hermit, as he seemed to be, beckoned to them and motioned that they should enter the hut. It was very dark, a thick stuffy dark as though a blanket had been pulled over his head, and for a long time Wattie could see nothing. The old man advanced and struck a flint and lit six candles which were ranged along a table which served as an altar. A shape formed on the ground before it, which, Wattie would swear, had not been there when they entered the hut.

Rob knelt on the ground beside it and drew back a cloth, and a white face gleamed at them. But Wattie was not close enough to see more than that. Then Rob let his fingers play over it like a man trying to recover a lost tune.

'Will you know more?' the hermit said, and he now spoke in the Inglis tongue. 'Will you know that which will confirm your worst imaginings even in the owl's hours?'

Rob bowed his head and did not answer.

'Or are you one of those who would rather live in the false world of fancy? Do you reject knowledge or dare search for truth even in a waste land?'

Without waiting for a reply, he pulled up the hem of the woman's skirt tearing it to reveal the long line of her naked legs. He inserted his hand between them and pulled the left leg apart from the other. He lowered the candle so that it lit up a mark on the inside of the thigh: it was blue in colour and shaped like a rat's claw and rather larger than a thumb-nail. 'Do you know what that signifies?' he asked. 'It is the Devil's mark made by Satan's teeth as a sign of admission to his hellish legion. See, there is the mark of the enemy against whom you have contended, the enemy of all mankind and the foe of virtue and true religion.' He moved the candle again and with his other hand tore at the cloth that covered her upper body. There, some three inches above the creamy breasts, a single teat hung like a piece of flesh that a child had tugged out of shape. Mark,' the hermit said, 'where she has given suck to familiar spirits . . . I have but one hope to offer you, one piece of comfort or consolation. The mark is more faded and the teat more withered than some I have seen. It may be that the wretch has abjured her dark Master. But I cannot tell . . .'

His voice died away in a mumble of Latin prayers and the candles flickered and went out.

Rob lifted the body and carried it into the woodland moonlight. He placed it down like a precious thing on a patch of grass fringed with anemones. Taking a spade from the hermit he began to dig. The task was hard for roots of tall trees spread and interlaced through the soil. At last, though, it was done and he lowered the body into the grave. He threw a handful of earth on top, and, straightening, asked the hermit to intone a prayer. But the hermit had vanished and the moon slid behind a cloud and darkness fell over the scene.

Wattie whimpered among the deerhounds and a bitch licked his salty face.

Rob gazed on Jean's sleeping face. They were miles from Hermitage. Their journey had been hard and swift and they had come to rest in a grey upland. The night was bitter cold and Jean, wrapped in sheepskins, huddled against him. He could not sleep, for his mind was busy with what she had told him when they halted for the night. Her words returned to him only in fragments and he had tried several times to stem their flow. He knew, he told her, the heart of the story; it had come to him through countless small signs and hints and he knew it as a man who has lived in the same valley all his days may learn to read the weather. He could not halt her, however; the confessional flow was like a river in spate, breaking down the banks of ignorance with which they had protected their lives, spreading over their whole history as floods drown a countryside.

She fell in love with him, she told him, when she first saw him in the inn in Jedburgh. She knew her love to be hopeless for she had already divided herself from that side of life. She was already an initiate. Did he understand that? No, of course not, it was beyond understanding by any who had not served the master. If only she could convey to Rob what it meant; the Church he knew was a cold dead thing beside that joy and surge of life her Master promised. When she received her initiation . . . she paused, the colour drained from her face and she began to tremble. He leaned over and kissed her on the corner of the mouth. She clung to him like a frightened child and then resumed. She never thought to see him again after that morning when he rode out of Jeddart bearing his father's body, when she had held up her mouth to him like a flower stretching to the sun.

She worked in the inn. She attended the sabbats and she nursed the twin secrets of her faith and her love for him that would never again be fulfilled. She was, in an odd way, happy. And then she received a command, which, because it chimed with her desire, she was overjoyed to obey. She did not know then why she had been chosen and, like a fool, she never thought of it. It was not till Rob and Clym had ridden for England, and she was already the mother of her child, that she had known of the curse laid on him. It was Mollie who told her, one day when she was angered with her, as she often was; and, at her words, the veil of mystery was torn. Jean saw that she was being used. And she fled.

Even as she spoke, Rob wondered and was puzzled. It was not quite how Mollie had told the story of her departure. But he let it pass. He had no need to concern himself with questions of what was true and what was false. If there had ever been a time for that, it was long by. He and Jean were bound together, by everything that had happened to them, everything they had done, even by whatever had tried to tear them apart. He knew that completely now and stroked her hair.

She threw herself into the practice of her religion, hoping to find release, atonement – she couldn't give it a name – in abandoning herself to it. But it was vain. Even in ecstasy, she saw Rob. And they knew that in her heart she had gone away from them. And resented it. And in their resentment she felt her faith dying and turn sour, so that she feared for Wattie, and had fled them; to the gypsies, as it happened, and once with them, arriving as she confessed, in a state that was near demented, she had felt gradually the sense of freedom growing upon her, for she seemed to have escaped the wheel on which she had been bound. But then Rob found her, and, though her heart went out to him, in pure and welcoming love, yet hope died at the same time: she knew herself still to be a captive of her fate.

And now, saying this, the words tumbling over themselves in a cataract of confused feeling, she wept. The tears froze on Rob's sheltering and comforting hand; and at last she slept.

But he remained wakeful all the night and listened to the wind chase through the bare branches that seemed to touch the sky and the water gallop through the valley below. Words formed in his mind:

> 'Cauld as the stane dings the spade
> like a sair wound in my breast
> Whaur the howlet braks the corbie's lee
> I'll lay my luve tae rest . . .
>
> Come wind, come rain, the warld is room,
> The reid hawk flies frae east tae west,
> But oh my heart stings sair and toom
> This night I lay my luve tae rest

It began to rain before dawn, a steady drenching rain borne from the west on a biting wind. The hills crouched round them, their tops fringed with a mist that the wind could not shift. They made but slow progress, for both were stiff after the previous day's exertions and the long confession; and Rob's sleepless night had drained both of their strength. They marched too without purpose. The fear they had carried with them from Hermitage, a fear that had hastened their steps, had died on them, but it had been replaced by neither hope nor intent. They moved simply because they could not have remained still in that vile weather, and because, even if that had been different, both felt condemned to movement.

They saw no one all day, no living soul and little enough sign of any life. Once, where the track descended, they came on a heron in a little pool, one leg drawn up, fishing with an air of abstraction. When it saw the wanderers it gave them a long contemplative look, then seemed to shrug its shoulders as it extended its wings and, with a heavy beat, soared out of their life and then out of sight, lost in the gathering mist.

Both were hungry, though they said nothing of that, and Rob knew that Jean was weakening. They must find some rest and sustenance, and it was with relief that he at last saw a wayside farm grow out of the gloom.

At first he thought it deserted. There was no answer to his knocking for a long time, and he was about to desist and look for something with which he might perhaps force the door when he heard footsteps. He pulled Jean against him and they waited in the wet cold while someone struggled with a bar on the other side of the door.

Wattie saw the long level of a moonlight lake. Mist swirled around the hilltops that surrounded it, but the water lay bright and tranquil. There was a boat moored by its edge, just where a rock path descended from a chapel that stood in a grove of yew trees. A figure approached the boat, a tall dark man. The moon showed that he was smiling, and, seeing that smile, Wattie shrank back, trying to hide himself in the veils of mist that all at once enveloped the water's edge. His limbs trembled, and he heard the shriek of women. Their voices rose from the waiting boat in a long cry of despair.

It was an old woman opened the door to Rob and Jean. She was dressed all in black, and bent half double so that she had to arch her neck in order to look them in the face. But she received them without surprise, as if they had been expected. A pot hung on a rail over an open fire which let smoke rise to a hole in the roof. The mean room was full of smoke itself, which stung their eyes, but the smell from the pot was rich.

Still wordlessly, she gestured to them to be seated and ladled soup into two wooden bowls which she set before them and fetched each a horn spoon. A grey cat with a torn ear leapt on to the table and settled itself between the bowls.

Rob put a spoon to his mouth. The broth was hot and good and nourishing. At that moment a crow, tethered to a perch in the corner of the room, cawed.

Five women rose from the waiting barge and each, as she stepped on to the land, curtsied to the waiting man. He raised each to her feet and folded her in an embrace. Then he turned and all followed him up the winding track till they were lost to sight.

Rob was distressed to see that Jean could not eat. Three times she lifted the spoon to her mouth, and three times replaced it in the bowl, untasted. He urged her to try to eat, and she returned only a tired smile and a sigh. The old woman had settled herself on a stool by the fireside and the cat left the table and rubbed itself against her legs.

The scene cleared and Wattie could not follow the procession as it wound its way up the hillside. The man led the way. Music sounded, a thin piping that sang to Wattie of lost causes and broken hearts.

The old woman was looking at Rob now, and at last he knew her. Jean's eyes were on him too, and he read pity and grief in her look. He tried to rise to his feet, but his legs were heavy and a heaviness too stole over his whole being and dulled his spirit. He felt the cat's eyes pin him there. Was the old woman smiling? Her lips were moving and a low muttering which he could not interpret came to his ears. The world was reduced to this spot of dim light in surrounding dark. And that instant he heard footsteps without, and it seemed as if the wood fell from the door and let the night enter the room.

*

A hawthorn tree formed itself on the ridge, clear against the starry sky. It spread from east to west, and on either side a body swung in the soft breeze. The sky greyed and was touched with pink, and footsteps receded with a slow echo from the hilltop, and the troop drew down back to the lakeside, and, with a heavy sweep of garments and deep sighs, all embarked on the boat which put out over the water, disturbing a flight of duck and watched by a lone heron. The women's cry, now a wail of lament that seemed to come from the very heart of things, sounded over the water till the boat disappeared from sight; but where it had gone or how it had been swallowed up was hidden from Wattie; and when he turned his eyes back to the hillside, the tree was bare.

Silence sounded about him, stretching itself over the whole world, and only the boy was a living witness, only the boy felt its weight.

BOOK TWO

BOOK TWO

I

The early days of a great family may be lost to record. History begins where legend leaves off, but for a generation or more the two are intertwined. Rob Laidlaw, the Minstrel, flits through the mists, you can catch his tune in the lonely hills and valleys and in the old wives' tales. The curse imposed on the family hangs light on his memory, for there are no black deeds in his story, and it shapes itself, or was shaped, through many tellings, till at last the figure of Rob is released from all fact that can be ascertained, and flies free in the imagination. So it is right that his end should be uncertain, a poet's vision, and that it should be filtered to us through the dreams and tales and snatches of verse attributed to the boy Wattie. It is a story which you can believe in not because you have reason to suppose it happened just like that, but because it is the right shape, as a ghost story may be.

But history is another matter, an awkward, unformed mess, and lives which are caught up on the great staircase of history can be messy things themselves. Sometime about the date when Rob disappeared into the hills with his Jean and was never seen again (though stories of their flitting hither and thither belong to many places and at least three parishes claim to have been the scene of his death), the other Laidlaws planted firm feet in History. You can read about them in Manorial Rolls, and, in the case of Maurie, the Privy Council Records. They became actors and victims (for in History actors are also victims, no man shaping the world to his desires, but being shaped himself even while he fondly imagines he is the architect of his own destiny). The story of Maurie, Young Clym and the bastard son of Isobel Laidlaw and Edward des Moulins whom they called Dandy cannot be told without telling also of the struggles for political power in the England and Scotland of their day. Even Wattie, fey creature as he was, infringes on History. And Will?

Well, Will was always marginal, but even Will, who had drifted back from France and found refuge as Maurie's dependent, was not free of its working.

So they were involved, all of them, in the great business of their times, and affected by it. Matters like the relations between Scotland and England, the course of the French War, and the struggle for authority in both the northern and southern kingdom, matters that historians can reduce to abstractions and considerations of cause: these were real and actual to them, they provided opportunities and challenges; they made and destroyed them.

Even so, history and legend can be ill to separate. For instance: Maurie was a liar; indisputable fact, but which of his memories were false and which true?

He told a story, for example, of his involvement in the death of King James I of Scotland, he who would have had the key keep the castle; and his story was vivid enough, taken down by clerks, repeated by them, so that you can read of it in the history books.

The Cardinal, Maurie said, had entrusted him with a secret mission to the King of Scots. A hint, he breathed to the Lady Clare, was offered that a knighthood should be his reward for its successful accomplishment. He smiled at her, wary, high and predatory as a soaring hawk.

'You must know,' he said, 'that things go ill with our arms in France. Some blame the incapacity of our commanders, others their dissension. Now, our master, the Cardinal Bishop, fears lest the rascal, or, as he says, weasel Scots will renew their old bond with France. They are fools if they do, for it has never served them well. Nevertheless the danger is there. Accordingly, I, yes, even I, have been asked to travel north to initiate discussions. I may promise to surrender Berwick, Roxburgh and the other territories north of Cheviot in order to secure peace in the north. It is a bold game, and I am the man to play it.'

'Maurie, little crookback,' the Lady Clare lay on her couch and fondled the terrier that lay in her lap, 'you do not need to speak to me in that pompous tone. Go north, little crookback, but give me a kiss first and remember the dangers that face you in your native land.'

So two weeks later Maurie rode with a company of twenty

men past the abbey of Jedburgh, under the gate where his father had entered to his death, along the old Roman road, past the three-headed Eildons till, as the light faded, he arrived at the great Cistercian Abbey and was received in purple and gold where he had once skulked as a thin insignificant boy. He knelt to the abbot John of Fogo and, as he told Clare, again felt his sword twist in the monk's belly 'on that day when I began my march to fortune'.

As for the abbot, whose self-importance had swollen with the years, he was bent to pay all honour due to the Cardinal's envoy. It mattered little that he was a man of no personal account. John of Fogo admired the subtlety of the Cardinal's judgement and delighted that the man had come first to him.

'It showed,' he wrote in a letter describing the meeting, 'the gravity of His Grace's enterprise and intent, for it has been wisely observed that the more noble and magnificent the ambassador, the less likelihood there be of serious business.'

'My Lord His Grace knows,' Maurie bowed lowed again, 'of your Lordship's zeal for peace and steadfast friendship. Even as the weathercock turns with the wind, so does your Lordship incline to what is right.' He rubbed his hands together and resumed. 'He is convinced that no Englishman can persuade King James of the folly of his course, of how ill he would serve his kingdom by renewing that alliance with the false French.'

It delighted Maurie to address the Abbot in the purest French he could muster though he knew that both would converse more happily in their native tongue. The Abbot bowed in appreciation of the compliments, and informed him that they would broach their discussions formally in the morning.

'Now,' he said, 'you must feast with us,' and led Maurie into the refectory, a long handsome high-vaulted room, and placed him on his right hand.

'The wine,' he said, 'is Rhenish, and the salmon from the silver Tweed that flows beneath our walls.'

Maurie knew fine that the river was brown, not silver, and found the wine thin and sharp, but he praised both fish and wine, and took pleasure in his own circumspect modesty.

The fish should be succeeded by a fatted calf.

The Abbot questioned him closely, with an eagerness that bordered on the impertinent about his lord the Cardinal. Maurie answered with a caution worthy of his diplomatic role. The Cardinal was all that was great and honourable, he said.

Even as he spoke he must have seen again Henry of Winchester, all wrapped in furs despite June heat, his face pale, his hands trembling with the disease already eating into his life, and again felt that thin arm round his neck and heard the whispered words: 'Burgundy has deserted us in France and now the timid and vicious mongrel dog that is the King of Scots seeks to lick our blood. Would you wish to arise Sir Maurice?'

'Aye, that I would . . .' the words had come from Maurie's heart.

Then the Cardinal had smiled, 'I have a grant here of the manor of Cleckington in Yorkshire made out in your name. It is yours, this lordship, and a knighthood too, if by this time a year hence, you have rid us of this troublesome king and seen our northern border return to its customary – and satisfactory – instability. And here, my son, is your warrant, a safe conduct, a diplomatic passport under the Great Seal of England, made out for your greater security in the name of Maurice of Cleckington, which will carry you safe, in God's name, through the whole realm of Scotland.'

So now Maurie smiled and bowed and acknowledged the abbot's civilities and dreamed of his own greatness.

In a hot August sun he gazed over the valley of Tweed shimmering in the heat. King James had assembled a force of unprecedented size: to seize Roxburgh or invade England? A general levy had gone out through all the Border country and lowlands of Scotland, as far north as Fife, Angus and the Perthshire glens summoning all able-bodied men between sixteen and sixty with the exception only of shepherds, cattle-keepers and those who served ecclesiastics.

The army's tents stretched as far as Kelso and Maurie's passport was questioned by a Highlander who looked ready to have his head first, and his document verified later. But he was restrained by a lean, pale-faced man who came forward and took the chestnut's bridle.

'A rough reception,' he said. 'My Hielanders have nae mair comprehension of documents, passports and laisser-passers than o' the English tongue.'

He fell to examining the document, screwing his eyes up.

'The Great Seal of England,' he said, 'an unco thing. But I see this credits you with being the emissary of His Grace of Winchester. Weel, sir, I hae little time for that sort of Grace or any other if the truth be told. Nevertheless, seeing you here with all the appurtenances of diplomatic state, and seeing that I myself am fully cognizant with all the rights and duties that are enjoined on me by all the articles of war, I shall bestir myself to see you safe in our camp, and be grateful too to do so, for, if your cause and purpose here is what I think it may be, I may even extend a hand in friendship to you.'

'And I to you, sir,' Maurie replied, 'if you will let me know to whom I have the pleasure of speaking, for my purpose is to advance that which is in the common interest of our two kingdoms.'

'I am glad to hear it. My name is Graham, Sir Robert Graham of Strathearn, and, with these words, he held out his hand.

They rode through the outlying part of the camp. Neither spoke, and Maurie had leisure therefore to admire the force King James had brought into the field. It was surely over-large for its nominal purpose, and yet hardly strong enough either. It lacked the engines to storm the castle of Roxburgh perched on its great rock; yet there were more men than was necessary to blockade it, so many indeed that it would be as difficult for the besieging army to provide for them during a prolonged siege as it would be for the defenders to withstand one.

And then – or so he often recounted – it struck him that nothing was happening, nothing at all. The huge force had been assembled – he passed through platoons of Highlanders gazing in wonder at the soft pastures of the valley; brigades of blue-bonneted Borderers, some busy at their horse lines, others in silent groups; past gay pavilions of nobles – he could put a name to half the coats of arms he saw: Crichtons, Livingstones, Hamiltons, Douglases (ah, Douglases), Kers of Ferniehurst, Gordons of the Merse and of Strathbogie, Grahams and Graemes, Homes, Murrays and Elliots; he passed pikemen and archers tending to their weapons, swordsmen sharpening their blades on a whetstone that a farrier had set up; other smiths paring horses' hooves and shoeing them. He heard minstrels strumming harps, pipers trying out airs, and monks and priests chanting psalms; and yet nothing of any significance was happening. The earthwork thrown up in an earlier siege was hardly manned. It was overgrown by nettles, docks, thistles, bracken and cow parsley which remained undisturbed. The mighty army had been brought together for a purpose never seriously entertained or already forgotten. Or was it an army of invasion which would soon leave only a detachment here to hold the English troops in the castle while the vaster part turned to cross the Border?

The next morning Graham presented himself at the tent allocated to Maurie and offered to escort him to the King.

'You will get,' he said, 'but little satisfaction. The king is as thrawn as an old sow as will have her way through a hedge, fence it how you may.'

There was no smile on his face to suggest that his words should be interpreted as any sort of rough tribute to the king.

King James was seated at a table in the open air. He had grown fat in the last years and his face had a look of discontent such as men can acquire who are certain of their virtue and baulked of their desires. He was flanked by half a dozen lords, among whom John of Fogo nodded to Maurie in the manner of one uncertain whether to acknowledge an acquaintance.

'He might have been shaking a fly from his web,' Maurie said.

King James looked at Maurie a long time before addressing him in a querulous tone which still kept the Cockney accent he had acquired in his English captivity.

'We have studied the letter from our reverend uncle which you have brought us,' he said, 'and we find nothing therein to satisfy our just grievances.'

'Your Grace,' Maurie said, bowing, 'lay your grievances bare upon this table and I am empowered by my commission given under the Great Seal of England to treat with you.'

'The cause of war,' King James snapped, 'is not here, but in France. My daughter is, as you well know, married to the Dauphin of France, and her just inheritance is threatened by England's obstinate refusal to abandon her claim to rule our old and well-loved ally.'

('He used to sing a different tune,' Maurie would interpolate in his recital, 'when he rode beside Harry of Monmouth and happily hanged Scots who fought for that same well-loved ally. But learn this,' he would add, 'Kingdoms and Great Ones have no friends, but only interests.')

So, hearing the king's words, Maurie lifted his head and spoke so that all around could hear: 'Your Grace, you have assembled a mighty army, greater even than that which King Edward led to be vanquished by your noble ancestor The Bruce. I am to tell you that my lords of Winchester and Bedford, Regents of England, view this willingness to break the peace which has long subsisted between our two kingdoms – to the benefit of both, aye, the benefit of both – with foreboding. And I am instructed to repeat the offer privily made before now: England will surrender this castle of Roxburgh if you will consent to disband this army and renew the seven years' truce that has now expired. As for France, consider well, sir, what I ask you; what has Scotland ever gained from that alliance? What has France to offer that can compare with the friendship of England, or that can contribute in like manner to the peace and prosperity of this kingdom?'

Maurie's voice would ring out over the years as he repeated this speech and savoured the memory of his glory. King James, he would say, turned pale as wax, and his fingers drummed on the table, and then he swept to his feet and marched off.

'Whom God wishes to destroy he first makes mad.' Maurie pushed a flagon of wine across the table to Sir Robert Graham. 'A thrawn pig in a hedge indeed.'

'Aye,' Graham said, drinking, and waited.

Maurie sighed. 'I think, my friend that you have little love for King James, and also that you are ready to be a good friend to England, which readiness is no more than a recognition of where the true interest of this kingdom lies, but will not go unremarked or unrewarded by my master.'

He let silence fill the tent. A wasp buzzed around the lip of the wine jug. Graham tugged at the corner of his moustache. The afternoon had stilled the bustle of the camp.

Maurie sighed again. 'The key shall keep the castle and the bracken bush the cow. Such was the king's promise was it not?'

'Aye,' Graham said. He brushed the wasp away. 'And there's mony a dungeon door in Scotland that the key keeps also. I ken that weel enough, having spent years myself under lock and key at the royal pleasure, and now . . .' He drank his wine and smacked his lips.

'Now,' Maurie said, 'England will be a good friend to all those that restrain the king.'

King James summoned Maurie to dine with him, gave him venison, Burgundy and a lecture on Statecraft; told him to carry to the Cardinal his loyal affection and the assurance that if England abandoned all claims in France, he himself would be blithe to renew peace with England. He smiled as he said this, fat, self-confident and sure of his wisdom.

'Statecraft,' Maurie said later and often, relapsing into the Scots he was usually careful to eschew, 'I wadna gie a docken for his grip o' thon.'

Sir Robert Graham brought the aged Earl of Atholl and a number of knights, Grahams, Murrays, Kerrs and Somervilles, to Maurie's tent. In the owl's hour he heard their litany of grievances, promised England's favour and dealt out silver.

A week later, King James abruptly broke camp. No reasons were given. The campaign was over before it had begun. Men hurried back to harvest their crops.

The sequel is quickly told. In a bright false spring of February next King James visited the Abbey of Blackfriars in Perth with all his household. They played tennis in the soft weather. King James ordered a grille to be placed over an open drain down which they had been losing their tennis balls. At night in his chambers he played chess while the Queen and her ladies embroidered cloths.

Maurie would pause in the telling of the story here, and smile to think of their happy security.

The king's chamberlain saw that all dined well. The friars took pleasure in supplying the first of the season's salmon to the King. He pushed aside the chessboard and talked with his architect of noble plans to embellish his castle at Linlithgow. The architect sketched a design for the rood screen in the royal chapel.

No one heard or at least attended to a disturbance at the outer gate. Their first alarm came with the sound of running feet. The architect – 'prudent man' Maurie would sneer – slipped from the room. Someone called for the Royal Guard, 'who all lay drunk or drugged or bought.' The queen caught her breath and turned mortal pale. The royal party exchanged glances of dawning fear. A rug was pulled aside with a quick jerk of hope and the king slipped through a trapdoor into a passage which would lead him out of the abbey by way of the tennis court. The queen cried on the chamberlain and at that moment they discovered the bar had been removed from the door. 'Up then springs the Lady Kate Douglas – the heroine of the evening. What's her arm if her deed will save the king' – Maurie smiled over the dinner table and refilled his glass. But her heroic act only delayed the king's determined fate. Her screams of pain were hardly heard as the murderers burst into the room. Sir Robert Graham looked round with wild eyes; his uncle, old Atholl, struck the queen on the mouth. The gang halted, perplexed. Then Graham threw back the rug and indicated the trapdoor. Down bundled his men. The women's cries were silenced by sounds of scuffling and yells of pain. Graham himself descended into the dark while Atholl seized the goblet that had been the king's and drained it. A head appeared through the trap. A man pulled himself up, leaned over and heaved. Another pushed himself up to join him. Together, they hauled the King's body into view.

They flung it on the floor, splashing blood. Graham, his face red-smeared, emerged from the black pit. He stood looking over the king (there were twenty-eight wounds in the body, they later counted, sixteen in the breast alone). 'And sae may all tyrants die,' Graham said. The queen crouched in the gloom.

So Maurie told the story, often, more and more frequently as the years passed until his household gulped more wine and closed their ears to hear him embark on it, and left the listening to guests. But truth? Make believe? Embroidered fancy? Was he old enough, important enough,to have been entrusted with such a mission then? Or – what is more likely – was he an unimportant member of an English embassy who nevertheless did take it on himself to give encouragement and promises of English support to Graham? Was he an undercover agent provoking disorder in the northern kingdom, before, with his growing success, he elevated his role? Much good however that promise of support, if given, did Graham; he and Atholl were both racked before execution. There is no record that they implicated

Maurie. However, England gained from the king's death, for Archibald, Earl of Douglas, made lieutenant of Scotland, negotiated a twelve years' truce between the two nations. Maurie claimed a hand in that too.

One thing supports his assertions, and is well attested. He attended court about this time. The young King of England's sword rested on his shoulder while Maurie looked up into eyes of the palest blue he had ever seen. The youth faltered in his speech . . . 'for that you have striven for peace with our northern neighbours,' he muttered, dwelling on the word 'peace'. He turned away and appealed to the Cardinal who leaned forward and whispered to him, 'for your zeal on our behalf,' his voice sank, 'I dub you knight. Arise, Sir Maurice.'

The Cardinal pressed the charter granting the manor and lands of Cleckington into eager hands.

'Peace,' he said too. 'Peace with honour on our northern frontier.'

'So perish all enemies to Your Grace,' Maurie said.

He had passed by Cleckington on his road south: a gaunt peel-tower on a hillock in a marsh where bitterns croaked.

And this too is certain: some years later Maurie paid a visit to Clartyshaws. What took him there, trusting – and it was a bold trust – in his English safe conduct, is a matter for debate. It can hardly have been sentiment, though on arrival he protested that he wished to see his mother's grave. He sought certain information about Rob and was pressing in his enquiries: Rob who had escaped him twice had come to occupy and perturb his thoughts; Rob represented the one enterprise in which he had failed, and Maurie valued his infallibility. Curiosity played a part: he wanted to see the next generation. Yet this was hardly enough. More likely, for Maurie was ever devious, he wanted to probe possibilities. It had occurred to him that his family in Scotland might represent an advantage, if he could find the means to use them. Maurie had fallen in love with the idea of conspiracy, that powerful drug. He had long reached the point when he preferred to travel by crooked routes.

His reception was cold. Young Clym had been brought up to distrust him, to nurse revenge for his father's death, and, when he saw his enemy ride up to his doorway and spring unconcerned off his horse with a confident flash of a smile, his own hand went to his dagger hilt. But Clym was cautious. He knew by his own nature that Maurie would hardly have dared present himself there without taking precautions, and that the satisfaction of revenge was likely to be brief. The Douglas·would scarce stand by his vassal, for the Douglas valued the new friendship with England, and his own fears and hopes would ensure that he would regard any assault on this English envoy as an affront to his own dignity and a threat to his own security. So Clym's hand fell from the dagger and a smile of welcome slid over his face.

As for Maurie, he was impressed by his nephew. Whatever Young Clym might be, he was no fool like his father.

'So', he said, 'the father has bred another man,' and clapped Clym on the shoulder. 'You call my father – your grandfather – to my mind, nephew. A rare man, of ardour and capacity, though confined in a little world. But, you, I fancy, will hardly be content to live your life within the limits of this little glen and mild ambitions.'

That night after supper, when the table had been cleared and the company dismissed, he resumed his theme. To interest Clym, he talked of the great men with whom he was acquainted. It pleased him to be indiscreet.

'I soon knew, nephew, that I had erred in attaching myself to Edward des Moulins, and saw that he would amount to nothing. So I detached myself, and look at me now.' He stretched back, displaying his furs and jewels, and watched Clym's face for envy and admiration. 'We are entering, nephew,' he said, 'on a time of change which offers opportunities to rising men. Everything in the two kingdoms is in a state of flux. That,' he said – and Clym was tempted to believe him – 'is why I have come here. Yes, there has been a rift in the family and I wish to make amends. It is ill that families are divided against each other, and, now that you have told me that my brother Rob – who was, you must know, the chief cause of dissension – has disappeared and in all probability is dead, why then, there is no cause for this destructive feud to continue. Believe me, nephew, I have never wished it.'

Then he discoursed on the grand politics of the day. They were entering, he repeated, a period when all was in flux. England was still embroiled in the French Wars, as Clym must well know. It might be news to him however that many of the wisest men in England despaired of success. It was against nature that England should hold down France, against nature and reason. His own master, the Cardinal, had not yet realized this, but the Cardinal was an old man and dying and stuck in a vanishing age. He let a note of sadness and admiration enter his voice as he spoke, but then, he sighed, great men too easily were caught in the glory of past deeds. He himself however was certain that the French War was already lost. What would happen then? First, many soldiers, released from the French War and bred to no trade other than arms, would be let loose in the country. Why, his own brother Will, whom Clym might hardly recall, was such a man. Now they would have no difficulty in finding employment. No fear! Many lords were only too eager to recruit their personal army. Why, he already had a small force at his own disposal. And the time was ripe. There was a crisis impending in England. The King, Henry VI, would never be a man, not a real man. He commanded little respect. Men said he had a wandering eye like his grandfather, the mad king of France. It was too likely. Heredity would out. And of course, Clym must know, Henry's claim to the throne was not unquestioned. There had been no rightful king since his other grandfather Henry Bolingbroke had deposed King Richard. Well, right was not everything. It mattered not a tinker's curse as long as the king was strong. It would have been a rash man who had challenged Harry of Monmouth's right to the throne. But when the king was girlish, and a baby in his feelings and given to falling on his knees and babbling prayers, it was a different matter. He lacked authority, and when he was also associated with a course of policy that had failed, with defeat and dishonour in France, 'why then, my lad, look out for squalls. There are strong men with a better right to the throne. There is the Duke of York for one, and there are great rich and greedy men who would set him there – someday. It may take five years or ten or twenty, but there is trouble brewing in England, and I mean to have a hand on the spoon that stirs the broth.'

Then he turned to Scotland. The power of the Crown had ever been precarious there, he said. King James had tried to assert it, and where was he now? The new king was a bairn. There were noble families as rich as the king and maybe more powerful and served by more loyal retainers. In particular, there was the great House of Douglas, to which Clym owed allegiance. There would be – there was no way of avoiding it – a mighty struggle between the House of Stewart and the House of Douglas. Appearances suggested now that the Douglas might prove the stronger, but appearances could lie. They had many enemies besides the king, families who were jealous of their power and greedy for their lands. And if the king was a man of resolution, why then, he had a power in reserve: he could grant the Douglas lands to another lord, and that man would fight fiercely to hold them. It would behove Clym to be wary how firm his loyalty held. 'The wise man reads the weather ahead,' Maurie said, tapping the side of his nose, and Clym nodded. He was impressed.

The second listener was more than impressed. He was elated. This was Dandy, the son of Edward des Moulins and Isobel. He had grown into a tall handsome boy who combined something of his father's fineness of appearance and his mother's peasant strength. He had red-gold hair that fell in waves from a rather narrow head, big long-lashed blue eyes and a soft sensuous mouth, but his jaw was set in a determined fix, his legs were long and strong and his hands big and capable. His air was often sleepy and he moved with a lazy athletic stride, and he was waiting, with a resentment directed at Clym and a certain contempt for his cousin's caution, for life to begin. He knew Clym disliked and resented him too, and he was eager to be off.

The next morning, as dew still lay on the grass and on the branches of the wild cherries and rowan trees around the house, he sought out Maurie, and pleaded with him that he be allowed to ride back to England with him, 'for I am like a hawk mewed up here, or a horse that is denied a gallop,' he sighed.

Maurie looked at his nephew and liked what he saw. The boy admired him and had been excited by his words. He breathed in the morning air.

'Would you not be afraid,' he asked, 'to ride with a man that has a curse on his head?'

Dandy threw back his head and laughed.

'Have you not heard, laddie, of the family curse?'

He reached up and tweaked the lobe of the boy's ear.

'The terrible family curse,' he said, 'that threatens me with an awful fate.'

Dandy shrugged his shoulders. 'Curses,' he said, 'old wives' tales.'

'It was an old wife that cursed me, and who knows? It may extend even to your generation.'

'A man like you,' Dandy said, 'is shairly maister of his fate.'

'A lad like you could not give me a better answer.'

Dandy smiled. 'Then you will take me? I am eident to see my father too.'

'I think, lad,' Maurie said, 'that you are already twice the man your father ever was, or will be. He's a poor bit of work, your father, but you lad, we might make something of you.'

He let his hand rest on the warm young flesh of his nephew's arm and was pleased to see him blush with pleasure.

'Aye,' he said, 'it will please me if you ride with me, lad, but first I have business to conclude with Clym.'

The boy laughed again. 'Why do you laugh?'

'I'm thinking, uncle, that even you will find it easier to broach business with my cousin than to conclude it. He's a canny chiel, Clym.'

'And so am I, lad, canny and subtle. But Clym and I have interests in common, and he's wise enough, I'm thinking, to be mindful of that.'

'Weel,' Dandy looked serious, 'as lang's you dinna trust him.'

'I'll trust our common interest, but not a step more than that. But I'm grateful, lad, that you are concerned for my wellbeing. We'll agree fine, you and me, and I shall open a golden future to you.'

II

Wattie fell into a decline after the disappearance of his father and mother. He was rescued from it by the intervention of the Lady Mary Douglas, a daughter of the Tineman, a girl who had never married (rare though such a state was among those of noble birth who had not chosen to take the veil), but devoted herself to poetry, good works and religion. She was attracted by what was fey in the boy, his gentleness and the sense he gave of being set apart from other children. So he grew up in her part of the household and was schooled by the Lady Mary herself, and, informally, by her old wet-nurse Janet. Janet was a treasure-house of tales about that other life which – most men knew, though some, like Young Clym preferred to deny – marched side by side with the world of ordinary sense. She told him of faeries and bogles, of the brownies that watched over households, of lonely places where no wise man would abide by night, and of houses cursed to successive generations. She raised in him a deeper awareness of the shadowy world where the imagination could gallop like a horse free of the bit. He learned of the kelpie that stood in the summer evenings by Yarrow ford and carried any child rash enough to lay a finger on him off to Faeryland. 'And do they ever come back?' he asked Janet, wondering perhaps if Jean and Rob had fallen to the kelpie's lures. 'Gin they do,' she said, 'they are that changed as to be fair transmogrified, and their ain mither couldna tell them.' Then, since the boy was given to dreaming and night terrors, he began to form the notion that maybe he was a kelpie child himself. He chose not to speak of this, and perhaps because of his silence, his difference from other boys became more marked. He had strange memories and dreams to perturb him.

As he passed beyond childhood the idea faded; yet something of it remained all his life. He often seemed to be looking at experience from a distance, seeing it through a screen. He was thus early cast, by what had befallen him and whatever unconscious impulses worked on his nature, as an observer rather than actor.

Yet, with all this, maybe because of it, he possessed a rare charm. There was no sign of selfishness in his behaviour, and he was gentle with no hint of weakness. He soon became more than a pet of the Lady Mary. She admired the way he had with the birds and beasts. He could manage even the wildest hawk, though he took no delight in hunting them. Once, when they had a falcon so wild and savage that even the chief falconer said there was nothing to be done with the brute but wring its neck, Wattie offered to take charge of it, and within a fortnight the bird was sitting on his shoulder and nibbling at his ear as if it had been his lady's pet linnet. He had a blue hare for three years which he found frozen in the snow and tamed so that it lay in his lap like a cat and would sleep wrapped round his neck. Stranger still, even the dogs were happy to accept the hare and do it no harm. There was never a dog did not recognize Wattie as a friend. The fierce mastiffs that spent most of their hours chained in the courtyard would let him pull thorns from their paws or ticks from their heads without the murmur of a growl; and he had always a brace of pepper-coloured terriers at his heels which slept nose to nose with the hare.

He acquired too a knowledge of herbs and flowers and everything that grew which, as the Lady Mary often said, surpassed that of any physician. It seemed as if he knew it by nature, for he had a quickness of apprehension like a wild animal's.

For all his charm there was that which remained distant and mysterious in him. He was known as a dreamer, and his dreams had a terrible urgency and reality. Throughout his life they set him apart; even rough men were a little in awe of him, as of things beyond their understanding.

The Lady Mary was determined that Wattie should add book-learning to his store of knowledge, and so she arranged for him to take lessons with her two younger brothers (the children of the Tineman's second marriage), William who had succeeded his uncle Fat Archie as the sixth Earl of Douglas, and David. A fourth member of the little class was their cousin Malcolm Fleming of Cumbernauld who had been sent to be educated in manners, learning and chivalry with his great cousins, acting also as the young earl's page. The four boys studied French, Latin, Logic and Rhetoric together, and the Lady Mary read them tales of chivalry and recited the country ballads, many of which she had herself had from Wattie's father Rob. They practised archery – the sole sport in which Wattie excelled, for he eschewed even angling – and learned to ride hard, though Wattie stood by, a mere watcher, and took no part in the martial exercises which his three companions regarded as the most important and rewarding part of their education. For several years the four were all but inseparable, except that Wattie had formed the habit of disappearing on his own into the hills and higher reaches of the valleys for days on end. It could not be an equal relationship, for there must be something of condescension in the way the earl and his brother (and young Malcolm too) regarded their companion; and yet they were impressed by him too, for they recognized that he had qualities they would never possess for all their wealth, talents and pride of birth. Malcolm Fleming might well have been jealous of Wattie's charm and influence, for he regarded the Earl William with a hero worship that amounted to adoration, but he too felt tender and protective towards him, and at the same time strengthened and enriched by his friendship.

The young earl was perhaps a little spoiled by the devotion he aroused, but he was the sort of boy who seems worth spoiling and can hardly avoid it. He was a sharp contrast to the unlucky Tineman and that dull ox Fat Archie. Men said that he was a throwback to the Good Lord James who had fought alongside the Bruce and founded the fortune of the House, or to the second earl that had died so chivalrously at Otterburn, the dead man who had won a fight. Young William delighted all. He was good-looking, fair-haired, blue-eyed with a rather pale lightly freckled face, stocky but athletic, a good horseman and better archer. He was a serious boy, conscious of his position, but aware that he had duties as well as rights. He had certainly a good conceit of himself, but no more than was proper and was neither loud nor boastful. When he made any violent physical effort – leaping a burn or putting his horse at a dyke or tilting with a lance – his tongue would protrude between his lips. Wattie used to wonder if the day wouldn't come when he bit its end off, but his affection warmed whenever he saw this happen, for he took it as a sign that the young earl would achieve things by the utmost effort and have to work for his successes. Of course all the young girls were in love with him, but, by the age of sixteen, he didn't yet show much interest in them; he was preparing himself to be a great warrior and a worthy Earl of Douglas, and Wattie loved him for it.

The king himself was still a boy for he had been hardly six when his father was murdered. Fat Archie had been his first guardian, and all might have gone well had he lived, but now the two Keepers, Livingstone and Crichton, who divided the power in the kingdom, viewed the young Earl with anxiety and jealousy. They feared the steady growth in Douglas power, and they were aware too that the old Comyn claim to the throne (which had led the Bruce to murder the Red Comyn before the altar in Dumfries) was now vested by marriage in the Douglases. They watched the young earl approach splendid manhood, and they twitched and sweated at the sight.

Their power was too unstable to risk open war in the kingdom, and so they resolved on policy. In high summer they sent messengers to Newark where the young earl and his friends were fishing, stalking and hunting throughout the Forest of Ettrick, inviting him to Stirling Castle, of which Livingstone was Keeper, 'that they might confer in all amity and to some purpose concerning the grave affairs of the kingdom.'

Young William was proud and happy to receive the message, for he took it as a sign that he had attained manhood, and so he rode out at the head of a troop of five hundred horse, all gaily caparisoned in the July morning, with flags flying and the Black Bull's head of the earl's banner streaming in the breeze, and a piper playing them across the water. Young David Douglas, at his brother's right hand, rose in the stirrups and let out a great cheer and the watching crowd returned it. Malcolm Fleming rode on the earl's left and the whole troops jangled and clattered merry as a carnival.

They rode up Yarrow and the water sparkled and danced to their tune. Before St Mary's Loch they turned right and set themselves to the hill–track that would lead them over to Tweed. The sun blazed down and dispelled the morning mist that had clung about the valleys and the high tops at the hour of departure. The men sang marching songs and the deer on the moors fled from the sound of the brave music. Joy and good humour carried them all the ride to Stirling.

But Wattie did not ride with them. A fever had come on him and he tossed in bed, passing from anxious sleep to tormented waking, troubled in mind and body.

Roses bloomed in the Stirling gardens and Sir Alexander Livingstone led out his young daughter to press a rose on the earl. She blushed rose-coloured herself and sank a curtsey.

'My lord,' the Keeper said, 'we are rarely honoured by your presence,' and the earl sprang from his horse and raised up the girl and embraced her; and all the people cheered to see, as the chronicler put it, 'such peace and content reign in their summer Scotland'.

The earl smiled at the people and waved to them, and his brother shouted his joy, and Malcolm Fleming of Cumbernauld threw silver pennies and groats among the townsfolk. That night they feasted on salmon from the Forth and lamb from the braes of Balquidder in the great vaulted hall of Stirling Castle, and all went merry as a marriage bell, the Douglas men drinking deep and merry in the carefree joy of their reception.

Wattie dreamed a grey dream in a mist. He stood alone in a long valley looking on a broken church in heavy silence. He had come too late and the knowledge oppressed him, and then a vixen howled in the pine-woods.

But the king, it seemed, was not at Stirling as they had been promised he would be, and would not ride there. The Douglas walked in morning sunshine with Sir Alexander Livingstone in the castle rose gardens, and Sir Alexander took him by the sleeve and spoke to him.

'In confidence,' he said. 'I maun hae a word in confidence, and I hae to warn you that thon sly tod Sir William Crichton has nae sic a friendly speerit to your lordship as I hae. Na, na, my lord, if there be twae men in the kingdom that render him feart and distrustful, they are the Earl of Douglas and Sir Alexander Livingstone. It was sair wark, my lord, to hae him append his name tae my friendly letter, and nae sooner had he done it that his face gaed white as a hoar-frost and his feet grew cauld as January, and he sware he wadna let the bairn-king oot o' his sicht or Edinburry Castle. There was nae reasoning wi' him, for he is as obstinate as he is timorous, and sae he sits there now glowering wi' dark suspicions of the baith of us, like an auld wife hearing noises by her hen-run. Sae, my lord, gin we are to bring this business to fruition which, I trust, we are baith agreed maun be done gin the affairs of Scotland are to be satisfactorily settled, why then we maun to Edinburry, where I trust we may by God's Grace allay his suspicions and bring him to reason.'

'To Edinburgh' the earl said. 'So be it.'

'Yet I'm thinking,' Sir Alexander muttered, 'that it will no calm his fears gin you come wi' sic a retinue.'

Wattie cried on the Lady Mary and called on her to stop the earl. 'There is danger, fell danger, lies in wait for him'; and the Lady Mary, chill at heart to hear these words, and trusting to his vision, sent a messenger on a fast horse to warn her brother.

The young earl lifted his chin and looked Livingstone in the eye. 'I bring my men,' he said, 'to do me glory and to give them pleasure, nae to impose my will or protect my body. If their mere presence will distress Sir William Crichton and gar him unfit or unwilling to do our business, why then, Sir Alexander I shall blithely leave them here in Stirling provided you will be kind enough to furnish them with meat and bed.'

Wattie sank in a deep sleep from which none would rouse him for a day and a half.

Malcolm Fleming of Cumbernauld picked a stone from the hoof of the bay mare that would carry the earl. He weighed the stone in his hand and cast it into a bush. 'Gin the horse fell and threw my lord and brake his head, that would, to my way of thinking, be a happier fortune than what I fear awaits him in Edinburgh. I hae tried,' he told young David Douglas, 'tae warn him that Livingstone and Crichton are twae wolves, the tane tae be trusted nae mair as the tither. But he just gies me a bonny smile, serene and high as the summer sun above, and . . .' he choked on the memory, and took a moment to recover, 'will you no, Davie, try your skill at the arguing?'

Young David Douglas tilted his chin in his brother's manner. 'There's never a Douglas doesna dare do what he's been dared,' he said, 'and, Malcolm, there's nae a man in all Scotland would dare lift his hand against the Earl of Douglas.'

The earl accordingly left five hundred armed men in Stirling Castle and with his brother and Malcolm Fleming and a mere handful of servants rode down the bank of the Forth with Sir Alexander Livingstone by his side. In the hot noon they saw the tower of Edinburgh Castle rise on its rock before them, and Sir William Crichton received them at the gate with all manner of dignity. The young king skipped from foot to foot to see them, the red birthmark on his cheek shining like a beacon on the Eildon Hills. He said to the brothers, 'Welcome, a thousand welcomes, for I ken fine you will be my truest friends as your ancestor the Good Lord James was to my great forefather, the Bruce. Now,' he said, in a changed tone as one who has completed his lesson and may turn to pleasure, 'come and play skittles with me.'

So they played skittles in the back court of the Castle, with much laughter, till Sir William Crichton came out in all his ample rotundity to bid them come to dinner.

'The trust you show in me', he said to the Douglas, 'gars me greet wi' joy.'

Wattie woke in a painted chamber and what he saw he saw with all the clarity of nightmare. The vision shook him with sobs and terror and again he cried on the Lady Mary and a boy ran to fetch her.

'I hae seen the most awfu thing that can be in this warld,' he said. 'I saw the Great Hall of Edinburgh Castle wi dust dancing in the sun's rays, but a' the walls ran wi' blood and nane there could see it. And there was my lord and young Davie, baith fresh and bonny as a May morning in Yarrow, and lauching and louping wi the young king. And the king's fiery face was lit up with the pleasure of their company like the red evening sky. The three of them were that joyful that even the dour faces of the Keepers couldna dull their joy. But Malcolm wore a face like a friar in Lent though nane of the others observed nor heeded him. And then my een went black and I couldna see. But the picture cleared and I saw that the darkness was a Black Bull's heid they had laid on the table afore them, the hair curling atween the horns. 'What means this?' cries my lord, leaping to his feet, 'what means this? What treachery hae we here?' But there was nae answer and I coud hear naething but the buzzing of wasps and flies and I could see nae mair but the rumple of curly hair on the back of the bull's heid and the cruel shine of the bull's horns.'

They took the Earl Douglas and his brother David, who had ridden in that morning blithe as swallows, out of the Great Hall, and they hustled them under a narrow gateway by a line of men-at arms, across the back court where their skittles still lay as they had fallen, and through a low arch to the Great Court where a block stood with a big masked man beside it leaning on an axe.

'What manner of justice is this? Of what do we stand accused?' cried out the Earl.

But there was none took it on himself to answer.

Only Crichton said, 'We hae a priest ready to shrieve ye.'

'Will you kill us both?' said the Earl. 'Then let my brother die first. He is young. Spare him the misery of haeing to see me suffer.'

They were rough hands that did the deed, and the priest's voice broke as he implored mercy on the boys' souls. A half-hour later Malcolm Fleming of Cumbernauld was jostled past the bodies of his friends, as if by an afterthought, and joined with them in death.

Wattie murmured, 'It is owre.'

The Lady Mary wept. 'God grant we meet wi' Crichton afore he finds his way to hell.'

> Edinburgh Castle, towne and toure,
> God grant thee sinke for sinne!
> And that even for the black dinner
> Earl Douglas gat therein.

III

The Cardinal, Maurie's patron, was dead. The French Wars went from bad to worse. The Lady Clare, married a second time to a sixty-year-old Northumbrian baron, was again a widow, now holding a dozen manors or more in her own right as well as the wide Boscobel estates she controlled as the patrimony of her near-imbecile son, whose tongue lolled from his twisted mouth and whose eyes shifted in vacant stare as a caged animal's might. At the age of fourteen he stopped growing at no more than an hand's breadth over four feet. He passed most of his time in a tower room playing at marbles, for his mother hated him to be seen in public.

'It disgusts me to know that that came out of my body,' she said to Maurie.

'Nevertheless,' he said, lying in a huge four-poster bed in the castle of Mirabel, as May morning sunshine made the big-vaulted room dance with the exhilarating sweep of the moors beyond, and the chatter of little birds sang a spring melody of new life, 'nevertheless,' Maurie sighed, the poor brute must marry.'

'And who would have the likes of him? Can we find a maid deformed herself?'

'It is necessary,' he said, 'necessary.'

'Enough of politics, my little crookback.' She pushed her thighs, which were still firm and rounded, against his, and drew his hands under the counterpane, directing his fingers to their accustomed pleasure. Her open mouth sought his, their tongues met in play, and she felt him grow hard, and eased him in, with a low moan, and they rocked, making the two-backed beast, joined easily in the flesh, as they had been in all but marriage since soon after Boscobel's death, and as they had from the first been joined in spirit. . .

There were clouds beyond. The State shifted like a house

built on foundations of sand. A group of fishermen seized William de la Pole, Earl of Suffolk, and a lord of the King's Privy Council, and dragged him screaming from the boat he was boarding for France. They hauled him over the grey beach where a north-easterly kicked the sand in his face, slung him over the gunwale of a rowing-boat and chopped his head off with six blows of a rusty axe. 'What a world we live in,' said pious folk when they heard of the crime and crossed themselves and said that there was no respect for degree now. 'What would be next?' they asked. Edward des Moulins, who had been of his company, threw himself at the fishermen's feet, and licked their salty boots to save his life. From that hour he sat, day by day in Castle Greer, turning it over in his mind, drinking the red wine of Bordeaux in an effort to forget what that moment meant: that no rank could protect the princes of a crumbling state; that neither furs nor jewels, nor great offices nor broad acres, were a sure armour against fear.

But in a crumbling state the bold man can rise faster. Maurie licked that knowledge. The Lady Clare lay by him, her head cradled in her swansdown cushions, and let her fingers play in the warm damp between her legs. She turned on her side and tickled her finger along Maurie's upper lip. 'Taste and smell,' she sighed. 'But who would take the idiot child?'

'No child,' Maurie said, drawing her head back on his shoulder. 'No child. Rather ask who would not see his daughter wedded to the broad acres of Boscobel. It is an alliance, my love, that the greatest lord would not disdain. More than that, it is a measure we can hardly delay to take, for sides are forming for the contest that will surely come. Our choice is of great significance. It will make or mar our future.'

'Are we not happy as we are?'

She drew her damp sticky finger again along the sharp line of his jaw and let it dance on his lips. 'Are we not happy as we are?'

'Listen, my love,' and he spoke to her again as he had tried before, elaborating the argument he had set before his nephew Clym. The French Wars were lost. All their actions must be based on that premise. There would soon be no more English Empire in France. And, when wars were lost, when they resulted in disaster and humiliation, then the whole fabric was torn and shaken. 'You know,' he said with that tenderness which he kept only for her (and she for him) 'what will happen? Unruly solders accustomed to nothing but war will seek whatever master would feed and pay them.' The government had meanwhile lost the confidence of nobility and gentry. The king was weak-minded and indecisive; the wife Suffolk had chosen for him, Margaret of Anjou, had a strong will but knew nothing of England and was hated as a Frenchwoman. 'I have seen her,' he said, 'bare her teeth like a she-wolf.' And in the wings waited Richard of York. He must strike for the Regency, if not the throne itself. Which side,' Maurie asked, 'do we back?' That was why the idiot's marriage was urgent. It would align them on one side or the other, open . . . opportunities.

Clare grew more and more excited as he spoke. Her hands again sought him. Again she pressed herself against him, and called out.

Edward des Moulins had married. His wife was a Beaufort, bringing him close in blood to the royal house. Maurie had done more than encourage the marriage, he had played a part in its arrangement. 'It does not commit us,' he said to Clare. 'But it may be useful.' As for Edward however, his own usefulness was declining. He moved in bemused state from castle to castle, rarely sober, but now rendered so slow and silent by wine that his condition passed as one of great dignity. He was loaded with honours: knight of the Garter, Privy Councillor, Member of the Court of the Marches. He acquired an army of a thousand five hundred retainers, foul-mouthed, blood-stained and cynical veterans of France.

Young Dandy approached Maurie more than once to ask him to make intercession on his behalf with the man who was after all his father. 'Might I not rise by his side?' he asked.

'Pish and tush, lad,' Maurie would say, 'you will travel further and faster with me than in that broken-down train. Trust me,' he said, and smiled on the boy and held him close. 'Trust me, for I have a tenderness for your interest.'

Edward was given a command in France. Maurie wondered that he dared accept it, for he knew him to be a coward. But vanity won, 'as it always does,' Maurie said; 'there is no quality can pull down vanity.' Edward's army disintegrated in the course of one summer campaign. Supply failed and they became mere pillagers on the already wasted lands of Picardy. When, by a blundering accident, they encountered a French army in a summer rainstorm, they fled in abrupt confusion. Sir John Talbot, the last fighting commander in France, met the fugitives and lashed out at them with the flat of his sword. He told Edward des Moulins that a capon priest would make a braver show than he had. Edward looked at him as if he did not hear. His eyes were pale and his mouth hung open as if he waited for a servitor to funnel Bordeaux wine in him. But Bordeaux was long lost now, and English merchants had to pay a high price for Gascon wine.

'You see, lad,' Maurie hugged Dandy to him, 'how wise I was to keep you from your father's side.'

'You have eyes for your nephew,' Clare told Maurie.

'Eyes?'

'You look at him as that filthy priest Brother Ambrose used to gaze on his catamites.'

'Pish and tush,' Maurie said. 'I have eyes for none but you, my lady, nor ever have nor shall.'

'Aye, but,' she sighed, 'I have seen you look . . .'

So had his brother Will, all the more clearly because he found himself eyeing Dandy in the same manner. Will had grown fat in the years Maurie had kept him cooped in Mirabel, 'like a capon'.

'You ken, Dandy lad,' he said, 'he keeps me here, not out of any love – na, na, there's nae love lost between Maurie and his brothers – if either of the other twae be living, which you tell me they arena, and why should I no' believe you, lad . . .' He reached before him for the flagon and carefully, his hand still shaking, filled his mug. 'Do you ken why he keeps me here? It's because as lang as I am safe and secure and free to drink myself to death, Maurie feels safe. He aye laughs, ye ken, at the proposition that we are born to be hanged, cursed to be hanged, all four of us, but in his heart, there is nae laughter, in his heart he believes it – as – here's the jest, laddie, as I dinna. I have seen owre muckle to believe in fate. I have seen my dear maister the Marshal Gilles de Rais choose his ain gait to Hell, and I ken fine he could have ta'en another road had it pleased him. So I hae nae time for the tale or curses of auld wives, nane at all, though it pleases me well enough to pretend otherwise to Maurie. For you see, lad, gin you had seen the hauf I hae seen of the terrors and cruelties of life, you'd be fine pleased to settle down in a cosie bield, even though you had a hauf-mad brother to act as your jailor. For that he's hauf-mad, laddie, I dinna doubt. He's eaten up with ambition and the lust for power, and it behoves you to walk warily, like a canny youth, while you bide with him. He's ta'en a fancy to you, lad, and I would advise you to do whatever he asks and pleasure him, or you'll find Maurie to be a far caulder enemy than he has ever been a warm friend.'

He nodded and winked and pinched the boy's cheek, and though Dandy did not understand the innuendoes, he smiled agreement. This uncle was not much of a man, but he had known the French Wars, and Dandy could not have enough of his stories.

Maurie rose from his lady's bed long after noon, and returned to his chamber to work with clerks on his accounts. It gave him a deep pleasure, sharp and intense as sex, to see his wealth increase. He worked for three hours, and then dismissed his clerks. He lay back and smiled. A spider was spinning a web in the corner of the wall and the window, and Maurie admired the certainty and intricacy of its work. It spun out a strand of silk, a strand then and the work was complete: delicate, strong and powerful. He rang a bell and told the page to fetch him his nephew.

Dandy lounged in, and, without waiting to be asked, threw himself on the couch by the window. Maurie smiled. The sunbeam danced on the boy's downy cheek. He had watched him that morning in the practice-ground riding a tilt, and seen him unseat an experienced knight. And but for Maurie, he would be only a rough farmboy who rode a shaggy pony on cattle raids.

'I am pleased with you,' he said, 'you do me credit.'

A rosy blush stole over the boy's face. Maurie twisted his fingers round and round.

'I have seen you speak with your uncle Will,' he said, 'my poor brother. It is a kindness of me to keep him here, for the world has treated Will badly, and he is now fit for little. He went to seek his fortune in France – and look at his fortune. He is not a man to take seriously, lad.'

'He has good stories to tell,' Dandy said.

'Oh stories . . .' Maurie waved his hand. 'One thing I have observed, child, is that those who are great storytellers are rarely men of whom stories might be told. The wise man is secret. He says little of what he has done, and less of what he hopes to achieve. And yet there are times when it is proper to speak.'

The boy lay quite still and waited. Was he impressed? Impossible to say. Perhaps he had already learned the strength of secrecy. Perhaps he was a boy who knew all things would come to him. Maurie's nails bit into his palms: the boy didn't know what it was to be a cripple, he was at ease in his body.

'Times,' Maurie repeated, 'when it is proper to speak. You know what I have risen from, for you were raised in the same peel, stuck in the same waste land and surrounded by the same midden. You can measure my rise to this perilous seat. I have watched you in the evenings, I have watched your face when the minstrels tell the tales of chivalry, and I envy you. Does that seem strange, Dandy, that I should envy you? But I do. I envy your ability to be stirred by them. But then I fear for you too. The world does not resemble these tales of heroism. It is a harsh place where each man is at risk. Remember that. Now listen. Tomorrow I ride to Castle Raby. Do you know whom I shall meet there?'

Dandy shook his head, saying nothing and keeping his eyes fixed on Maurie's face.

Maurie paused: 'Richard, Earl of Warwick,' he said.

The boy looked at him.

'Have you not heard of him?'

Again Dandy shook his head and watched his uncle.

'Warwick,' Maurie said, 'is the great man that will be. His sister whom they call the Rose of Raby is married to Richard, Duke of York, but Warwick is twice the man that York is. He is a man after my own heart, no simple minded soldier but a sage and politic man, as the Cardinal was. He is a man, Dandy, as I can do business with.'

'And what business will you do?' The boy's gaze flitted out of the window; sounds as of a game rose from the courtyard, hearty laughs, shouts and cheers.

Maurie said, 'Pay no heed to that. I am offering you excitement such as no game can equal. I am offering you indeed entry to the greatest game of all, where the stakes are the exercise of power or the traitor's block. Have you heard of the Countess's son?'

Dandy's eyes drifted back to look at him. 'Aye,' he said.

'And I see you have heard that he is a mystery. Your Uncle Will will have spoken, he was ever a blatherskite. There is no mystery, lad. The boy is an idiot. But he is an idiot who is heir to great possessions, and I go to Raby to arrange his marriage. There!' he threw himself back in his chair. 'To arrange the marriage of such a creature with a great heiress will test even my powers. And you shall ride with me. It is time you tasted the great world.'

'He'll do it,' Will said. 'If Maurie has set his heart on it, he will do it. But walk cannily, Dandy lad.'

So, on an August morning, Maurie, in surcoat of gold and purple and mounted on a Spanish jennet, with Dandy at his side as a squire, rode at the head of three hundred armed men, some wearing the Boscobel livery, and some fifty of them in his own livery of Cleckington, over the drawbridge of Mirabel, and turned south. They clattered through the village, and Dandy, delighting in the adventure, did not notice how the villagers turned away from the sight of them, or glowered at the ground as they passed. They rode all day, and the light was fading and an autumn nip entering the air when the great towers of Raby rose before them. The castle could be seen at some two miles' distance, and Dandy's heart leapt at the size of it. Something of Maurie's mood had communicated itself to him, but the boy's excitement was a simpler thing. He rejoiced at the swing and movement of the enterprise, and throbbed with the message of the future.

The gate was thrown open to them, and they rode into the courtyard and dismounted. A squire bowed low and greeted Maurie with elaborate courtesy such as Dandy had never seen. Maurie responded in an austere manner, with curt nods of the head. The squire led them along corridors hung with Flanders tapestries depicting boarhunts and tournaments, to a great high hall that was already chilly despite the log fire that roared there. He invited Maurie to sit but Maurie shook his head.

Then a stocky square-bearded fellow in dark cloth with a gold chain round his neck emerged from behind a screen. He looked Maurie up and down. 'You have ridden easy,' he said, 'we expected you an hour back.'

He spoke in the harsh accent of the English Midlands. 'Tell your master,' he snapped at the squire, 'that my lord of Cleckington is here. Bestir yourself.'

The squire, a slim dark youth, flushed, turned away and departed, indignation expressing itself in the set of his shoulders and his exaggerated willowy walk. 'That lad needs a good kick in the arse. Truncheon,' the man said, 'I am Truncheon, his lordship's man of business. I suppose you are a sort of man of business yourself.'

'I am a man as others can do business with.'

'A good answer, a very good answer. I approve of it. Business then is our business and we shall waste little time, nay no time at all, on polite preliminaries. You can do the politenesses when his lordship appears. But I am a plain blunt man who says, "to our muttons, and gloves off". He smacked his thigh. 'What say you, friend?'

'I say: good business makes good friendship.'

'A good answer again. I approve it. Well, sir, his lordship has studied your proposal, and given thought to it. Much thought, much bending of the brow and much listening to sage opinion. My opinion. He is of course pleased and honoured at the suggestion of an alliance with a family so old, distinguished, even revered . . . but you know all that, friend, you could give the same speech word for word. Business, there is no need for the likes of you and me to parley in this mealy-mouthed manner. We are men of sense such as can leave that diplomatic airy-fairy arsy-versy language to princes and clerics. Are we not? Business eh? Brass tacks, eh? They say the lad's an imbecile.'

'Near complete,' Maurie said.

'Excellent. A good answer. An excellent answer. You're cool about it. I do like a man as speaks his mind. Have some wine.'

'You talk of diplomacy,' Maurie said, 'Well, friend, what is this marriage but diplomacy, and it's an ill start, I reckon, to begin with a lie.'

A laugh rang out behind him. He turned, and Dandy turned too, to see two figures standing in the doorway. The one who had laughed was a tall yellow-haired boy. The man beside him, about a yard away – it was his habitual distance, as Maurie was to learn – was of medium height, a medium colour, medium looks; and when he spoke now, did so in a medium, unaccented voice.

'You are ill-mannered, my lord,' he said. 'Pray, my lord of Cleckington, forgive the child. May I be permitted to introduce my nephew Edward, Earl of March, the son of Richard, Duke of York. Unfortunately, he thinks his high birth excuses his ill manners.'

'No, but really,' the young earl advanced with a wide smile, 'you must indeed forgive me, my lord. I was laughing with pleasure and admiration. I am so tired of hearing mannerly lies.'

Maurie knelt before him and kissed his hand. 'I am in no way offended. To be tired of lies so young must be accounted virtue. I spoke but truth, and if it pleases you, why then I am glad, my lord. Allow me in my turn introduce my nephew, Andrew Laidlaw, though he has not yet a handle to stick to his name.'

The young Edward smiled again. All his life he would disarm criticism with that smile, and enliven the company. That smile and his animal vigour would make men forgive his cruelty, laziness and selfishness when he became Edward of England. But now the Earl of Warwick said to him, 'Quite, quite, truth is to be prized, but we men have business to discuss. Go and play at knucklebones, my lord, or' – he flapped his hands – 'or something, and take our young guest with you . . . Shoo, shoo.'

'There,' he said, when the boy had left the room, 'is the next king of England bar one. A wild and graceless boy, you may say, but with such a king as that boy will be we would not even now be losing our empire in France.'

Maurie nodded. Did Warwick believe that? If so . . . it was against nature, common sense and political reality that England should rule France. Surely Warwick must know that? If he didn't . . . but as for what he said of the boy . . . Maurie thought of the cold timid hand and the small thin voice that had dubbed him knight, and could see that other boy standing tall and straight and golden and commanding with the crown of England on his head, a picture – there was no reason not to form the picture – the lord of Cleckington by his side and offering counsel at his table . . . and nodded again.

'You are frank, sir,' the earl said.

'My lord, there is a time to conceal truth and a time to speak it. Now I could gain nothing by the former course. My lady of Boscobel, whose beauty and merit you know well, and whom I have faithfully served for many years, has deputed me to act as her ambassador. My lady has a son. That son, is as I say, dim-witted. He is worse than dim-witted. Yet he is lord of great estates, which must be safeguarded. He needs therefore a wife. That wife must have a father who is a great man. And, in return,' he said, 'the great man will receive in these troubled times, a loyal ally. My lady's estates are of no inconsiderable value, and we keep, all in all, more than two thousand men at arms at our disposal.'

'And so you come to me,' Warwick said.

'And so I come to you, my lord, as . . .' Maurie spread his hands wide, palms extended to the heavens, 'my lord, what can I say without flattery? And you are too great a man to serve with flattery. My lord, my lady trusts me, yet my birth is humble and I am no born Englishman, but from a northern stem. As such, I have, my lord, no hereditary antipathies. I served the Cardinal who trusted me. But, my lord, the Cardinal is dead, and there is little merit in the House of Beaufort.'

Warwick frowned. 'Is it in your interest that you seek to promote this marriage?'

Truncheon kicked out his legs to draw attention to himself. 'Permission to interrupt, sir. We have been given a good answer, an excellent answer. And, sir, you have penetrated to the truth, to the very kernel of truth. It is indeed in our friend's interest to promote this marriage, and that, sir, is why I approve it. Never trust a man, sir, who does not act in his own interest. He's a scoundrel, sir, such a man is; you can never tell what he will do next, sir.'

'That's as may be,' Warwick muttered, 'as may well be, as a general rule. But particular instances, particular instances . . . and then there's another matter. My daughter, the Lady Alice, is but a girl, they say she's a beauty though I can't tell myself.'

'That she is, sir,' Truncheon said, 'a regular beauty, with the pure complexion of the Easter lily, I'll vouch for that, and a sweet nature too. There is not such a girl in the north of England, and if there is no such girl in the north where we breed fine women, why then sir, there can be none to match her in the south neither. There,' he turned to Maurie, 'what do you think of that for an answer, sir?'

'A very pretty answer, sir,' Maurie said,' and a pleasing one, and yet perhaps it does not catch the drift of his lordship's thoughts. . .'

'The drift of my thoughts . . . quite . . .' Warwick muttered again.

'The drift of his thoughts . . . that's a fine phrase, a monstrous fine phrase, I'll be bound. By our lady, sir, if you will allow me to say so, speaking as a plain man, you understand, you are uncommon shrewd, sir, with an uncommon gift for words, sir. Fine words and fine sentences . . . the drift of his thoughts, there's a phrase indeed, and what might the drift of his thoughts be, sir?'

'Why,' Maurie said, 'if I may be allowed . . .'

'Allowed, sir. By all means. Perfect freedom here, sir . . .'

'Thank you . . . allowed to interpret what I believe his lordship may be thinking, but is too gentle and polite and mannerly to say. His lordship may think he is caught in a double role. He is a man of state, but he also a fond father. The man of state looks at the broad acres of Boscobel, his eye gleams at the coats of the men-at-arms, he sees the coming troubles of the realm, and he says to himself, "this is a timely proposition. This is a fair match will secure my power," and the man of state rubs his hands in approval. But the fond father shakes his head. The fond father loves his daughter and is loth to see her bound to an imbecile.'

'So that's what it is, is it?' Truncheon said. 'That's the drift of your thoughts, is it, my lord? A bonnie exposition, sir, but a fine pickle you have placed my lord in.'

'What's for the best' Warwick said.

'Why, my lord, I ask you to trust me,' Maurie said. 'Trust me. Can you imagine I would let harm come to your noble daughter?'

'A question,' Truncheon said, 'a good question, my lord. Would he indeed? No, he would not, my lord. And why not, you ask. Because, my lord, our friend here has an eye to his own interest. As he should have, as a man unmistakably should have. There's your answer, my lord, and a fine one. A shrewd one.'

'Our friend Truncheon understands me,' Maurie said. 'My lord, it will be but a marriage in name only. We shall of course require that the Lady Alice resides at Boscobel, but, believe me, my lord, her husband shall not be permitted to touch a hair of her head . . . or lay a finger on her.'

'There,' Truncheon said, 'there, my lord, I ask you. Can he say fairer? No, he cannot, And is your drift arrested? Why, yes, my lord, it is. And is there more to be said? No, my lord, there is not. We have an agreement, and there need be no departure from it, by jot or tittle.'

'And so,' Edward Earl of March said, 'I draw a line through my x's and you have lost again.'

'Lost, have I? It's no muckle of a game, is it?' Dandy smiled.

'No muckle? What a strange way you talk; do they all talk that way in Scotland?'

'Near all,' Dandy said.

'Well, you're right, if it means what I suppose it does, quite right. How tired I am of such games. How I long to be full grown. And how these old men talk! My uncle Warwick thinks himself the fount of wisdom, and certainly he drenches you in the course of conversation. But words, words, words . . . when I am king, I shall put a stop to words.'

'When you are king. But will you be king?'

'Aye,' Edward said, 'that I will.'

'But there is a king.'

'A poor saintly creature, no sort of man at all. You look as if you can ride and fight. He can't. Would you like to wrestle?'

'Here?'

'Why not? They will talk for hours.'

'But tell me first how you will come to be king.'

'Well,' Edward said, 'in the first place you must know that we have a better title to the throne than the House of Lancaster. Though it is true that my great-grandfather Edmund, Duke of York, was but the youngest son of Edward III, while the so-called King Henry is descended from the third son John of Gaunt who was made Duke of Lancaster, you must not forget that I am also descended from his second son Lionel Duke of Clarence. You see, Lionel had no sons but only a daughter Philippa, who married Roger Mortimer, Earl of March. That title is permitted to descend in the female line, and it comes to me through my mother who is the direct descendant of Lionel and then Philippa. So you see I am descended from two sons of the great king, one of whom was older than John of Gaunt. So that I clearly have a better claim to the thone, and besides, I should be a good king, while the so-called King Henry would be better set to his prayers in a monastery. Are you listening?'

'Aye,' said Dandy, 'I heard every word.'

'And did you follow me?'

'Aye.'

They were sitting on a broad window ledge halfway up the staircase. The narrow window gave on a little enclosed garden, and twice as Edward talked, Dandy had seen a girl pass below. He was watching for her again now; and there she was passing under an arch cut in a yew hedge. She was of medium height, with dark hair worn loose and a pale creamy face of the most perfect oval. Her eyes were dark – or so it seemed to Dandy – and her lips curved to form a bow. She glanced up at the window. Her eyes met Dandy's. For a moment their gaze held, and his world stopped still, and the earl's words became a mere mutter as of the wind in distant tree-tops. Then, continuing her walk, she was out of sight, and he waited for her to return. When she did so, she looked at him again, and he thought he saw a smile form at the corner of her mouth, and the lady with whom she was walking (whom he had not noticed before) twitched at her sleeve, and a blush like a young rose of the palest pink crept over her cheek.

Forgetting rank, he tugged at the earl's sleeve. 'Who is that?'

'That? Oh just my cousin. My Uncle Warwick's daughter, Alice. It's her marriage your uncle has come to arrange, isn't it. For my part,' Edward said, 'I intend to marry for love, unless my love will have me without marriage. Of course when I'm king she probably will. If you're king you can get all the girls you want. Not that my feeble cousin tries. You should see the girl they've married him off to! A virago, a perfect virago, my dear, as Eustace – that's the molly who showed you in – would put it. He's quite a wit, Eustace, even if his sister will be a man before him. Not that his sister is at all like a man either, just a manner of speaking, you understand. But Alice is all right, shall we go down and talk to her. To tell you the truth, there's a little friend of hers called Joan, who I rather fancy. She's more than all right, and what the soldiers call a nice little armful of fluff.'

The girl must think him a clod. He couldn't think of anything to say, and when she asked him a question, he stuttered out an answer in the thickest and most incomprehensible Scots. But she smiled at him, and her smile was friendly and encouraging. Meanwhile he was aware of young Edward laughing with the girl Joan – who had appeared as it were from nowhere as soon as they entered the garden – and putting his arm round her waist and squeezing her till she giggled. And all he could do was gaze at the Lady Alice as if he had been a mooncalf. Yet the more he gazed, the rosier became her cheek, and the more reluctant she seemed to break away. He supposed later that they must have found something to say, but he couldn't think what it was, any more than he could have described what she was wearing.

And yet she showed no sign of wishing to leave, but talked in a manner to put him at his ease. What she said he could never have reported, but the sound of her voice, light and laughing as thistledown, and yet soft too with no thinness in it, stayed with him and disturbed his dreams that night. She was a girl such as he had never met before, had scarcely even envisioned.

Maurie's dreams were of a different order. As a sign of his good will and appreciation – and as a bribe to safeguard future conduct? – the great earl pressed jewels and the deeds of a manor on him. 'He is indeed a great man,' Maurie assured Dandy as they retired to their chamber; but if Dandy had been older, wiser or even less occupied with the picture of the Lady Alice, he might have read irony in his uncle's tone. 'And a great booby too,' he might have added, 'The young earl however is another matter.'

'Did you speak long with the young earl, lad?' he asked.

'The earl? Oh aye . . .' Her walk had a grace in it that the angels might envy; if he had been a poet like his uncle Rob! She had smiled straight at him as they parted, like a rose unfolding;

and yes, there had been, he was sure of it, an appeal in her eyes. Was she asking him to stay by her?

'Cling to the young earl, nephew. He will make your fortune . . .'

Cling to the earl's cousin . . .

In the morning the simpering squire Eustace told Maurie, with much roundabout apology, that could not hide a smirk, that a certain friar sought an audience with him.

'Some tedious affair of charity, I'll be bound,' Maurie said, 'but, well, yes, you had best show him in. These crows,' he said to Dandy, 'are persistent as a terrier with his eye on a scrap of fat.'

The curtains parted. He heard a gross chuckle, and a long lean man with grey greasy locks like rat's tails sidled into the room, and, in a manner that was not typical of his order, made a deep exaggerated bow to Maurie.

'You have become a great man, I hear,' – the voice was throaty and amused – 'that hobnobs with princes. Would you have a moment, a little hour, for an old friend . . . an old confederate?'

'Brother Ambrose,' Maurie cried, 'I had thought you dead. Well, men say that the Devil looks after his own, but he shows no readiness to take you, eh.'

The friar loped towards him, seized him by the shoulders and hugged him to his body. He sat down and slung his feet over the table. He smiled broadly and eyed Dandy.

'It's a pleasure,' he said, 'to renew acquaintance with you, my little Scot. And who's your bonny boy?'

'My nephew Dandy.'

'But not a papal nephew, eh?'

'Dandy, you may leave us. The friar and I will wish to have a crack about old times, which do not concern you. Run along.'

'Mind you,' the friar said, watching Dandy lounge from the room, 'both in Rome and Avignon you find more than one kind of papal nephew. A bonnie boy indeed, though, let me relieve you of all jealousy, not quite my sort. I can too easily imagine him riding in battle.'

'Enough of this foolery. What do you want?'

'What but what you told the boy? A crack about old times.'

'What we did together in the past is best left unspoken.'

'Prudent man. But not forgotten, eh?'

'You did me a service and were paid for it.'

'Second instalments are not unknown. Come, my friend, we have done much together. You'll not spurn an old friend and . . . accomplice.'

'Your word against mine,' Maurie looked him in the eye, 'whose would be believed?'

'Yours,' the friar sniggered. 'Yours, my lord, for a time.'

'A time long enough to see you . . . out.'

The friar touched his lips with his fingers and blew a kiss across the table.

'Let us not quarrel. I have not come here to make demands, nor offer threats. Merely to offer my ever so humble and yet useful services. Come, my old friend, great man as you have since become – and again I kiss my hand to your achievement – may there not be occasion for you to require my deft and peculiar talents? Who can tell what . . . tool . . . a politician may have need to use?'

His smile was eager, ingratiating, shameless. Maurie sniffed again the atmosphere of that steamy tavern beneath the Minster walls; he saw the friar slobber his embraces over the blond boy – what was his name? Nick, that was it. To his surprise he was pierced by a shaft of jealousy. How had the man lived these many years? He compared that imagined life to his own watchful and laborious ascent. Had he been cheated of something desirable, some satisfaction that might have been promised him, by his own demanding ambition? He felt he was no longer young; he had mounted a great staircase, and the view extended widely in all directions; but the steps were wet and slippery with blood, and, when he gazed abroad, the landscape showed a wilderness of dead ashes.

He said, 'I have to thank you for restoring my brother Will to me.'

'Ah Will, poor Will, no sort of man, but I hoped you might find him of use. Or, if not of use, then of comfort. And did he tell you? I saved him from the gallows. He was near suffering with the rest of the Marshal's entourage. An interesting man, de Rais, but a fool. He had to delve beneath the surface, and was not content to enjoy, as we are, what is tangible and real. He sought a different sort of power than you, old friend. A power such as no man may safely hold. That it exists and may be seized, I have no doubt, but the wise man shuns it, the wise man seeks to reduce the mysteries of life, not to embrace them. I have my own skills, greater and more subtle than even you can realize, but I flee the sort of knowledge the Marshal pursued. And your poor brother was like a village idiot in such a galley! But if he had been hanged, would you have slept at night? I have been keeping my beady little eye on you, old friend, and on your family. A man like me has a wide acquaintance, and there is little I cannot discover if I set myself to it. If Will were hanged, only you would remain. Is that not so? And would you then sleep easy at night? For, my friend, while wise men like you and I shun the shadowy side of life, the dark knowledge of those who are ready to traffick with what Holy Church calls the Devil, and others call the old Gods or the Dark Master, we are still too wise in the intricate paths of life to ... deny its reality. So, friend, I did you that service, and I have no doubt you keep Will safe.'

He leant over the table and seized the jug of beer that had been placed there for Maurie's breakfast. He took a deep swig from the side of the jug and ran his tongue over his slobbering lips.

'You remember poor Nick,' he said. 'He's dead, poor lad. He became a master carver and made the mistake of settling down. An unwise course for a lad with such tastes. It did for him.' He wiped a tear from his eye, or pretended to do so. 'Now, as for me, I have always liked to keep on the move. But I've no doubt a man of your wide concerns can arrange for that. On the other hand, I grow old and suffer sadly from rheumatism in winter. So, old friend, I seek your protection. I'm too old to live on my own wits now.'

Maurie nodded.

'Good.' He took another swig of beer. 'Thin ale, Warwick keeps. Thin ale, but then he's a thin man. I have a boy in tow. That will be all right though. He has a rare talent, a genius for architecture. He'll build you something beautiful, something to make you remembered for centuries, if you give him his chance. Robin he's called, Robin Cochrane.'

'I've no plans for building,' Maurie said. 'Not in stone anyway. Nevertheless you are welcome. The time may come when I have a use for you again.'

IV

The Black Dinner could not break the power of the House of
Douglas, for that was founded on their wide estates rather than
the life of the earl himself, but it seemed to have shattered
Wattie's wits. Men looked at him with a certain awe, for it was
soon known that he had 'seen' the earl's murder. For a long
time after it he seemed to live in another world. He suffered
from terrors at night, and in his waking hours was easier with
the dogs and other animals than with his fellow men. The
Dominican inquisitors sent by the Pope had long left the
country, but the Bishop had Wattie summoned before him to
examine him: it was not forgotten that the boy's mother had fled
under suspicion of witchcraft, and strange stories still went
round the country of how she and Rob Laidlaw had died. The
Bishop's clerk was all for having his master charge Wattie with
heresy, to encourage the others, if for no other reason, and he
might have succeeded if the Lady Mary had not intervened to
save him. All the same not even her protection could prevent
Wattie being watched with suspicion. Then she retired to a
nunnery, and begged him to come and settle at the convent
gate, for she feared for him, and not only loved him, but felt that
in some way that she could not explain she was responsible for
him. Wattie, however shook his head at the suggestion, though
he could give no reason. But then he wasn't a boy to whom you
looked for reasons.

The murdered boy's Uncle, James had become Earl of
Douglas. He was a man whom few respected, and was generally
known as James the Gross, a fat lazy creature, given to eating
and deep drinking, and now hardly able to sit a horse above a
slow amble. Yet he was hard and tenacious too. He did nothing
to avenge his nephews' death, and men shook their heads and
said he had been privy to the murder. If he knew of these
rumours, he did not let them disturb him. He was after all Earl

of Douglas, and he stroked his great paunch and let them mutter as they chose. He had his own ideas of policy and of how to advance the family's interests. He patched up relations even with Crichton and Livingstone, letting them know that he understood the Black Dinner had been 'an ill-chancy affair,' when hearts and fears had ruled heads, and he could not see why it should not be possible to resume an old friendship unfortunately broken. The two Keepers had no doubt erred in their suspicion of his nephew, but he could not deny that the boy had been rash and arrogant and given them cause. So, with soft words and soft ideas, he let matters slide, and was deaf to the mutterings of discontent that ran through the Douglas lands.

But he could be angered, as Wattie Laidlaw soon discovered. Gross James had not inherited all the Douglas estates, for the western lands had passed to the murdered earl's sister, the Lady Margaret. Gross James could hardly abide this, and it was his ambition to reunite the estates by arranging the marriage of Margaret (who was known as the Maid of Galloway) with his eldest son William. It was a mark of Gross James's politic skill that he had broached this proposal without disturbing Crichton and Livingstone, though they had been pleased enough to see the division of the Douglas inheritance. But Wattie Laidlaw, who had brooded bitterly on Gross James's betrayal of the boys who had been his friends, burst out in anger, and cried that 'the Maid micht as weel lick the innocent blood spilled in the yard of Edinburgh Castle as mairry the Fat Man's son.' Hearing this, the earl banged down his tankard of wine, and struggled to rise from the table. He ordered the daft boy to be seized and brought before him, and he cursed him in terms that men said were 'a sair affront to his ain dignity and proved his guilt moreover.' He had Wattie tied to the tail of a cart-horse and whipped three times round the market place in Selkirk. 'Let him learn tae lick his ain blood,' glowered the earl, as he watched the lash rise and fall and tear strips from Wattie's back. 'Sicc an insult frae my ain vassal, a bairn whae has eaten the Douglas meat and saut all his life.' He smiled to hear Wattie holler with pain like a wounded hare, and when at last the boy was released and fell in a whimpering heap that shocked and horrified the townsfolk, Gross James commanded that he should betake himself to the Abbey of Melrose and there do penance throughout the forty days of Lent. 'And niver dare present yourself again at any castle held by the Earl of Douglas,' he cried.

And so, with wandering steps, Wattie found himself at last back at Clartyshaws.

Young Clym greeted him with a black face. 'You daft gomeril,' he said. He himself had nothing to quarrel with in his new lord who was, he said, 'a douce quiet body that would dae naebody ony hairm gin they keepit their mou' shut,' and he told Wattie time and again that he must have been 'fair demented tae blether yon gait. And,' he added, 'there's nocht for you at Clartyshaws, for this is a decent seemly place, and we are quiet folk that want nae part of your crazy fancies.'

Wattie said nothing to all this, but nevertheless he bided most of that summer at Clartyshaws, though for days on end he would disappear into the high woods. It was as if the clarity with which he had envisioned the Black Dinner had marked him with an awful knowledge which frightened him and which he knew he could not escape. He was at the mercy of powers he could neither understand nor control. He had tasted the extreme savagery of man.

Young Clym, as he was still called, though he showed less and less sign of youth, meanwhile attended Gross James to excuse his kinsman's conduct and assure the earl that he had no part in it or sympathy for his views. Gross James, possibly discovering in Clym a man after his own dull heart, possibly merely happy to find at least one vassal who did not blame his failure to avenge his nephews, took a fancy to him, and rewarded his loyalty and good sense with a gift of the peel-tower and lands of Aikwood on the lower Ettrick, which some two hundred years before had belonged to the wizard and philosopher Michael Scott; not that Clym had a mind for the like, or a care for it either. Aikwood had an heiress, Anne Scott, and it was necessary of course for Young Clym to marry the girl. He was in no mood to demur at that condition, for the lands were wide, the connections good, and the young girl not positively unfavoured. So, in this manner Young Clym himself got a scrap to fall from the Black Dinner, and he rubbed his hands and warmed his heart at the thought of his new estate. The poor girl may have thought differently of the affair, and little enough of the bargain wished on her, but no one thought to consult her feelings, and the match was made and celebrated. Anyway she died in premature childbirth within seven months of the marriage, and thereafter Young Clym sometimes called himself Scott of Aikwood. He appears under both names in the rent-rolls and charters of the period.

Despite this, Clym looked on the Douglas with a wary eye. He had been impressed by the warnings given by his uncle Maurie. Though he did not trust the man, and had been brought up to hate him, and to look to revenge his father, a man of his ambition could not fail to admire Maurie's success and to listen to him. Maurie had told him to beware the Douglas, because there could not be two kings in Scotland, and the power of the Douglas threatened the Crown. 'The Douglas and the Stewart cannot lie easy in the same bed,' Maurie had said, and Clym could not forget the words. While Gross James lived, there might be no danger for Clym in the Douglas bond. Things might be different when he was gone.

So Clym sat in his new keep and reckoned up his gold and his head of cattle, and eyed the world warily. He kept in touch with his uncle across the Border in occasional communications, and he was pleased that Maurie had taken Dandy off his hands. For all that, and for all that he admired Gross James's refusal to revenge his nephews, Clym could not forget the duty his mother had enjoined on him. Maurie had been responsible for his father's death, and he had been brought up to hate him. However politic he was, the thought disturbed Clym. There were duties, he believed, a man could not escape without putting his soul in peril. So he watched, waited, and accumlated. 'You mauna cut the corn ere the grain is full,' was one of the phrases with which he larded his meagre conversation. He had a stock of such utterances; they committed you to nothing. It was hard to get a live opinion from Clym, even though you tickled him like a trout.

Gross James did not last long, dying after an Easter feast when he gobbled oysters brought from the Solway beds, and he was succeeded by his son William, who had all the Douglas dash and ambition that the Fat Man had lacked. The marriage proposed by Gross James between William and the Maid of Galloway now went ahead, for the Church's prohibition of such consanguineous unions counted for little, and was easily set aside when a Douglas was involved. Others might view this reunion of the vast Douglas estates with apprehension, but the Douglas vassals were pleased and proud, though Young Clym shook a wary head and closed one eye to indicate that others might say what they liked, but he saw rocky water ahead. Wattie however now reconciled himself to what had happened, seeing the Maid herself was willing. She had been a friend and ally since childhood. If she had been coerced into marriage by Gross James, Wattie would have sighed and kept his distance, but now he presented himself at Newark Castle in the autumn where they held a hunting party, in the knowledge that he would be welcome.

They bided there all the September and October, and the young Douglas surrounded himself with retainers to be counted in their thousands. Early in the morning the earl's huntsmen rode out with the deerhounds, and they drove the red deer into the side valleys, and the great men, the earls and barons and knights rode after them, and there was mighty slaughter under the hill-brows. Day after day it continued as the leaves turned crisp and golden, crimson red and pale yellow, and the sun shone from the frosty mornings to the red of evening on the earl's hunting, till they had killed enough to provision his households through the winter. Late every afternoon the carriers rode up on their little hill ponies and gralloched the deer, and slung them over the ponies and brought them down to the castle; they carried some into the neighbouring valleys to other castles that must be provisioned too. Fleshers were waiting in every courtyard to hang the beasts,and days later, quarter them and salt them. It was an enterprise as important as harvest.

Each evening there would be feasting in the great hall of Newark, and that was not just a time for pleasure and enjoyment, for the young earl was a masterful and ambitious politician, and this gathering of his followers was a time for counsel, encouragement, reassurance and planning. He was surrounded by his family too, for Gross James, whatever his failings in other respects, had proved himself a potent sire. Earl William had four brothers: Archibald, Earl of Moray; his twin James who was made Earl of Avondale; Hugh, Earl of Ormond and John, Lord of Balveny. They all had something of the Douglas fire mysteriously lacking in their father – except, it was presumed, in his marriage bed.

Talk at the earl's table was free and often wild. Wattie, who had attached himself to James of Avondale, attended it closely. Again and again it returned to the question of relations between the Crown and the House of Douglas. There was tension in the air, a mood of expectancy, founded on the assurance that great changes were afoot in the realm. One morning, while they rested from the hunt on the high tops, Wattie said to Lord James. 'Do you ken why your cousin, my ain lord and the friend of my boyhood was so cruelly murthered?'

'I think we do. It was the jealousy of the small man that will blot out the sun.'

'Aye,' said Wattie, 'and yet it was mair as thon. There mauna be twae kings in Scotland, and yet ony Earl of Douglas is fain to be the tither.'

'And yet, Wattie, no Earl of Douglas has ever been a rebel. No Earl of Douglas has set himself against the king. The greatness of our House was founded on the friendship of the Good Lord James with the great King Robert the Bruce, and when the Bruce inheritance passed through King Robert's daughter Marjorie to the House of Stewart, the allegiance of the House of Douglas passed unquestioningly thither too. Show me the man that will deny me that.'

'Jamie, Jamie,' Wattie said, 'you canna believe that life will aye run a straight gait. Were the Earls of Douglas brothers in bluid to the Kings of Scotia, it wad nae mair prevent things fa'in' oot as they will fa' oot than a proclamation that the sun should shine wal keep off the rain. Jamie loon, there are cruel times ahead. I hae had an inkling of days to come when the women shall weep and strang men groan wi' pain. I see naething clearly but what I see brings the saut tear tae my ee.'

'And can this be averted?'

'That I canna tell. And yet I ken this full well, that in ony extremity of life we maun act as though we had the free will tae determine what will be.'

'And so?'

'Sae, Jamie, ye maun act in politic fashion. Ye maun form a bond wi ither noblemen for your ain protection. Ye maun brak the concord atween Sir Alexander Livingstone and Sir William

Crichton. It will be ill to do, and ill medicine tae swallow, but for dire diseases the remeid itsel may be bitter. Mind well what the Dukes of Burgundy hae won for themsels in France. Gin you fail to brak the bond atween the twae wolfish keepers, I fear ye'll sup anither Black Dinner. Mark well what I say, and remember I hae listened, I hae obsairved, I hae reflected.'

Wattie's advice caught no more than the mood of the moment; the minds of the Douglas brothers were already tending in that direction. The family had, they knew, reached that point of greatness when it must either dominate the State, or submit to authority and suffer dismemberment. The Black Dinner had proved the fear that the Douglas aroused; it had shown how that fear translated itself into ruthlessness. The chief of the family stood in mortal peril unless he took measures to guard against his enemies.

So, as Wattie had urged Lord James, they first moved to detach Livingstone from Crichton; then formed a bond with David, Earl of Crawford, the greatest baron north of Forth. Meanwhile, by a mixture of generosity and threats, they secured the allegiance of the Borderlands. The earl sought the support of the Church by announcing that he would free the monks of Melrose from his jurisdiction. Canny men like Young Clym muttered that no good would come from setting themselves against the king, but wilder sparks were delighted by the new mood of unrest. Clym sat fast in Aikwood, glowering at the wall, but a band of Douglas retainers rode into England, burning farms right up to the walls of Carlisle, and rode back driving two hundred head of small red cattle before them.

That raid provoked an English response. Henry Percy, later to be the third Earl of Northumberland, crossed the western border at the head of an army of veterans from France and his own retainers. Hearing of the proposed raid in Mirabel, Dandy begged Maurie to let him ride with Percy, but Maurie shook a wary head, and said there would be fighting enough to come for matters of more importance. Meanwhile the young Douglases sang themselves to battle at the head of all the Blue Bonnets of Ettrick and Lauderdale, Teviot, and Yarrow and Annandale, and wild Liddlesdale too. They met Percy at Gretna and gave him a bloody head, for the veterans of France had no stomach for this kind of wild warfare.

There was a ferment in the land and Young Clym hated it. This sort of wild activity made a man's acres sit loose about him. No good could come of it. Moreover, Clym had thought deeply about these matters. He could not believe that his master of Douglas could prevail against the royal authority. And what anyway had the House of Douglas done for the Laidlaws of Clartyshaws? Gross James had, it was true, made him lord of Aikwood, and Aikwood was a noble tower and its lands were good; but then Gross James had only acted like a Douglas. And, again Clym brooded, had not the Earl of Douglas failed his own father, and allowed him to stumble unsupported to his death? What did he, Laidlaw of Clartyshaws and Oakwood, owe the House of Douglas? Little enough, when you thought long on the matter. And they could not win, he was sure of that.

The Lent following he went to make confession to a priest at the Abbey. He brought gifts and the knowledge that he was regarded there as a devout son of the Church and a man who could be trusted. His conversation was such, though guarded, that the Abbot summoned him to his presence. Clym entered on the dialogue warily, for he knew the benefits the Abbey had received from the Douglas, and he knew his own doubts might be ill regarded. Yet there comes a time when a man must say 'my duty is to my ain self and bairns.' Clym rubbed his hands, and thwacked his arms against his sides. 'A man should be maister of his ain fate,' he muttered.

John of Fogo was long dead, and the present Abbot was a little man, gleg as a sparrow with fluttering hands and twittering speech. 'Men tell me, my son, that you doubt your lord's intent,' he brought out at last after many preliminary hems and haws and meaningless inquiries.

Clym stiffened his shoulders and raised his head to look the Abbot in the eyes. He coughed twice. 'Aye, that I do,' he said.

The Abbot twitched twice, and said nothing.

'King's rule,' Clym said, 'is daecent rule for daecent men. The king's ain feyther said "the key shall keep the castle and the bracken bush the coo." Aye, my lord abbot, he did, and Scotland was then a daecent canty place where honest men could live an honest life. I ken fine that is how it should be, and there's nae fairmer or honest man would tell you different, gin he dared to speak the truth. A' this riding and raiding is braw wark for wild and harum-scarum lads, but it's ill for honest folk. And these are true words, my lord.'

He waited. The Abbot shifted in his seat, tugged at his ear and twittered something in an undertone to the monk who sat beside him. The monk nodded and left the chamber. 'My son,' the Abbot said, 'we have a visitor to our abbey who would be blithe to hear your words.'

He led Clym up a twisting stair to a high-vaulted room where a thin priest sat shivering by a fire piled high with roaring logs.

'This is the man we have spoken of,' the Abbot said, 'a Douglas vassal who fears the earl's intent.'

The thin priest extended a pale hand shining with an episcopal ring. 'A wise man in a mad Scotland,' he said. 'Let me hear your views, friend.'

Clym repeated what he had said to the Abbot, and the thin priest nodded. 'Do you know who I am?' he said.

Clym shook his head.

'My name is James Kennedy,' the priest said, 'and I am Bishop of the Holy See of St Andrews. Yet you find me here, seeking refuge with my brother of Melrose. And why, you may ask. Because I have been driven from my palace and from my ministration to my flock, by that same Earl of Crawford with whom the Earl of Douglas has sealed a bond. What think you of that, my son?

'I think, my lord, that them that winna respect the rights of the Haly Kirk will respect naething.'

'A good reply – from one who calls himself a simple farmer. Would that our nobles of Scotland thought as you do, my son! I am cousin to the king, being nephew to his father. I have travelled far, in France and Italy, and have sojourned with the Pope at Avignon, and I nowhere heard wiser counsel than King James's for, if there is no authority, there is no true freedom, there being no security for life or property. Here in Scotland, we are cursed and sore afflicted with a false freedom which is properly termed licence and we are cursed and afflicted by false loyalties. Men follow their liege lord even blindly into rebellion. I am come here to the Borderland to urge the Douglas to break his treasonable bond. I am glad to have met one honest man at least with the courage to refuse to follow him.'

'Weel,' Clym said, brushing his fingers across his cheek, 'I

220

canna promise exactly that, my lord, for you maun see that I hae my ain immediate interests tae protect. A man's first duty, you will tell me, is to God and the Kirk, and his next tae the King, and these are grand words, but happen they're true, it yet seems tae me, that he has aiblins a prior duty tae his ain skin, and tae his hearth and the weans it bields. Natheless, my lord, happen I can keep my ain cattle siccar in my ain bracken-bush, I gie you my word I winna mairch wi the Douglas. And I wish you weel in your mission to the earl, though I maun warn you that I canna gie muckle for your chances of success. The earl is a thrawn young man, and eaten up wi pride and the glamour of his warlike prowess.'

'Spoken like a man and an honest man,' the Bishop said. 'You have done well for yourself today, my son. Remember always that you have a true friend and well-wisher in James Kennedy. And now the Lord be with you, and with your spirit.'

He held out his hand and Clym knelt to kiss the ring.

V

The Lady Alice Neville wept for three nights before she left her father's house. However often the earl explained to her, with the patience and clarity on which he prided himself, that her marriage was necessary, and that she was entering on great possessions, he could not comfort her. It had been impossible to hide from her that her chosen husband was a monster, and when Maurie suavely joined his reassurance to her father's, the tears fell faster. She looked on him and saw a lean grey little man, with the twisted face of a cripple and an eye like cold iron, and felt afraid. Even his voice made her tremble, and when he laid his hand on her sleeve she shrank away. He smiled, and took her hand and kissed it before taking his leave, and his lips seemed to her like the touch of a rat.

'You are alarmed now, my lady,' he murmured. 'It is but natural, but trust in me and I shall see that you come to no harm. Your life will spread before you like a meadow covered with the flowers of summer.'

She turned to her cousin Edward, but he laughed at her fears.

'You must do as your father says, Alice but you are a green girl to have such terrors. I may be only a boy but I know something of the world. The lord of Cleckington is a wise and skilful man.'

'He is a slimy monster,' Alice sobbed, 'and I fear him as I would a serpent.'

'What a fool you must be, cousin, to speak like that. How can you be so blind? This marriage is the summit of his achievement, and he would rather cut off his right arm than have any harm befall you. In arranging this marriage he binds himself and the great estates of Boscobel to the Houses of York and Neville, and that is a great stroke of policy.'

'But,' her heart sobbed, 'I crave for love and I am to be married to a monster.'

There was only one face that did not fill her with fear or disgust. She could not look on her father who had betrayed her. She despised her cousin Edward who had no mind for her fears. She loathed and trembled to see the cripple who had ensnared her. But the boy who had come with Edward to the garden, and had looked at her in a manner that called a blush to her cheek, who now rode a yard behind her, was different. He alone, it seemed to Alice, saw her as a girl, and not as a pawn in the great game. She bit her fingers and pictured his dawning smile.

Dandy experienced a new feeling: tenderness. He pitied the girl as much as he desired her. Her face floated before his eyes at night and he heard her soft voice in his dreams. He made excuses and found occasions to speak to her merely to have her sweet face before his eyes and her low cool voice in his ears. He burned with indignation at the thought of what they had condemned her to endure, and of what they had denied her; and then of what he was himself denied.

'Pish and tush,' Maurie said, 'the girl will come to no harm. It will be a marriage in name only.'

'Can we bring him to the altar?'

The Lady Clare flushed to the roots of her hair. 'I cannot bear to look at him,' she said, 'I cannot let my eyes rest on him. It disgusts me to think that that crept out of my womb – and what pain I suffered to bring that forth.' She laid her hand in Maurie's lap. 'Little crookback,' she said, 'it is, as you know two years since I have seen the beast, and I cannot endure ever laying eyes on him again.'

Dandy plied his uncle Will with wine, and then more wine. He drank cup for cup with him, till his wits were loosened, and he spoke wildly, things that were better left unsaid and that it was fortunate Will would never call to mind.

They drank deep into the night, while the castle lowered silently about them, and the owl cried through the black waste, and the dogs lay asleep at their feet.

'Never cross Maurie,' Will repeated for perhaps the tenth time that night. 'Never cross Maurie, for those that do so are ill served. You may think it craven of me, nephew, to hae sic a dread of my ain brother, but from the days when we were bairns thegither, I hae kent there was that that was uncanny about him. Never till my dying day shall I forget the look on his face as he brought the flat of his sword doon on the shelt that carried the Gudeman of Hangingshaws, and saw the shelt gallop off leaving the man swinging from the tree – a man that Maurie murdered, as sure as I hope to be saved, for sheer pleasure of the deed.'

But Dandy was persistent – he had the Laidlaw stubbornness that Will lacked. And he knew what he wanted, and pressed Will to deliver. Will had access to the idiot, for there was something in Will's dullness that the idiot seemed to recognize, and they had found that Will could pacify him even in his wildest moods.

'I'll nae dae it,' he said again and again. 'Maurie would flay the skin frae my back.'

But Dandy begged him and urged him, and at last he consented.

'We'll take some wine wi' us,' Will said. 'The idiot likes a sup of wine and it maks him easier.'

'Where's he kept?' Dandy asked, 'for he's that well hidden that in a' my time here I havena learned that.'

'Aye,' said Will, 'he's keepit fair away, and for gude reason.'

Dandy followed him down three flights of twisting stairs. Will carried a lantern but shaded it as they went. Dandy felt his way along the dripping wall, and they seemed to be descending into the bowels of the earth. It was black as hell, and there was no sound but their footsteps echoing behind them. Once Will stopped to listen, and then they could hear the rustle and scraping of rats' claws. At last they came to a heavy metal-studded door. Will produced a huge key from his belt and fitted it in the lock. It groaned as he turned.

'Are ye prepared?' he said and pushed the door open.

Dandy could see nothing. Will uncovered the lantern and held it aloft. They were in a small room about ten feet square. It seemed to be quite bare of furniture and at first Dandy thought it was empty.

'What manner of trick is this?' he cried.

'Hist,' Will muttered. 'Keep your voice down. Loud voices alarm the puir cratur.'

Then, as his eyes grew accustomed to the dim light Dandy

made out a heap of rags piled in the corner. The rags shifted and he saw they covered a body. It moved again and he heard a rattle of chains. It moved again and a face appeared. It was a tiny head, the size perhaps of a year-old child's, and shone white and beardless in the light of the lantern. Dandy drew back in horror: not even in travelling fairs had he seen such a travesty of a face. The creature had only one eye, and the right side of the face ran smooth and unmarked from brow to chin. The nose was flat and wide-nostrilled, but the huge gaping mouth twisted downwards to the left corner of the chin.

'Aye,' Will said, 'yon's the lord of Boscobel.'

'And,' Dandy breathed, 'they would marry thon pure young girl – to . . . this . . . this mockery of nature.'

'He's the lord of great possessions,' Will hiccuped.

He moved forward and clapped the rags just below the head. They stirred in response, and heaved upwards. The tiny head was seen to be mounted on a trunk of massive proportions. The shoulders and hands would not have disgraced a blacksmith, but when it struggled to its feet Dandy could see that it was mounted on grotesquely short, if also very thick, legs. The whole thing could not have stood more than four feet high, and of that the trunk made up at least two-thirds. It was broad too, and it whimpered to see Will.

'Aye, cratur,' Will said, 'and you're blithe tae see us, poor besom that you are, inasmuch as you can be thought capable of pleasure.'

He thrust out the wineskin, and the monster (as Dandy thought of him who was Lord of Boscobel) heaved it to his slobbering mouth, and gulped, the wine spilling down the chin.

'I've seen enough,' Dandy said. 'I did not think it could be as bad.'

'Na, na,' Will said, 'but you would hae me come, and noo we're here, we'll keep the poor cratur company.'

The Lady Alice lay in a green meadow by a slow river. She was quite alone and plaited daisies into a chain as she listened to the lapping water. There was a scent of thyme and wild camomile and her heart was still as the evening sky. A solitary horseman appeared on the hillside across the stream. The sun lit up his face and she saw that it was Dandy. She made no sign but waited his approach. Behind him, on top of the hill, as he moved into the shadows, the sun touched a broken chapel with fire. The horse's hooves swished through the dewy grass as it picked its way circuitously to the water. With no aid from its rider it stepped into the stream. She held her breath, but still the boy seemed not to see her though he was moving towards her. She half-rose to her feet, and, as she did so, the sun dropped beneath the hill, a night breeze blew so cold that she hugged her mantle round her body, and man and horse vanished under the black water.

She gave a cry and woke shivering.

Maurie lived in a fever of activity. It seemed to him that he had come to an end of waiting, that all his life had prepared him for the opportunities that now lay within his grasp. For the first time even his mistress lost her hold on him. He looked at her and saw a woman who had withered on the tree. She plied the hare's-foot over her scraggy neck, and complained of stomach pains. She suffered from night fears, and spent hours with her confessor. When Maurie chided her she looked at him with dull resentment and made no reply.

'What ails her?' he said to Brother Ambrose.

'Timor mortis conurbat illam, which is to say, my lord, that she is beginning to look on life as a foreign country, and to fear that she will be called to judgement for her sins.'

'Sins?' Maurie said. The friar chuckled.

'You and I, my friend, may be robust enough to bear the weight of our actions. Not all are so fortunate. Your lady is no more of our company.'

'The plague upon it' Maurie said. 'Can you discover what she confesses to her priest?'

'Rest assured. Her sins will remain locked up in his breast.'

Meanwhile preparations for the marriage went on apace. The contracts were signed. Maurie was named administrator of the estates; Lady Alice's dowry was consigned to his care. There was a constant coming and going between him and Warwick, Truncheon acting as the intermediary trusted by both parties. 'Very soon,' Maurie thought to himself, 'very soon . . .' His fingers itched, and the Lady Clare's coldness hardly perturbed him. York would be Regent – or perhaps more – Warwick would rise with him and he himself . . .

There came a knock at his door and Dandy entered. Maurie greeted him and bade him take a seat. The boy frowned. He had lost some of the bloom of youth, and Maurie found himself looking at him differently. He was pleased to be able to do so. There had been something disquieting in the tenderness with which he had regarded him; it was like riding against your enemies without a breastplate. Now he saw only a young man, capable certainly, but not now . . . what was the word . . . vulnerable? Dandy was still his man, but no longer called for his protection. Maurie smiled; he had been in danger, he knew it now. 'He who forms an attachment is lost,' he scribbled.

Dandy said, 'I have that I maun confess to you, uncle. And I am near afeared to do so.'

Maurie waited; let the boy find his own way to tell him.

'I've seen him,' Dandy said.

'Who do you mean?'

'I mean, I've seen the . . . thing you keep chained up.'

'Have you now?'

'Uncle,' Dandy hesitated, 'uncle, how could you do it?'

'I'll not pretend,' Maurie said, 'that I do not understand you. I'll do you that courtesy. And I'll not pretend that I feel no sympathy for your indignation. You're but a boy and ignorant of the world. Maybe I have spoiled you. It's natural you should feel as you do, natural enough. I daresay you have a fondness for the girl even. And I'll not blame you for that. But it must stop there, and you must listen to me. Now sit down. That's an order, and listen.'

He waited till the boy had settled, and himself got up and limped to the window. It was a grey afternoon without, but the sky was clearing from the west, and there would be frost that night. From the pool by the grey willows below the castle, a heron rose, and Maurie watched as it flapped its slow wide-winged way across the sky and out of sight. He drew his furs round him.

'She's a pretty maid,' he said, speaking almost as if he had forgotten the boy's presence, for he continued to gaze out over the afternoon and his voice was quiet, 'and may well deserve better. But what are women for? They are for us to use as we use our horses, here for our service. Ladies of high degree are pawns in affairs of state, and so this marriage has been made, and for that reason it must go on. I have sworn to her father that she will come to no harm, and that it will be a marriage in name only. But the alliance this marriage represents is the heartbeat of myself. I have struggled, I have made myself what I am, from nothing, and I will not be baulked now. This marriage, which is my making, binds me to Warwick, and Warwick is pleased to be bound.' He turned back to face the boy. 'You daft gomeril, do you think I shall let a boy like you set himself against my plans? I have a tenderness for you, boy, how I cannot tell, for I long ago resigned the cares of blood, and chose to go my solitary way; but still I have a kindness for you, and yet, as the Devil is my witness I had sooner see you bound to a horse's tail and whipped all the way from York to Berwick or the Carter Bar ere I would let you set yourself up as an impediment to my plans. And who did you persuade to lead you to my lord of Boscobel?'

Dandy shrank from his tone. He felt a fear which he had never known in his life, and which he was never to forget. With the fear came shame, as he heard himself confess Will's part in the affair.

Maurie laughed: 'He was ever a useless fellow, and to blame Will is to confess your own guilt. But we'll hear no more of it. The marriage will go on, and your fears are groundless. The lass will come to no harm. But, mind this well, boy, you will yourself do nothing that might sully her honour. I'll not have Warwick say we made a whore of his daughter.'

Dandy had no answer. But he fumed, and suffered. He knew that Maurie was wrong. Though he accepted the ruthlessness of politics, and, as the future would show, was capable of great and thoughtless cruelty himself, nevertheless he revolted from Maurie's argument. The girl should not be used in this way. How he would prevent it he did not know, but he had made up his mind.

He had of course fallen in love. He could not see her without excitement and though his tongue still froze when they had opportunity for speech, he knew she felt the same. The air quivered between them, and he was amazed that others should be blind to their passion. He was her knight, and he saw her as a maiden about to be sacrificed to a dragon, as certainly as the heroine of any of the tales of chivalry with which the castle minstrels were ready to charm his ears.

The days drew on towards Christmas when the wedding was intended to take place. Snow fell on the hills, then on the lower moors, and at last lay thick in the courtyard of Mirabel. Maurie worked late hours in his chamber and Dandy sat with his uncle Will and drank and thought of the Lady Alice lying in her chamber, and of how he might contrive to see her alone. He dared not confide in Will, for he had learned the truth of Maurie's judgement that Will was a blabbermouth, and he had no friend in the castle whom he could trust.

At last one night, perplexed to the point of desperation, he made the direct approach. Having ascertained that Maurie was occupied in his own room, he slipped up a back staircase and knocked on the door of her chamber. One of her women opened the door and would have denied him entry, but he thrust past her and into the room.

Alice started up on seeing him. Her women had been tending to her hair and it lay loose on her shoulders. She wore a white shift, and looked at him in wonder. He couldn't tell what fears ran through her mind, and, in an ecstasy of excitement and apprehension, dropped to his knee before her. She drew back then catching hold of herself and seeing the expression on his face, stood absolutely still. She waved her hand to silence her ladies. 'You should not be here.'

He swallowed, and shook his head. 'Lady,' he said, 'I hae come to offer you my help.'

'Your help?'

'My help and my service.'

She was thinner than when he had first seen her in the rose garden of Raby, and there were dark hollows in her cheeks. She looked pale and fragile and afraid, and he longed to take her in his arms, but dared make no move which might be false.

'Alas,' she said, 'and how can you help me? How can any man help me?'

He did not move. 'Lady,' he said again, and paused . . .

'I am condemned by my father's will to this mockery of a marriage.'

'There are lands beyond Cheviot,' he said, 'if we could win away.'

They halted on that word 'if'. Both were for a moment appalled by the dangers and rewards it held; both were struck to silence by the understanding that had come upon them. She stretched out her hand and stroked his cheek. He clutched it and pressed it to his lips.

'So little time,' she sighed.

'And so you dare?'

She looked round to canvass her ladies, but none dared meet her eye.

'Are you sure, my bonny boy?'

Brother Ambrose laid his tankard of ale on the table, and seized Robin Cochrane by the elbow. He pressed his thumb and forefinger on the nerve till the boy squirmed and squealed with pain.

'Are you sure, laddie?' he asked again, and released him.

The boy pouted.

'That hurt. Of course I'm sure.'

'Clever boy.' The friar slipped his hand under the boy's tunic and pinched his buttock. 'Clever boy. Come sit with me, and tell me all.'

'Promise you won't be angry,' the boy said, settling himself on the friar's knee and putting his hands round his neck. 'Promise you won't be angry, no matter what I say.'

'Young limb of Satan,' the friar planted a smacking kiss on the boy's lips. 'Young limb of Satan, artificer of genius and delight, tell me all. Reveal your lust, depravity and treachery and it shall only bind you the more powerfully to my heart.'

'Well, then,' the boy said, returning the friar's kiss. 'Well then . . .'

His story was simple. He had been happy, the boy said, to follow his lover's instructions, and try to ingratiate himself with Dandy, all the more because he found him – he giggled – very desirable. It had piqued him that Dandy seemed indifferent to his advances of friendship, all the more because he was quite certain – again he pouted – that Brother Ambrose was right in asserting that the boy was not wholly given to girls. 'He has so much ardour,' he said, 'that I knew that, if aroused, he would be full of passion, for he loves himself and I know that from the admiring way in which he strokes his hair.' But, no matter what hints Robin dropped, and what seductive glances or suggestions he offered, Dandy remained insensible. So then it seemed to Robin that the only thing to do was to take him by storm, and he had accordingly three nights before slipped over to Dandy's couch, intending to join him there and convinced that, in the dark of night, his enticements and charms would not be resisted. Then, to his surprise, he had found the couch deserted. So the next night he had watched, and seen Dandy slip away and had followed him. Where? To the Lady Alice's chamber. He had seen him enter, and, mindful of his duty to Brother Ambrose, had concealed himself to await his departure; which had not taken place till many hours had passed.

'And why did you not come to me then?' the friar asked.

'I wanted to be sure.' The boy tossed his hair out of his eyes. 'Besides. I was curious. And jealous. What has that whey-faced girl that he should prefer her to me?'

So he had watched again last night, and followed him. Only this time – he blushed – Dandy must have been more wary and on his guard, for suddenly, as Robin turned a corner, he found his throat seized and there was Dandy standing over him, with an expression of fury on his face.

'He called me "little spy", and harsher names, and threatened to thrash me within an inch of my life if he ever caught me following him again.'

Then, though Robin chose not to tell this to the friar, Dandy swung him round and gave him a great boot on the backside which sent him flying down the stairs; and then laughed 'that's nobbut a taste, you popinjay.'

'And I hate him,' he said, 'him and that witch who has enchanted him.'

They had talked the matter through. Haltingly at first she had confessed her fear and loathing of the match; he had disclosed his passion. She allowed herself to be embraced, while her ladies protested in a manner that hardly hid their pleasure or their fears. Then she dismissed them to wait in the antechamber, and for a long time the boy and girl sat holding hands and hardly daring to go further. Little by little however they advanced their love. He was like a man released from a dungeon into sunlight. 'A proper pair of turtle doves,' crooned one of the ladies who had risked a peep round the arras. 'A pretty sight and well suited, and well does our sweet lady merit such a pretty boy,' her companion sighed, 'and yet we must not let matters go too far.' No, my dear, but they are still some way short of that stage.' And the two women hugged each other in the joy of their complicity.

For half hour perhaps joy drove out fear and the present eclipsed what was to come. But long before dawn they were seized with renewed alarm. What after all was to be done? Alice swore that her ladies were to be trusted and that of course was just as well, for they had already seen so much that a word from them would doom the pair. Since they were trustworthy they must be consulted, for both, Alice assured her lover, had an experience of the world that they lacked themselves.

That was true enough, no doubt. But their experience was nevertheless not such as could suggest a plan. Indeed they seemed only able to perceive difficulties. No, they advised, it was impossible that Dandy should go to Warwick and reveal the enormity of the proposed match. The earl was a politician first and last. He had weighed the affair and knew well to what he was committing his daughter. (Alice shed a tear and was happy to let Dandy kiss it away). There could be no doubt, they said, that he had sought information about her proposed husband. He would not have relied merely on what Dandy's uncle told him. Therefore he was fully committed to the marriage. And at that, they too wept; which solved nothing and advanced the argument not at all.

Their present course was folly. They were agreed on that, Each stolen visit offered a new risk. And yet they could not deny themselves the pleasure of these hours together. Dandy had not dared mention his encounter with the friar's boy, lest Alice panic and refuse to see him; so he convinced himself that the meeting had been fortuitous and that the boy suspected nothing.

All the same he had doubts. To allay them he sought out Robin and, looking embarassed and wanting to kick the boy again, apologized for his outburst of temper. The boy fluttered his eyelashes at him and smirked, and Dandy tried to keep a smile on his face. The boy made an unambiguous suggestion and Dandy nodded, sick in the stomach, but able to tell himself that all was well and that Robin didn't suspect the truth.

But the truth could not be hidden long. Dandy was shaken from his confusion of shame and disgust, lust and tender longing, by a peremptory summons to his uncle's presence. He found Maurie attended by Brother Ambrose, who leered at him as he entered. Maurie sat behind a heavy table, his fingers playing with the relics which dangled on gold and silver chains from his neck. When he spoke, his voice was quiet as a hawk's flight.

'I trusted you,' he said, 'aye, and indulged you, foolishly, called you nephew, and would have made a great man of you; and now my friend here brings me reports of charges laid against you which would see you excommunicated by decree of Holy Church, surrendered to the civil power, which is myself, to be sentenced to be flayed, gelded, hanged and disembowelled.

'I do not understand. Of what do I stand accused?'

'Sodomy, nephew.'

'A vile sin,' the friar said, 'which stinks in the nostrils of God and Man.'

'You would never . . .' Dandy paused, crimsoning.

'Never say I would never,' Maurie said.

This is a vile conspiracy . . . to conceal . . .'

'Your true offence? But it will serve, I promise you, nephew.'

'Our witness,' the friary said, 'your partner in shame, is all contrition. He sheds copious tears, throws himself prostrate, babbling to the saint and the Mother of God for intercession.'

'What will you have of me? Not my life, uncle?'

Maurie snapped a relic from its chain.

'How dared you,' he said, 'come atween me and my purposes? How dared you endeavour to set aside what I have willed? If you were a man and not a lad, if I did not – for some reason which I cannot fathom – retain a certain tenderness for you, I would break you . . . But . . .'

'But I have advised my lord,' the friar said, 'that your sins are but the follies of hot youth . . . and such a youth.'

He smiled again. Dandy dropped his gaze.

Maurie said, 'You have till darkness to be gone. And you may thank God knows what for my . . . unexampled clemency.'

'Thank rather the bloom in your cheek,' the friar said.

VI

Dandy reproached himself all the ride north, and reproached Alice too. If his nerve had failed, so had hers. They should have risked all. They should not have delayed. He paused at a wayside inn, and when a man asked where he came from and whither he was going, turned his face away, as if in shame.

Alice would have had him run for Ravenspur and a ship to France. There were great opportunities, she had heard, for a young Scot of good birth and bearing, in the Company of Archers which guarded King Charles and in whom alone he trusted. Dandy, setting aside the matter of his love, was sorely tempted. To move into a new world, to cut the tether that held him to the past – it was certainly a prospect ... but ... he paused on the thought. To follow that course was to abandon all hope that he might be able to take his revenge on the uncle who had thwarted him and chosen to inflict such horror on Alice. And so he had turned his horse's head to the north.

It was a slow cold wearisome journey, for the snow lay over all the land and a keen wind blew from the north-east. It bit into his face, so that his eyes watered; but at least offered some excuse for his tears. He saw Alice's face before him: the dark eyes, the pale and cream skin, the curving lips he had possessed and been robbed of. He had no words for his grief, no words to salve his pain, but as the wind snapped at his face, and his horse struggled through the snow, anger filled him, driving out sorrow, and was then itself replaced by fatigue and the demanding difficulties of the journey.

Of course he made for the Douglas. There was nowhere else, no other lord to whom he might attach himself. And he was made welcome, for the new spirit of adventure which reigned there now that Gross James had given way to the young earl meant that young men such as Dandy were in demand. The experiences of the last weeks had toughened and matured him.

The sunny and open-hearted boy who had ridden south with Maurie was no more; instead Dandy now presented a grim face to the world, and there was a wild zest in him that made him a natural leader and one who had little care for the consequences of his actions.

He soon had the opportunity to prove himself. There was a man named Kerr, a small baron holding an estate near Jedburgh, who crossed the Douglas over a strip of land which was also claimed by a Douglas vassal. This Kerr, like many of his family, was a dour thrawn pig of a fellow, accustomed to having his own way, and ready to boast that he feared neither King nor Douglas. When the Douglas sent knights to remonstrate with him, tell him to give up the land and keep a civil tongue in his head, he turned black with rage. When they assured him, as they had been instructed to do, that if he gave way in this matter, and thereafter showed himself respectful and sensible of their lord's authority, he could thenceforth rely on the Douglas's protection, he uttered a great roar, like an infuriated bull, lowered his black head, which was round and hard as a cannon-ball, and rammed the first knight so mightily in the midriff that he fell off the bridge where they were debating and toppled into a muddy stream. Then Kerr snatched up a great axe and swung it round his head, yelling that he did not give a docken for all the Douglases the black Deil had ever spawned; and he presented so fearsome a picture that not one of them cared to be the first to challenge him, but all took to their heels and scampered off in disgrace and confusion.

As might be expected, this incident made a great stir, and all those, who for one reason or another, had cause to fear or resent the Douglas, made much of it and took heart. And, worst of all, laughter rang across the Borderland from the walls of Berwick to the Solway Firth. There were many toasts drunk to Kerr in that harvest's ale.

Young Dandy heard the laughter and measured the mockery. He saw the earl's frown, and saw his chance to gain distinction.

Two weeks later Kerr rode into Jedburgh to the sheep market and made ready to sell his flock. Dandy, with a band of a dozen scallywags he had recruited, took note of this, and stationed his men round the ringside. Whenever Kerr was seen to approach a man he hoped might buy his sheep, the man soon found himself surrounded, jostled and menaced. This happened half a dozen times, and on each occasion the likely buyer drew off, some putting forward the excuse that the sheep were of poorer quality that Kerr was accustomed to produce, others making no excuse at all but just slipping off with a quick glance over the shoulder. Kerr was quick to see what was happening, but, being (as all knew) pig-thrawn, said nothing and just kept approaching buyers. But all the time he looked grimmer and grimmer, and men watched, some happily, others uneasily, to see what would happen. Finally, Kerr's command of his temper snapped. He turned on Dandy, whom he had identified as the ringleader, and abused him roundly. No one later disputed that Kerr had made the first direct approach. His hand went to his dirk. Dandy gave him the smile of a boy who has got his way, and, without a word of warning, whipped out his own dirk and thrust it into Kerr's belly. His men crowded round the big man, their dirks jabbing at him, like a flock of angry birds. At last they let him fall. His blood trickled across the market place and into the gutter.

Dandy wiped his dirk on a piece of sacking. 'So perish all enemies of the House of Douglas.'

'Obedience is the fruit of fear,' he said as he rode home.

That episode made him a man of note, and bound him tightly to his earl. As for Douglas himself, he now regarded a trial of strength in the kingdom as inevitable. That feeling was general. Wattie summed it up when he was heard to say that his lord maun back his claim to the hilt, or live scorned and despised by all true men. He shook his head as he spoke, for Wattie was never warlike, and men's knowledge of his nature made his words all the more impressive. So Douglas, who was ever mindful of the fate that had befallen his cousin on the day of the Black Dinner, now renewed his solemn and indissoluble bond with the northern earls of Crawford and Ross. They swore to stand by one another, against all men, the king included; they went that far: to name the king himself in their bond.

This was rank and open treason, such as sent a shiver down the spine of all prudent and timid men. Young Clym, hearing the news, told his beads, counted his money and stayed close at home. Then, to fortify himself, the Douglas called on all who loved him and owed allegiance to him to prove their faith by swearing their adherence to his league. Many tumbled over themselves to do so – Dandy among the first of them – for to such the prospect of civil war was deeply attractive. A few canny ones held out. Some offered excuses, if timidly, others held silent and hoped their defiance might pass unnoticed. Young Clym pondered the matter two or three days, weighed his lord's chances and crossed the Border into England. That was the measure of his alarm, for, in doing so, he left his estates to the tender mercies of his master. But he was taking the long view of things, as was ever his nature.

Dandy, hearing of his cousin's flight, at once went to the Douglas and asked that Clym be declared to have abandoned his estates with his allegiance to the Douglas, and that therefore Aikwood and Clartyshaws devolved on him.

'You have proved your merit but once,' the Douglas replied. 'Prove it again, and we shall see.'

Dandy fell to his knee. 'What you command, I shall perform.'

Others had been less prudent and less fortunate then Clym. One bonnet-laird by name Maclellan of Bombie, declined to take the oath, and was rash enough to remain at home. 'We maun encourage the others,' the Douglas said calling Maclellan to Dandy's attention.

'There are mair lands as Aikwood and Clartyshaws,' he said, and Dandy smiled, and called the men who had helped him deal with Kerr to horse. They rode by night and surprised Maclellan at his morning porridge.

'Finish your parritch,' Dandy said, 'for whae can tell, Maclellan, gin you will sup the night.'

Then they bound him to a horse with his hands tied behind his back, and carried him to Douglas Castle, where he was confined.

Maclellan's wife had screamed at Dandy till he threatened to have her ducked in her own well if she didn't hold her tongue, but, as soon as he was gone she took more practical action. She despatched her son (whom she had hustled to the hay-loft to keep him out of Dandy's sight) to the King's Court at Linlithgow, 'and mind well,' she said, 'that you speir for your feyther's uncle Sir Patrick Gray, whae is captain o' the King's Gaird and the yin man can save your feyther. O these are waeful times, but haste ye, son.'

Sir Patrick heard what his nephew had to say and at once

demanded to see the king. King James, who was fully aware of the danger of the bond between Douglas and the northern earls, of the threat to his own authority and the danger of his position, recognized that he must support Sir Patrick or lose the respect and support of his own followers. Nevertheless he hesitated. The birthmark on his cheek, which had earned him the name James of the Fiery Face, shone red as the evening sun, but his fingers tapped the table at which he sat. Then he rose and walked up and down the chamber several times, while Sir Patrick waited.

'My lord,' said Sir Patrick.

'Aye aye,' said the king flapping his arm at him in his perturbation.

'My lord,' said Sir Patrick again, 'gin the Douglas is permitted to seize any lord he pleases whae has the courage to put his lealty to Your Grace above his duty to the Douglas, why, then, your Grace will find that there will be few . . .'

'Do you think I dinna ken that?' cried the king. 'Do you think, Sir Patrick, that you are dealing wi a blind man that doesna see the lie of the land? And, yet, Sir Patrick, your nephew is the Douglas's ain vassal. There's no mony of our great lords would thank me to come between them and their vassals. . .'

'By our lady,' Sir Patrick said, 'Your Grace may think yourself fortunate that no mony of your great lords have yet set themselves against you. And yet, how many will continue to obey you, gin they see the Douglas is permitted to make his own law?'

'Aye,' said the king, twisting his fingers together, 'and how and if the Douglas doesna heed our commands to release your nephew?'

'Why then,' Sir Patrick said, 'he is guilty of the grossest treason.'

'Which he is already,' the king replied, 'by reason of his bond with the Earls of Crawford and Ross, and there is naething I can do about it, no, nor dare do. Nevertheless, Sir Patrick, for the love I bear you, I will consent to do as you ask.'

And so Sir Patrick rode south, and, on the second day, arrived at Douglas Castle as the earl was sitting down to dine. He rose from his chair and embraced Sir Patrick as if they were old friends.

'I take it kindly of the King's Grace,' he said, 'that he has sent you here, for there is no man I respect more highly than you Sir Patrick, and none whom the whole kingdom holds in higher respect neither.'

'Aye aye, my lord,' Sir Patrick said. 'these are fine words. But fine words will fly nae feathers. I hae here a letter delivered under the royal seal commanding you to deliver my nephew of Bombie intil my hands.'

'Your nephew is it?' the Douglas said. 'Weel, now, and that is a great relief to me, for I give you my word it is a sair embarrassment to me to be obliged to gie lodging to the rash chiel. But Sir Patrick,' he smiled 'you hae ridden hard and lang, and you canna hae dined. Now it is weel kent that it is ill tae come between a man and his dinner, and a thing that offends the very laws of hospitality. Forbye, besides your nephew, there is muckle matter of great concern to the affairs of the kingdom to be discussed atween you and me. Yet there is nae gude talk to be had atween a full man and a fasting. Therefore you shall dine first on our gude Galloway beef and a cup of red wine or mug of yill, whichever is your fancy, and then we'll to business.'

So Sir Patrick sat down to eat, lulled by the young earl's friendly words and smile. And, as he did so, the Douglas beckoned to Dandy, and spoke to him in an undertone. Dandy slipped from the Hall and down to the dungeons to make the prisoner ready.

It was a spring evening and warm and light when they rose from the table.

'Now,' the Douglas said, 'for form's sake you maun gie me the king's letter for I would never have it said that I declined to read the king's words or neglected them.'

So he read it, and smiled again.

'Weel, Sir Patrick, though this is written in peremptory style ill-befitting the Earl of Douglas to receive, yet, for the love and respect I bear you, I shall grant your request. Come with me and I shall deliver the Laird of Bombie.'

He took Sir Patrick by the arm and led him out of the hall and down the stairs and out on to the Castle Green. A dark shape lay there by a block of wood and Dandy and another half-dozen men-at-arms stood by.

'What hae we here?' asked the Douglas, and Dandy stepped forward and drew back the cloth to reveal what lay beneath.

'Alas, Sir Patrick,' the Douglas said, 'you are come too late.

Yonder lies your sister's son, but he wants the heid. However, as the king requests, I yield him to you. Do with him what you will.'

Sir Patrick Gray looked the Douglas in the face. He looked at Dandy and the men-at-arms. He looked long at his nephew's body. He signalled for his horse which was led up to him. He put his foot in the stirrup and swung himself into the saddle. Then he leant down and said: 'My lord Douglas, as you hae ta'en his heid, you maun dispose of the body yourself. It is nae mair use to me than it would be to the poor loon that was leal to his king, and has suffered for that lealty.'

He spoke slowly and quietly, as if in sorrow rather than anger, and he turned his horse's head and walked it to the castle gate, leaving a silence behind him in which there was something of shame and horror. Only when he was under the gate and could see the ribbon of road stretched before him did he rise in his stirrups and turn himself round to cry out: 'If I live, my lord, I shall see you are rewarded for this crime.'

And then he dug his spurs in the beast and clattered over the drawbridge putting it to the gallop as soon as he hit the roadway.

VII

Clym found it hard to sleep at nights. He was forever tormented by fears for the security of his lands. He dreaded the revenge the Douglas might have taken. Would he not have given them to another? The thought made Clym toss and turn; and yet, no matter how perturbed he was, he was sure he had been wise in his judgement. The words of Bishop Kennedy echoed in his mind: 'there is no security for property without true authority.' And then Clym grew bitter and resentful: it was a fine state of affairs when a solid man like himself had to scamper for his life like a hare chased by hounds. What was the Earl of Douglas better than a thief in the night?

It irked him to wait on events, and yet what else could he do? He sat hours in ale-houses drinking little and pondering the matter, while his eyes searched the faces of other travellers. And, as he did so, he refined his thoughts.

It was impossible that in the long run the Earl of Douglas should defeat the king. Would he not therefore be wiser to make his way back to the north, and present himself at the royal court? He would be secure too. And yet he always came back to the same point: he would be insignificant. He had nothing to offer.

Another man might have preferred to leave the matter to chance. Even Clym considered doing this. Several times, as he sat at the table, he took a coin from his pocket and balanced it on his thumb with his thumb nail crooked behind his first finger. He could send the coin spinning and abide by its decision. For was he not insignificant in England too? What had he to offer anyone?

At that question, to which he found himself recurring time and again, Clym's mood would become ever sourer. He cursed the Douglas who had cheated him of his security by his rash ambition. He cursed his fathers who had not provided him with a bigger patrimony. He cursed the king for his feebleness. He cursed the barmaid who drew his ale and laughed with the other customers of the tavern. In short Clym cursed the whole world that had arranged itself to spite him.

What, he asked himself again, could he hope to achieve in England? He had had some thought of seeking help from the des Moulins or offering his services to them. After all, he reasoned, they had an old claim on the Douglas lands. The king might have to call in English help to subdue the Douglas, and the price of that help might easily be the restoration of their claim. And yet, wasn't it too distant in time? And why should that benefit him, even if it happened? His own father after all . . . but Clym thrust that thought aside.

Nevertheless he did present himself at Castle Greer. He was received with suspicion and treated as another beggarly Scot. He persevered. He found a sergeant who promised, in exchange for a small bribe (the smallest possible), that he would arrange a meeting with the Lord Edward. 'If I find his lordship sober,' the sergeant added, making Clym regret his coin.

He spent three weeks kicking his heels in the castle outskirts. He lived cannily all this time, avoiding conversation lest he come on an Englishman eager to pick a quarrel with any wandering Scot. He dined as inconspicuously as possible at the bottom table, among travelling riff-raff, and there was nothing in their conversation to encourage him. He began to realize that England's troubles were such that few would care what happend north of the border. There was a storm brewing here too. His hand tightened on his tankard of ale. Was the whole world in conspiracy to cheat him?

He looked up at the high table and saw the Lord Edward, a scarecrow of a man with lank grey hair like rats' tails and a slobbering mouth which he couldn't keep away from the wine-flask, and the sight dismayed him. How could he have thought that rescue might be found in such a quarter?

And yet there was no going back. With the greatest caution he sounded the sergeant, as the only man who might be thought to lie under any obligation to him, about his uncle Maurie. The sergeant laid his finger to his nose. Clym took the hint, and that night the pair of them sat in a little ale-house beneath the town wall of Greer. He grudged every pint the sergeant drank – at his expense. The man was loth to speak of Maurie, even though he had promised to do so. Clym asked him if he was afraid.

'Afraid? Is it a beggarly Scot, a mean farmer – for such you have told me you are – in dispute with his lord and running for fear of his life from him – that has the insolence to suggest that Will Nym, who has served in the French Wars like his father, aye, and grandfather before him, who had been bred to the trade of war, and . . .'

But at this point he lost the thread of his involved sentence, and sank his lips in his beer-mug.

'You know not what you ask,' he muttered.

'You have seen the Lord Edward,' he said at last, 'aye and judged him, and judged him fairly, I'll be bound.'

Clym nodded his head.

'And have you asked yourself what brought him to this pitch?'

'No, that I hanna. I judged he was ever thus.'

'Not he,' the sergeant said, 'the young Lord Edward was as bonny and blithe a lord as you could have wished to see. But he took the crabbit Scotchman of whom you ask, that is now Lord of Cleckington, to his bosom, and he would have been better advised to lodge a viper there. That is the cause of his undoing, that and the crimes in which the Scotchman has made him an accomplice. I tell you, friend, you had better preach heresy and trust yourself to the mercies of Holy Church, than to such a man.'

'And yet, men say there is a curse on him,' Clym said.

'That he is accursed I cannot doubt. And yet many a man carries a curse to a long distant grave, for I have observed that them that are deeply cursed are often like to live long.'

'From what you say, my uncle has lived long enough.'

'He will live longer. Yet if I were to survive myself long enough to see him with a rope round his neck, I believe I could die at peace.'

'There,' Clym said, 'we are at one. Help me to that day, and you will be rewarded.'

'Pish and tush,' the sergeant said, 'and what reward could I look for from a mean Scot like yourself that grudges me every mug of ale?'

Clym swallowed the insult. He would swallow many such. He

said: 'I have a special reason for my hatred of my uncle,' and then he paused as if afraid that he had said too much.

The sergeant rose from the table. 'If that is so, my friend, you would do well not to blab of it. No tavern is a safe place. And as for me, I wish to hear nothing of it. I have no desire to cross my lord of Cleckington.'

Clym brooded on this conversation. It brought home to him how great a man Maurie had become, and suggested at the same time that he might be wise to dissemble his feelings for Maurie and even look for help in that quarter. Yet he paused, impressed by the sergeant's warning.

He turned all these matters over in his mind, unable to bring himself to act. Then, one afternoon, as he was standing by the well in the great courtyard, he became aware of an unusual bustle, and crossing to the battlements, saw a troop of horsemen approaching from the north.

'More of your beggarly Scots, friend,' Will Nym said, digging him in the ribs with a familiarity Clym resented, but pretended not to notice.

'I'd rather see them come this gait in peace than as they usually come,' another sergeant muttered.

The troop, consisting of perhaps two dozen men, trotted up to the drawbridge, the horses' hooves kicking up clouds of summer dust. The men themselves were all coated in dust, their faces dust-grey, their breastplates smeared and caked; even their horses seemed to blow out clouds of grey powder.

Their leader was a tall young man with a lantern jaw. His grey eyes were streaked with blood, but, despite his fatigue, he roved sharply over the waiting faces in the courtyard. He swung himself off his horse, and, without a word, walked stiff-legged to the well. He drew up the water and slaked his face. Only then, as the water formed rivulets through the dust, did Clym recognize him as Archibald Douglas, Earl of Angus, a cousin of his own lord and head of the collateral branch of the family which was known as the Red Douglases. Without hesitation or forethought, Clym advanced and dropped on his knee before him.

The earl let the bucket of water fall over the rim of the well.

'Clym Laidlaw of Aikwood and Clartyshaws. I hae the honour tae present myself to your lordship.'

The address was awkward, for Clym did not know how best to make it, but his voice was firm and he held the earl's attention.

'Aikwood and Clartyshaws . . . are you a vassal of my cousin?'

Clym swallowed.

'I was born so, my lord.'

'And yet I find you here.'

'Aye, that you do. I hae lodged here these many weeks.'

'These past weeks? Braw weeks to be furth of Scotland. Aikwood and Clartyshaws, I'll hae a mind to you. Meanwhile I hae urgent business with the Lord of Greer.'

He moved as a man accustomed to command, for all that he was still young, indeed barely twenty, through the crowd, which fell away from him on either side, and so entered the castle. Clym fell in behind and entered in his train.

There was confusion within. Though Angus had in fact sent a messenger on ahead, the purpose of his visit was scarce understood. Moreover, the messenger had arrived when Edward des Moulins was deep in liquor and all attempts to sober him had been unsuccessful. Accordingly Angus too now had to kick his heels, till a young man of his own age came running in hot, breathless and excited. This was Edward's son Henry, who had been hawking when informed of the visit.

The delay gave Clym the chance to speak with some of Angus's men. They were all, despite their weariness, in a state of high excitement, and their tale, though confused, excited Clym himself.

All Scotland, it seemed, was in a ferment. Had Clym heard of Sir Patrick Gray and the Laird of Bombie? The tale was soon told him, and he felt his own neck bristle. But what followed was stranger and more terrible still. 'Naething like it in the lang annals of Scotland,' one soldier said, shaking his head.

King James, as might be expected, was fell angry when he heard of the insult accorded to his letter and the captain of his guard. But the king, though quick-tempered, had something also of the subtlety of his much-feared father, the Poet King. He said nothing to Douglas of the Laird of Bombie, but let that matter pass. Sir Patrick Gray caused masses to be said for the soul of his murdered nephew, but King James was silent even when he heard that the Douglas had bestowed the lands of

Bombie on that scapegrace ruffian Dandy Laidlaw. Instead, the king passed many hours in conference with the Bishop of St Andrews – Kennedy, 'him that's the deep yin,' the narrator said nodding his head at Clym.

The upshot of their debate was that the king sent another letter to the Douglas full of affectionate language and couched in the most mild and politic terms. He explained how he was sore puzzled by the league his dear cousin of Douglas had formed with the northern earls, they being among other things demonstrate enemies of Holy Church, as was proved by the scandalous treatment they had offered to the Bishop of St Andrews. Moreover, said the king, such bonds threatened the tranquillity of the kingdom and that peace and order which must be the aim of all good men like the king and the earl of Douglas himself.

'Oh it was a bonny letter, mild and loving in manner and matter. And I myself saw the king smile as he delivered it to his messenger.'

'And what was the Douglas's response?' Clym asked.

'Ah well, that was not all of it, it seemed. For the king had ended his letter by suggesting that the earl should come to Stirling Castle to discourse anent his bond, and allow King James the opportunity to allay any cause for complaint that the Douglas might imagine to exist. But Earl William was canny. Na, na, he says, shaking his neb, the last Earl of Douglas whae dined in the king's house wasna able to digest his dinner.'

This was not a response to please King James, who had never ceased to feel guilt because he had been made the unconscious instrument of that murder. When he read these words in the earl's reply, the red mark on his cheek flamed in anger like the summer sun declining over the western hills or a beacon lit on the Eildon Hills to warn of the approach of an English army. He howled of the insult the earl offered his king.

'Do you not trust me?' he wrote angrily. 'There is no other man from whom I would stomach such an insult, and yet for the love I bear you I repeat my friendly invitation.'

'Do I no' trust him,' said the Douglas, when he had read the letter to his men. 'I wadna say that I rightly do.'

'And why should he?' one soldier interrupted the story to say, scratching his head. 'And what for should he? Put not your trust in Princes, it is written in the Holy Book.'

And so the argument proceeded.

'This is an unco stour you're in,' says the king, 'forbye putting a black affront on the Lord's anointed.'

'Natheless,' says the Douglas, canny-like.

'Weel,' says the king, 'affront though it be, this whole affair is more important even than my royal and offended pride.'

'Therefore,' the first soldier told Clym, 'he gied the Earl a safe-conduct, stinking wi the maist solemn promises that niver a hair of the Douglas heid wad be hairmed. Nae skaith, the king promised, should come to Douglas or ony man in his retinue.'

Receiving this, the Douglas found his own pride challenged.

'So the Douglas garbs himself in braw new claes of scarlet and green, and hies him to Stirling wi a blithe smile on his bonnie face. And they dine thegither in amity, with niver a black bull's heid to be seen, wi' a dozen lords of the Privy Council, and a' lauching and fleerin' like swankies roond the hairst stacks. Only Sir Patrick Gray sits glowering with a Sunday face, or like an auld wife looking on a bonny lass.'

Clym pictured the dinner and wondered at the rashness of the earl, and, as he wondered, admired his own judgement for having declined to follow so foolish a lord. He urged his informant to come to the heart of the story.

'Patience, and we shall win the end,' the soldier said. "What ails Sir Patrick," asks the Douglas, inflamed it may be by the French wine. "Niver heed Sir Patrick," the king replies, "he's aye a dour deil." And they all share in laughter at the expense of the Captain of the Guard, whae sits there like a skeleton at the feast. Then, eftir they've eaten, the king raises a goblet of wine and proposes that they a' drink a toast to his noble guest. The wine is downed, though Sir Patrick winna lift his cup tae his lips. There are mair toasts and a' is merry as a marriage bell. Then the king claps his hand on the Douglas's shoulder. "There's just ae thing disturbs me, cousin," says he, "and that's this league you hae made wi the Earls of Crawford and Ross. I dinna like it. It's clean contrary tae the allegiance you owe me as your king, and forbye, it's fair detrimental and odious tae the peace and tranquillity of our fair realm of Scotland. Therefore, cousin, I maun ask you tae brak it."

247

'"Na, my lord," the Douglas answers, "ask me onything but that."

'"Ah but," the king says smiling still, "I have nae other request tae make of you, but this I maun hae."'

'At this a grim look comes in the Douglas eye. "I'm thinking," says he, "it would no' be canny tae brak my bond in the absence of my confederates. Nae canny, and a sair dishonour tae me also."'

'Then he goes on to tell the king, but with a sharp look at the bishop, that they all three regarded it as a gude and necessary security for the just government of the Kingdom."'

The soldier paused and passed his tongue over his lips. There were beads of sweat standing out on his brow.

'What then?' Clym asked.

"Wull you no brak it when I speir you?" cries the king, and the richt side of his face is a' crimson wi' his rising wrath.'

'"That I will not," says the Douglas, speaking quiet and standing straucht.'

'The fool,' Clym said. 'He could have gien his word. It would have cost him little.'

'Maybe so,' the soldier replied. Again he licked his lower lips. 'The king asked again, and again the Douglas denied him. Then, "By heaven and St Andrew," the king shouts, "gin you winna brak your bond, then this shall." And with these words, he stabs the earl wi' his dirk, first in the thrapple, so that he heaves forward choking blood, and syne in the belly. And Sir Patrick Gray ups wi a battle-axe and hacks the Douglas in the heid, crying "tak this for Maclellan", and all the other lords standing by begin to dirk the body too, just to prove their zeal for the king's cause. Only our ain young earl of Angus doesna strike a blow, but, being a cunning tod, though young, says not a word of protest either. The body fell at last and they stood round in silence as though amazed by their work, and twae soldiers entered and heaved it out and threw it in the moat.'

The story stirred even Clym's dull phlegmatic nature. The soldiers' excitement communicated itself to him. It had been pent up during their long ride and now bubbled over. Yet, unresponsive though he normally was to others' moods, he realized that they were also doubtful and horrified. They were rough men, bred by their trade to have little scruple or pity, but something in the king's breaking of faith disturbed them: there had been a breach of honour and hospitality they could neither understand nor forgive. Clym thought that the king's desperation had over-ridden his sense of honour; that seemed comprehensible to him, for the king had a higher duty. But what would happen now? The earl had four brothers. They were certain to seek revenge. Clym shivered. This murder brought his chances of returning to Aikwood no nearer. Which side would win? And why had Angus ridden South? He had, by the soldiers' account stood apart at the moment of the crime. He was the king's man, but he was also a Douglas, albeit belonging to another branch of the family, and there had, Clym knew, been rivalry between the Black and the Red. On whose behalf had he crossed the Border? Clym must find an answer to that question before he moved.

Henry des Moulins, deputizing for his father, had listened to Angus's narrative. He was shocked, far more deeply than the soldiers had been. It was barbarous and dishonourable and worse. He could not forget the story his father had so often recounted trembling in his cups, of how the Earl of Suffolk had been seized by rude fishermen and beheaded with clumsy blows of a rusty axe over the side of a boat. He looked at Angus with horror. How could an eye-witness speak so calmly of such a murder? And a man of his own age moreover!

Angus smiled. 'These things,' he said, speaking French to emphasize his diplomatic status and perhaps to impress on the English lord that, though his story might be barbaric, it was no barbarian who had told it, 'these things can be blown out of proportion. That happens easily. I have come to England, at the king's request, to try to forestall a response that would be damaging to both kingdoms. We know that trouble is brewing here too, trouble indeed of a similar nature to that which my Douglas cousins incarnate. The same thing is happening in France, I believe. I am told there is a phrase current there. It is "the over-mighty subject". Such men are like poison to a kingdom. They corrupt the body of the realm. My cousins, the Black Douglases, are precisely that: over-mighty subjects. Now, the king has scotched the snake, not killed it. The Douglas power remains, awesome and undiminished, a terrible threat to tranquillity and order. Already the king, alarmed, has drawn back from the full significance of his desperate act. He has essayed to make his peace with the brothers of the dead earl. Vain hope, you may say; with justice. Such peace, after such a deed, can only be shortlived. However, I have a purpose here in England, and act on royal instructions. I am here to advise, nay, even to warn, England to do nothing to succour the delinquent family. It is not, I would urge you, in your interest to see civil strife in Scotland, for, if you should judge it so, we shall be tempted play the same game south of the Border.'

Henry des Moulins listened, impressed by the young man's assurance and grasp of politics. He promised that he would convey the message to his father who was unfortunately indisposed, but who had, as the earl must know, great influence at Court. As for him, he understood the import of the earl's message, and was grateful to him for expounding it so fully. He could see that it would be in no way to England's interests to support the Douglas, and indeed shuddered at the thought.

'Moreover,' he said, 'perhaps I may remind you that my own family has claims on certain of the Douglas estates . . .'

'I am aware of that,' the earl said. 'So is King James. It is why I directed my course to Castle Greer.'

'So you fled South.'

Angus looked Clym in the eye, and Clym experienced what he had never know before: an inability to hold another's gaze.

'I came south,' he said, 'for the line of the Upper Tweed was held by the earl's men, and there was no safe way I could win across it and gain the king's court. And therefore, though I risked the sequestration of my lands, and couldna tell the fate of my beasts and bairns, I crossed the Border rather than pit my name to the earl's traitorous league, and I hae been mewed up here like a hawk in a kirk belfry ever since, kicking my heels and pining sair at hert tae be awa from my ain acres. Your coming, my lord, has been fair as welcome as Easter tae yin that has starved through Lent.'

'Is that the case,' Angus said, 'and why did you direct your feet to Castle Greer?'

'Weel,' Clym scratched his head, 'they had to gang some airt were I no to bide in ditches like a gypsy. And we hae family connections, blude is aye thicker than water, as they say, if no as thick as parritch. Yet I canna but say that the warmth of my reception here has been nae better nor cauld parritch.'

'You hae connection?'

'Aye, summat remote and dishonourable, but real enough. The Lord Edward, ye maun ken, had his way wi my deid feyther's sister – the lass is deid tae – and indeed their bye-blow, my ain cousin Dandy, is yin o' the Douglases' bauldest reivers.'

'A thin connection, true enough, and one that the Lord Edward might not choose to hae called to mind. I had thocht you might mean summat else. As for your cousin Dandy, not for naething was my ain Black cousin ca'ed the King of Thieves. Weel, my laird of Aikwood, you are fortunate to hae fallen in wi me, and shall ride wi me. But hanna you a cousin who is now a great man in England?'

'There is my feyther's brother, but I ken naething o' him.'

'That is ignorance better remedied,' and Angus held out his hand to Clym.

VIII

Often now the Lady Clare woke screaming in the middle of the night. She cried for her ladies and bade them fetch Maurie. When he came she held his hand tight and, in the broken muttering that had become her habitual manner of speech, complained she was as sick at heart as she was of body.

'My neck is as scraggy as an old fowl's,' she sighed, 'and I know you can no longer love me or desire me. And yet think what I have done for your sake and by your command. I have imperilled my soul for you, Maurie, and I see Hell gape before me. As I lay here, I heard spirits howl in pain.'

'It was but the dogs in the courtyard.' he said, 'you have had the nightmare. These are foolish fancies.'

'No fancies. The spirits of the damned cluster round me, and cry that my lot must soon be as theirs. Why did I listen to you? Why did I not suffer my lord of Boscobel? I have been cursed in this life with the monster that was spewed out of my womb and I am damned to all eternity for the foul murder to which you suborned me.'

'These are idle fancies,' he said again. 'The fruits of your disordered health. I shall send Brother Ambrose to physic you in the morning.'

She drew back among the cushions. When she spoke again it was in a whisper. 'Never him. I cannot look on him without horror and loathing, as the instrument of my damnation, as you, whom I loved madly, were the agent. And now you have withdrawn even that love from me, that formerly sustained me in our evil-doing.'

'Withdrawn my love,' he said, 'never that. But Brother Ambrose shall physic you. There is none wiser.'

'As he physicked my lord of Boscobel!', and she broke into heaving sobs that racked her thin body, and twisted to and fro on her bed as if a spirit indeed inhabited her frame and struggled to escape.

The mood passed, and she wept more quietly, while all the time Maurie sat by her bed and watched her.

'I would curse you,' she said, 'for what you have made of me, only no curse of mine could add to the fearful retribution that awaits you. I approached the Virgin while I slept and threw myself on the cold stone before her and licked her naked feet in the misery and anguish of my repentance, but she drew back without a word and I was left naked and afraid in the dark.'

Again she shook with terror and remorse, and again Maurie said only, 'This is foolishness.'

The weight of the great sleeping castle hung round them. The night's silence was broken only by the mailed feet of guards on sentry duty below. Maurie rose and looked out of the window. The first grey light of the summer dawn stretched empty to the hills. In a little he could make out their line. A dog barked in the town below, and then a cock crew.

'I have seen you look at her.'

He pretended not to hear.

'I thought to warn her, and then . . . why should she . . . not suffer as I have suffered?'

Odd how the cock's cry cut the night; odd the memories it summoned into being.

'This jealousy is foolish,' he said, without turning round. 'It is your sickness which speaks, nothing else. The pain of your body has disordered your mind. None will believe you. Who would heed the ravings of a woman as ill as you are?'

The cock cried again. A sentry threw out a challenge. He could hear the first bustle of the morning from the little town.

'But I warn you . . .' Still the voice came from the bed. Would the woman never be silent? '. . . She will be your match. I have watched her, seen her look at you, and that . . . loathing and dread which I have now only learned, she already knows.'

'Peace,' he said. 'You have robbed me of my sleep, and yourself of yours with your foolish prattle. The friar will physic you. Do not repeat these slanders. Boscobel died long ago, in another life. None suspects anything, do not torment yourself.'

'It is not I who do so, but the devils from hell who tear at my very being, and would drag me to their everlasting torments.

253

Let me see a priest. Let me see a priest that I may confess my evil and hope for salvation.'

'You shall see no priest but the friar. And do not speak even to your women of these suspicions you entertain concerning me and your daughter-in-law.'

'Daughter-in-law . . . after such a marriage . . .'

And she wept again, for her sins and her fears.

He crossed to the bed and looked down on her. What a strange thing life was that the most infinitely desirable of bodies should grow so noisome. He sniffed corruption in the musty chamber, a rank whiff from the bed where they had delighted to pleasure each other. His hands tightened. His gaze fixed on her neck. To stop himself, he dug his nails deep into his palms till he almost cried out with pain. Her sobs racked her body, then at last subsided to a feeble whimper. This was the extremity of being, in filth and fear.

'I have a lust for green apples, and there are none to be had.'

'Patience, my love, the mood will pass.'

Maurie pressed her against the trunk of a pear tree and fondled the full breasts that swelled out of the white gown. Bees buzzed in the trees and surrounding flowers.

Alice sighed, 'I could not have thought that you could pleasure me so. I never dreamed that any man could do so.'

Her black ringlets brushed his cheek. He pushed his hand further down into the cavity between her breasts. He was drunk with her as he had never been before. Her mouth opened against his and he felt passion run through her as they strained against each other. He drew her from the tree and guided her into a rose-fringed arbour. There he kissed her again, then drew back to let her soft luscious lips play on his, fluttering like moths. They sank to the ground, on the warm grass. He knelt by her, and laid his head on her belly which was already swollen, then pushed up the taffeta gown so that he might gaze enraptured on the white young yielding thighs. He pressed his mouth against them and licked, tasting her youth and lust, feeding his own and sweetening his age.

'You have bewitched me,' he sighed, and heard her moan, 'or you me . . . more, more, don't stop, more,' till she cried in ecstasy, and he looked up at the shadowed casement of the Lady Clare's chamber.

'Oh,' she cried again, 'oh, I had never dreamed . . .'

'Confess,' he said, 'confess my jewel, that an aged lover can pleasure you as no youth can. Is this not better than what my nephew Dandy had to offer?'

Her arm crept round his neck and drew his face to hers.

'Sweet witch of my heart,' he murmured.

The child must be born, and born in wedlock. Maurie, having lived fifty years for himself, impelled by the strength of his will and his ambition, was now consumed by a new desire: he wanted a son, and the boy must be openly his.

June made the courtyard lazy. The mastiffs slumbered. Guards nodded in the gateposts. Cocks were silent. Serving girls took brief sun by the castle well, flirting in summer idleness with lounging soldiers. The heavy hour of languid noon lay upon them.

'An ominous hour,' Brother Ambrose sighed. 'When temples are deserted and untrodden by worshippers, and pagan devils stalk abroad as they do at midnight. An hour when the weight of mortality presses heavily on the soul.'

'Not on his lordship's it would seem,' Robin Cochrane giggled. 'I saw him lately in the rose garden with the young lady.'

Brother Ambrose hovered over the bowl in which he was concocting a potion.

'He would do well to beware of that maid,' he said. 'I have warned him, and yet what can such a warning avail? Men are bound by their own nature, and their course is fixed by every irredeemable act they perform. No man, not even I, is now safe with our lord, and, when this matter with the Lady Alice has run its course, he will be maddened like a rabid wolf, snapping at all. You look pale and out of sorts, boy. Are you still pining for your Scots lad?'

Robin picked a spot on his chin, and tossed his head back. 'Not I. Why should you think I would pine for one who does not appreciate me?'

'Is it a fit of the sulks then?'

Again the boy tossed his head. 'Not that. If I am low-spirited

255

it is because I feel my talents are wasted here. You promised me my lord would let me build something for him, or at least work on beautifying what is already there. But there is no work for me here, nor ever will be that I can see.'

'Only that,' said the friar. 'You relieve my mind. And yet, my dear, I know it is a great thing of which you complain. Perhaps you should seek employment elsewhere.'

'Are you tired of me, Ambrose?'

'Light of my heart and of my eyes, how could I be? But I love you so deeply that it grieves me to see you wretched.'

Towards evening there came a cry of horsemen. Lady Clare heard it as she lay in her darkened chamber. Maurie and Alice heard it steal over the orchard where they lay entwined in the declining sun. Both had slept long, and Maurie woke resolved.

'I am Archibald Douglas, Earl of Angus.'

'I am honoured,' and for once Maurie's polite response was truthful. He felt himself honoured; the man who has attained dignity and high rank in a foreign land only realizes his full achievement when he meets his compatriots. Maurie found more satisfaction in being treated as an equal by the beardless Earl of Angus than in his acceptance by the mighty Warwick.

He had his servants bustle about, setting wine and meat for the travellers.

'No business till you have supped, my lord,' he urged; but Angus would have none of it. He was ever a man to come directly to the point, and he had no small talk; he was uninterested in sport or personalities; when he could not speak business he was silent.

'You come from Greer?' Maurie said. 'How did you find my lord Edward?'

'Sick. We saw only his son.'

'Sick. Like his sister, whom God preserve.'

'The Lord Edward's sickness, methinks, came frae a bottle. My Lord, you hae heard of the death of the Earl of Douglas?'

Maurie nodded.

'A moment of rare rashness, 'he said, 'an imprudent act.'

'A necessary deed.'

Maurie raised his eyebrows.

'Say you so?'

256

'Reason of State,' Angus kicked his shoes under the table, and disturbed a sleeping hound. 'Reason of State. The earl, my cousin, poor fool, threatened the stability of the whole kingdom. There could be no peace while he lived, unless he abandoned his pretensions, whilk he would never do save with death.'

'It is rarely wise for kings to act as their own executioners.'

'What does it matter who strikes the blow, so long as the blow be struck. The courage to act is given to few men. We are fortunate to have a king who does not shrink from what must be done.'

'Maybe so,' Maurie said. 'And why have you come here, my lord? To what do I owe the honour of this visit? Come, let us be frank with each other. I hate a secret and diplomatic man.'

'No one,' Angus said, 'or so I hae heard, has greater influence than you with the Earl of Warwick, and so wi the Duke of York.'

'You have heard flattery, nothing more.'

'You are owre modest. Now we ken fine – you will pardon my Scots leid for you were well acquaint wi it in youth, sir – we ken fine that the duke and earl wield great power in this kingdom, for the king's miserable state is well kent too. Maybe the earl is a greater man than the duke, and it's the earl, men say, that you hae by the lug. Therefore, and for this reason, I hae come to you, my lord, to urge you that you may counsel the great men o' this realm to leave weel alane, and no meddle in our Scotch affairs, and sae give neither succour nor yet counsel to the new Earl of Douglas.'

'You speak plain, my lord, and it seems to me little like a Douglas yourself.'

'I speak as a Scot, sir, and yin that kens our country needs a strang hand. We are ill folk tae govern and yet maun be governed. I speak as a Scot that hopes to see King James mak gude his feyther's promise.'

'I knew his father,' Maurie answered, 'a narrow, obstinate man, who would not be advised. Pray, my lord Angus, that the present king be not similarly formed.'

As the meeting broke up, with the promise by Maurie that he would ponder these affairs and meet again to discuss them further at supper, Clym Laidlaw stopped Maurie in the doorway, plucking him by the sleeve. Maurie turned, sharp and offended, but found his importuner loth to relinquish his hold.

'Bide a moment, uncle. Do you no mind me? Clym Laidlaw of Clartyshaws and noo of Aikwood also, your ain brither's son.'

Maurie took half a pace back. He waited till all others had dispersed and they were alone together.

'My nephew Clym,' he smiled. 'I have had ill luck with nephews, aye and with brothers too.'

'I hae come far, sir, since you paid us a visit at Clartyshaws.'

'Aye,' Maurie smiled. 'That you have, and the years have passed, adding grey to your hair and rheumatism to my joints. Do you serve the Earl of Angus?'

'I serve no man but my ain interest.'

'Come with me.'

Saying this, he turned round and limped ahead of his nephew, leading him into a small antechamber furnished only with a deal table and a pair of three-legged stools.

'You are bold to come here,' Maurie said, taking a jug of sweet white wine from a cupboard, where it had evidently been placed for his readiness, and pouring two mugs.

'Aye,' Clym sipped the wine. 'And you were bold to come to us at Clartyshaws.'

'My mother's house,' Maurie said.

'Just so,' Clym nodded. 'I was brocht up, uncle, by my sainted mother in the knowledge of the awful truth of my feyther's death. I kent frae the days I was a bairn of how he rade into England in search of justice, that the wrang my Lord des Moulins did our family wi your ain aid and abettance might be revenged. I mind him ride forth myself, and I mind fine how I watched the valley gate for a feyther that would never return. And now, a man past his age then, I hae come to England, an exile frae my ain lands, and stand afore you to ask for that same justice. I hae seen the Lord des Moulins myself, and a puir peely-wally cratur it is too and sae I turn to you, uncle, to demand just recompense for the ills I hae suffered.'

'Justice,' Maurie said, 'come, man, sup your wine. It is, I promise you, the best canary.'

Justice, he thought, is a better word, and an easier word, than revenge. Justice is something which can be bought and sold.

He looked across the table at the heavy-set figure, at the dour beetling brows, and the obstinate line of the mouth, and said to himself, 'Here is a fellow with no warm sympathies. There is nothing to fear from him. He is a man who will ever count the cost of an action. A man of business, like myself, but also a man, compared to me, with but a narrow experience of life.'

'Your poor father,' he said, 'was a fool. Now I am persuaded you are a man of sense. But he . . . he rode into England on a foolish raid. He was taken and imprisoned in accordance with the custom of the Border, but no sentence had been determined when he tried to escape, and was killed accidentally in the attempt. I had no part in his death, nephew. I will not pretend it greatly grieved me, for we were divided early. Our ways were separate. I rode south to seek my fortune, while he bided at Clartyshaws, which is now yours.'

A frown crossed Clym's face, which Maurie noted.

'As for the wrong your father imagined my lord des Moulins did the family, why it was but the way of a man with a maid. Men of the world such as we are will never stir up a stour over the like. Besides, the lass was willing and doubtless lay with others. That is the history, but history of long past events. We are not men to brood on what is done with. How come you to England?'

Clym, expressionless while his uncle spoke, now recounted his tale. Maurie questioned him closely: on his exact reasons for leaving Scotland, on his relations with Angus, on his understanding of the likely course of events in the northern kingdom. All the while he spoke he fingered the relics (a fingerbone of St Aidan, a medal of St Cuthbert, a reliquary containing the dried blood of St Bridget) which dangled from his neck-chain.

At last he said, 'Nephew, while I admit no responsibility for your father's misfortune, and therefore acknowledge no debt to you, yet blood, as men say, is thicker than water, and the ties of blood must always appeal to our sentiments. You are, from what you say, a prudent and perspicacious observer. You could do me some service, and yourself also. The great Earl of Warwick, whose humble servant I am proud to be, will richly reward a man who supplies good information to us from Scotland, and I myself, for my own purposes, will supplement his generosity if the same, and perhaps additional, information is made available to me. Do you understand me, nephew?'

Clym glowered across the table. 'I understand you wish me to become a spy.'

'Spy,' Maurie said, 'is a harsh word, but an honourable and hazardous profession. Does my offer tickle your fancy?'

Will the trout take the worm? Clym's mouth opened, and, it seemed to Maurie, snapped on the hook.

Three days later Clym left in Angus's train for Raby Castle. He took with him a letter of recommendation from his uncle addressed to Warwick. He saw the sun shine on his future.

The night before leaving however he had an encounter which might have perturbed a man less sure of his own abilities. He was accosted by a bent grey-haired, grey-bearded fellow whose hand shook and whose breath stank of wine.

'Men tell me,' he said, 'that you are Laidlaw of Clartyshaws.'

The old man's voice quavered. Clym looked at him with disgust.

'Then,' the old man continued, his eyes filling with tears, 'you are indeed my own brother's son. You maun be Young Clym.'

Clym looked at him with amazement.

'Man,' – and now boozy sentiment almost rendered the old man's speech incomprehensible – 'do you no' ken me? Your ain uncle Will?'

'How should I ken you?' Clym said. 'I had thought you dead.'

'Not so, though,' he hiccuped, 'in wretched state, dragging out a pitiful existence, I might as well be in the grave, but no . . . and yet how should you ken me. You were but a tousle-headed bairn when last I clapped eyes on you. Why, man, but it does the heart good to see you and be minded again o' the bonnie braes o' Ettrick and Yarrow, and the water rinning free and clear, and a' the deer in the hills of my ain country. Oh, nephew, how my exile's heart pines for the hills and burns of hame.'

He meandered in this lachrymose vein for several minutes while all the while Clym sought to detach himself. The old man spoke warmly of Dandy and asked how he had never told Clym that his lost uncle was to be found in Maurie's household. Clym shrugged a dismissive answer, but Will persisted, talking almost at random, but again and again recurring to his longing to see Ettrick once more.

At last, however, he said; 'And yet I never shall. I ken that fine. I whae have fought many years in the French Wars, and proved myself in mair battles than Tweed has tributaries, am mewed up here, a prisoner in fact if no in name.'

'And how is that?' Clym asked, his attention caught at last.

'How is that you say? How indeed. Simply, nephew, that my brother Maurie, that is become a great man, cherishes my presence and protects my person. And why' – here Will lifted the leather-jack of wine that hung at his waist and, directing it to his lips, gulped, letting some of the wine trickle down his chin and then searching it out with his tongue – 'Why,' he resumed, 'it's no love precisely and gin you ken Maurie you wouldna believe me were I to say it was. Na, na, Maurie gars me bide here – for his ain safety. You'll have heard tell, nephew of the curse laid on us four brithers by the Gudewife of Hangingshaws, auld witch that she was. All four of us wad die at the rope's end, she promised. Clym is gane, and they say Rob is gane, and that leaves Maurie and me, and it's his belief, or superstition, that as long as he keeps me secure here in Mirabel, nae skaith can come to him.'

'And why,' Clym asked, 'does he no' despatch you with a dagger in the guts, which, it seems to me would surely brak and so disprove the curse?'

Will shook his head. 'Aye, you may well ask as I have asked myself. Sometimes I think he sees me as a kind of talisman. Then I wonder if perhaps he fears that any action of his own wouldna hae that effect. He is fell superstitious, Maurie, you ken. Even in your brief converse you maun hae seen the way he keeps fingering his wee bit relics. He is a deep and puzzling man, though he is my brither. I canna tell the reason, though I fancy he aye hopes tha my auld friend, the gift o' the pagan God Bacchus, will carry me off. But oh, nephew, I am loth to depart without again letting my gaze fall on the braes of Ettrick and feeling the cool breezes of my ain calf country.'

'And why,' said Clym, who had been meditating a plan while his uncle rambled, 'should you not do so? I canna hae you ride wi me the morn for I accompany my lord of Angus to Castle Raby, but when I hae again won my ain estates, I shall devise a means of sending for you.'

Hearing this, his uncle slobbered kisses on his hand, to Clym's considerable disgust, and it was only with difficulty that he prevented him from folding his arms round his neck and transferring his display of affection to his own mouth and cheeks.

'But, mind this well,' Will said, as they parted, 'Maurie is a sly and cunning tod, and nae to be trusted. Gin he has conferred some benefit upon you, rest assured, nephew, it is his own purposes he hopes to advance and never yours.'

This warning echoed in Clym's mind the next morning, as, inconspicuous in Angus's train he took the road for Raby and his future fortune.

Maurie drew Brother Ambrose aside after Matins. 'You look glum, my friend.'

'I am bereft,' the friar said. 'That imp Robin has ridden off with the beggarly Scots. Leaving me with barely a word.'

'Come,' Maurie smiled, 'he had outgrown you, friend. Besides, have I not remarked the looks you lay on that yellow-haired page of the Lady Alice's?'

The Friar giggled. 'You were ever quick to notice, from that first encounter in the York tavern. A delectable piece indeed. But quite sadly unresponsive. Would you believe, friend, that he regards me simply as a vile corrupt old man?'

'A boy of discernment and true judgement. Nevertheless, old friend, why should you be denied? I may find the means of indulging you.'

'Provided?'

'Precisely.' Maurie played with St Aidan's fingerbone. 'The Lady Clare's disorder of the blood does not improve.'

'Alas.'

'I do not think she can recover. And yet she lingers, painfully.' The friar tapped the tips of his fingers against each other.

'A noble lady whose summer has departed. "Carpe diem" as the pagan poet has it, or "Labuntur anni". Alas. How fortunate, my lord, for both of us was that distant encounter in York. Now, listen, I have a potion distilled from herbs grown in the high valleys of the Alps, the secret of which was granted me by an old woman of these same mountains. It is a sovereign remedy for the blood. The mountaineers are wont to nibble these rare plants, or drink the liquid distilled from them. In doing so they derive great benefit, a pure blood, a clear skin, and a tolerance of the thin mountain air. But those unaccustomed to the medicine from early youth have been known to receive it differently. What is benign for the mountaineers is oft times malignant for them. Nevertheless there is a chance, a plausible chance that it may remedy disorders of the blood. It is certain, friend, that it will arrest them one way or another. Do you desire me to try my skill and the effect of the potion on my mistress?'

'It is necessary. Without your aid she cannot recover, but she may live to the autumn.'

'And I have seen what my lady may not yet have remarked may be born by then. So we shall arrange matters to our common satisfaction. His name is Hugh, I believe. The very fair one, the cherub, not the sly beast with the reddish tinge. He would be no conquest. Hugh, a tight-buttocked little beast. Let us,' the friar flapped his bony fingers, 'loosen all. You loosen his morals, I shall loosen the grip of the disorder on my lady, and then those delectable buttocks. Come, let us drink, friend: to Science and Sodomy.'

'We are agreed,' Maurie said. 'One other thing however. The potion must be administered privily, for my lady has a strange suspicion of you.'

'Strange indeed. Let it be done thus. It suits my nature.'

The Lady Alice alternated between joy and grief, panic and rapture. Her ladies were disturbed by her state of mind. They debated whether to inform Warwick of his daughter's condition, but neither dared approach him. They watched their lady tossing in her bed. It was very hot without, for there had been no rain for many weeks, and thunder now threatened. The level of the water in the moat had fallen away, disclosing a greenish slime which stank. Frogs croaked all night, and the stench of the town's ordure rose to the castle and offended the ladies' nostrils.

'She still pines for the young Scots lord,' said Dame Bridget, who did so herself.

'Poor lass,' her companion, Dame Eleanor sighed, 'She has done great wrong and it pains and torments her.'

'They say there is a case of plague in the town.'

'There is plague in her heart, poor lamb.'

Dame Bridget damped a cloth and wiped Alice's brow. Alice moaned at the touch and turned over to rest on her side. Her feet kicked below the silk coverlet.

'When the child is born . . .' Dame Bridget began.

'It is better,' Dame Eleanor whispered, 'it is better, sister, to say nothing of that. Who knows whether our words and speculations do not enter her poor disturbed mind.'

'She has done great wrong,' Dame Bridget echoed her companion's words, 'and yet I cannot think of her as a sinner.'

'Poor lass. Here sister, take a cup of wine.'

She passed the mug of sweet canary to her friend and for a little they sat and sipped in silence.

'There is the owl. How busy the night is. They say the Lady Clare is worse.'

'Her life is despaired of, they tell me.'

'Poor woman. Now she, unlike our lady, had indeed been a great sinner. They say she screams like a lost soul, and visions the torments of hellfire awaiting her.'

'And well she may, for that she will burn throughout eternity I cannot doubt.'

'The monster she bore is proof of how she lost the protection of the Virgin.'

The two women were silent, each perplexed, fearful and turning the same thought over in their mind.

'And what of him?' Dame Bridget asked at last, 'does he scream of nights? Does he know the terrors he has brought on the Lady Clare, aye, and on our sweet lass here too?'

'Never him,' Dame Eleanor affirmed. 'He has given his soul to the Prince of Darkness, and we all know how Satan cares for his own.'

'Think you that?'

'That I do.'

'Has he then bewitched her?'

Dame Eleanor took up her embroidery. For some minutes she stitched, elaborating an exquisite pattern, while her companion waited, accustomed not to interrupt, and knowing that her question had not been disregarded, but was rather being deeply pondered.

'There is more than one kind of witchcraft and more than one magic,' Dame Eleanor pronounced. 'Who can say what has been worked on our sweet lass?'

Again she resumed her work and again her friend waited.

Then Dame Eleanor rose, and, taking her scissors, snipped a lock from the Lady Alice's hair.

*

264

Two nights later, the two women watched their mistress drift into the dream-troubled sleep that was all she ever seemed to attain. Then, when it seemed that she was as settled as might be hoped, Dame Eleanor donned a travelling-cloak and mask. Her friend put her ear to the door and listened.

She turned back, 'I do not like your mission,' she said. 'I do not like the dangers you are running.'

Dame Eleanor smiled. 'There are dangers which we dare not shirk. Besides, all is prepared. Gaspard is at the postern gate, and he owes me a favour on account of the potion I gave his wife last winter. He will escort me out of the castle, and my pony waits below. As for the guards at the outer gate, they have all drunk by now of the medicined wine we sent them.'

'But if they tell?'

'Why, they believe the wine is a gift from the Lady Clare. None will suspect us. Why should they?'

Dame Bridget wrung her hands. 'I do not like it. What if my lady wakes and asks for you?'

'Why then, as we agreed, I am sick of a migraine, and have retired. She is, even now, a loving soul. And will understand. Sister, I do not like this enterprise, but our lady's safety and even her soul is at stake. Come, kiss me, and bid me God speed.'

Half an hour later Dame Eleanor, accompanied only by a boy whom Gaspard had procured as a guide, rode out of the little town, mounted on a stout moorland pony, and turned her face to the hills. The summer moon was up and cast a dancing light over the sleeping world. She rode easily humming a little tune and occasionally, when shadows loomed alarmingly, murmuring a prayer. They met no one and the country through which they passed became ever more wild until there was no sign of human habitation. A fox, going about its business, paused a moment on the little track to look at them; then judging they offered no danger, sat down to lick under its leg, before trotting into the broom by the pathside. A little later they disturbed a family of roe at the edge of a pine-wood; their white scuts sparkled in the moonlight as they scampered into safety.

Then the path turned up a little valley where there were no trees, only a few stunted bushes, and great boulders littered the strip of level ground between them and a gurgling stream. They were climbing now, and the ponies' breath rose in misty clouds.

Mist lay along the water too, and the birds were silent. There was no sound in that valley but the panting of the ponies, the clatter of their feet on the loose stones, and the muttering stream. Once Dame Eleanor caught the boy looking at her as if in alarm, or at least a wonder that was touched with fear, but she leaned over and laid her hand on his arm to calm him.

They came to a point where the valley divided. Without hesitation, she turned the pony's head to the left, up a narrower glen, which, in a little, round a bend, opened into a mountain plateau. On the far side of the plain, perhaps half a mile away, they saw a group of trees, pines also, all leaning to the right. Beneath them nestled a cottage. There was a candle in the window.

Dame Eleanor gestured with her whip to let her companion know that this was their destination.

Outside the hut she dismounted, and gave her pony to the boy to hold. The door opened before she could rap on it, showing that they were expected or at least that their arrival had attracted attention. She entered and the boy was left to support his fear of the night and this lonely place best he could.

IX

How did King James sleep the night after he murdered the Earl of Douglas, and what did he expect from that action?

Wattie brooded on these questions. He was nervous and unsettled, but it was that sort of unsettlement, produced also by alcohol, which let him see things with that strange distorting definition that a full moon can lend the countryside. He was no soldier: he had hardly the stature which might make men seek his counsel. Yet, in his disordered fancy, he saw the king as a man now outlawed from all morality who must be regarded as a wild beast, dangerous to all, the proper victim of any true man. And yet if the Douglas moved, did they not invite their own destruction?

'Crime calls aye to crime, and murther lets loose murther and disorder on the land,' he said. 'We have a duty to avenge our slaughtered lord but how if the fulfilment of that duty destroys us in our turn?'

The new earl was the murdered man's brother James. With his high carriage and yellow hair worn over his shoulders, James was known as the fairest man in Scotland and the bravest knight. The great Burgundian chevalier De Lalain had once crossed the seas to challenge him in the lists; they had fought *à l'outrance*, and it was the Burgundian who was unhorsed. That however was but mimic war. Wattie had ever loved and trusted the new earl, and now he pitied him, torn apart by duty and prudence. Wattie stared at the black wall of the future, and felt naked; his powers had deserted him, and he could read nothing there.

The earl announced that King James had speedily summoned a Parliament of all those nobles, churchmen and burghs known to be hostile to the Douglases, and that Parliament had said the king was blameless: the earl, 'by manifest treason and conspiracy', had been guilty of his own death.

'I read the fine hand of Walter Kennedy in that verdict,' the new Earl said.

'Weel,' Wattie said, 'it is an unco strange and unheard-of felo de se that dirks himself six-and-twenty times and maks a great reid gash in the back of his heid. But whatten answer will you mak, my lord?'

'Whatten answer can I mak tae sic lees,' the earl sighed, and sank his face on the table before him, and began to sob. Wattie knew he was weeping not for fear or even despair, and not even for his murdered brother, though he had loved him, but out of bafflement.

They were alone in a room together high up in the castle, and it seemed to Wattie that they were alone also in the knowledge of the import of the choice that faced the earl. And his heart went out to the Earl James in pity.

The clamour of voices and the ring of steel rose from the courtyard below. They looked out and saw a crowd of some fifty or sixty men all brandishing weapons and shouting loudly. Wattie's own cousin Dandy was among them, and it was Dandy leapt on a mounting-block, so that he stood head and shoulders above the crowd, and from this position broke into a harangue.

They could not catch his words but saw he was waving a parchment. Then, he lifted his face to the castle wall, and all the crowd looked upwards too, and gave a great cheer.

The earl drew back from the window. 'There's nae answer to your fundamental question there, Wattie, for we may never ken what the king thought to win, but you maun admit there's an answer tae my immediate predicament. I canna bide at hame while my brother lies without Christian burial, and I canna, indeed daurna, thole the disgrace of sic inaction.'

He marched down the winding stair and out into the court-yard. Wattie followed him. 'Wae's me for the House of Douglas,' he muttered, 'that was ever sae bonnie and fair, and wae's me for my puir Earl James, but, come what betide, I shall be leal to my trust.'

The crowd parted, in a sudden silence, to allow the earl to approach Dandy, who still stood on the mounting-block with the parchment held out before him as during Lent priests carry big crosses in processions of penitents. Then, seeing the earl, Dandy fell on his knees before him, still brandishing the parchment and crying out, 'I hae here, in my very hand, that damnable promise of safe-conduct given by that villain and coward James Stewart miscalled King of Scots to his "trusty and well-beloved Earl of Douglas", and I hae also' – he fished in his belt and pulled out a bloody rag, – ' a fragment of the sark that same Earl William was wearing when he entered Stirling Castle under the protection of this same safe-conduct. Whae among you can gaze on these, this damnable safe-conduct and this pitiful rag, and still lie peaceful in his bed? Whae among you can find a sure bield in Scotland now that miserable country, is ruled by sic a perjured and murderous king?'

The Douglas stretched out his hand. For a moment it hovered lily-pale in a shaft of sunlight breaking through the clouds. He took the promise of safe-conduct. He took the bloody rag and pressed it to his heart. Then thrusting the relic within his shirt, so that his murdered brother seemed to lie against his heart, he drew a dirk and rent the parchment in two. He threw both parts in the air, caring nothing for where they might fall, and turned back towards the castle.

Only a few boys and youths, eager for any adventure, dared into the streets of Stirling when it was known that the Douglas men had broken down the West Port. Most of the townsfolk, fearing that they could now look for no help from the royal garrison in the castle, barricaded themselves in their houses behind bolted and reinforced doors. The churches were locked likewise, and only the taverns remained open, their landlords surmising that to lock them would not protect their wares, while if they stayed open and assumed a face of welcome they might even be paid for what was drunk and would otherwise be stolen.

Dandy pranced at the head of the invaders. He stood up in his stirrups, and waved his sword. Behind him he led an old grey mare, – 'a spittle jade', the chronicler tells us – that was dragging the king's safe-conduct (which had been sewn up at Dandy's insistence) behind it. The parchment trailed through the dust and bumped against the piles of the burgh's dung, and, as he paraded up and down the streets and three times widdershins round the Mercat Cross, Dandy cried out that they were bringing the king's honour at the tail of a carthorse. All was done in order, for this was a demonstration, not a wild folly, so they marched for a good half-hour round the town, that every street might see the king's honour, and judge it at its true value. They marched right up to the castle walls; but the gates were bolted and the drawbridge raised. Many a face looked down from the battlements, some fearful and some defiant, but neither the King nor Bishop Kennedy nor Sir Patrick Gray, nor any of the nobles dared appear on the walls. There was no exception, for the Earl of Angus, whose pride was such that he could not have borne to hide his face, was engaged on his English embassy. Dandy cried on the king to come and view his besmirched honour, but there was no response. He hauled the dung-smeared parchment up, waved it aloft, spat ceremoniously upon it, and called to a man whom he recognized on the wall, 'Is it you, Sir Angus Kerr that I see there, and do you pride yourself on guarding a king that values his honour so highly that he will adventure nothing to rescue it? Shame on you, and shame on your perjured and murderous king.'

Sir Angus Kerr looked black as thunder, but made no reply to the taunts.

The Douglas men had meanwhile been drawn up in front of the castle in battle order, and now the earl himself rode out before his men. He drew a document from under his cloak and began to read in a loud and ringing voice, throwing out his words that some at least of those on the castle walls might hear him. He recited the grievances and injuries done to his family, how two earls, his cousin and his brother, had both been foully murdered while trusting guests of King James. 'Sic hospitality' yelled Dandy, but the earl quelled him with a look. Then speaking in a most solemn voice, he announced that he formally abjured all allegiance to the King of Scots and offered homage to the King of England if he would now march north to restore honour and order to Scotland.

He paused, but there came no answer from the castle; only the grim walls and the silent soldiers looking down as the sun moved westwards. The earl nodded his head, as if satisfied, and delivered the document to Dandy, who, with the grey horse still following, rode forward to the outer gate of the castle and hammered on the door with the hilt of his sword. And still no one moved above. Still there was no reply. It was as if Dandy had approached an enchanted castle. Then, sheathing his sword,

270

he drew a dirk and stabbed the document of renunciation into the wood. The hilt quivered and then was still. The document hung there that all might learn how his subjects had judged James of the Fiery Face unworthy to rule them.

Dandy turned, his eyes dancing in that bright still girlish face, and, with a loud cry the Douglas men debouched from the open ground in front of the castle, swarming into the streets and vennels of the town. Only a small contingent remained drawn up in order to guard against any sally from the castle. If Stirling was the king's own burgh, that summer night it was given over to the wild men from the Border. They made free of it, and with relish. Houses were fired and looted, girls and women raped, casks of wine uncorked (the innkeepers' hopes of payment proving vain). Yet it was no mere uncontrolled savagery. All night Dandy and one or two of his lieutenants moved among their men, directing affairs, so that any onlooker might have realized that he was watching a planned military operation. Stirling, they had determined, should be taught the king's unworthiness. The king had dishonoured his promise of safe-conduct; therefore Stirling and indeed the whole kingdom should learn how the king could not protect his own town from the righteous anger of the Douglas. 'Burn the coo in its ain bracken-bush,' cried Dandy. So, when women screamed and rooftops blazed, the reality of the Douglas wrath and the force of their revenge should be carried on the night winds to the king crouching in fear in his castle.

Early in the morning Dandy began to call off his men, beating them out of the taverns and bawdy-houses, haling them from the beds of honest burgess-women whose husbands had been bound and compelled to watch their wives' disgrace, and ordering them to collect their loot and make ready to march. He gathered them in the market place, and then, as a final gesture, nailed the soiled and tattered safe-conduct to the mercat cross.

Then they turned their horses' heads to the southern hills.

Yet Dandy's exhilaration faded on the homeward ride. They had done nothing decisive; it had only been a gesture; and it angered him to realize, that to judge from the contentment on the faces of his chiefs, it was understood as a victory. It began to rain. The mist closed round them and he felt a sourness in the stomach. Dandy knew again an urge to destroy. He wanted to tear to pieces a world that was not ordered to honour him. He was hungry for more than food and drink, and now, each step his horse took away from Stirling seemed to insist that they had accomplished nothing substantial, but that the king would recover his position.

Certain of this, he rode up beside the earl and plucked him by the sleeve, telling him they had made a mistake, that they should return, and lay siege to the castle, that they should force the king to his knees. But the Douglas only smiled.

King James had certainly been alarmed by the Douglas raid. He could not escape a feeling of humiliation. There he had been, the King of Scots, cowering behind the battlements, not daring to show his face, while wild men from the most unruly part of the Borderland sacked and burned his own town. And yet he put a stay on his temper. Men said it was shame drove the red anger out of his fiery face, but it was more like prudence. He listened to the advice of Bishop Kennedy. 'Hasten slowly,' said that careful prelate rubbing the fur of his sleeve. 'You'll no land a muckle fish like the Douglas if you dinna play him patiently.' The bishop pointed out that for the moment many men sympathized with the Douglas. 'But we can put that right,' he said, and ordered all the clergy to read from their pulpits the treasonable bond the earls had made, which had provoked the king's slaying of the previous earl. 'Hasten slowly,' said Kennedy again, 'and let your words be honey.'

Accordingly, King James sent messengers with bland faces and blander words to the Douglas to assure him of the love King James still felt for 'the noblest knight of our kingdom' and of the trust he would still be happy to repose in the earl. At the same time he tenderly reminded him that Parliament had concluded his brother's death had been justified. He promised also that the Stirling raid would be forgotten. No reprisals would be exacted for any crimes committed on that day when men had taken leave of their senses.

That was one side of the king's coin. The obverse wore a sterner face. That August when the harvest still stood in the fields, he collected an army from Fife and the Lothians, the braes of Angus and the western lands, and marched towards the

Border, giving out at first that he planned a raid into England. Yet no summons came to the Douglas, and the next they heard the king was in Peebles. Thence he marched down the Tweed to Yair, where he crossed the river and then turned up the Ettrick by way of Selkirk and over the hills to Dumfries. Eight peel-towers and more than a score of farms were set ablaze; crops were burned in the fields, sheep and cattle driven off the hills, and all the while the Douglas brothers, taken by surprise, sat fast in their castles and dared not move.

The soft answer had been followed by firm action. King James had outwitted them. The wild young men like Dandy might chafe, and indeed Dandy three times charged at the head of a little troop against the stragglers of the royal army, but the chiefs of his party grew ever more anxious. They began to fear that the Stirling raid had been a blunder. That show of their strength and that defiance had alarmed many, who now turned to the king, whatever his crimes. The Douglas's renunciation of his allegiance and his appeal to the King of England had roused what patriotism there was against him. The aggrieved man had put himself in the wrong, and now he felt it. Unnerved by the king's march, by the support he had, and by uncertainty as to his next intentions, by the end of the month the earl presented himself before the king in Dumfries. He knelt to his sovereign, and in a cracked and trembling voice formally expressed his forgiveness for the murder of the Earl William. Some, like Dandy, were disgusted by this, but others took a more practical view summed up by the old wife who asked, 'and what for should he no' forgi'e him, since that same dirk-thrust made him Earl of Douglas himsel'?' He even bound himself to enter into no league against the king, but again as the old wife put it, 'eftir what's happened, whae wad think to jyne him?' In return the king was gracious. He raised up The Douglas and embraced him. He promised even to secure a dispensation from the Church which would permit Earl James to wed his brother's widow, the Maid of Galloway, and so enable the Douglas inheritance to remain intact. It was observed that at mention of the dispensation, Bishop Kennedy smirked.

There followed three years of freedom from civil strife. In this time the earl was even employed as an ambassador to England, where the misgovernment of the Lancastrian king was hustling

273

the country to revolt. This honour, Douglas told his brothers, was proof that he was now in the king's confidence.

Wattie shood his head: 'A man deprived of his wits is fair like to be lost.'

Douglas hardly noticed that the king was working to form his own league, and in this blindness showed himself unlike his murdered brother. Not for nothing did they call Earl James 'the last knight in Christendom'. He had a simple and honourable nature and did not even see that his cousin Angus avoided him. All attempts to open his eyes to the encroaching danger were vain.

These years of peace led Dandy back into the riding life. Though Earl William had promised him the estates of the unfortunate MacLellan of Bombie, that promise had been lost in the aftermath of the murders. Young MacLellan, who had risen to fetch Sir Patrick Gray, and thus precipitated his father's execution, inherited the estates, and Dandy was left a landless man. Late every summer he took the hill roads south at the head of a band of ruffians. There were at most a score of them, and these rides were his delight: he loved the crisp early mornings with their hint of autumn when the hills rolled away green and golden till in the far distance they shaded into a misty blue; he loved the sharp smell of horseflesh and its sweat, the clatter of hooves down a stoney slope; he loved also the cries of terror that arose from the valley farmhouses; the shrill yelps of priests whose churches he was about to despoil and whose robes it amused to rip off leaving them dancing up the hillsides in their sarks.

Yet it was on one such occasion that he received a check. He was on his way back from a raid over the Border, but, hearing that an English troop was guarding the ford over Carlisle, and that another had been despatched to guard the pass over the Cheviots into Liddesdale, he turned up a little valley on the west side of Kielder where, by some chance, he had never found himself before. They were all in a foul temper for it had been a profitless ride. They had, it was true, taken a head of cattle, but, falling in with an English band of superior numbers soon after turning for home, had lost them and been forced to run for their lives.

So, when they saw the squat tower of a little church and a manse beside it nestling by the edge of a wood of pine, ash, alder and hawthorn, they were eager to take what compensation they could for their earlier loss. Even in such a lonesome place, a priest might have a few head of beasts they could reive, and so, as Dandy was wont to put it, 'restore him to that Christian nakedness which is befitting to all that follow a holy calling. For it is surely against the wishes of our Saviour that his servants grow fat while warriors starve.'

There seemed no one about, and no beast either, but Dandy rode up to the door of the manse and gave it a great rap with the hilt of his sword. Silence followed, and he hammered again, and this time, after a moment's hesitation came the sound of a bar being removed.

The door opened just wide enough to disclose a young face. Dandy couldn't be sure at first if it was boy or girl. He saw only a pale skin, big doe eyes under a ragged fringe.

But the voice was a girl's, and clear and sharp as a March morning as she asked him what he wanted with them. They were but poor folk, she told him, and if it was meat they were seeking she had none to offer.

'Maybe the priest would ken where some micht be found,' Dandy said, smiling down at her from his horse.

'The priest is a dying man,' she answered, 'and my mither, his housekeeper, lies dead within. You could serve as a burial party, I'm thinking.'

One of Dandy's men plucked at his sleeve. 'Let's away. It's the plague.'

The girl looked Dandy in the eye. 'It's no the plague,' she said, 'for I ken fine what that's like. It's another fever. Have you any skill in medicine?'

'De'il a bit o' it,' Dandy said. 'And are you all alane in the house, lass?'

'That I am, but for the priest on his deathbed.'

'And are you no afeard tae open the door to me and my men?'

'Afeared?' she answered. 'It would take mair nor a troop o' Border callants to frighten me, but I am, sir, in a sair extremity, and would be pleased if you would take a look at the man, for that he is dying I canna doubt. And I am sorry, sir, that there is nae food nor drink to offer ye, bar a pickle of meal and the end of a barrel of saut herring that has seen better days.'

'Well,' Dandy said, 'you're a lass of rare spirit, whatever else, and I'll be happy to oblige you.'

He dismounted, and making a sign to his men that they should remain where they were, followed the girl into the little house. It was a poor mean sort of dwelling, and there hung about it a stench of death and decay that made Dandy want to spew, but the girl marched before him with her head high, and no tiredness in her step, as if she had not spent days and nights nursing and wondering what was to become of her. She led him to a back room. It was dank and cold and the only light was given by a single tallow candle that stood on a small table by a pallet bed. As his eyes grew accustomed to the dim light he was able to see the man who lay there. He saw a wasted ascetic face that still had something of nobility in the high brow and Roman nose, but, when he laid his hand on the man's brow, it came away wet, and the man's eyes were lost and wandering. He felt hot and yet he shivered.

'Is that a priest you've brought then, Nell?' asked the man; and the weakness of his voice told Dandy he had not long to live.

'You ken fine,' she said, 'that there is no a priest within a half-day's ride, and it's no likely yin would happen by.'

'No likely indeed,' the man said, 'for I have been but a poor servant of the Lord myself. Well, I must die unshriven and trust in the Lord's mercy that he take the intention for the deed.'

'You have but few sins to answer for, feyther,' the girl said.

'And is that word not a sin itself,' the priest answered, 'seeing that I am indeed your father in the flesh as well as in the spirit?'

'And if that is a sin,' she said, 'I canna believe it is a great one, for you have aye been a good man, and a kind one, to me and my poor mither.'

Saying this, her self-control gave way, and she began to cry.

'Lassie, lassie,' the priest very slowly and with difficulty made the sign of the Cross, 'dinna grieve for me. Who is this man then?'

'I'm but a rider whae has happened by,' Dandy said, 'and sad tae see you baith in sic a plight.'

'A Scot by the sound of you,' the priest murmured, 'and so it is better perhaps not to enquire too closely in what you do this

276

side of the Border. If the Lord has sent you to be a comfort and stay to my lass, then that may be indeed a token of his grace.'

'And that,' Dandy said with a grim chuckle, 'is mair nor I've ever been ca'ed afore.'

The priest made a noise that might have been an answering laugh or merely a sigh, then sank into sleep again. The girl dried her eyes and stood up. She was slim and pale, the tears had made streaks down a dirty cheek, and she was dressed only in grubby shift of brown cloth. Her feet were bare and her head uncovered, but there was a nobility and fortitude in her bearing that Dandy was drawn to. 'Here,' he said to himself, 'is no well-born girl whose courage will fail in danger, but one a man could rely on.'

She looked him in he eye, then turned away needing no word to confirm her fears. Indeed her father's certainty of his own approaching death had already removed any hope of recovery. She offered to make a brose for Dandy's men with what little meal she had, but he said only, 'they carry meal anough for their purposes.'

'I'll no be needing what we hae, for I canna stay here,' she answered.

'Where will you gang?' he said, but she could offer no reply.

Instead she asked him, but this time timidly, if his men could bury her mother.

'The Kirkyard's no but the other side of the wall,' she said.

'Have you spades?'

The girl accompanied Dandy and two of his men into the churchyard to show them where the grave should be dug. She led them to a corner of the plot beyond a line of yews to where a hawthorn thrust ragged branches into the evening sky.

'She would wish it here,' she said, 'where my brothers lie. But I would not have you thinking he has not been a good priest as well as a good feyther, for a priest is . . .' and then she broke into sobs again. Dandy put his cloak round her, and made to lead her away, then, setting her to rest against an upstanding tombstone, turned back to the men who had already started to dig.

'Dig deep and wide enough for twae,' he said.

The priest had wakened again and seemed momentarily

stronger. Nell told him what they had been doing and he nodded his head.

'Poor Margaret,' he sighed, 'she has aye had a consciousness of sin. I'll no last the night,' he said again, 'and it is my pleasure to think we winna be long parted and I'll be there by her side to answer for the baith of us. Nell, lassie,' he said, 'the gentleman might like a sup of wine. And I'm lief to wet my lips too. There's no muckle left of a gift was gi'en me by my patron, Sir Roger de Bracy, when he rode back from the French Wars wherein, poor man, he suffered mightily.'

When Nell had left the room in search of the wine, the priest caught hold of Dandy's hand.

'She's a good lass,' he said, 'and it seems to me that you hae been sent here for her comfort. Tell me naething of yourself, for I can see mair nor I might like to ken, save only ae thing. Are you wed, man?'

'No, that I am not,' Dandy answered.

'Nor yet betrothed?'

'Nor that neither.'

'Just so,' the priest, with a painful effort, heaved himself into a sitting position. 'And would you marry my lass?'

Dandy paused. The man was in full possession of his senses. A keener look had returned to the eyes that examined Dandy.

'You ken naething of me,' Dandy said.

'I can see you are a man.'

'That can be said of any.'

The priest answered with a thin disbelieving smile.

'There are men and men. Some are wolves, some weaklings and wastrels, and only a few go properly by the name of man.'

'There are those,' Dandy said, 'whae would ca' me in your first category.'

'Doubtless. Nevertheless, it is because you are a proper man that I make this request. I have lived much in the world, my son, for I was not always as you see me now. In my youth, I was a soldier, serving even with my patron, Sir Roger de Bracy, in the French Wars, and eek in those wars against the pagan Lithuanians that we properly term Holy Wars, if any slaughter of our fellow men be rightly so called. It was my wish to fight also with the blessed King Matthias of Hungary against the ravening Turk, and even to venture the doomed city of Byzantium to strike a blow for Christendom there.' He paused, swallowed heavily, and for a moment closed his eyes; then, rallying, continued, now in a harsh and rasping tone as he struggled for breath. 'I have not much time. Will Nell never return with the wine? Quick, though, before she comes, for I would rather have your answer in her absence. Thus do we arrange things for our women. It was not to be. I was prevented, doubtless, by the Lord's wish, to serve him there, and instead translated, as a priest, to this narrow sphere. Why, I know not. Yet I have laboured here these twenty years. The girl's mother accompanied me, and that set me apart from my fellows, not, you will understand because I was a priest with a concubine – many of my brothers so console themselves in the loneliness of our calling – but rather because the poor woman was a foreigner. We came together in Hungary. Oh but she was lovely then, my poor Margaret. And now she is gone, and I am slipping to join her, and Nell is all that is left. I tell you this, my son, that you may know I am accustomed to judge a man. You have a wild face, but a strong one, and a candid eye. Is your heart given to another?'

For a moment Dandy was unable to answer. His natural impulse was to lie. The memory of Alice still disturbed him, but he had kept it a secret thing, ashamed both of the resentment he felt against her and of his enduring desire. But, looking at the dying priest, he found himself unable to conceal the truth, and told his story. While he was speaking the girl brought in wine, and poured two cups, and then, obedient to her father's signal, left them.

'My son,' the priest said, having let a long silence elapse while he pondered Dandy's words, 'my son, I am honoured by your confidence, but, if you are willing to take my daughter, I do not think that your first love and the oaths you swore to her should act as impediment, either in law or honour or according to any knightly code.'

'Muckle I care for knightly codes.' Dandy said. 'But what makes you think your daughter would hae me, were I willing, which I'm no' saying I am.'

'And what else is to become of the poor lass?'

'I winna hae her that road,' Dandy said. 'I'll no marry her

out of pity. And I would think, frae what I hae seen o' the lass, that she wouldna be eident tae tak me thon gait either.'

The priest touched the wine with his lips. 'Thin,' he said, 'thin and sour. But everything tastes thin and sour to me now. I am ready to be gone. No, my son, while it is true I might have such thoughts, my Nell is not one to fear the world. She will aye set her face boldly against it. But I saw the look she cast you, and I hardly doubt that she would be willing.'

Dandy rose and walked two or three times up and down the little room. He stopped at the end of the bed. The priest met his eye. 'Well, sir?'

Dandy drew his dirk from its sheath, and weighed it in his hand. He smacked the blade three times on his left palm, then thrust it home, and raised his mug of wine. He held it towards the priest as if it were a pledge.

'I'll dae it,' he said, 'as lang as the lass is truly willing.'

'Thank you, my son, and the Lord bless you and keep you.'

The girl was reluctant at first, and reproached her father, but when she was silent and saw the look in the old man's eyes, and when Dandy took her by the hand, and with his right hand held her chin level so that their eyes might meet, a smile, almost it seemed against her will, broke out; and, as she smiled, she seemed for the first time to Dandy a woman, and not a girl.

'Sunshine after rain,' the priest said.

'I canna think,' she said.

'Dinna try,' Dandy interrupted her, and bent over to kiss her lips. 'Dinna try. Feyther, will you marry us even now?'

'With all my heart, and in the full knowledge that I do God's bidding.'

The marriage and the wine seemed to revive the priest. For a little he talked freely. His talk was all of the past, and, as he spoke, there was spread before Dandy the whole map of Christendom. He saw the low waste marshes of Pomerania and felt the biting wind that blew thither from the remote mystery of Muscovy; he heard the Danube roll over the wide Hungarian plain, and saw huge herds of wild horses gallop, manes outspread, till they disappeared in the mists rising from the river. He heard troops of worshippers sing the glories of the Three Kings of Cologne, he saw the twin towers of Chartres rise splendid, affirmative and awful, across the waving cornfields, and he walked in imagination the marbled floor of the great Roman basilicas, St Peter's, St John Lateran, St Mary the greater, and St Paul outside the walls. Most magical of all, he beheld the onion domes, the crowded bazaar, the long and intricate walls of the fabled city of Byzantium crowned by the majesty of Santa Sophia, and now, only two years before, taken by the Turks. Again, the priest lamented his own failure to attain Byzantium, 'the last lost jewel, the second Rome, the great city where Christ rose triumphant over the Ancient World.' Tears trickled down his cheek as he spoke of Byzantium, and Dandy felt the narrow confines of his own life.

A rising wind shook the trees in the churchyard and howled round the manse. It was thick dark outside and still the priest talked. Then for a little he slept, and, seeing this, Nell too closed her eyes; but Dandy watched through the night with all these splendid images jostling in his mind.

The priest woke again. For some time Dandy did not observe this till he felt the old man's gaze fixed upon him.

'Tell me what you will of yourself, my son. I am too weak now to do more than listen.'

To Dandy's surprise he found himself telling the story of his life. The words tumbled out. Admissions he had never made to anyone now flowed. No doubt the certainty that his listener was near death loosened his tongue; but the urge to confess is always powerful, and, in Dandy's case, being so long denied, seemed all the sweeter.

At the first mention of Maurie he observed the priest's face tighten.

'You hae heard tell of my uncle then?' he said.

'I did not realize who it was you spoke of when you told me of the lady to whom you first gave your heart. A little man, with a raised shoulder, who is forever fingering the relics of saints which he wears on a chain round his neck.'

'Aye, that is Maurie. You have maybe met him.'

'No, never, but I know much of him. Many years ago, how many I cannot tell, I travelled some days in the company of a certain friar. A lewd libidinous fellow, who disgraced the noble order to which he belonged, and the saint – ' he crossed himself, slowly, with an effort that was clearly painful – 'whose name it bears. He was a swaggering foul-mouthed rogue who boasted in his cups – a nightly condition it seemed – of the crimes he had committed. One night he spoke of the man you tell me is your uncle, and there was a note in his voice such as I have never forgotten. He had, it seemed, done fearful things at this man's behest, and yet this friar, who was so contemptuous of all that was good and worthy, who despised also most of the great ones of the earth, stood in awe of this Maurice whom he styled the Baron of Cleckington. His voice quivered when he spoke of him, and I heard in his tones a mixture of fear, envy and respect. I have never forgotten it, and have always remained curious about the man who could inspire such feelings in a rogue, who, with this sole exception I would have said, feared neither God, man or devil.'

The speech tired the priest and brought on a fit of coughing which woke Nell. She wiped his brow with a damp cloth, held the wine cup to his lips to allow him a sip, and begged him not to tire himself.

'Alas, my dear,' he sighed, 'I shall soon have rest enough.'

Even so he drifted for a little into a doze, and when he recovered, observed with pleasure that Nell too was asleep again.

'There is something I maun speir,' Dandy said.

He paused a long time, and then, laboriously, in the manner of one unaccustomed to explore moral questions, set forth the whole story of his relation with Maurie and asked the priest if he would be justified in seeking a revenge that was likely to end in killing his uncle.

'You maun think it strange' he said, 'that a wild reiver like me, whae has, as I maun confess, sent a score of souls tae meet their maker, should misdoubt on sic a matter. Yet those I hae slain, I slew in armed combat, and I ken fine that my uncle wad never venture his skin in battle. Therefore, if I am to encompass my revenge on him for all the ills and evil he has brought on my house, aye, and I maun confess, on the Lady Alice too, I maun be ready tae kill him in cauld blood. What say you to that, feyther?'

The priest did not reply. For a long time he lay silent, and Dandy wondered if he had perhaps not heard his words, if he had drifted into sleep – but then he saw that his eyes were open

– if perhaps he had at last slipped away. But no, his lips were working, and he spoke at last, though with greater pain and difficulty.

'Murder is wrong, and I can give you no easy answer. It is a sin that cries to heaven. And yet to kill a murderer . . . revenge, my son, is a kind of justice, imperfect, dangerous, for in its execution the first cause is too easily forgotten and swallowed up in the deed. I have little wisdom in these matters and can give no easy answer. And yet, because I see that the matter is important to you, I must try. Revenge, I say, is a sort of justice, and a man like Maurice of Cleckington is a soul given to the devil. We are enjoined to cast out devils, but you must beware, my son, that the same devil does not enter your soul.'

Dandy seized his hand and kissed it. 'Thank you, Feyther, you have made my path clear. And I may tell you, I ken fine from your description whae thon friar was, and I maun add that if the opportunity is granted me tae separate his heid frae his shoulders I will no be laith to tak it.'

Then he touched Nell on the arm and woke her, and indicated that she should look to her father; and when she rose, he left them to be alone together at the last.

It began to snow as they buried the priest by his Hungarian woman. It fell in slow fleecy flakes, and before the last spadeful of earth was thrown back on the grave, Dandy's men were casting anxious eyes to the hills. It would be ill to be caught here on the wrong side of the Border. Yet Dandy would not hurry Nell. The girl had a right to her last devotions, her prayer for the dead souls. He watched the snow fall on her face and turn to liquid as if the skies were shedding tears which she was too proud to weep herself.

The winter that followed was perhaps the happiest of his life. For the first time he knew tenderness without the fear that had run through his love for Alice. He had married Nell out of pity and a strange sort of respect; he had married her perhaps because of what her father had shown him of a world he had never known. In a few weeks though he found he loved her; he had, by pure chance, discovered a spirit that matched his own.

'Will you let me ride with you when the snows have melted?' she asked him.

'Lasses canna ride nor reive,' he teased her.

She kissed his eyes. 'Maybe this one can.'

'It's a lass's task to bide at home and mak the kale brose.'

'I'm no ordinary lass. Oh, by St Mary, how I wish I had been born a boy.'

'You do not,' Dandy touched her lips, 'for, gin you had, you wouldna be in my airms and my bed.'

She bit his finger. 'Happen I could be your page . . .'

'And what would the likes of me do with a page, forbye . . .' he ran his hand under her shift. 'There's nae page could offer me what you do, my love . . .'

'Am I really your love, really and truly?'

'That you are . . . my ain true and single love.'

The snows thawed early that spring. By the end of February the dykes were clear and only the top of Cheviot glinted white. James of the Fiery Face gathered an army in blustery March and came south at a ringing trot to Melrose. He had bound to him all the lords of central Scotland and many from the Border, and he had with him Gaelic speaking warriors from Perthshire and dour plough-boys from Fife and all the men at arms of Lothian.

An outlying shepherd ran to Aikwood Tower to warn Young Clym that the royal army was encamped by the Abbey lands, and Clym, who had been waiting the news, buckled on his sword, summoned a score of his men, and leaving half of them to guard the tower, marched down the water with the rest to pledge his loyalty to King James and so secure his future.

He presented himself to Angus and was welcomed by him with more honour than his status merited, for Angus knew how needful it was to flatter any Borderers who came to the royal camp, and so encourage others to desert the Black Douglas. He presented Clym to the King's grace himself and set him on his right hand at supper.

The king's move had taken Douglas by surprise. The earl looked white as a swan's back and all around was dismay and dissension. The earl saw destruction yawn before him. His hand rested on the pommel of his sword, but he feared to draw the blade. Instead he sent his brother Archie (who was his twin, though unlike him in temperament, for Archie had no more sensibility than a Galloway stot) to the king to ask what terms

284

he demanded. King James smiled to see him come, but declined to receive him. Word came back to the Douglas that his brother had been clamped in irons and carried to Edinburgh Castle. Guilt further corrupted the earl's resolution.

His other brother John urged him to action. At last he ordered his vassals to assemble at Hawick. He withdrew there, hoping that delay would soften the king's temper. But the wind still blew sharp and the stinking vennels of the little town made it a cold place, and a hopeless one.

Dandy, meeting his cousin Wattie in a tavern, was all fire and frustration. But his fire warmed few. The camp was gripped in apprehension. Wattie sat a long hour while Dandy ranted, himself gazing into the smouldering fire.

'What do you read there?' Dandy asked him.

'Cold ashes and a grey morn.'

Dandy smacked his sword blade against his riding-boot.

Wattie said: 'When the gude Lord James won Roxburgh Castle in the time of the Bruce, he garred his men disguise themselves as black kye to deceive the English, and noo we sit penned up in Hawick, like kye at the shambles.'

'No me,' Dandy cried, 'we'll strike a blow that will win oor lives yet.'

Still they withdrew and as they marched to the south-west, the wind, nipping their heels and never shifting from the north, carried the reek of burning farms and keeps and homesteads. And then came word of another royal army that had marched south by the western route.

'We are caught atween the claws of the crab,' the young Lord Hamilton who had stood with Dandy at Stirling Cross said to him. 'We maun nip ae claw afore they close on us.'

The Douglas sipped his wine, nodded his head and gave no orders.

Wattie felt pity for him, but Dandy was not alone in expressing rage, contempt and bewilderment. With Hamilton he again forced his way into the earl's presence where he found Wattie strumming on his harp while The Douglas sipped at the red wine.

Hamilton said: 'My lord, you maun order a battle or we maun a' hang separately.'

Dandy said: 'My lord, I hae twae hunder' men ready to fecht, but they canna move on their lane.'

The Douglas stroked his breastplate. The firelight flickered and a log died. Wattie plucked the strings of a lament and Hamilton marched to his lord and shook him by the shoulder: 'Wull you no' gie he order to move?'

'Against the king,' said The Douglas, 'whae sware me to peace?' And he turned his eyes back to the fire.

Clym filled his lungs with the smoke from the keeps and his eyes sparkled in the light of the burning farms. Every step he took in this fierce raid was a stride into a richer more powerful future. His fortune shone brighter than the fires, bright as the king's face.

'It is lost,' Hamilton said to Dandy, 'all is lost. The great House of Douglas is rotten in its foundations and its glory has vanished. What will you dae?'

Dandy looked at the solid figure, and then over the vacant moors. 'What is there for a man to dae but stand by his lord and be slain by his side?'

'Friend, I hae still lands tae save. My house may have been burned, but my lands are wide and I shall hae sons that maun be provided for. Come, ride wi me, friend. We have fought well thegither, we hae ridden far and wide, stirrup tae stirrup, and hae stood shoulder tae shoulder against the royal tyrant. But the game is lost, and there is nae need for the pair of us to submit to our ain destruction for the sake of a lord that willna stir tae save himself. It is time, friend, to shuffle the cards and deal again. Let us try a new cast of the dice. Ride wi me again, Dandy, tae the king's camp, and I'll warrant we may yet arrange things there to our advantage.'

'You hae lands to save, my lord,' Dandy replied. 'But as for me, I hae nocht to care for but my gude opinion of myself. And I hae a rare conceit, my lord, that would hae me gang to my grave thinking proudly of my ain person.'

'Very well,' Hamilton said, 'I can rest easy in the thocht that I hae done a' that friendship requires of a man.' And, with these words, he took leave of Dandy, summoned his men and rode out of the camp. No man made a move to stop him.

*

286

In the pall of night, with a cloak over his head, the Black Douglas slipped out of his crumbling army. Wattie rode by his side on a little pony, and there were only two boys, pages of the Douglas, who completed the party. They rode in silence, the boys gripped with cold and fear, and the Douglas with his head lowered. They were miles clear before day broke.

Word had come that the king had sent on outriders to guard the Border passes that none of the trappened army might slip through the net. So they bent their course to the west, coming by the afternoon within sight of the Solway water. They marched its shore till they came to a little village where they sought a boat. The first man they asked was overcome by fear and bolted himself in his hut denying knowledge of any craft, but towards evening they found a stouter or greedier fellow who, on recognizing his lord of Douglas, demanded silver before he would put his little boat to the water. Drawing his cloak closer round his head, the Douglas left the arranging of the business to Wattie. He sat all afternoon over a jug of wine in the tavern, and in the fading light of the afternoon he may have traced his journey from the spring flowers of childhood through the memory of his great encounter in the lists with the Burgundian to this hovel stinking of fish; he may have begun the thirty years' making of his soul. The moon dipped behind heavy-banked clouds as the water lapped against the bow of the little boat; the Black Douglas crossed over into England and landed on the margin of History.

Dandy woke to the news of the earl's flight. Before the sun was up men were trickling from the camp. Others were bridling their ponies with the haste and oaths of fear. On the distant hills he could see the flags and tents of the royal army. Hamilton would be there, attending to his beard and whiskers before requesting an audience of the king, and then, despite the swagger with which he would enter his Grace's presence, making humble and humiliating submission. Dandy's cold hands trembled as he buckled his sword belt. Nell approached brushing sleep from her eyes, and he envied her the trust that had let her find repose. He held her to him and looked over her shoulder at Amos Rutherford, his oldest riding companion.

'Hae the beasts saddled and gar the men mak ready.'

'Aye, Dandy, that I will, though I see no place to run.'

'We dinna run. We ride in orderly warlike fashion tae the hills.'

Their route took them through a pass a bare mile below the royal army, but the valley road was shielded by a beech wood, and, certain of their day's triumph, the royal captains had been careless of their dispositions. Only a handful of troopers guarded the ford that would let Dandy and his men pass behind the king's position and make for the wild moors of the upper dales of Tweed.

A challenge was thrown out from the ford, and Dandy stood high in his stirrups to let them see with whom they had to deal. An arrow whistled by his head. He lifted his hand and ordered the score of men that had remained at his command to take the ford at a sharp downhill canter. Nell rode by his side, her knee almost touching his. He settled his lance and made straight for the sergeant of the guard. The man hesitated as if he would offer fight, and then wrenched at his horse's head and turned tail, clattering through the water. Dandy dug his spurs into the pony's flanks and put it hard at the braeside. The sergeant's horse baulked at a line of gorse bushes and reared. The man struggled to control it and, in doing so, half turned the beast towards Dandy. Dandy levelled his lance and thrust its point under the sergeant's chin. The horse lost its footing. Horse and man slithered down the slope, the movement dislodging the lance from the sergeant's neck. They gathered speed in a whirl of hooves, flying mane and flailing arms. The sword slid from the sergeant's hand. They careered down the hillside to disappear under the peaty water of a pool some thirty yards below the ford. Dandy turned his pony, smiling. His men had scattered the guard. Half a dozen riderless ponies were making off up the opposite slope. A number of bodies lay at the waterside. Nell gazed at them. Her stomach hollowed at the thought that any one of them might have been her man, or the son she had not yet borne him.

Clym tore at a mutton bone. There was a happy and complacent mood in the camp. Even Clym had smiled to see Hamilton make submission, and captured men driven in at the sword's point. Angus too had smiled as he promised to reward his loyalty. Clym dreamed of fat lands and fat cattle.

X

The bell tolled a long Requiescat as shadows crept round the castle wall, and maids-in-waiting knelt in prayer by the Lady Clare's bed. That scene, lit by candle with flames wavering in the draught could still disturb Maurie's sleep. He told himself, often he had no regrets. He had, as always, acted in accordance with necessity. Yet he knew that, in creaking his finger at Brother Ambrose, in giving him that decisive nod, he had performed a deed which stood alone in his history; its consequences assailed him. Clare was dead, as others had been, by his will – ah yes, indeed, but from Necessity also; and yet it was not the same, not as it had been with others. Even Ambrose, he knew, felt that: the friar's gaze fell on him like a Bill of Attainder, a judgement against which there was no defence.

'Pish and tush,' he muttered, fingering St Aidan's relic, 'pish and tush, is it possible one death can be so unlike another?'

In the howdumdeid of night he had descended from his lady's chamber, descended while her waiting-women still mumbled their prayers, to the dungeon where her idiot son was confined. 'Hail, lord of Boscobel,' he smiled, and turning to his gaolers, said, 'unless you feed a light, it will die. But there is, friends, a time for all to enter the darkness.'

He had sent messengers to Warwick to acquaint him of all that had come to pass, and to assure him of the love he felt for him and of his constant duty to the Lady Alice. They brought back, as he knew they would, his commission: he was confirmed in his wardship of her, her lord, and a – stroke of unintended and thoughtless humour – their heirs, and also as guardian of the vast estates; bidden also to take such care of the Lord Boscobel as may be deemed necessary.

'Come, my love,' he said to the Lady Alice, 'you must see him once that you may know from what I have saved you.'

Did she think: 'To what you chose to condemn me'?

Her head rested on his twisted shoulder, and she wept.

That night she swore her ladies to secrecy, and told them all she had seen, and all she had been constrained to do. She had said, then 'I am caught by my own sin in my lord's sin, and I am filled with horror at the thought of my own corruption. The child in my womb is surely accursed too. How does my lord think it may be born? And if born, how acknowledged? Would he blazon my shame to all the world? Have his own deeds turned his wits?'

'My child,' Dame Eleanor said, 'the world is made and ordered by men, in their cruel image and for their own delight. And yet, child . . .'

'And yet?'

Lady Alice held a mirror to her face, and watched her breath cloud it.

'And yet, child, there is another world, that marches by this one, and there is another route, another way.'

The glass cleared.

'What do you know Dame Eleanor, of such matters?'

'Child, I have ventured on the road, and can show you where it starts. There are rocks and precipices and many perils, but at the end there is a promise of enlightenment and wholeness. Do you wish . . .?'

She paused. Alice blew again on the glass and watched as it cleared, slowly from one corner.

Maurie studied the letter his ally Truncheon had enclosed with Warwick's commission. It confirmed what he suspected. Affairs of State were approaching crisis; the king's misgovernment was growing intolerable; the skirmish at St Albans between the adherents of the Duke of York and the King's men had settled nothing; Maurie should hold himself ready, to recruit troops, to wait Warwick's call to arms.

An uneasy truce held. Yet snow clouds loomed. England, no less than Scotland, was nervous, and apprehensive; it was weather when men's hands flew to their dagger-hilts. The House of Lancaster had suffered failure on failure since heretic-burning Harry of Monmouth had brought his cold life to a cold grave. His wretched son was now as complete an imbecile (men said) as if he represented a judgement on Harry's cruel life and his

grandfather's usurpation. Why, he was no more fit for government than the idiot chained in the dungeons of Mirabel. Yet to
dispense with him was dangerous; it is ill to move against an
anointed king. Everywhere, in castles all over the realm, men
weighed the odds. The queen, that she-wolf of Anjou, would
fight for the rights of their son Edward, Prince of Wales.
Meanwhile bands of soldiers, discharged on the disgraceful
conclusion of the French Wars, which had left England with
only Calais as a reminder of the English Empire in France,
roved the land seeking, and finding, employment.

The wind, though, blew hard from the north. Maurie had no
doubt of that. He made this clear to his old patron Edward des
Moulins, who had come to Mirabel to assist at his sister's burial.
'Abandon the House of Lancaster,' he urged. 'It is a decayed
tooth in the mouth of England.' Edward, however, was mulish:
he talked of honour (honour!), even in his cups. (And he was
rarely out of them.) Maurie sighed. Did Edward not see that
there was only one law in such affairs, the law of power? Sixty
years back this had dictated that men follow Henry Bolingbroke
and abandon Richard of Bordeaux. Well, the House of Lancaster had held the throne these six decades. But now their grip
had loosened and would not be renewed. Could he not see that,
and did he not agree that Government was necessary? King
Henry could not provide it. How, Maurie asked, can we protect
property unless there is firm law? On the contrary he urged, 'we
are compelled by the lack of governance to provoke lawlessness
ourselves. So men-at-arms sit in our hall, and no man's life, no
man's estate is secure. The key shall keep the castle and the
bracken-bush the cow. That was what King James promised the
Scots, and though we worked against him in our own interest,
his intent was good, wise and politic.'

He leaned across the table and removed the wine flask from
des Moulins' grip.'

He looked at his old friend's pale, cheese-coloured face, and
sighed.

'I have heard,' he said, 'that the old enemy of your family,
the Earl of Douglas, sought refuge at Castle Greer, and that you
turned him away. You were wise to do so, not because he was a
rebel to his king, but because he is a broken man, doomed to
failure by his own incapacity. And yet, my lord, you court the
same fate yourself. Come join with me, bind yourself like me to

the Earl of Warwick and the Duke of York, and so ensure the fortunes of your house.'

Des Moulins reached for the wine flask again. He gazed on Maurie as if on some strange unfamiliar being. In his ox-like manner, moving through the months in vague fuddled state, des Moulins found himself lost in a world which contradicted his instinctive trust that things would never change: that he could not lose his position of honour. And yet, in the nightmare that disturbed his rest, he knew this was false: time and again, he woke screaming, his own screams echoing Suffolk's as the fishermen dragged him across the wet sand to the boat that would serve as his execution block. And he had seen The Douglas too on his knees in the dust before him. He was afraid, and to calm his fear refused to admit what these things signified. He stared at Maurie, who had been his servant, his sister's lover, with whom he had shared a past that no longer seemed to have any meaning, and who seemed at ease in this new world that denied himself.

Maurie said to the Lady Alice: 'There is no profit in trying to persuade him. He is fixed in his course which will land him in the mire.'

Edward roused himself once. He asked to see his nephew. Maurie smiled and led him down the twisting stair. He saw Edward shiver as the chill caught him. His foot slipped on the slimy cobbles and he almost fell, steadying himself only by gripping Maurie's arm. They advanced into the inner dungeon. The idiot, barely illumined by the lantern Maurie carried, crouched in his own dung. He raised his head. His uncle fell back a step.

'Does he know nothing?'

'Nothing. He neither knows nor feels, and in the last week, he has ceased to eat.'

'He fled in fear,' Maurie said. 'It was as if he saw himself reflected in the white eyes.'

'Lord,' she said, 'will the idiot die? When will he die? It would remove a weight from my spirit.'

'He will die,' Maurie said, 'before our child is born.'

*

Maurie was near sixty, but his vigour seemed only to increase. His neck rarely felt the rope that Gudewife of Hangingshaws had promised him. He would wake by Alice and feel every morning spring. He would ride out across their wide lands and nurse the thought of his son's inheritance. He no longer marvelled at what he had achieved, for his past had grown distant to him. When he lolled in Church during the service and heard the priest descant on hell and the day of judgement, or on the awful need to repent that a man might die in a state of grace, the words held no meaning for him; he was above and beyond such matters.

Then, one week in November 1460 the idiot at last expired, having been denied food for thirty days. Only Will had any tenderness for the wretched thing, and it was Will who made himself responsible for its burial, and paid a priest to say a mass for such soul as it might have had. The following night the Lady Alice miscarried again, this time of a daughter. Maurie shrugged his shoulders ('it was only a girl'), and allowed none to see that he felt himself cheated. For Alice, however, her second child's death seemed like a judgement: conceived in lust, rather than love, in a union marked by sin and deceit. She could hardly bear to look on Maurie.

He however was caught up in the great world. That summer had seen sporadic fighting over England. It had been a time to take sides, and the White Rose of York had suffered a sore check. Had his judgement been wrong? The pompous, complacent Duke of York, eager for power and respect, yet fearful to seize what he would have, was defeated at Wakefield, his timid head struck from his neck on the field of battle, and then hung from the walls of York with a paper crown mocking his pretensions.

Maurie ordered Mirabel to be prepared to stand a siege and sent messengers to Warwick to let him know what was intended. The rain and mud of November cut all approaches to the castle. No attack was likely till spring; yet he could not relax. He had not anticipated this, and he knew, that, unlike a great lord, his fortune depended on continued success. Let him stumble once, and how joyfully boots would trample his face in the mud. It was no time for woman's wails and tears. Everything for which he had struggled was at risk. The Lady Alice marked his indifference to her grief, and chalked that against him too.

Winter set in hard. The land was locked in a forty days' frost. Red deer came out of the high woods and down to the valley farms, then beyond them into the villages and even to the fringe of the Castletown. Four soldiers of the guard were found frozen to death; after that the guard was withdrawn to the hall itself; no army could move in that ice-gripped country. Lust and love both perished in the bitter cold; it cracked all Alice had ever felt for Maurie and left him in her eyes an icicle old man. He himself, taken in that bleak December beyond sex, beyond food and beyond drink, sat in a tower room wrapped in bearskins from the Baltic and martin's pelts, his gaze fixed on the dancing fire as he waited for spring to unlock action.

Brother Ambrose died on the eve of Christmas. His last boy, the lady's page, drew a rough cloak over his face. No graves could be dug in the iron ground. His body was added to the growing pile.

Maurie had become an object of fear. His origins were quite lost. There were few now who remembered that he had been a Scot, few who recalled from what meagre stock he had sprung. He existed as a force, an expression of naked will, malignant, dreadful, acute. Even hardened battle-scarred veterans froze at his quiet rebuke. Men felt for him the awe which is occasioned by the being who accepts no restraint on his own will. No matter how cautious he might be in action, the sense emanated from him that he would always dare more than another. So, in the sergeants' mess, all winter, there was speculation which way he would move: when spring came.

Then, on a goose-grey January noon, a messenger presented himself at the main gate of Mirabel. He gave every sign of having ridden hard and far, for his horse was coated with sweat and mud, and almost gone in the legs. The man himself had to be held up when he dismounted. He was revived with a mug of hot ale, and brought before Maurie.

It was a moment before he recognized him as Truncheon. Seeing his condition Maurie felt afraid: was he in flight? Had Warwick himself been taken? Had the Lancastrians, under the Duke of Somerset, nipped conspiracy in the bud? And, ever as these fears flashed through his mind, it came to him angrily how Edward des Moulins would triumph in his timid and stodgy adherence to things as they were. But, restraining these questions, he clapped Truncheon in an embrace and led him towards the fire.

'I landed in the Humber,' Truncheon said, and Maurie, hearing these words saw the sun of York break through the clouds.

'I was pursued twenty mile. Lord, lord, I am too old and infirm a man for such games.'

'Forget your aches and age, friend. What is the news?'

Truncheon smiled, lay back in a chair and kicked off his top-boots. He held his feet to the fire and toasted them. 'I can feel the blood flow,' he said.

The news was good, if they could keep their nerve – 'aye, and our hearts too' a few weeks more. Edward, Earl of March, now, after his father's death, Duke of York, was gathering an army in the Low Countries, an army of Brabanter routiers, Flemish pikemen, Burgudian kinghts as well as those Yorkist retainers who had followed him across the sea. It was formidable, experienced, and like no army that had been seen in England for thirty years. Truncheon smiled. And what of Warwick, Maurie asked. Well, Warwick was lying low and tranquil, Truncheon said. Warwick was careful, and safe. But his agents were out. The whole North would rise. Maurie, too, must seize this chance for fame and fortune, a chance such as would never present itself again. They looked at each other, their eyes holding, and both smiled. There was – Truncheon let his fat tongue rest on his lower lip – only one question. Warwick was, as of course Maurie knew, a warm family man. He wished the Yorkist party to be bound together by the holiest of bonds. He was of course York's uncle, and had already arranged that his daughter Margaret should wed her cousin George; but there remained the matter of the Lady Alice, whose husband, Truncheon sighed had turned out so unfortunately but was now, he gathered, no longer with us. What, Warwick wondered, was to be done with the Lady Alice? She was too great a lady to be left a widow.

Maurie said: 'Humble though I be, my lord of Warwick could find no more faithful husband for his daughter than myself, nor none that would secure her interests better, or is more tender and steadfast in his devotion to my lord of Warwick.'

And Truncheon smiled again, clapped him on the back and said, 'The very words I hoped to hear, friend, and spoken like a man.'

Spring blossomed full and fecund. Before the daffodils, Edward of York landed at Ravenspur. Maurie marched to meet him, leaving his wife in command of Mirabel. The sun shone on the tall son of York who leaned graciously from his six feet to embrace the Lord of Boscobel. Warwick too purred at his new son-in-law (who was older than he was himself). The army advanced in a clatter of colours on the despondent Lancastrians. Maurie was put in charge of supplies, and revelled in the task, commandeering food, drink, weapons and transport from reluctand lords with a quiet menace that made them shed their unwillingness and hurry to assist. York's youngest brother, Richard, only twelve but already wise in the vicissitudes of fortune, attached himself to Maurie: 'one crookback to another,' men said, out of hearing of both. Maurie grew accustomed to finding the boy's dark almond eyes fixed on him, and enjoyed their homage. There was something there, he thought, of his own temper: a ruthlessness and competence that pleased him.

A snowstorm blew up at Towton in the first week of April. The wind howled white in Lancastrian faces. Frozen hands dropped swords and were unable to pull bowstrings. The Yorkist cavalry with the young Duke sitting high in the saddle lurched down the gentle northern slope and fell on the Lancastrian mass. For a moment it seemed that the battle would be brief. A fragment of the Red Rose broke, only to drown in the deep and muddy river. The others, seeing this, resolved to stand to their fate. The struggle lasted a grim morning and the river ran blood down to the water meadows below the bridge.

At last the duke rode back up the hill to the little gathering sitting their horses by a chantry. Warwick dismounted at his approach and the others followed suit. The great earl bowed himself low and kissed the duke's foot. He looked up at the mounted boy. 'We have this day made you master of England, Ned.'

His choice of pronoun did not disturb York's smile.

'I have you all to thank,' he replied, and at that moment the

snow stopped, the clouds parted and the sun lit up the landscape, dotted as far as the eye could see with fleeing and
pursuing men. Screams and shouts rose to them, but to the little
group on the hilltop the scene below was distant as in an
illuminated manuscript framed by the greenwood of the English
Midlands. There was never kingdom so thoroughly won in one
morning's fight, for there was no doubt in any mind that they
had only to march on London now, and that they would do so
to the merry note of drum and trumpet.

And in London they would find him who had been king
almost since birth.

In the half-light of early evening the Lady Alice awaited the
gypsy woman whom Dame Eleanor had promised should tell
her fortune and restore her life. She dreamed of what she had
missed, of how life had cheated her, and, in the clarity of
solitude, saw who had marred her life.

The Tower crouched over the London river, and narrow streets
huddled round its walls. Booths selling cooked food – pies,
pasties and steaming sausages – nestled against the outer walls
of the fortress on the city side. Boats and barges bobbed and
jostled each other on the water and a brown scum collected at
its edge. Maurie waited in the prow of a rowing-boat; it was
almost thirty years since he had last come here to confer with
Henry of Winchester. The people thronging the gates raised a
cheer for the duke. So would they have cheered had he been
brought here in irons, Maurie thought.

Hands were held out to help them disembark. The duke
brushed them aside and leaped on to the grass, which was
fringed with lilies. 'I prefer these English lilies to those of la
belle France,' he cried. A raven pecked its way towards him.
The duke threw back his shoulders, raised his mighty head with
the yellow hair shining, and addressed the crowd; 'Good Lon-
doners,' he began, and they cheered again. He spoke of peace
and justice and the restoration of true order that trade might
flourish and all men live at paeace with their neighbours. The
words came, he told them, from his heart which overflowed with
love and gratitude to his people and his Saviour. Who could
believe such stuff? Maurie wondered. The keeper advanced with

the keys of the Tower lying on a red velvet cushion. He knelt before the duke who reached forward and placing both hands on the cushion took it from a surprised but unresisting grip.

'My lord Boscobel, of Mirabel and Cleckington,' he called out. Maurie, with some difficulty because his back was stiff and his right knee ached with rheumatism, climbed out of the boat. He knelt before the boy who was his lord. The duke, balancing the cushion on one hand, extended the other to help him to his feet.

'Take these,' he said, gesturing to the keys, 'we appoint you keeper of our Royal Tower, being assured that no man will better acquit himself of the manifold duties this place entails.'

The Lady Alice, with Dame Eleanor in attendance and the old crippled gypsy woman leading the way, slipped out of the side postern of Mirabel by dead of night. The moon was not yet up, but a north-easterly wind sent heavy dark clouds scudding across the sky, yielding passages of a strange violet light against which still bare branches of the hill wood rose up. They travelled quickly, so quickly that they were unaware of a girl who followed them. The Lady Alice moved as if unconscious of the dangers of the night, seeing only what was in her mind's eye, though Dame Eleanor twitched at her sleeve and muttered warnings. The third member of the party murmured constantly under her breath in a strange language that neither of her companions understood. Meanwhile their follower, intent on escaping observation, found she had to hurry to keep them in sight.

In a little while they were in the wood and the ground had levelled and they were following a rough and overgrown track that ran alongside the stream. Here the noise of the water enabled their pursuer to keep closer order, which seemed necessary to her lest she lose them in the trees. They left the stream behind them and climbed again, until, having reached the brow of the hill, the gypsy paused, like one seeking direction.

The wind dropped and the branches were still. The cry of a storm-bird came to them and the gypsy nodded, as if she had been awaiting the signal and, turning always to the left, resumed her path, but faster now. Their route wound through a pine wood, spiralling, and they climbed onward in silence. Dame Eleanor found herself short of breath when they halted again, but, catching her mistress's look of excitement, as if she awaited splendid and yet frightening things, held back her complaint. Before them a ride led up to a strip of the western sky. The moon swam clear of clouds, and the sky was broken by a jagged tower.

They entered a clearing and were surrounded by women. They pressed against them with warm caressing hands. Breath, fragrant with odour of camphor, fanned their cheeks. The unknown women embraced them and one drew back the hood from Lady Alice's face, and drew her soft long fingers down milady's cheeks, and a sigh, as if of rapture, was uttered. The same hands then drew the Lady Alice aside and placed her on a stone bench that ran round the tower. Dame Eleanor looked from face to face and saw none she knew; yet one advanced on her and addressing her by name made her welcome. There was honey in her voice and she looked on Dame Eleanor with love.

'We have waited long to see you,' one said to the Lady Alice.

The woman who had been following them saw all this from the position she had taken up behind a wall that ran along the south side of the tower, and which had once no doubt encircled it. Then she saw them give a cup to the Lady Alice. She drank from it. The sound of soft laughter and soft loving voices came to her, and, for a moment, forgetting why she was there, she felt herself to be an exile from delight. Then the whole company formed itself, without any word of command being audible, into a column and they entered the tower, the Lady Alice being escorted as a guest, it seemed, of honour. When she was sure all had gone in, the follower crept from her hiding place, and, mounting the stone bench, looked through the embrasure.

There were a dozen women, or more. All had stripped the garments from the upper part of their body, which were now bare but for garlands of wild roses and mingled herbs that they had hung around their necks. There was an open space behind the tower wall, which, the follower saw, was bounded by a ring of crumbling masonry. At the far end sat a tall dark woman on a raised bench or throne. She held a silver dish in her left hand. It was lifted high so that its face was directed to the company, but the watcher could not see if there was any design on it. The moonlight fell on the woman's face which was pale, calm and lovely as the Virgin's in the chapel at Mirabel.

In turn each of the women approached their enthroned queen or priestess, and kissed her upraised hand. Then each laid at her left side gifts they had brought; bread, eggs, wine, oil and silver. They trembled as they did so, and the woman leant forward, her robes fluttering dark green in the candlelight behind her, and kissed each woman on the lips, and then indicated to each of them that she should kiss the dish which she held in her left hand.

When all the women had performed this ceremony, which was accompanied by no word or note of music, two others led the Lady Alice forward. She knelt, and the queen laid down the dish and leaned forward. She drew her hands down milady's face, cooing like a turtle dove, and then, with great care and gentleness, as one performing a holy ceremony, removed the upper part of her clothing. She caressed her breasts and the watcher caught a murmurous pleasure on the night air. The queen drew milady to her and they embraced, their mouths locked together in an exchange of tongues. Then milady stood upright before the queen, and the two women who acted as her attendants slipped off her skirts and out her shift so that she stood in full naked loveliness before her majesty.

The woman on her left took her by the wrist and led her toward a flat stone raised some two feet from the ground, as it were a tomb. It was covered with a rich cloth and there was a pillow of soft spring flowers at one end. The woman indicated with a loving gesture that milady should lay herself on this couch, and she obeyed, smiling.

She stretched out her legs and parted them and the whole company uttered a deep sigh. The queen rose from her throne, and crossing the rough ground with a curious floating motion, and carrying a wand in her left hand, pressed herself on milady, cooing and caressing all the intimate parts of her body. She began to work the wand and milady cried out and the other women moaned. Then they paired off as for a dance, but instead lay on the ground and began to pleasure each other, as their queen pleasured milady. The watcher, again forgetting why she was there, felt a deep ache of loss and longing, and would willingly have leapt up and joined them. Prudence and fear restrained her, but, she said later, 'it seemed to me as if unimagined valleys of delight were beckoning, and yet I was denied entry . . .'

Milady cried out, a piercing delight such as the watcher had never heard or thought to hear from any mortal being, and all the women cried out too, and the moon danced in the sky. There came, as from a great distance, the sound of galloping hooves, and led, it seemed, by no human hand, a troop of milk-white palfreys appeared. The women rose from the ground and mounted them. The candles were extinguished, someone struck up a wild tune on a stringed instrument, another sounded a horn. Last of all the queen and milady rose from their bridal couch (as it appeared to the watcher); together they mounted the same milk-white mare, milady in front of the queen. All the women cried out, and the mare that carried the queen and milady leading the way, all galloped out of the broken enclosure and careered down the hillside. The breeze carried the sound of hooves, the blowing of horns and the cries of rapture over the woods and to the distant hills. For a long time the watcher remained where she was, frozen by fear, wonder and envy. At last silence resumed, and the watcher, lifting her head saw only a vast emptiness and the dark shape of the broken tower.

'Where is he?' Maurie said.

'He? You mean the king?'

'I mean Henry of Lancaster that was king.'

'No skaith will come to His Grace, will there? The Tower was surrendered on that understanding, was it not?'

'Skaith?' Maurie said, and took the nerve in the man's elbow between his thumb and forefinger. 'He will be well attended.'

Maurie was led into a high-vaulted chamber. The window looked over the grey expanse of river and the walls were hung with Arras tapestries depicting hunting scenes. Three figures sat in the room, as if they had stepped out of the tapestries. There were two old women sewing at a table. They did not lift their eyes from their work as Maurie entered. A thin man, dressed in black, his head shaved, for he had been suffering from ringworm, knelt at a prie-dieu gabbling prayers. Cries of lightermen came from the river, but, when Maurie let the door clang behind him, there was only silence but for the quick persistent gabble.

Maurie said to the women: 'Bring him to the table and set him down, that I may speak to him.'

The first woman said: 'His Grace prays. Do you not see that? It is wicked and sinful, against all the laws of Holy Church, to interrupt the poor man at prayer'; but her companion rose, smoothed her skirts, and crossed the room to him that had been king. She knelt beside him and put an arm round his shoulders and whispered to him. The shaven head shook. She renewed her coaxing, until at last, with the utmost reluctance and with shy backward glances, like a good child being removed from its toys, the man allowed himself to be led to the table and eased into a chair.

Maurie sat opposite him. He looked at the pale eyes, and they could not meet his, but flickered aside as a hare's might. The thin hands, mere bones held together by a veil of skin, moved on the table. The finger ends picked at each other. The nails, bitten back to the quick, were flecked with dried blood, blots on the grey parchment of his skin.

At last he who had been king from birth spoke, so low that Maurie had to lean forward to catch the words.

'She has no cause to be angry with me. I have prayed all night to the Virgin that she would not be angry. I have done all I can to avert it, and have prayed, but have no wish yet to desist from prayer. Why did you lift me from prayer? Do you not see that I must pray for my miserable soul and for all the wretched of my unhappy realm? I have more prayers to offer to my Lady that she will intercede on behalf of her unfortunate and unhappy servant.'

The woman who had lifted him up leaned towards Maurie and said, 'It's the queen's anger he fears, sir. If you can persuade him she's not coming back you will find him as gentle and willing to please as a newborn lamb. For that is what he is, sir, as helpless as a lamb. If it wasn't for Mistress Margery and me here, I don't know what would become of him.'

'Does he understand nothing then?'

'He understands the queen's red anger right enough.'

'Does he know he is no longer king? Have you told him that?'

'Lord bless you, sir, as if that would matter to the poor babe. They have put too much upon him, the poor soul, and that's the truth, that's why his wits have fled him. He has no care for earthly things now, it's a heavenly crown that his mind, such as it is, poor thing, is set on winning, and it's a long time since he has given any thought to that other business save when the queen compelled him.'

'He knighted me,' Maurie said.

'Did he now? That would be long ago. He hasn't been able to bring himself to touch even the pommel of a sword these seven years.'

'Does he eat?'

'Curds and whey and a wee bit bread, that's all. Enough to keep body and soul together, though he would fain let his soul run free, poor child that he is. Not that I would wish that to happen, sir, not yet. He's a saint, sir, and Mistress Margery and me are that fond of him, sir, why he is no more trouble than a baby, except when She troubles him.'

'Well,' Maurie said, 'she has fled to the north, they say. He will not be troubled by her again.'

Mistress Margery shook her head and spoke for the first time: 'She'll not rest, my lord. She has a wild and tireless nature. She'll not accept defeat.'

The other woman, Dame Bridget, whose voice was soft and western, her hair white as a Swaledale fleece, said, 'But no harm will come to the poor man, will it? You see, sir, what an innocent it is.'

He who had been king plucked a rosary from the deep pocket of his surcoat, and his lips quivering, like a rabbit chewing, told his beads.

'He thinks of nought but his poor soul,' Dame Bridget said again, 'and yet it's sure I am that there's no stain bigger than a violet's head on the poor misused creature. Oh it has been a rare grief to him to have been a king.'

'Well, it's a grief is spared him now,' Maurie laughed. 'Mind, ladies I promise nothing, but it is presently in no interest of the king's to alter his condition.'

'My brother George,' young Richard who had been made Duke of Gloucester said to Maurie, 'is of opinion we should kill Henry of Lancaster, he says that while he lives my brother Ned will not be recognised as king by all, the late king, usurper though he was, having been crowned and anointed by Holy Church.'

Maurie smiled. 'And what say you, my little prince?'

'I say,' the boy piped, 'he can do us little harm alive, and may yet wound us dead.'

'Expound your reasoning.'

'There are two parts to my argument, my lord. In the first place, while he lives and is our prisoner, those who love him will hesitate to raise their hand lest they endanger his life. Therefore our present clemency is our greater security.'

'And the second part?'

'Is this. He has a son, my cousin whom they style Prince of Wales, now in flight with his mother of Anjou. While his father lives, he can claim only the empty title of Prince; if his father were dead, he could style himself king. Furthermore, his liberty of action is now circumscribed by the tender care he must demonstrate for his father's life. For these reasons, I controvert my brother George. Am I right or wrong?'

Maurie looked at the boy's set yellow face, marked its knowledge of pain, bright eye and thin decisive mouth; he had had no such pupil since he first instructed the Lady Clare.

'You are altogether right, my prince, and wise in your judgement. Prince is, as you say, an empty title, a vain thing, and this fugitive prince defends a lost cause which loses adherents daily. Smile, little Duke of Gloucester, the stars in their courses mark our triumph, all things have come to fruition, the sun of York shines on the land, our ambition flourishes and the outlook is fair for England and for ourselves.'

XI

James Kennedy had styled the Black Douglas 'the king of thieves', and after his flight, the thieves scattered. Most are as lost to legend as to history, and only occasionally does a name surface. There were half a dozen years in which nothing is heard of Dandy Laidlaw. Mothers in Stirling, and other parts too doubtless, might couple his name with that of the Douglas in the threats they used to quiet their bairns, but nothing is known of his whereabouts in these years. He may have continued in the upper reaches of Tweeddale, and since he appears in no document it is assumed that he remained a landless man, keeping body and soul together on a diet of cattle reiving and sheep stealing, contriving certainly to escape both famine and the gallows.

There was though another tale that was current in his branch of the family till that died out in the seventeenth century. This told of how, mindful of Nell's heredity and intrigued by it, he left the kingdom and travelled across Europe to her mother's land of Hungary, seeking his fortune there and failing to find it, but fighting in a mercenary company in the wars against the Turk. According to this story he even took part in the last defence of Constantinople, and was wounded by the side of the last Emperor of Rome: yet this cannot be, for the city was taken some two years before the Douglas's defeat. Nevertheless the tradition is strong, and Dandy may well have been one of the many Scotch soldiers of fortune who adventured in Eastern Europe.

Meanwhile his cousin Clym prospered, being well rewarded for his abandonment of the Douglas. After King James of the Fiery Face was blown to kingdom come by a cannon which exploded at the siege of Roxburgh, the real power in the realm was held by the cautious and subtle Angus, and Clym rose by his side. By the middle 1460s he was on his way to becoming one of the great men of the middle Border.

These were years of peace with England, and Clym flourished in the peace. He had never had much time for the old traditions of his house. He saw that money could be made more safely by honest trade than by reiving and Clym had a warm taste for gold. He formed an alliance with a group of merchants busy in the cloth trade and he had too an interest in a trading-vessel that sailed out of Eyemouth. Berwick merchants too knew him as a douce and careful investor in their enterprises, and though there were many in the Borderland who despised Clym for his peaceful ways, there were others who nodded their head and called him a wise man 'who aye kennt the airt of the wind'.

One day, in early summer, a messenger presented himself at Aikwood demanding to see Clym on a matter of importance. Clym, thinking there might be profit in it, agreed to see him, but was dismayed when the messenger proved to be only a lad of sixteen or so. His dismay deepened when the boy revealed that he came as an emissary of his cousin Dandy, and that Dandy had sent him to propose a meeting and to tell Clym that he recognized the error of his ways and wished to make an accommodation with lawful authority.

Clym's first instinct was to send the messenger on his way, preferably with a couple of blows. 'It shows little respect,' he said, 'tae a man of my position that he should send sic a callant tae me.' There was something, he reflected, in the choice of such a messenger which was an expression of Dandy's old impudence; it was as if he was laughing at Clym even while he sought his help: for certainly Dandy had little hope of a pardon unless his cousin interceded on his behalf. The choice of messenger indeed sharpened all Clym's old dislike of his cousin, a dislike which was (though he would hardly admit the fact) sharpened by his awareness that Dandy had always laughed at him. Besides, he had no wish to be reconciled to his cousin; the only news of him which he would have wished to receive would have been word of his death; and indeed, not having heard directly or even indirectly of him, he had hoped that this would have occurred. To be reminded of Dandy was bad enough; to have the reminder come in this impudent guise worse still. He glowered at the boy.

'The rogue can lie in his ain mire,' he said, 'or swing at the end of a hempen rope for all I care.'

But then Clym's prudence stayed him. He was never one to make quick judgements, and it came to him that it was just possible that Dandy might indeed have something to put before him. After all, he thought, Dandy had no more warm a feeling for him that he experienced himself. They had never seen eye to eye. So it might be that if Dandy now made approaches to him, it might be worth listening to what he had to say. Dandy was admittedly a fool – his whole career showed that – but he was not without a certain wit; he knew Clym well, and therefore he must know that Clym was not like to help him unless he himself was able to put something in his cousin's way.

So, instead of giving vent to his first impulse, he drew his cloak round him, nursed his long chin on its fur collar, and bade the boy speak on.

But the boy smiled: he had said his say. His master sought a meeting, and he could go no further than that. Except this: he had been told to add that if Clym was loath to meet his cousin, Dandy would then be obliged to make his approaches elsewhere, and if he did so, Clym could be sure that he would regret losing the opportunity offered him.

Clym glowered again. 'Tell your master, if sic he be, though I hae little respect for the judgement of a loon that follows sic a scapegrace, that I will see him. I will laith see him safe here at Aikwood within a sennight.'

Again the boy smiled. 'Na, na,' he said, 'my maister, as I am blithe tae own him, tellt me to say that he has nae wish to impose upon your lordship's hospitality. He will bide for you by St Mary's Chapel on the day afore the full moon, and, gin you dinna come he will tak' his wares elsewhere.'

With these words the boy, acting, Clym surmised, on instructions, turned on his heel, and left him. It tried Clym hard to let him depart; yet he could see no alternative. But he marked this insult against Dandy too.

Six days later the larks sang and the peewits swooped and the curlews called on the moorlands as Clym trotted up the valley at the head of some fifty men. He had spent the past week seeking information about the size of Dandy's troop, knowing that to approach him with too large a force would probably

cause him to retire into the wild hills, while to come with too
small a one would put himself in danger.

The loch spread out before them in the sunshine and the little
chapel stood hard by it, but there was no sign of Dandy and his
men. Clym, gazing over the empty country, ordered his sergeant
to deploy his men in such a way that they could if necessary
defend the church.

The morning wore on bright and blue. Clym rested in the
chapel porch and kept his eyes fixed on the hills. He felt an
unaccustomed throb of excitement and impatience. And yet he
told himself that there was nothing Dandy, a landless outlaw,
could offer him which would bring him profit. It was ever
Clym's way to discount his hopes in advance.

Towards noon he saw a troop of no more than a dozen
horsemen come down the sheep track on the other side of the
valley. He ordered his men to stand to their weapons. The band
halted. The horsemen circled, and seemed to be engaged in
discussion. Then two figures detached themselves from the rest
and advanced at a low walk towards them. Clym's son, Clym
the Third, approached his father and said, 'It seems, feyther,
that your precautions are scarce needed.'

'Think you so? Weel, lad, there will be an arrow trained on
Dandy's breist the while we talk, and I'm thinking that we will
hae a better and truer debate as lang's he kens that. Ye maun
be mindful that we are no dealing with an honest man the day,
but with yin that is as crafty as a tod and as trustworthy as a
serpent.'

And, saying this, he got to his feet and clapped his hand on
the boy's shoulder.

'Aye, cousin,' he sang out to Dandy, 'and hae ye come here to
submit yourself to the king's justice?'

Dandy dismounted though without giving any sign that he
had heard Clym's words. It was only then that Clym realized
that his companion was a woman, and he frowned to see this,
for he realized that Dandy felt secure in some advantage that he
held. Dandy handed his horse to Clym's son, and nodded to his
cousin as a neighbour might across a garden fence. He lounged
towards the chapel and sat down on a stone bench, as easy in
his manner as if he was settling himself outside a tavern, and
waited for Clym to join him there. His will prevailed, and Clym,

shrugging his shoulders, yielded the advantage he had thought to hold, and joined him.

Dandy chewed on a stem of grass and looked sideways at his cousin, and told him how he had heard that he had become a great man.

'I wad never hae thocht it of ye,' he smiled, 'Ah weel cauld parritch can smoor a fire.'

'Gin you hae come here tae insult me wi' bairns' mockery,' Clym said, 'I'll hae you strung up on yon rodden tree.'

He pointed to a lonely rowan growing by the lakeside, but Dandy continued to smile. 'You'll no dae that,' he said, 'for I maun tell you that gin I dinna return tae my men safe and sound, aye and afore the sun sets this evening, there will be consequences that will make you smart with grief and anger at the opportunity you hae lost. I gie ye fair warning of that, cousin, and you will understand them fine when you hear the tale I am about tae unfold.'

With that, he smiled again, clapped Clym on the thigh, called for ale (which Clym would fain have denied him, but dared not do so), drank deep, ran his hand over his lips, and began to speak.

They were travelling (he said) back from a cattle raid into Northumberland. They had had little success, for the word of their raid had gone out and even the dullest peasants had driven their beasts to safety. So, barring a fat merchant from Flanders, whom they had robbed and beaten, they were riding home as lean and hungry as they had travelled south. He shook his head at the thought, and drank some more ale.

'Haud your wheesht, Clym,' he said, 'and be patient. My tale will interest you yet. I swear it.'

So, he resumed, their mood was sour. And, as it happened, the weather matched it. Usually of course neither wind nor rain would distress them, they rode as easy in foul weather as in fair. But, when they had got clear of Kielder and into Liddesdale, their necks stiff from looking back to make sure that they had shaken off their pursuers, the rain turned to a downpour, huge black clouds as heavy as the king's hand surged up, the lightning flashed and the thunder crackled and boomed. It was no weather for riding, and, judging that any pursuers who might have given chase would care little for it either and have abandoned their track, they turned up a side valley, for Dandy remembered that there was a deep cave there which would offer them a bield. Night was approaching too and they clattered up the burnside, splashing and scattering loose stones in their haste to win a refuge from the storm. (Clym cracked his knucklebones with impatience, but Dandy still smiled.) Then it happened that a flash of lightning tore the sky apart and rived a hawthorn tree which burst into flames like a witches' sabbat; it lit up the mouth of the cavern halfway up the steep brae and so revealed the tall figure of an armed man guarding the entrance. They reined in their horses, in awe or horror, for in the wild light he seemed to be no mortal man, but their desperate state stiffened their nerve and they put their horses at the hillside. The man challenged them, which, Dandy said, was some relief for it suggested he was but a man, since a demon would be quick to cry out a welcome to them. He therefore shouted that they came in peace and were only travellers seeking a bield for the night. But the man remained obstinate. He would not, he said, permit them to enter, and he levelled a sword at Dandy to show that his words would not lack support. But Dandy was too quick for him. He was off his horse and grappling with the man and sticking a dirk in his side before the guard had completed the backswing of his great sword, and so he was dead before he could cry for help, if help there was. He crumpled to the ground and the way into the cave was clear.

They advanced behind drawn swords. A dim light flickered ahead. It revealed three figures crouched round a fire of twigs and heather which half-filled the cavern with smoke. The slightest of the three leapt up, his hand at his belt from which dangled a dagger. Even in that light Dandy could see he was only a boy. Nevertheless he sang out a challenge in a voice that had hardly broken and, when there was no immediate answer, called out 'Hugo'. Silence held a moment. 'I misdoubt he'll hear ye,' Dandy said, and, understanding his words, the boy darted forward. Dandy grabbed him by the forearm, so hard that the dagger fell to the ground and the boy sank to his knees. Dandy relaxed his grip, first kicking the dagger into the shadows with the side of his foot. 'Ye're a wild lad,' he said, and ye'll win yoursel a dirk in the gizzard ere it feels a razor gin you carry on

310

this gait. Aye, and I'll send ye on to hae a crack with your freend Hugo.'

The boy lifted his head. 'Take your hand off me,' he said, 'I'll have you know that I am of no common blood.'

'Is that so?' Dandy laughed, liking his spirit, 'but I'll hae you ken, laddie that it's an uncommon situation in which you find yourself. Now bide easy,' he said, and took his hand off the boy.

At that moment the man by the fire advanced in a fearful twittering scamper to tell the boy to be silent. Dandy, his eyes now used to the light, took stock of the pair of them. He saw a brave boy with a snub nose and unruly curly hair and a peely-wally thin fellow that was like, as he put it, to piss himself in his terror. 'It's the wrang yin o ye's the bairn, I'm thinking,' he said.

Then the third member of the group spoke. This was a woman, and she had a strange foreign sort of voice, Dandy said, looking hard at Clym. She rose up from the fireside by which she had remained crouching throughout this scene, all in dark clothes, with a grey poll, like a hoodie-craw. There was some-thing in her face that cut off Dandy's laughter, and he fell involuntarily to his knee before her. The shadows flickered on the walls of the cave and he saw the woman reflected there. She stretched out her hand and drew the boy to her and held him close. Dandy felt her scrutiny.

'You are wild men,' she said, 'I see that well, but you do not have wolves' faces. I throw myself on your mercy without restraint or concealment.'

Dandy fell silent and looked Clym in the face.

'Dae ye ken whae she was?'

A fish jumped in the water and the air was filled with the rattle of a grasshopper, and the scent of heather, wild thyme and camomile. Still Clym did not reply. His thick hands pressed themselves together and his slow mouth moved without opening like a cow chewing the cud.

Dandy nodded, and took up his story.

There was something in the woman's manner which held them abashed. She seemed to ask them for nothing and it appeared that she would have felt insulted by pity, and yet they pitied her, and did not move.

Then she spoke again. 'You see before you,' she said, 'the

unfortunate and ill-used Margaret, Princess of Anjou, Queen of England and France. Though I might rail against the evil winds of fortune which have swept round my life as a river in flood may carry all – beasts, stacks, crops, fences even trees and walls – before it, I disdain to do so. Nor shall I howl against the ingratitude, wickedness, cowardice and treachery of mankind. I shall not even bewail the plight of my captive and sainted lord, Henry of Lancaster, sixth of that name to be rightful King of England. I shall not seek to impress you with my state or my royal blood. Instead, I stand before you, wild men as I see you to be, at your mercy. This brave lad, whose will would have slain you had his body been equal to his spirit, is my son Edward, Prince of Wales, the last and sole hope of the House of Lancaster. We throw ourselves on your mercy, though your faces and manner proclaim you to be fierce and lawless robbers; yet you cannot be more cruel than the treacherous nobility of England. I take you to be outlaws. Therefore I seek your protection, being myself cast out and deprived of all that I have known, reduced to misery and thrown into the cold night of exile and defeat by those who now command the law of England and hold my poor miserable lord their prisoner.'

'Aye,' Dandy said, 'it was some speaking, sich rhetoric as I hae never heard frae priest nor poet.'

'And whae's this?' I said then, pointing at the ither loon.

'This,' says she, 'is a' my train is reduced to. He is the lord Henry des Moulins, and he makes me mindful of that property of geometry which clerks call "reductio ad absurdum".'

'At whilk,' Dandy said, 'the queen lauched, and I likewise thinking it seemly, though fair bemused by what she micht mean.'

'Weel,' Dandy said to the queen, 'happen we are a' indeed naked men and women in fortune's winter. Happen, Your Grace, my men and me are hungry, and it may be that we'll take better counsel when our wames are fu'.'

He broke off, and looked at Clym. 'Aye,' he said, 'it was my opinion that my tale wad make you loup like a saumon.'

Indeed Clym was on his feet and scanning the little group on the farther hillside as though the queen might be among them. 'But I'm no',' he added, 'clean gyte. The queen's grace is lodged in a safe place, and I hae come merely to speir of you what should be done.'

Margaret had been anxious of course that they should be led straightway to King James's court, and Dandy had at first been near ready to take the risk. But he hesitated. There were, he reckoned, too many men there whose fingers itched to put a rope round his neck, and there were trees at Falkland and Linlithgow with stout branches from which a man might be set to dance in the air. Even coming with such a prize in hand, Dandy feared he would not be safe. Yet – and he emphasized this – he was determined to do the best he could for the poor lady. Had he come on the queen in all the majesty of power, he would happily have seized her jewels, slit her son's throat or (more likely) held him to ransom; but her lonely and destitute condition, and the boy's spirit, had touched him. The spark of chivalry, an essential element in his nature, though half smothered by his struggle for a place in the world, had been kindled. He would therefore do what he could for fallen greatness, and he was encouraged in this resolution by Nell. Hence the approach to Clym.

He didn't know just what he hoped for. He distrusted Clym of course, and resented and even feared him. Yet the more he brooded on the matter, the less risk there seemed to be in turning to him. It was not that he believed in the old saw about blood being thicker than water; in his experience it ran just as easily. But if he didn't trust Clym, he nevertheless had confidence in his ability, experience and ambition. He knew he had something worth offering his cousin.

At the same time Dandy hadn't fought his way through life without acquiring a good store of knowledge of men and women. There was something in the queen that he could depend on. She was hard and fierce doubtless, and those who had named her 'the she-wolf of Anjou' had hardly erred. Nevertheless there was, he believed, quality there. She would requite a service done to her, if that was within her power, just as surely as she would revenge an injury. So, if Dandy could put himself in the position where he might aid the restoration of her fortune, she would not forget him. She would see too that Clym did not cheat him. That encounter in the dark of the cave might cause the sun to shine again on his own life, which had languished in the shadows since the day the Douglas had fled to the Solway shore.

As for Clym, he was hardly moved by the story of the ruined queen and gallant prince, but his mind was working. Even as he listened to his cousin's tale, he was pondering the attractions of different courses. He could do as Dandy suggested. That would be easy and safe and he would be well rewarded, for Angus would be happy to welcome the royal pair; the King of Scots was after all still, in name at least, the ally of the House of Lancaster, and there was advantage for him in aiding the defeated party south of the Borders: Scotland could only gain from England's division and weakness.

Then there was another course which tempted him, disturbingly. He had always played cannily; yet now there opened before him the prospect of great influence. What would his uncle Maurie and his Lord of Warwick give for the surrender of the fugitives? He chewed that prospect with the zest he brought to the task of extracting the marrow from a bone.

And then he was stopped in his cogitation by another thought. There were many who failed to understand Clym; they thought that because he was dour and silent and had an eye to the main chance, he was without the warmer emotions. Yet this was not so, and there is more than one kind of self-gratification. Clym had never forgotten the morning when his father had ridden south to bring Maurie home to justice, and the memory of that evening when Rob trailed up the road to Clartyshaws, alone, with the news of Old Clym's death was warm. His mother had sworn him to revenge his father. She had said, 'See to it, my son, that Maurie Laidlaw, that traitor to God and his own blood, gangs til no easy grave'; and Clym had sworn the oath. It bound him still; in the night watches when he was distressed by fear of the fires of hell, this unrequited oath preyed on his mind, and came between him and sleep. And now . . . had the Lord delivered his enemy into his hands? Might he not bait a hook with Margaret of Anjou and Edward, Prince of Wales?

He said to Dandy, 'We hae crossed swords in the past, cousin, but this day our interests march thegither. We maun trust each tae the ither.'

'Aye,' said Dandy, 'just so. And you'll let me ken when you hae had word frae the king?'

Clym looked at his array of armed men. 'No sae fast, my bauld warrior. What's tae stop me frae seizing you even now, and hauding you fast? This wife you ride wi can carry the news back to your ain men, and hae them bring up the captives.'

'Aye, aye,' Dandy smiled. 'Your trust rins a lang wye, cousin. But, forbye what I tellt you at the start o' this colloquy, you canna think I am the man that is ignorant of your nature, and sae unlike tae take precautions. In the first place, I maun tell ye, that for a' the men ye hae wi ye, ye'll be hard pit till it tae win your way back doon the valley. Yarrow ford is narrow and ill-won, and it is held ahint you by three score men, a' hardened fechters in a heist of battles. The Swire road too is held at a narra point. And, in the second place, gin I mysel dinna return frae this encounter, why then, nae matter what message is brought purporting tae come frae me, Amos Rutherford kens fine what he is tae dae. And that, cousin, will be action such as will ripe a' advantage frae you, and deprive you of this road tae fortune that I hae opened tae ye. Na, na, cousin, ye ken fine that our interests march thegither. Dinna let your dark and crooked nature tempt ye yo deny this. I shall bring the Queen of England tae ye, and him they ca' Prince of Wales, only when I learn you hae arranged for their reception by King James, and when you bring me a full pardon for a' misdemeneours I may have committed. Play me fause, cousin, and you will no live to play again.'

He got to his feet, certain of the force of his argument. He nodded once to Clym, beckoned Nell and they strolled to their horses. Clym looked at the ground and chewed slowly.

XII

Maurie suffered from an ague in the damp air of the Tower. He lay listless and fevered through the summer. When he recovered, his left fist was clamped shut. He could not prize the fingers far enough open to grasp the reins of a horse's bridle. He consulted physicians. Some said it was but the progress of age, others looked more darkly and muttered that it lay beyond their understanding and their science. He began to feel oppressed by the Tower; the stench from the river was making him ill, he said.

Then the king brought him relief. His relations with Warwick had cooled. He sought a reliable lieutenant in the north. Though he knew Maurie to be an ally of Warwick, he knew enough of men to see that that alliance was not of the heart. He sounded Maurie out, dangled an independent greatness before him, and Maurie emerged Lord President of the Council of the North.

Within a week he took the old Roman road out of London. For the first days he travelled in a litter, but the breeze from the hills seemed to invigorate him, and though his hand hardly relaxed, it did so sufficiently to enable him to sit a horse again. All along the line of the road peasants bent over scythes in the broad fields and their women moved doubled up to bind the sheaves. The road was busy with troops of mules and ponies laden with the northern woolpacks for the London exchange, with merchants going fussily about their business, with returning pilgrims from the shrines of St Alban, and St Thomas at Canterbury. Such soldiers as they encountered marched under the happy discipline that King Edward imposed on the south and midlands. Maurie rode part of the way with an abbot returning north, and purred to hear him praise the king's government and the peace it had restored to the land.

The young Richard of Gloucester accompanied Maurie too, as far as Castle Raby where his mother Cicily Neville, Dowager

Duchess of York, awaited him. The boy's face wore a sullen look at the thought of this return to his mother's apron-strings, but Maurie chafed him into good humour.

'Come, Duke,' he said, 'the work I go to perform in York will be your work soon. I go only to prepare the way for you, to warm your seat. Fret not. I am an old man, and the north is a great wild country that calls for more energy than I can long provide. I have spoken to your brother the king, and we are agreed that you will be my successor.'

'What of George? He is older than I.'

'Older, Duke, but not wiser. Your brother of Clarence is an amiable lord. I can speak frankly to you for I know you love him. But he is infirm of purpose and wild in judgement. You require a cool head to govern the wild lands of York and Northumberland. Clarence will not do. Remember that my judgement is unclouded, for Clarence is my wife's sister's husband. That does not blind me to his weakness. He is moreover bound to his father-in-law, my lord of Warwick, and ... and ... between ourselves, Duke, the great earl has, it is well known, done great service to your brother the king and feels that no reward can match it. Yet beware, Duke, the man who has a high opinion of his own deserts. As for yourself, respect your abilities and achievements, but be not proud. School yourself to take no heed of your own merit, for such can blind a man to the realities of State. No man, Duke, merits more than he can hold.'

'What, my lord, has become of my cousin of Lancaster whom they called Prince of Wales? Is it really true that the King of Scots is ready to help him?'

'The King of Scots is a child, younger than you. There are wild men at his court, but wise heads too. They will talk loud, but there will be no clash of iron. We need not fear open war.'

'What need we fear then?'

'What a lad you are for questions, Duke: What are we to fear indeed? Treachery and disloyalty are constant alarms in life. Let your brother the King's Grace beware traitors.'

'Surely no one would turn against Ned . . .'

'There is the matter,' Maurie said, 'of his marriage.'

They were silent. The words 'the king's marriage ' had that effect on members of the Yorkist family, and no wonder. King

Edward, described by one of his own chaplains as 'greatly envied in the lists of Venus', had long resisted Warwick's efforts to marry him to a French princess. 'I have brothers enough to succeed me, uncle,' he said. 'Moreover, while I remain unwed, my condition remains a diplomatic counter of some value. Marry me off, and I am but another wedded man.' He would smile at Warwick as he spoke thus, and never observed how his uncle scowled and nibbled at his lower lip. In such speeches however the king was less than frank. He had encountered what was new to him: a woman whom he desired but could not conquer. This was a silver-gilt beauty called Elizabeth Woodville, the widow of a knight who had adhered to the Lancastrian party and been killed at Towton. King Edward laid court to her. She lowered her bashful eyes. He pressed his suit. She smiled like a cat licking cream. He employed all his powers of fascination and she said that she was deeply honoured. He threw back the curtains that concealed the royal bed, and she admired the furnishings. The king itched with frustration. The court caught the infection and itched with him. Warwick brooded on the matter and turned a darker shade of grey, and Elizabeth Woodville, whose pale cheek knew no pink blush of embarrassment, murmured of the sacred duties of motherhood and the requirement for a widowed mother to preserve unblemished chastity and reputation. It was a comedy, but one that grew more bitter. At last the king gave way. He proposed marriage. The virtuous widow hesitated. Would he not, she asked, be wiser to wed a foreign princess? Edward tried to seize her and drag her to a couch. She gazed at him from under her long and irreproachable eyelashes, and sighed that she could never marry a man who did not respect her virtue. So, with a groan, he respected it, and they were secretly married the next week; but, though a few knew of the wedding, he had hardly dared to tell Warwick.

So, no wonder Maurie's mention of the royal marriage cast a gloom over young Gloucester. He had touched on the one matter that threatened the Yorkist supremacy and the family's grip on the throne.

Though Maurie had been riding six days when he reached York, and did not gain the castle till the afternoon light was dying and the vale was hidden in the mist of twilight, he hardly rested before summoning a meeting of his council, refreshing himself only with a mouthful of bread and pickled herring and a cup of sweet canary wine. The dozen members of the council could not all be assembled, and only four sat at the table.

Two were strangers to him, two well known. He remarked on that. He observed too that, because of his great age – and, weary from his journey, he looked old and withered – his would be but a brief tenure of office. His successor would be a royal prince. Of necessity he would be young and without experience, though – he assured them from his own knowledge – possessed of the highest qualities; it therefore behoved him – and his trusty councillors – to ensure that when the north was handed over to his royal care, he should find it in a condition of order and tranquillity. There must be peace on the Border, or as near peace as that troubled and disputed land could know. What was the news from Scotland?

One of the councillors – it was the new Bishop of Durham – hurried to answer. There was no danger, he said, to be feared from the Scots. The leaders of their council of regency, the Lord Boyd, his son newly created Earl of Arran, and the Earl of Angus, were all sincere in their desire to maintain peace and friendship with England. The Lord President, he said, could take his word for it.

'I have stayed too long in the south,' Maurie said, 'as keeper of the Tower of London. I would have blithely headed north had I realized that the Golden Age now flourished here. Come, my lord bishop, do not deceive yourself as to the sincerity of the Scots. The Scot is sincere only as a weasel is sincere in its desire to suck the eggs a fowl lays.'

The three other councillors tittered to see the Bishop's discomfiture. Maurie turned his gaze on them, and they fell silent.

'What word of her who was usurping Queen of England and the pretended Prince of Wales?'

'None,' said a knight. 'They have vanished as if off the face of the earth.'

'They are presumed dead,' the bishop said.

'Strange presumption. My lords, I tell you this: we can feel no security and there will be no true peace till they are laid by the heels. If, as I guess, they have found refuge north of the

319

Border, then we may look for trouble. Be assured that it is in Scotland's interests to foment dissension in England, and they will neglect no opportunity to do so. Ergo, it is likewise in our interest to disturb the northern kingdom, to set vassal against lord, baron against king, son against father, brother,' Maurie licked his thin cracked lips and sucked in his breath, 'brother against brother. Such is our interest and our policy. Do not then, my lord of Durham, intrude your sincerity within it. And you, sir,' he turned to the knight who had spoken, a red-cheeked, red-haired ruffianly figure, 'I charge you to prepare me a report of all the rumours concerning the whereabouts of that self-styled Prince of Wales.'

Maurie summoned his lady to York Castle, and with her his brother Will.

'I am glad to see you in good health,' he said to Will. 'I had thought my good red wine would have carried you off ere now.'

'Na, na,' Will said, 'you maun mind, brother, that our promised fate is different.'

'Come, Will,' he said, 'you are not still brooding on that old wife's words. They are a long time fulfilling themselves, are they not. Why are you looking at my hand?' he asked his wife.

'I was wondering,' she said, 'how it had come about, and what measures you had taken to cure it.'

'It is,' he said, 'but – natural infirmity of age. Why, did you hope for more?'

'I wish nothing but your health, my lord.'

That night Maurie and his lady lay in the only chamber in the castle that offered any semblance of comfort. They had made love, but angrily, without tenderness, as though he wished her to submit to whatever is dirty, exhausted and ugly in old age, while she attempted to put his old age to such tests of performance that it must confess itself at last defeated. The opposites which had formerly attracted them now disgusted both. Afterwards they lay in cold silence, each triumphing because submission to the other's will had been again resisted; the war remained frozen in siege.

Politics, Maurie knew, had once cemented what lust had joined; and now politics would crack that cement.

His mind dwelled on the rift that was developing between the king and her father.

He drew his nails down her flank. This woman had come near to overpowering him. She had promoted the one deed that he found himself regretting. Surely she had bewitched him? When he had commanded the friar to break his old alliance with the Lady Clare he had murdered his own youth at the same time. And now the woman for whose sake he had done this reminded him that his joints creaked, that his limbs were always cold and that the grave waited for him.

The wind howled round the tower. Maurie felt his wife tense by his side. Should he force her again? He stretched out his bony hand, and, as he did so, felt the other tighten.

XIII

The crowd surged round the Lord President as he rode back through the streets from hunting: he held a nosegay of herbs – rosemary, lemon thyme and dried basil – against his nostrils to guard against the stench, and the risk of infection. In his old age Maurie clung ever the harder to life. The town had been in a bustle that morning with the rumour that the Scots had advanced south of Bamborough. His own information assured him this was not so, and it was to show himself unconcerned, and so allay the rumour, that he had ridden out.

Back in the castle, a page pulled off his boots. Another pressed a goblet of sweet canary in his hand. A third massaged his neck, for a day in the saddle told against him now. A fourth tripped up with a letter.

Maurie told him to read it aloud. The boy blushed and replied that it was marked for his eyes only. Maurie sighed and dismissed the other pages. He took the letter from the boy and broke the seal.

'Who delivered this to you?'

'A beggarly Scot, my lord.'

'Have him brought before me.'

'Immediately, my lord. There are two other men, Scots also as I think, who seek, or rather crave, an audience.'

'Let them wait. This has a more promising air.'

He waved his hand to dismiss the boy, and read the letter again.

It was from Clym, his cousin or nephew, he could scarce remember which. The manner was clumsy and ill-written, but the matter – that was . . . he searched for the word . . . enticing? The writer announced that he expected to have, within the next days, the renegade self-styled Queen of England, and her son who called himself Prince of Wales, in his hands, in his own castle. Clym professed himself in a quandary. Should he surrender them to his distinguished uncle, who might wish to have this opportunity to bring peace to his country, or should he rather hand them over, as they wished, to the King of Scots? Being loth to do aught which would disturb the tranquil relations then subsisting between the two kingdoms, to their general good, Clym sought his most distinguished uncle's advice; and perhaps proposals. Not so ill-written after all, Maurie thought.

'Here is the man, my Lord'

Maurie saw a crop-headed lout glowering at him. 'You are the man who delivered this letter.'

'Aye, that I am.'

'Do you know its contents?'

'Not to speak of knowledge, sir.' The man scratched his head. 'Seeing as for ae thing the seal is no' broken, and for another that I canna read. But knowledge, as you maun ken, my lord, is a wanchancy thing when it is a matter of affairs atween great persons. Furthermore, a body canna help but surmise and conjecture, and, seeing as Gabriel Nixon, sic being my name' – he ducked his head towards Maurie – 'is no only a gleg observing man, but yin lang acquaint wi his ain Master's affairs, and sae I wad wager a Galloway stot tae a broken-mou'ed gimmer, that ony surmise I micht hazard wad hit the mark.'

'Then, my friend, take a sup of canary – or would you rather ale? – and sit down and give me the benefit of your opinion.'

The two Scots who were kicking their heels as they waited for an audience with the Lord President played dice in the corner of the Great Hall. The one who held the dice-box said, 'If I throw a pair of sixes I shall recover my estates.' He rattled the bones and his long grey hair fell ragged over his eyes.

His companion shook his head. 'If you throw right, my lord, happen we may get dinner, gin we ask cannily.'

In the Castle of Mirabel, the Lady Alice, who had fled thither to escape her lord's attentions, waited for the old Gypsy woman who had promised once more to lead her to their queen. The light was fading and she had come to prefer that half-light in which she could dream of what she had missed. In the half-light, what had been imposed on her – an idiot and this cold man who now appalled her – seemed half to belong to another half-life. She had been cheated of much, and of more, but in the dusk could surrender to other dreams. In the gathering dark she tasted the honey of revenge.

Maurie was in high humour at the table, a mood which cast an intense and chill dread over his entourage. He placed Gabriel Nixon at his right hand (which offended a visiting abbot who should have been that evening's guest of honour), and he teased his pages, which made each tremble lest he offered the wrong response, or lest the teasing should slide into the sarcasm which fell like a lash from his tongue and tore the skin off them. But there was none of that tonight. Maurie smiled and laughed and chaffed them, and after the meal even remembered the two beggarly Scots who had sought an audience. He asked the fourth page where they had been put, and was told they had eaten their dinner at the bottom table among the grooms and stable-hands.

'Have them brought up,' he said, and then felt Gabriel Nixon's hand fall heavy on his arm.

'What is it?'

'Do you no' see? Do you no' see whae it is that makes his way towards us? Why, my lord, you see approach you the very ruin of nobility. Though it is now some twelve or fifteen years since I hae cast my een upon that countenance, yet I canna be mistaken. What does the Earl of Douglas, that was lord of lands frae Clyde tae Cheviot, in this humble and miserable state? Are there nae lords in England to hae a tender care for fallen greatness?'

'Is it indeed Douglas?'

Maurie ordered the two Scots to be led into an antechamber, and commanded Gabriel to follow him there. He settled himself in a carved oak chair behind a table, and did not move as the earl entered. Instead he saw the earl hesitate, saw him quiver as if he would turn away, and smiled to observe how he trembled, waiting for the Lord President to address him.

The page drew a curtain beind the Scots to exclude the noise from the hall. He placed a five-flamed candelabrum on the table before his lord, bowed low and withdrew.

'My lord Douglas,' Maurie said, 'it grieves me to see you in so abject a condition.'

Once he had seen – a long time ago, when he was a youth – a swan die, on the marge of a loch, with pine woods behind, in a November dusk.

'Whence have you come, and where have you journeyed these many years?'

The earl's eyes shifted away. He gestured with his left hand, a movement that began as if it would be a great sweep that would dispel everything which had destroyed him, and set the past aside; but the gesture was not completed. His hand dangled in the air, and he could not speak. Instead his companion, fixing Maurie with a candid blue eye (not wholly sane, as it might be, but unafraid) replied on his behalf: 'To Rome, my lord, on pilgrimage to the Holy Shrines where the blessed saints Peter and Paul were rendered martyrs to the Faith, and syne these weary feet of ours hae hied them to the Holy Land itself, even to Jerusalem, and these knees hae scraped the skin off o' them on the floor of the Holy Sepulchre, and we hae worn our feet bloody on the via dolorosa that leads to Calvary. And now we are returned, our vows fulfilled, and my poor lord, whom I hae sworn to serve all the days of my life till he receives the balm of release frae earthly pains, seeks your gracious intercession that he may go home to lay his banes in our ain country. For it is his desire – aye, and mine too – tae breathe again the caller air of our Border hills afore we die.'

He spoke, keeping his gaze steady, but the Lord President disregarded his words, and himself addressed Douglas again.

'My lord of Douglas, you have suffered for your ill policy and your blindness to your true friends. But it is too early to prepare your soul. All that is lost may not be retrieved, for we cannot regain time, but much may yet be recovered. I have news to hand which, when I act upon it, may yet serve to restore you to your earthly glory.'

'Na, na,' the earl's companion said, 'we'll nane o' that, my lord is beyond a' that. The cruel whips of life hae flayed a' the flesh frae his back. He canna thole ony mair tribulation.'

'Enough,' Maurie said, 'who is this wretch to come between great lords in the discussion of affairs of state?'

'I am thinking,' Gabriel Nixon, said, 'that this is yon Wattie

Laidlaw that is a cousin of my master's whilk was brought up in Douglas Castle by the Lady Mary and was driven, men say, clean oot o' what few wits he ever had, by the word of thon Black Dinner that young Earl William was garred tae eat in Edinburry castle, and I'm thinking too that frae the manner he speaks naething since has served tae drive them in again.'

'A cousin of your master's? I think the worse of Clym Laidlaw that he lets the fool travel the roads.'

He tinkled a bell that stood on the table before him. Two men-at-arms entered.

'Take this insolent Scot. Flay him well and throw him in a dungeon. You cannot teach a Scot manners, but, by St Aidan, you can make him rue his lack of them.'

Then Maurie called one of his pages. 'Take the Earl Douglas,' he said, indicating the heap of rags. 'Lodge him in the guest room of the West Tower. Let new garments be set before him. Have my barber trim his beard.' he sniffed. 'Let him be bathed too.'

Left alone with Gabriel Nixon, he said: 'The game moves my way and your master's. You will ride tomorrow, and this is what you will tell him.'

The next day Maurie was seized by a fever and confined to bed. His hand had tightened again. He raged at his illness, cursed his physicians, and tired himself. A rumour ran round the castle that he was like to die. He caught something of the mood from the nervousness his attendants displayed, and cursed them the more roundly. There was no one he could trust. He felt the cold breath of a solitude that was strange to him. He had always felt himself a man apart, but this had been determined by his own will. Now, it seemed to him, circumstance controlled his freedom as never before.

Yet he roused himself, pale, shivering, and so feeble that he required the support of a page's shoulder to let him stand upright, on hearing that Richard of Gloucester had arrived in the city.

The prince was agitated. He stood at the window overlooking the yard, and picked at a wart on the back of his left hand. He snapped at the page to settle his master and leave them alone.

'Warwick has discovered Ned's marriage,' he said. 'You

know, none better, how my uncle prides himself on his ability to
conceal his mind. Well, when he learned of the marriage, he
abandoned all restraint, and cursed Ned to the four winds. His
vanity shrieks aloud.'

He hobbled across the room with his rapid lame motion that
made them think of a spider.

'Ned has been a fool. He allowed our uncle to proceed with
the arranging of the marriage to the French princess. I asked
him how he could be so daft. He smiled and said he had been
sure the French would not agree, and in the meantime, he said,
"It amuses our Uncle Dick and keeps him out of other mischief."
Well, the amusement has vanished, and Dick is mortally
insulted. He swears the queen must have practised witchcraft;
in the next breath he accuses Ned of being selfish, self-willed,
self-indulgent and deceitful. "After all I have done for the House
of York," he cries, "I set the crown on your head." That is his
refrain. So what's to be done? Ned smiles, as he always smiles,
and confirms Uncle Dick in his honours, and tells me our uncle's
humour will soon pass. He is mistaken. You must agree he is
mistaken. I know my Uncle Dick, and so do you. He is a man
who lives in his self-esteem, and depends on the esteem of others.
He will not laugh off so public an insult, he will brood and plot
revenge. But when I tell Ned this, he only laughs. Am I not
right however?'

Maurie rested his elbow on the table, his head on his hand.
His body ached with fever.

'You are right,' he said, 'Your uncle cannot be trusted now.
You know the name he delights in: the king-maker. Which king
will he seek to make?'

Maurie was overcome by a fit of coughing which wracked his
frame. He had to fight for breath, and struggled to articulate.

'There's George,' Gloucester said. 'He is married to Uncle
Dick's daughter. But George would not betray Ned. We stick
together, we sons of York.'

'Warwick is a politic man. He would never kill the king to
install George in his stead. But he might let George think he
would, and tempt him with the Crown. But if he is to betray the
king, then he will need more than that slender fraction of
Yorkists who would follow George. He must turn to the House
of Lancaster. But, listen, and I will make you privy of a secret,

327

which you must reveal to no one, not even the king. I have reason to believe that I shall shortly have the boy Edward of Lancaster, whom they call the Prince of Wales, and his mother of Anjou, in my hands. So, you, my Prince, must ride to London, and when I send you word, you must be ready to cut off the head of the House of Lancaster. Aye, indeed, we approach the hour when the mad Henry's prayers must be answered and he be admitted to Abraham's bosom. Come, my prince, fetch me my seal and I shall give you authority to command my lieutenant of the Tower to deliver him to your care, and so to eternity.'

Maurie chafed, waiting for Clym's reply. The game was all but in his hands. Yet events which he could not control swirled about him. Triumph beckoned, just out of reach; he cursed Clym for his delay, cursed King Edward for his folly, cursed his wife for his condition. He sweated at night, assailed by vile dreams. Hearing the wind blow like a lost and angry soul round the castle, he heard the dead voice of Brother Ambrose question 'Suppose we have wagered amiss, my friend? Suppose hell gapes before us.' 'Pish and tush,' Maurie had said, with a wave of the hand; but devils' faces gleamed in the dying fire.

He sent a messenger after Gabriel Nixon, urging Clym to make haste to surrender his prisoners. It must be done, he knew, before his nephew learned what was in store in England, before he guessed that others might pay a higher price for their Prince of Wales. He strove to force open his left hand, by an exercise of will, that he might be able to grasp his opportunity; but the fingers were held fast. In the morning he gave orders that horses and a litter be prepared, that they might ride to Mirabel. He would wager all on a single cast.

XIV

Dandy was troubled. There had been no word from Clym, and
Queen Margaret's temper was suffering. She told Dandy that
they were all three no better than his prisoners, and demanded
that he take her to the court of the King of Scots at once. Her ill
temper chimed with his own fears. He regretted his approach to
Clym, and feared he was preparing to cheat him. Yet he dared
take no other course. He begged Nell to try to placate the queen.

She hesitated. She wanted to do as he asked, always, but she
could not believe he had been wise to turn to his cousin. She
had never known Clym, but she knew of him; and she knew –
she had felt – how he hated Dandy, and would do him a mischief
when he could. Then she had come to admire the queen. There
was a savagery there, certainly, and a wicked pride, and she
could well believe that in her time of power, she had been harsh,
unscrupulous and cruel. But now, when she saw her gazing at
the southern hills or watched her pace the escarpment in the
first light of day, or remarked the manner in which she looked
at her son, she found in her something that compelled admiration. Nell warmed to her refusal to submit to misfortune. She
admired her manner too; the arrogant Margaret had not been
brought low by her distress; but it had softened her. When she
spoke to Nell, it was as if to an equal.

And the third reason for her hesitation was that Nell felt her
own strength ebbing. She woke weary in the morning and there
was a pain in her breast that gripped her at intervals like a
mailed hand. She had spells of dizziness and when she recovered
she was so weak that she could scarcely speak. She had said
nothing to Dandy, but she knew that the queen had divined her
weakness and pitied her.

Nevertheless, because Dandy had asked her, she made the
attempt. She found the queen sitting on a fallen tree and gazing
to the south. The line of the hills ran misty blue. The sun was

up but the tops were not yet distinct. The grass sparkled, and wisps of mist lay in the valley. A whaup cried from the moor above. It was a morning of false spring, and without thinking, Nell said, 'On such a day it is good to be alive.'

The queen smiled, 'At my age, mornings grow briefer, and more precious. I have been thinking of my childhood, of the towers of my mother's castle and of the Loire winding through ribbons of poplar. If life could stop at such moments; 'carpe diem,' the Roman poet said – the rose of morning has died before the sun declines. This little valley is so calm, so beautiful that if one could sit here and forget the world, one might be happy. And yet, and yet . . . *'je meurs de soif auprès de la fontaine'*. Do you understand that, my dear?'

'I die of thirst beside the fountain . . . Yes, Your Grace, my dead father, God rest his soul, taught me the French tongue. And yet this valley of ours has seen blood run and heard women cry their grief.'

'Where is there free from pain and fear and sorrow? I have found no such place. In my youth my own fair land of France was torn by war, cruelty and greed, and now England is likewise distressed, and my poor lord . . . what do you know of the king, child?'

'I have heard he is a saint,' Nell said.

'A poor saint, that cannot care for his wife and children. I have watched you and your man, my dear, and, queen though I am, daughter of France and of Anjou, I have felt envy. My own lord has loved the Virgin more than he has loved me. Do you know what they call me, by what name they insult me?'

'Peace, Your Grace, do not distress yourself further.'

'How should I not distress myself when the whole world is so fashioned as to bring me nothing but distress? They call me "the she-wolf of France". Do they think I do not know that, and do you think I do not merit the title? Men are full of wickedness, the beauty of the world is a cheat. That I have learned, and now I find myself, an outcast, a fugitive, even perhaps a prisoner, here, at the extremity of the earth, because my lord is a saint and not a man. Not being one, he has compelled me to unsex myself, and play the wolf. Why will your lord not carry me to his king?'

Nell crouched by her and took the queen's hands in hers.

'Believe me, my lady, my lord is as true a man as walks the earth. He has promised to succour you, but alas his means are few. He is a poor man, and landless in law, for he does not hold this keep by right, and there is a price on his head. He is an exile in his own land. He dare not approach the court himself for he has enemies there who would string him to the branch of the nearest tree if he entrusted himself to them.'

The queen did not remove her hands from Nell's grasp. 'I know you are honest, and am therefore ready to trust your lord. And yet I have moments when I fear that he may be tempted to use us to his advantage rather than our own.'

'No,' Nell said, 'never Dandy.'

Gabriel Nixon rode the hill on his grey pony at a steady trot, that slackened to a walk on only the last steep stretch before the keep. Seeing the queen and Nell sitting there, he doffed his cap, and his bullet head shone in the winter sun.

'You're a brave man to ride here on your ain,' Dandy said.

'Never that. The bearer of good news has nocht tae fear.'

'Good news?'

'Aye, Your Grace,' Gabriel turned to the queen. 'My master has been in communication wi the King of Scots. Now, or rather – for I maun be honest and exact in my account – wi Lord Boyd that, as you may ken, rules the king. Now this was no' easy, and it was no' easy for my lord to win Lord Boyd to his way of thinking, for you maun ken that Lord Boyd is loth to disturb the peace and tranquillity that now prevails between this kingdom of Scotland and your of England; and the lang and the short of it is that the business was done. You and your son will be received with honour, gin you present yourselves to the King's Grace at Lauder a sennight frae now, in the company of my ain lord.'

Queen Margaret's face lit up. She called out for her son, the prince, and, when he appeared, embraced him. She kissed Nell too, and blessed her, but Dandy, frowning, gripped Gabriel Nixon by the elbow, and said, 'And what of me?'

'What of you?'

'Aye, there's nae person moves frae this place, till my wants are satisfied too.'

'And sae they are,' Gabriel said. 'I hae here a copy of a

331

pardon extended to you for all offences that may hae been committed and laid to your charge. The original will be gi'en to you, when you deliver this royal lady to my maister. Oh dinna look sae distrustful. You're a sma' man, no worth revenge, aside the glory that opens afore Clym Laidlaw. And in as much as you hae made it possible, my maister smiles on you also, and is ready to forgive all.'

Dandy turned his gaze up the valley. There was rain forming on the hills. 'Aye,' he said, 'we'll ride wi' you. We'll trust our cousin Clym.'

There was a weariness in his voice Nell had never heard. The light had fled from him. It was as if in the moment of what should have been victory he had seized to believe in his star. And, at that moment, she knew also the truth of what she had tried to conceal from herself: that this weakness of which she was conscious was the harbinger of death. She saw him ride off into a trap, and knew he feared it was a trap, and had attained a point of exhaustion where he was ready to surrender himself to whatever fate held in store. When he turned back to her, and took her in his arms and kissed her before the whole company, the music of that surrender sounded around them, as if they were alone in the waste place where they had first met.

> She kissed his cheek, she kamed his hair,
>   As oft she did before, O;
> She drank the red blood frae him ran,
>   On the dowie houms o' Yarrow . . .

Clym received the queen and prince with all solemnity. He greeted Dandy as a friend, and placed him on the queen's left hand at table. He spread a banquet before them: hill mutton and venison pasties and Gascon wine, ewe's milk cheese and oat bannocks. He spoke to the queen in his most courtierly tone, assured her he would see her restored to her rights again. He presented Dandy with the original of the pardon granted him by the King of Scots, and laughed to see his surprise.

'Did you think I would cheat you, then?'

Dandy made no reply, fingering the document.

'And if you did,' Clym argued, 'why then did you come?'

That night he despatched Gabriel Nixon south again, to appoint a meeting-place with Maurie. Then, with a smile, he revealed to Dandy how things stood. He told him the news that had reached him from England.

XV

The twin towers of Mirabel loomed out of the mist and rain. The horsemen clattered through the little town that huddled round the castle walls. Women and children watched them pass, but many of the women pulled back their children when they saw their lord among the horsemen; others spat when he was safely past. Pigs darted squealing into the vennels, and, as they passed the smithy, even the sound of hammer on anvil was stilled.

The steward had canary wine and dried fish waiting for Maurie. The wine settled his stomach, the fish restored his energy.

'Where is my Lady?'

The steward coughed and said he had taken the responsibility of ordering that she be confined to her quarters.

'And the waiting-woman?'

They went to fetch her. He sipped canary, and no one dared address him.

The woman, Margery, trembled. Her skin was stretched over her cheekbones and her tongue moved over bruised and swollen lips. Her eyes glistened with tears and a terror she could not hide. Maurie smiled.

'She has been tortured?'

'Put to the question, my lord,' his chaplain said, 'as you yourself commanded.'

'And revealed what?'

The chaplain drew a paper from his bosom. He read of how she had confessed herself compelled to accompany her lady to a desecrated chapel, of how she had there seen her lady meet and couple with the Queen of Elfland, of how they had performed monstrous rites, and of how her lady had lain with the queen and been pleasured by her.

Maurie held up his left hand. The fingers were clamped

334

together. 'Look,' he said, and tried to straighten them. They moved perhaps half an inch and then stuck. The hand shook with the effort.

'I have been accursed,' he said. 'This is witchcraft. This woman has done it, and now blames my lady.'

Margery screamed. All the men in the room felt the excitement of her terror.

'She must be subjected to a sterner test. I tell you, there is witchcraft here.'

Two soldiers dragged the woman to the door. A third cleared the way before them, and they hauled her down a staircase, her feet bumping each step; the screaming subsided into a series of yelps still more horrible to hear, if any of them had been prepared to admit the horror of what they were doing.

The cellar was lit by a branch of yellow candles. The woman was tied to a trestle table in the middle of the room. She was stripped, and tied down, on her back, her legs spread.

'Examine her,' Maurie said, 'for the devil's mark.'

'It has been done. There is no sign of it.'

'Oh, the deceit of devils,' the chaplain said, crossing himself.

Maurie picked up an iron rod and placed it over the brazier that filled the little room with near suffocating smoke. He smiled.

'You must not be amazed,' he told the chaplain, 'at the wiles of the devil, but I shall smoke him out. Is the rod hot? Give it me that I may tickle her.'

He applied the iron. She screamed as if to split the sky. Maurie placed his crooked hand where the rod had been.

'Loosen my fingers.'

She screamed that she could not, and he applied the iron a second time. Her body convulsed in an attempt to deny the pain, and her screams tore her head back, and she fainted. The priest applied a soothing unguent. The men sat down and waited. No one spoke. A page brought canary wine for the Lord President, and he sipped, keeping his gaze fixed on the woman. The priest wiped her brow and muttered prayers.

'Come, my daughter,' he said, 'speak the truth and shame the devil.'

She opened her eyes. 'It was my lady,' she muttered in a voice

335

beyond the imagination of all of them. 'She wished to cast a spell on him.'

'I think she speaks truth now,' the chaplain said

'How can we tell? I cannot put my lady to the question. We shall try her with the iron once again, and if she does not deny her words, why then she speaks truth.'

He hesitated. If Alice had not been Warwick's daughter . . . it was intolerable that he dared not act against her, intolerable that he should hesitate on account of that medium man, whom the king had offended, but had not troubled to destroy. If only Warwick were put down from his seat, or if he himself held Edward of Lancaster in his power, as had been promised.

'Is there no word from the Scots?' he asked, gazing north, into the night.

Frost returned. The land was held in its grip. Birds fell frozen from the trees at night, and the moat of the castle turned to ice so thick that a man in armour could have walked on it without danger.

The Lady Alice, confined in a tower room, denied her ladies, attended by nuns whose faces were as blank as the great wall of Mirabel itself, lived her night adventures in an imagination that was starved of hope. When she reminded the nuns of her birth, they remarked that temper brought a little froth of blood to the corners of her mouth, and that her nails bit into the palms of her hands. They made notes of these circumstances.

And then Gabriel Nixon rode up, his horse lame and himself shivering despite his furs. The news he brought made Maurie smile. He lifted his clenched fist in approval, and lodged Nixon in comfort, assuring him that they would ride together in two days.

Later that night a guard reported the approach of a troop of horse. Then it was not a troop, but only two men riding fast. They had been sent by Richard of Gloucester, and the news they brought was grim. Warwick had struck. The king was in flight for France. Gloucester urged Maurie to be loyal; the House of York, the message ran, would see its sun shine again.

'The King's brother Clarence has joined his uncle and father-in-law Warwick.'

'He won't make Clarence king.'

'No, my lord, Henry of Lancaster has been proclaimed king again.'

Maurie laughed for the first time in weeks.

The next morning his old ally Truncheon appeared at the head of a band of knights and men-at-arms. Maurie ordered that he be admitted, and his men lodged comfortably.

'They will want to drink,' he said. 'Receive them as old companions and encourage them to drink deep.'

Truncheon's hair was white, but his face was redder than ever, red as a cardinal's hat now, and he stood before the fire with his legs splayed to let him warm his fat arse, stood there as if Mirabel was his, and he expected Maurie to jump at his command.

But Maurie said, 'your master's mad.'

'He rules England,' Truncheon said.

'Making and unmaking kings and making madmen kings. He is mad if he thinks anyone will accept the half-wit as king again.'

'Henry of Lancaster presided at a council the day I left London,' Truncheon said.

He spoke like a diplomat who will defend what nothing but his brief would persuade him to defend.

'So I am no longer trusted?' Maurie said.

'I'm here. Myself. That's proof of trust.'

'Of a kind. But I was not privy to the plot. I am only approached when the thing is done.'

'You're his son-in-law.'

'Aye.'

'His other son-in-law Clarence is with him.'

'Clarence is a drunken fool, born to be hanged if he does not drown in Malmsey first.'

'You have long-standing connections with Lancaster yourself.'

'He knighted me. But, as to the rest, my lord des Moulins is dead, and his cheese-faced son is in the hands of the Scots.'

Truncheon sighed. 'We have done much together. I had hoped to persuade you. I have no wish . . .'

'No wish to do what you have not at present the power to perform? Very well, old friend, tell me this: what has become of the she-wolf?'

'Word has been sent to Scotland where she has found refuge.'

'Warwick will have her back? I tell you he has taken leave of his senses.'

'There is the boy, Edward, Prince of Wales.'

'You give him his title?'

'Naturally, since his father is king again.'

'And what of King Ned?' Maurie held his breath.

'Last heard of huddled in a fishing-boat in flight for France.'

'So he has escaped, given Warwick the slip . . .'

Was there ever, he thought, such a kack-handed conspiracy?

'You have brought me much to ponder,' he said. 'If my king has deserted me, I heed not scruple to desert him who was my king.'

'Spoken like a wise man. Have you wine, my friend?'

'Indeed yes, forgive me.'

He turned to his page. 'Bring me that flask of special canary. You will excuse me if I do not join you. I have an evil liver these days, and drink only boiled milk.'

He sat back and smiled as Truncheon raised the special wine to his lips.

He sent a message to Gabriel Nixon to be ready to ride that night. 'First,' he said, 'I have business which I dare not leave behind me.' He sent another messenger to France, to find King Edward, and assure him of his loyalty. Then he summoned the Abbot of Rokeby who had been brought to the castle a fortnight back.

'I know what you fear,' he told the Abbot, 'but you must choose between the nearer and the further fear. I am the closer. As for Warwick, by midsummer, I tell you he will be bones for dogs to lick. The sun of York will shine resplendent, and you, my lord Abbot, may ask what reward you choose. So, play the game, Master Abbot . . .'

The nuns had dressed her in white. They led her into the Great Hall where a dais had been set up at the north end. A black-draped table stood on the dais and there were three men sitting behind it: the abbot and two Dominican friars, with white narrow faces, hard-carved as stone saints. Six hands lay on the black cloth, and four were long and white, the skin stretched over dry bone; but the Abbot's were soft and plump and bejewelled, hands for rending the flesh of fowls. There was a

338

crucifix studded with garnets and rubies on the table, and the abbot picked it up and held it in front of her.

The nuns fell back, and she was left alone. The clerk read the catalogue of charges. He recited the evidence supplied by her waiting-woman, and, though her lips moved, she said nothing. The reading of the charges took a long time, and when she was asked what she had to say in her defence, she offered no word, but shook her head.

The judges argued among themselves as to whether her silence constituted a sufficient admission of guilt. She could not follow the argument. She sensed that a gaze was directed on her from the side, and that it was her husband, but she could not lift her eyes or turn her head towards him.

Then they brought in twelve women who, they said, had participated in abominable rites. Each wore a white shift and had a hempen rope round her neck. The Lady Alice looked at them and saw the same look in their eyes.

A friar said, 'All have confessed when put to the question, and we have notice of their depositions here. All state that the Lady Alice was the chief consort of her they call their queen. They did not weep even at the extreme pain of the question, for all affirm that they will be true martyrs for love of the hellish master whom they style their god. They have shown themselves impatient in their confinement to attain that moment when they can testify that they long to suffer for their master.'

The Abbot raised his fat moon face and asked the Lady Alice whether she united herself to these sentiments.

She replied in a soft voice that was yet clear as a bell. 'I know no master, only my mistress, and she can take many forms. I do not know by whose authority I stand here, being a lady of quality and the daughter of the mighty Earl of Warwick, and I know I am subjected to the malice of him who has been my husband. Yet in as much as I disown him and have known keener and unearthly pleasures, perhaps I stand rightly here. But I know this also: I will be none other than I am. I find too much content in my condition. And I trust in her to whom I have committed my soul and body.'

Then she lifted her head and sought to meet his gaze. But he turned away. There was a silence in the long winter room.

*

The faggots were stacked in the great courtyard, towards dusk.

'We burn their sin for their souls' sake,' the Dominican friar said. 'And you, by the punishment you inflict, do justice on behalf of mankind and in honour of Almighty God and in obedience to his will.'

'I accept the duty,' Maurie said, 'in my capacity as member of the Privy Council of His Grace King Edward IV and Lord President of his Council in the North.' And none dared say that the king's Grace was as like as not dallying with a serving-maid in the Flemish tavern where he crouched in exile, but all knew that Maurie was, by his acceptance of the judgement of the Court, on their behalf, exposing all to the vengeance of the Earl of Warwick.

The sky was filled with screams, and then, rising through the smoke, a hymn of unearthly praise. It was taken up, thinly, from some of the other pyres. The smoke choked it. The faggots crackled. The air was fouled with a horrid smell, and the flames died hours later in a sullen light. Snowclouds gathered, and men at arms crept back to the hall.

At midnight Maurie, with Gabriel Nixon and a dozen men, rode over the drawbridge heading north. He stretched out his left hand. The fingers straightened. Then he gripped the reins, and they rode into darkness.

XVI

Clym sniffed the dawn. It was bitter cold, the sky heavy with snow. He looked to the south, and saw no movement. They had been waiting three days now, and it had already been necessary to send some of the men back to fetch more provisions. He shivered in the cold, and cursed. The day before he had begun to wonder if his uncle would refuse the bait. He knew enough of Maurie to respect his wariness. And yet what was the reason for him to be suspicious: Clym had pitched his demand for gold high enough to prove his greed and his eagerness to deal with his uncle. They had nothing to fear. But he wished this waiting would end. A red hawk hovered in the sky, seeking its prey in an empty land.

Dandy lounged up. Clym had hesitated there too; in the end Dandy's refusal to commit Queen Margaret and the Prince unreservedly to his care had persuaded him to confide his secret. Dandy had been at first reluctant, Clym couldn't understand why.

'It'll be the first time you hae baulked at a killing,' he said.

'There's been owre muckle o' that, and he's kin forbye,' Dandy had said.

But his mood had changed, that night when Nell passed away between owl-light and cock-crow. Now all he said was: 'I'll ride to see you dinna play the queen false. I'll no trust ye, Clym, till I see her safe conducted to our king.'

In her last moments Nell had impressed on him his duty to the queen.

Two hours after daybreak a line of horsemen came dotting into sight at the far end of the valley.

Clym took his hand from his sword-hilt. 'He's brocht an army. They are owre mony.'

'And what did you look for?' Dandy said.

The wind blew from the north-west as the mounted men

picked their way down the far side of the valley, and along the burn. They stopped there, and scanned the hills, and seemed to listen for whatever the wind might tell them. Dandy sat on the ground beside Clym, wrapped in a plaid and with his head lowered, not looking at the troop that was approaching.

'They're owre mony,' Clym said again. 'We canna take them here.'

'And did you ever think you could?' Dandy said.

Clym settled his face, mounted his pony and rode down the hill to greet his uncle. He sat stiff in the saddle, his legs thrust straight into long stirrups.

'Hae you brocht the gowd?' he said.

'As promised.'

'Then we can talk business.'

'Where is the woman and her son?'

'We'll ride to them.'

Maurie's face clouded. 'They were to be here,' he said.

For a moment they looked each other in the face. Each read distrust in the other's air.

'You'll be quit of the business by nightfall,' Clym said, 'and on your road home. You hae my word to that.'

So they rode back into the hills and down a little valley which was touched by a gleam of winter sun, and was guarded at the north end by a keep. Maurie rode in silence, flexing his left hand, and with a smile on his face when he did so. Dandy did not approach him, but kept his face covered.

Smoke rose from the keep and when they reached it they found two sheep being roasted and jacks of ale ready for the company.

'Where is the woman and her son?' Maurie asked again.

'Bide your time and they'll be wi us,' Clym answered. All the ride he had run over the numbers of Maurie's men in his head, calculating the odds, misliking the answer. He had no wish for a fight; no wish to have to rely on Dandy and his wild men, though they were in waiting on the other side of the brae.

Gabriel Nixon drew him aside.

When they had finished speaking, Clym smiled. He ordered more ale to be served, and watched the men drink as he chewed on a rib-bone. His uncle sat near the fire, his furs pulled round his shoulders. He was as white as a bone that has lain long exposed to the weather.

'You'd best speak to Dandy,' Clym said to Gabriel Nixon. 'Tell him a' you hae tellt me.'

When Gabriel Nixon had told Dandy of what had happened in the last hours at Mirabel, and of what he had learned there, Dandy rose, and, without a word to anyone, left the peel-tower, and rode over the hill to collect his men. At the same time Clym sent Gabriel Nixon on another mission, and then approached his uncle. Maurie had drifted into sleep, but started up when Clym touched him on the shoulder.

'The woman and her son will be here before daybreak,' Clym said.

Maurie grunted his satisfaction and pulled the cloak more tightly round his shoulders. It was impossible to guess what he was thinking. Clym wondered in his dull manner what age the old man was. He had no means of estimating. The hall drifted into night and silence. Maurie's youngest page laid a peat on the fire, lest his master wake cold, and blame him for his condition.

In the howdumdeid, the blackest hour, moving with assurance though the night was moonless, Dandy's men crept through the scrub of birch and rowans on the north brae behind the peel-tower, and, their presence unsuspected, despatched the sentries posted at Maurie's order to wait his own entry to hell. Then they drew up around the peel, and sat down to wait for light.

Dawn was breaking when Gabriel Nixon rode up at the head of a little band. Dandy approached them, and helped Queen Margaret to alight.

'Is the King of Scots here in this wretched place?'

'No, my lady, we have some other business to settle first.'

Then, aware of the suspicion in her face, he softened his voice, which had been harsh with grief, anger and fatigue, and promised her that the business could only please her. Clym emerged to greet her, his face set, but a spring in his step despite his sleepless night. He fell on his knees before her, and kissed her hand.

'Your Grace,' he said, 'you will thank us for what we are about to do for you.'

The young Prince of Wales came forward. 'I do not understand.'

'You're nane the waur for that,' Clym said, 'but when you come tae understanding, then I'll thank you to recall what we hae dune for you.'

The boy looked at his mother. She bowed her head.

'We have no choice,' she said, 'but to trust in the honour of our friends.'

She turned to Dandy, and laid her hand on his arm. 'I was so sad to learn about your lady. She was one for whom I had formed a profound esteem.'

Clym led them into the hall of the keep. Maurie roused himself from sleep. Most of his men-at-arms were still slumbering. They lay on the earth floor while a few dogs picked for scraps about them, and snarled at each other over bones. The air was fetid and the silence disturbed by stertorous snores.

'I hae the honour,' Clym said, 'to present to you Her Grace, Margaret of Anjou, Queen of England, and Edward of Lancaster, Prince of Wales.'

Dandy's men filled the room, crowding through the door behind them, and then moving swiftly to disarm or seize Maurie's troopers. The few who were awake were too surprised to offer much resistance.

Maurie lifted his head, and made to rise, slowly and painfully, to his feet, but the weight of Dandy's hand descended on his shoulder, holding him down in his chair.

'What foolery is this? What do you mean by these titles?'

'Nae foolery,' Clym said, 'but aiblins a preliminary to a final reckoning, uncle. You hae done ill to trust me, that is a child of your murdered brother. And as for the titles, you ken fine what I mean by them: that the great Earl of Warwick has restored this lady's husband, the saintly Henry of Lancaster to his rightful throne, and that the usurper, Edward of York, whose servant you are, now hides his head in fearful exile. Did you think you could keep that news frae me and my warld?'

Maurie cast his eye round the company. He saw his soldiers helpless, saw the belt of grim faces aurrounding him, understood all. He licked his cracked lips, and raising his left hand in the air, flexed and unflexed the fingers, staring at their movement with what looked like wonder.